THE FOUNDING FATHER

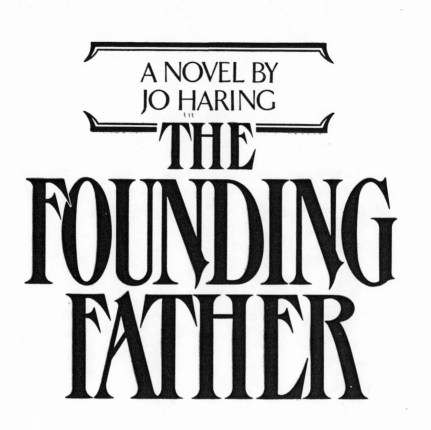

A NOVEL BY
JO HARING

THE FOUNDING FATHER

M. EVANS AND COMPANY, INC.
New York

This is a work of fiction. Except for certain well-documented historic characters and facts, all people and events in this story exist only in this book. Any similarity in names or events is purely coincidental.

Library of Congress Cataloging in Publication Data

Haring, Jo.
 The founding father.

 I. Title.
PS3558.A62418F6   1984   813'.54   84-13579
ISBN 0-87131-443-6

M. Evans and Company, Inc.
216 East 49 Street
New York, New York 10017

Design by Lauren Dong

Manufactured in the United States of America

9 8 7 6 5 4 3 2 1

For Bob Haring

PROLOGUE

"Who's those?"

"What?"

"Who's those?" repeated the little boy.

"I dunno. Watch whur yer steppin'," said the man. "Yer steppin' on graves."

"Is that bad luck?"

"I dunno," considered the man. "If it ain't, it prob'ly ought to be."

"But who's those?" persisted the boy. "Those with the big white tombstones? Was they important?"

The man shrugged. "Murphy," he said, "that's all I know, Murphy, died 1903. That's a long time ago—1903."

"Borned 1819. He was a old man, wasn't he? How old?"

"I dunno. I'd have to have a pencil and paper to figger."

"Don't nobody decorate their graves? There's four, see? Just alike. Four. Don't nobody never decorate?"

"I dunno. You have to ask yer ma. She prob'ly knows. Her or Grandma. They notice things like that, like decoratin' on Decoration Day. I don't pay no attention."

"They must a been important."

"Mebbe."

"To a had such big, nice stones. They must a been important."

"Well"—the man shrugged—"mebbe, but they ain't no more."

ONE

THE PRESENT

*T*he throng of last-minute Christmas shoppers is made up mostly of men, I observe. It always is. They are swamping the clerks in lingerie and jewelry and cosmetics. They always do. Christmas Eve morning is always a busy time in retail stores, and the steady buzz of the computer registers all but drowns out the ubiquitous Christmas music. It seems to me that the Christmas season in the store has not been quite the same since the old-fashioned cash registers with their happy ring were replaced by the programmed efficiency and no-nonsense buzz of these computers. The ring of the old-fashioned register was more Christmasy somehow.

I smile. It is not a thought I would voice. I am not a cynical woman. It is merely an observation, but when you own a chain of department stores such an observation would be viewed as crass at best. I learned long ago to keep things to myself.

I am not cynical, nor am I sentimental; particularly am I not sentimental about cash registers. I am middle-aged enough that I can remember when the cash registers themselves were innovative, when Old Levi had them installed to replace the pneumatic tubes that had always carried cash (almost never checks) to a harried bookkeeper in a loft overlooking the counters and wood floors of the original Murphy and Son Department Store, which was itself replaced several years ago by a Kentucky Fried Chicken franchise.

Pausing in the center aisle near a display of luggage that needs dusting, I notice some confusion near the cosmetics counter. The clerk is busy at one end of the counter and, I observe, is carefully trying to stay occupied with the customer she is serving. The reason for her preoccupation, I suspect, is the group at the other end of the counter, the group that is shouting at one another.

"How the hell should I know, I told you?" shouts the man.

"Well, you shure as shit ain't givin' me no clues!" says the woman.

One little girl has another little girl pinned to the floor, and a third girl is tugging on the woman's arm and mouthing the word "Mother," the way girls in their early teen years often do. This is definitely out of the ordinary, but out-of-the-ordinary things happen in retail stores just as they do everywhere else. It would not be the first family to get into an argument over a purchase, though, to tell the truth, most such arguments take place in small or major appliances and generally involve television sets or other electronic gear.

It is the makeup of this group that is arresting. It is the sort of family that usually shops exclusively in discount stores. Again, that is merely a personal observation that I would never make aloud. It is not intended to be judgmental. It is not even the clothing so much that marks them, although I am struck, as I often have been struck, that people who regularly shop discount stores tend more to polyester stretch fabrics and overweight than people who shop at better retail outlets. And I wonder again, as I often have, that women who are overweight do not seem to notice that such stretch fabrics reveal every roll and dimple—"cellulite" in some circles—on hip, thigh, and derriere.

The man in his plaid polyester pants and clashing plaid shirt, the pearlized snapped pockets and V yoke of which mark it as Western, is at least not overweight. And his billed cap with *CAT* emblazoned across the front, along with the rolled cuffs on the shirt, suggests, at least, that he has probably had more personal dealings with cows than those erstwhile cowboys who come in here for ostrich skin boots and leather coats.

The cosmetics clerk has not lifted her eyes at the commotion, though several other people have glanced in the direction of the woman, who is glaring defiantly at a display of Jovan before her. The man, his hands stuffed in his pockets as if to keep them from doing bodily harm to the woman, though the slump to his shoulders indicates that he never would, has moved around the counter to stare in some interest at the hair dryer in the shape of a six-gun. I have never liked that item. I feel that it belongs in a novelty shop. But the buyer for this department makes few mistakes, and it has sold well. So I have said nothing.

I move in behind the counter. I am no stranger to clerking. I don't do it often, but I am not embarrassed to pitch in. The situation needs some tactful handling.

My friendly "May I help you?" is greeted with a discouraged sigh from the woman in polyester.

"I'm lookin' fer a Christmas present," she says. "And I've just about looked ever'where and cain't find nothin'. Ever'where," she emphasizes, as if to say that she is at last at the bottom of the barrel and Murphy's Department Store is it. I know, of course, that that isn't true; that what she means is that she's hit every discount store and possibly J. C. Penney's and Sears without success and is now in the kind of store with which she is totally unfamiliar, in her panic at the approaching gift-delivering hour willing to venture even here.

"Perhaps I can help," I say. "I'm very good at picking out gifts. Who is it for?"

"A old woman. Very old. *His* grandmother," she says, indicating the man, his hands still hanging on to the change in his pockets. She does not even dignify him as "my husband," though I suspect he is. The three girls, the two of whom have at last stopped wrestling long enough to stare intently at me, have a look about them that suggests the genetic combination of these two adults. "She's old," the woman repeats, and there is for an instant a gently sad twist to her mouth against that pitiable condition of great age.

"She's alone," explains the woman. "After fifty-six years her man died and left her. This is her first Christmas alone." She says it angrily, as if the old fellow could somehow be found wanting for having died and left the old woman alone on Christmas.

"It's sad, to be alone on Christmas." Unaccountably I hear myself confessing, "My father died in August. I will be alone on Christmas for the first time, too."

I don't think the woman notices. She's glaring again at the man, who is fondling the blow dryer. It doesn't matter. I felt little grief at Lee's passing, less, I think, than I felt at Old Levi's passing, that many years ago. I suppose I felt depressed at both, depressed at so obvious an expression of mortality. And perhaps I have missed both father and grandfather occasionally; I can't really say. I keep busy.

"I don't want to get her just anything, just some old bath powder," mutters the woman in polyester, glaring again at the offending display of expensive toiletries the Jovan packaging engineers have so elegantly designed for Christmas consumption. "But, hell, what does someone that old want?"

It is plaintive, and I am arrested by the obvious caring of the polyester woman. It is unlike what I usually see in this establishment relative to gift giving. Most of the people I see selecting gifts, I suspect, are doing so more on the basis of how the gift will reflect on their own taste and image rather than of a genuine effort to please the recipient. One does not, I suppose, really expect overweight people in polyester pants to care like that. It is again the kind of observation I would never make aloud to anyone. Besides, Nanny wears polyester, and though she's not overweight, she is black. I know her to be caring in her own peculiar fashion. But then, one thinks of blacks as caring, elderly blacks especially, the "mammy" syndrome maybe.

However, Nanny loves smelly bath powder. I give it to her for every occasion, including this one, and she litters her bathroom with it. She also loves frilly chemises, which she wears in the winter under sweat shirts as she works around the house—sweat shirts that usually have a slogan displayed across the front. But somehow I do not think that Nanny's taste in gifts will help this situation.

"She's old," the woman had said. Old. Old is what Old Daniel is. That might offer a clue. "I have an elderly friend," I say. "He's in a nursing home; he's very old," I repeat. "I got him a book for Christmas, a picture book—photographs—of early-day Oklahoma. He's nearly blind and quite senile, but I think he will enjoy looking at the old pictures, even if he can't read the captions."

"Well, I don't know." The woman hesitates and then glances at the man. "You think she'd like a book?"

He shrugs. "I dunno," he mutters; "she ain't much a hand to read, I don't think."

"Perhaps," I suggest, following that path, "a photograph book, something she could mount her snapshots in?"

The woman looks interested.

"Mother," says the young girl, the one who looks embarrassed, pouty and self-conscious all at the same time, "she's got some old albums, but nobody don't ever put the pitchers in 'em."

"Wouldn't hurt you to do that," snaps the woman. "Get off your lazy ass long enough to do something fer someone else."

"Mother," mouths the girl again. Briefly I feel for her. Then I am inspired. "How about a photograph," I say. Then, lying, I add—maybe it's not lying; maybe it's something like creative merchandising—"We're having a special in the photography studio, a Christmas special, a family photograph—twelve by fourteen, color, for only $14.95." I pull the figure out of the air. Such a picture would run above fives times that sum in this store. The woman and the man glance at each other; there is a spark of communication.

"The special was actually over yesterday, I think," I say, and the woman looks disappointed, "but if I call down to the studio, I'm sure I can get them to extend it." I *know* I can get them to take such a photograph. I have but to say, "This is Elizabeth Murphy. . . ." My wish is their command.

"Well," drawls the woman, "when would it be ready?"

There is an immediacy to Christmas gifts. No one wants to have to tell the recipient that his gift has been ordered, is on the way.

"I expect they can have it out by early afternoon," I say, again *knowing* that they can. "There's not much photography business on Christmas Eve. Why don't you go down there? It's in the basement, between the credit offices and the beauty salon. I'll call so they'll be ready when you get there."

"Well, I thank you," says the woman, her gratitude genuine. "Come on," she snaps to the rest of the family.

"Mommy, are we goin' to git are pitcher took?" says one of the smaller girls in awe.

"Brush yer hair!" is the reply she gets. The family is suddenly strung out on the way to the escalator: the two little girls chattering eagerly, the older one looking pleased but self-conscious. The man, his jacket draped over his arm, is rolling down his sleeves, buttoning each in turn. He takes off his cap and runs his hand over his thin hair.

I call down to the photography studio, identify myself, explain the situation and start to tell the photographer that this is simply a seasonal gesture by Murphy's Department Stores, then, perversely, I decide against it. "They're friends of mine," I say abruptly. "Do the best you can." I would like to be a little mouse in the corner to witness his expression when he sees the crew I have sent him. "Charge them $14.95, but bill the remainder of the full amount to my account." I do not want his department coming up short on account of my generosity.

It is a generosity that I am at a loss to explain. I am not a particularly soft touch. I give huge amounts to various charities, institutions and whatnot. It's simply a part of being in business. I do my share and I walk past Salvation Army bell ringers without the slightest pang of conscience. So why this impulse in the name of Christmas spirit? I put it down to just that: impulse.

"It takes all kinds," the cosmetic clerk who has so covertly witnessed the proceedings says, grinning.

"Yes," I say. It is as noncommittal as I can make it. I hope that the old lady will appreciate it. I hope that she will like the photograph, and I try to imagine her expression of delight. I can't get the picture. Maybe she would be just as happy with a fifth of Old Redneck or something.

I pick up the phone and call down to the studio again. From the strained sound coming from the other end I take it that the photographer has viewed what he has to work with. "Throw in a good frame," I say, "at no extra charge. Something in the medium price range," I add, my business sense finally asserting itself, "and make it clear that the 'Christmas special' is over." I hang up. I do not want these people to go out spreading the word among their friends that Murphy's is having a Christmas special on family photographs.

I have my own shopping to finish, which was why I was out on the floor in the first place. I have David and Arlene's college-age children to buy for, but that will be easy. I will choose three sets of the current collegiate cliché for the two girls and a boy. The rest of my shopping is done. Old Daniel's *Pictorial History of Oklahoma,* Nanny's chocolates, bath powder and chemises, David and Arlene's framed graphic, and the hundred-dollar bond I always give to Leroy and Charlaine. This comprises my "family," though in truth none really are family and they're not even all the same color, and I laugh out loud as I think what David and Arlene would say if they knew I lumped them and theirs with Nanny and her son, Leroy, and his wife, Charlaine, as "family." It is a perverse thought that carries me through the rest of the short day.

It's Christmas Eve. I have no afternoon meetings, no phone calls pending. I call down to gift wrap and tell them to bring my wrapped packages, and I call the parking garage and ask for my car. The secretary has the afternoon off, but it doesn't matter. I like to do thinks for myself, anyway. I have plenty of work to do, but I can take it with me. I will stop by the club for a drink and a late lunch. There is no point in hanging around here late and furthering my image as a lonely workaholic. Personally I don't care, but images are a part of business.

My car is a new Lincoln: black; my cars are always black and always either Cadillac or Lincoln. I like the statement that a big new black car makes; it says, "I'm rich! So up yours!" I chuckle to myself at the quip and the black attendant smiles and says, "Merry Christmas." I tip him and wonder again if maybe it's time to switch to a Rolls-Royce or something else equally ridiculous. Caddies and Lincolns are becoming commonplace enough that the "statement" is not as loud as it once was. I recall that Lee always drove pastel Oldsmobiles. A pastel Oldsmobile does not make much of a statement. It was altogether fitting and proper that Lee drive such a car, I suppose, as he himself did not make much of a statement, either.

As I pull out into the parking lot, I catch a glimpse of the polyester family heading across the lot toward the battered pickup I assume to be theirs. They fit every cliché from polyester to pickup. At least they are not carrying bath powder; the large Murphy's shopping bag—the design of which cost a fortune in fees to a design firm in New York—at least holds an imaginative gift. I, I think wryly, am the one with the bath powder. I can small Nanny's gift all the way from the trunk of the car, I think.

No one in the family notices as I drive by. They are hurrying, and I suspect somehow that they are not from Tulsa, that they are country people come to town for last-minute shopping. I don't know, of course. I would like to see the picture. I wonder if the photographer caught them in some trendy pose, or if he had the sense to capture them as they were. Perhaps I'll check the proofs after Christmas. And then I think that this is maybe the only family picture they have ever had taken, and I suddenly envision distant progeny studying that ancient photo, taken at a defunct department store, of ancestors long gone and contemplating their polyester uniqueness. I grin at the thought.

I have no family photographs to speak of, except a few formal photos of Old Levi and Lee. Old Levi had a few grim old pictures of his family, the three Louisas—I give it the old-fashioned pronunciation that Old Levi did on the rare occasions that he mentioned that trio of women all named Lou-i-za—and his grandfather Obediah, the founder, I think, of this particular line of Murphys. That vague figure, Obediah Murphy, was the beginning, and I guess I am the end. Perhaps the descendants of the polyester family will know no more of them from that photo than I know of Obediah and the three Lou-i-zas from those dim and dreary photographs, which I had all but forgotten existed until Nany unearthed them recently in a box of old papers she found under the stairs. I remember them now only from that night so many years ago that Old Levi insisted I sit up all night while he went over his "book," which was little more than notes on his ancestry and his life, notes that are among those papers and pictures that Nanny found.

Well, Old Levi had gone strange by then, was approaching senil-

ity as well, and his late-night ramblings—agitated though they were—
didn't make much sense, and I remember them and the pictures only
vaguely.

I hope, though, that one of those little polyester girls has the good
sense to hang on to the picture and hand it down. Commonplace as it
is today, it might one day be of great interest to someone.

At the club I am suckered into a bridge game by people who don't
seem to want to go home for Christmas Eve either, and I stay too late.
By the time I leave, it is already dark and the air is damp and misty. In
this part of the Southwest we don't expect a white Christmas, a dry
one is satisfactory, but this has the look of a wet Christmas. The
ubiquitous Christmas lights shine through the mist as I travel up
Riverside Drive. They are, in the main, modest houses on this
stretch, but the lights through the damp are cheerful. People of modest circumstances, I have noted, have more sense about Christmas
decorations than the more affluent, who are always bent on making a
fashion statement, even with Christmas decorations, refurbishing ex-
tant bits and pieces of pagan ritual into trendy—that word again—
statements.

I am in a perverse mood tonight, and I think of Arlene's decorations and wonder what they will be—trendy, I'm sure. "Trendy" is a
word I hate; it is, what can I say, so "trendy" in and of itself. But
that's Arlene in a nutshell. David is a workaholic and Arlene is
trendy. They are a compatible cliché.

I pull off the Drive and up the steep incline toward the house on
the hill. It is the house that Old Levi built in the early part of this
century. From the top story you can view the Arkansas River, with its
nightly backdrop of city lights and refinery flashes. Until he died, Old
Levi occupied that floor, staring in his last years for long periods out
over the lazy, shallow, meandering river, which picks up speed only
as it nears the state of its name, rushing through Little Rock in a
sudden, libidinous anxiety to cohabit with that old lecher the mighty
Mississippi.

My ghosts are abroad tonight. I don't know why. Old Levi has
been in my thoughts more today than in months, years perhaps.
Maybe it is the Christmas season that does it, but in truth I have few
memories of Christmas. We ceased celebrating it at all when Old Levi
went strange, but for a few gifts that Lee would slip me on the sly. I
was a good big girl by then, big enough to realize that when you were
heiress to a string of department stores, Santa Claus was a bit redundant.

Perhaps it is this estate-settling business that David has been froth-ing over that keeps my pair of ancestors in my mind. Whatever it is, I wish that Old Levi would leave me be. I have work to do; I do not have the time to feel dreamy and pensive. I wish he would get back into my subconscious where he belongs. It is not my fault about the Kentucky Fried Chicken franchise.

Nanny is none too happy with me when I arrive. She tells me abruptly that my dinner is in the microwave.

"I had a late lunch," I tell her.

"In the microwave. Whenever you wants it," she says. She kicks the dusty old Seagram Seven box at the foot of the stairs. "You got to see to these here," she snaps. She has dragged that old box of papers out again. I think she is assigning me penance for some real or imag-ined sin. Nanny's nose is definitely out of joint. And then I remember that last year Lee and I took her out to dinner on Christmas Eve, a gesture on Lee's part that startled the both of us. Lee never paid much attention to Christmas or to Nanny or, for that matter, to me. I can't but wonder if he sensed that that would be his last Christmas. That is a romantic and therefore highly unreliable assessment. If Lee acted out of character, he had the right; for that was, to my knowledge, the only time he ever did.

I think we have a tradition here. I will take Nanny out to dinner one day next week. That will satisfy her, I guess. And perhaps I ought to look through these papers before tomorrow's dinner with David and Arlene so I can tell him if there is something relative to the estate among them.

"Ah'm goin' to ma room to watch the television," says Nanny, and without a glance she marches slowly up the stairs to her second-floor room. We share that floor, she and I. She has a nice room and bath and I have a suite, the suite where I grew up. I have lived in that suite of rooms all my life but for that brief period when I made my round-heeled way through college, surviving a pair of abortions—they were illegal then—and a bout with an incompetent shrink. He advised me that my problems stemmed from a domineering mother. In all fairness, the combination of fact and fantasy that I had given him did not make it clear at all that I had been raised by a pair of detached old men—Old Levi and Lee may have been father and son, but they seemed of an age to me—and a succession of bored housekeepers. I was bright enough to know what my own problems were.

I settle down to read the paper and feed myself from the micro-wave before I slip out to the car to smuggle the packages in. Nanny is like a child: she will rattle and sniff and fret over the gifts until she manages to wheedle their contents out of me. It's best not to let her near them until it's time to open them. I hide them behind the sofa so she will have to search before she finds them.

I have paper work to do, or I could go on to bed and read awhile. Then I recall the box of papers. I probably should check through them, so if there is anything, I can give David the bad news tomorrow.

I don't think it will take long, so I decide just to lug the box up to my room and sort through the papers before I go to sleep. David is determined to get into probate before the first of the year, and I hate to think what might happen if I should come up with yet another unregistered oil lease or piece of rental property. I think David will just about have kittens. (David's prone to having kittens on a regular basis anyway.) The day after Christmas, he says, he's going to hustle all this stuff over to the courthouse and be done with it.

"It has to do," he says, "with taxes, estate taxes."

Possibly. I think it has more to do with David's being a tidy sort who likes to have things all cleaned up by year's end, no loose ends spilling over into the new year. These papers, I think: I hope they won't yield anything that will unsettle David's plans. I smile. I would hate to be responsible for David's fathering a litter of kittens.

Nanny found the box to spite me, I think. I'll bet she knew all along it was there, hidden under the stairs with the old Christmas ornaments, the ornaments that Old Levi hid away after he went strange. I can't believe that Lee knew the box of papers was in there. He would never have left so unsightly a thing as an aging Seagram Seven box gathering dust under the stairs. He would have sorted, filed and tossed as needed. I am reminded of David. Had Lee had a son, I think, he would've been like David.

Nanny's already asleep, I'm sure. I can hear Johnny Carson's monologue punctuated by her thick snorts and groans. I smile again. No matter how long I live—no matter how long Johnny Carson lives—I will never be able to listen to him without imagining a backdrop of grunts and groans and snorts and whistles. I pause at her door, peek in, and sure enough, she's propped up as always, sound asleep in the direction of the TV. It's too loud. It always is. I turn the set off and ease Nanny's tough old body—it reminds me of beef jerky—back on the pillow and switch off the light. She'll be up before me.

Nanny claims to be part Creek, though to tell the truth I'd say there's precious little Indian in her, but she claims it and to be as old as the hills, and we both half believe it when I tell her that for certain she was never born of woman; she was carved out of a rock from the Osage Hills. She's a fixture, anyway, at all the Indian powwows, and she dances. If she's not part Indian, she ought to be.

I don't think the old Seagram Seven box will yield anything important. But Old Levi did hide away a lot of things that we've unearthed, things that Lee might have known were there and might not have. Lee wasn't dishonest. But we keep uncovering things that he never paid taxes on, and David moans about the Feds. I'm not worried. I was not twenty-one and not even living at home when Old Levi died. If Lee didn't pay inheritance taxes on things that he probably didn't know existed, it wasn't my fault. His either. He's dead now, and if his estate owes back taxes, so be it. I'll pay them.

The papers are all probably Old Levi's. Old Levi stored a lot of things in liquor cartons. There's still much to be said for their storage capacity. And from the look and smell of the box I'd say it probably dates back to "dry" days, run into Oklahoma by bootleggers or near-bootleggers—that is, people returning to the state from elsewhere, their car trunks loaded with illegal booze. I've heard bootleggers referred to as rumrunners, but I don't think so. Rumrunners were more romantic, I like to think, like pirates. There was nothing romantic about a bootlegger. They were just businessmen back in the days when the bootleggers and the Baptists formed this unspoken alliance to keep Oklahoma dry.

Everybody was satisfied then back before someone decided to go honest. The Baptists were certainly satisfied, and the bootleggers. And the consumers, who could call their favorite bootlegger and get hard liquor delivered to their doors cheaper than most other states could sell it in stores, they were certainly satisfied. But then there were those who didn't like the image, I guess, that the whole situation gave this progressive state—after all, we'd had to spend years living with *The Grapes of Wrath*—so they decided to go honest and vote us wet, and then nobody was happy with the situation, especially the Baptists and the bootleggers.

It was a little like Nanny's son, Leroy, when he decided to make Charlaine an honest woman and marry her; they haven't got along since.

I blow the dust from the box before I put it hesitantly on my bed. Not many people know it, but I'm sort of a designer-bedding junkie. People are impressed because I'm all business, middle-aged maybe, but liberated and rich, especially the rich part. But my secret vice is all these frilly and elegant bedclothes. Nanny complains about them, though not as much now as she did back before permanent press fabrics. But I can't keep from collecting them. I slip into the household linens stockroom with every new shipment and pick out a complete set or two—comforter, dust ruffle, sheets, pillow slips, bolster, the works—and charge it all to my account.

I like to work on my bed, but I suppose I'll have to finish this estate business with David in his office and sit with him at that intimidating oak desk, the one that belonged to Old Daniel when he headed the firm, and I suppose will fall to young Daniel when he joins David in the firm. Arlene wouldn't like it, I think, if I asked David over to help me get this ready for probate in the middle of my king-sized bed. And Lee, he might turn over in his grave if he knew that I had pretty well settled his estate in the middle of my designer sheets. He could never have understood such frivolity, he himself always so predictable. I remember with a smile what Old Levi had said about Lee unexpectedly one night—I don't recall the occasion even.

"Levi," he had said—that was not long after the war (people of my generation always call it "the war" as if there had been no other), after Lee had officially changed his name from Levi Murphy, and Old Levi—who was *old* Levi because his son had been *young* Levi—still was not used to calling Lee anything but Levi, "Levi, you know, was born in a Packard, in the backseat of a Packard. It is," said Old Levi and I love this, "the only truly imaginative thing Levi has ever done."

When I pressed for details—after all, being born in the backseat of a Packard was out of the ordinary—all I got was a curt, "We had not expected him so soon and we went for a Sunday drive." Early-day Oklahoma roads were real labor inducers, I guess. Some still are.

That was all Old Levi said, no other details. Lee's mother, my grandmother, Betty—Elizabeth—for whom I was named, died, I know, as a result of complications of that birth, which is probably why Old Levi was so reluctant to talk about the incident.

Whatever happened to my own mother, no one seems to know for sure, or at least ever told me. I know only that she left Lee when I was still a baby, carefully bettering herself, marrying up through the ranks, leaving Lee and Levi's modest dry goods store for an oilman and his fortune, and leaving him for a cattle baron and finally, at least when last heard of, settling down with a real estate developer in L.A. There was a frontier laissez-faire kind of attitude in early-day Oklahoma that held that a man (or woman) was justified in using any skills or talents to get ahead. Lee's wife, Lucille, apparently had some skill at marriage. No one has heard of her in years, nor have I ever made any attempt to trace her or her family. I am content, I suppose, to keep that part of my life a mystery.

It might seem strange that I would have so little interest in so important a part of my background, but I was never encouraged in that direction and in the last several years I have simply been too busy to think about it. Once I had reasonably sorted through all my own personal problems and adolescent trauma, I was flung headlong into the retail business. It is easy to get involved to excess. Perhaps before I die I will make that effort. I'm sure my maternal line could not be so hard to trace, nor my father's maternal line, about which I am equally ignorant.

At any rate, I know nothing of Lucille, not even her last name or the name of her father. Perhaps I am the one carved out of a rock from the Osage Hills.

I grew up with little female companionship or guidance. We had some housekeepers, shadowy figures. Nanny did not surface until I was nearly grown and Lee hired her to look after Levi in his declining years. Old Daniel's wife, Thelma, was a motherly sort, who clucked and worried a lot about me and often had me over to play with David. We are about the same age. I think Old Levi and Old Daniel expected us to marry. I was never interested. It was Thelma who explained to me about my menstrual period. But for her I might still be trying to figure it out. No, actually, she was so circumspect and evasive with her explanation—she had no daughter—that I wasn't really too sure what was going on, only that I'd probably get pregnant through no fault of my own no matter what I did.

I stare for a few moments at the dusty box and finally put it back on the floor at the foot of the big bed.

I am tired, and I tell myself I'll go through the papers first thing tomorrow before I go to David's for dinner.

Of course I don't. I sleep too late, and by the time I rise, Nanny is in a snit to open her packages. She has already found them behind the sofa, not so great a hiding place, I think, and has torn at the ends of the wrapping paper. She always does, but I have outfoxed her by having the gifts wrapped twice, first one way and then the other. She has been foiled in her attempt to peek at the end of the box for clues.

She is pleased as a child with everything, and I am pleased with the nightshirt, purchased at K mart, which she gives me. It has a slogan, CUDDLE ME, and the picture of a fuzzy kitten on the front. Nanny loves things with slogans. I tell her it looks very warm and she is pleased.

She is going to Leroy and Charlaine's for Christmas. Most of their children and grandchildren will be in attendance. I almost envy her. I have been to dinners at Leroy and Charlaine's, and they are always raucous and lively affairs, with much shouting and arguing.

The first time I went there with Nanny, many years ago, I re-call—I wore gloves and a pillbox hat, that's how long ago—it was for Thanksgiving and the children were all small. That experience was jolting. Almost immediately Charlaine and Leroy began arguing, about what I don't remember, loudly and abusively, Nanny chiming right in, siding first with one and then with the other, until Charlaine finally shouted, "Go on outside and fart around and see if I care." And Leroy slammed out of the house shouting, "That's just what I'm goin' to do, you high-yeller slut!" Charlaine stormed into the kitchen, Nanny right after her, both still shouting.

Fearing the worst—unfurled straight razors at arm's length at the very least—I looked around for my gloves and pocketbook. But before I could beat a retreat, Nanny strolled back in with the intelligence that the turkey was done and dinner would be shortly. She called to Leroy, who was puttering in the garage of the modest house, and he came whistling in and went straight to the bathroom and noisily splashed at his hands while children began to filter in. Charlaine was all smiles, Leroy was all compliments and the children were all noise and appetites. I have since learned that this is the way things are at their house. It is a noisy, argumentative kind of love, strangely excit-ing and occasionally unnerving to a spinster who spends most of her hours in a cavernous office or a silent mansion.

I offer to drive Nanny to Leroy's, but she has already called a cab. Nanny has great rapport with cabdrivers and she loves to ride cabs. I am suddenly left alone in the still house. It is not the first time I have been alone here; I have always been alone here, as a matter of fact, even when Lee and Levi lived. It is no great thing and I am a little surprised even to have noticed it and I climb the stairs to dress for dinner.

My undressed form is a little hippy and sags in places where it once didn't. It comes of getting older; there's little to be done. I certainly don't intend to panic and run off to a spa and work up sweats and such in the name of eternal youth. I am slightly disturbed, how-ever, at the dimples of fat—cellulite if you like—that I notice; it may just be the light. I recall the polyester woman, dimpled in her stretch pants, and grin wryly to myself. Let her who is without cellulite cast the first stone.

I wonder if the old woman has got her picture and if she is pleased with it. And, unaccountably, I am struck by a salacious thought, wondering vaguely how that polyester pair got those unappealing children. Did they make love on a wide bed, he searching through cellulite to find her? I have a hard time imagining them making love. Does he slip up behind her as she bakes bread or irons or folds clothes and pull down her polyester breeches and screw her while she continues, bovinely, her activities?

I laugh at myself and the train of thought rumbles on. Familiar people making love. I can't imagine, for instance, Arlene and David copulating—that's what they do, I'm sure. Polyester people screw; button-down people copulate, at least I'm sure that's what Arlene and David do. But trying to conjure that vision, I come up with Arlene outlining, between thrusts, her current decorating scheme or something, while David, mounted upon her, goes through the motions and mutters distractedly, "Uh, huh. Hmmmm," and shuffles simultaneously through a sheaf of papers, using her thoughtlessly as he might an electric razor or toothbrush.

Such bursts of imaginary voyeurism are rare. But if I have them, I suspect others do, too. It's called fantasizing in some circles and is considered quite normal. It's only that I project my fantasies onto others and remain detached myself. I learned that from that far-gone shrink.

David and Arlene live in the southeast section of the city, the new part, on a hill, their house new, newly decorated, newly landscaped. Arlene jumps from house to house, style to style. Nothing ever evolves; her decorating always looks as if it sprang full grown from the brain of an omnipotent interior designer.

I wonder if Old Daniel will be there. I take for granted that he will be; he always is, ferried from a distant nursing home in an ambulance for all such occasions. Arlene and David are kind to him, as kind as it's possible, I suppose, to be to a drooling, largely unseeing entity. That's unkind of me. There are sparks of life in the old man, dim sparks. I recall many years ago Old Daniel, who was then quite fit and alert, saying in response to something or other, "If I live to be a hundred." I had been surprised then, thinking that he must have been that already at least. How old he is, I'm not sure, only that he was a contemporary of Old Levi and Old Levi died, in his turn, during the Korean War. Old Daniel has lived beyond his turn.

I honestly think that Arlene would keep Daniel at home and hire a nurse—they can well afford it, if only by virtue of the retainer that Murphy's Department Stores, Inc., pays David's law firm—only Old

Daniel doesn't fit her decor. There are no hiding places in Arlene's house. Old Daniel would fit quite nicely, however, into my house, which is all dark corners and dusty crevices. I think it is peculiar that Arlene, who has such a passion for keeping house, would be the one with the sleek furniture, tubular and shiny, surfaces that dust could never cling to, that dust would slide right off of, and I, who have no interest whatsoever, beyond my designer bedding, in the house around me and abhor even the simplest kinds of household maintenance, would have a house that harbors dust, yea, even seeks it, actively recruits it. There are dusty places in my house, far corners and crevices of dark decorative molding that probably have dust that predates me, dust that came with the house. I have no idea whose idea it was to install that molding, dust catchers—no woman's, I'm sure. Old Levi fit well in that environment, and Lee; Old Daniel would look as if he belonged right there with all the musty closets and mahogany paneling and heavy furniture.

Arlene often chides me about redecorating or remodeling. She's gone as far as to wander through my rooms, outlining ambitious projects for letting in light and opening up spaces, a town house to end all town houses. I just laugh when she does, and tell her I haven't the time to worry with it. Perhaps. Or perhaps I just don't want any light let in to illuminate the dusty crevices of my life. That dust, after all, is all I have of a past; but for those few faded photographs and memories, I am completely unattached in the universe. I think of Nanny and Leroy and Charlaine. They are certainly not unattached.

Nor are Arlene and David, though the contrast between Leroy's and David's families is great. I have never really gotten acquainted with David's children, though I've known them all their lives and am, I think, godmother to one or two of them. There is a strange distance between me and that generation, the generation that wears labels on its jeans and logos on its pockets. Danny, named for Old Daniel, is the only boy and the girls are Marci, with the diminutive *i*, and Brooke, a soap opera heroine's name with a superfluous *e*.

I have presents for all of them, Old Daniel included, and I lug them to the door, where David unburdens me of my packages and places them under the Christmas tree. It is a decorator tree, all tied with white bows and hung with silver balls.

After a cup of eggnog and a toast or two to the holidays, we open our gifts with the obligatory exclamations of gratitude. Arlene and David have given me an arrangement of silk flowers. It is quite lovely and, I'm certain, custom-made and not purchased at Murphy's. Arlene is clever at finding things that couldn't be bought at Murphy's, one-of-a-kind sorts of things.

"I have something for Old Daniel," I say.

"He's sleeping. He won't be out for dinner," says Arlene.

"He drools," says one of the girls matter-of-factly. She has dark hair. I didn't remember that any of David and Arlene's children had dark hair.

"Marci," says her mother testily.

Marci with her diminutive *i* and Brooke with her superfluous *e*. The world is full of unnecessary vowels, I think, too many vowels and not enough consonants.

"Well, Mother," says Marci, "it's true. Who wants to sit and watch him drool and spit over his food?"

It is not said with a lack of compassion, but only as an observation. Marci, I have already noted to my surprise, has a more brittle wit and intelligence about her than her name or her hairdo would suggest. Her hairdo is identical to that of the majority of teenaged girls I have seen, and I have wondered more than once if there is a law about which I am ignorant that requires girls of a given age to wear their hair in a prescribed manner. Her sister Brooke, of the superfluous *e*, apparently lays no claim to wit or intelligence, although she is adept at bored shrugs. Danny, like David, seems perpetually detached, coming to life momentarily only at mention of a televised football game.

When the conversation lags, unusually early into the meal, once the preliminaries concerning the ambience of the meal have been dispatched, Arlene says, "Your grandfather and Mr. St. Cloud were boyhood friends, weren't they, Elizabeth?" She always refers to Old Daniel as "Mr. St. Cloud."

Danny and Brooke ignore the remark, but it is Marci of the dark hair and diminutive *i* who glances around and considers. She has probably heard that information all of her life, for Arlene is given to bringing it up whenever she feels a hostess's responsibility to draw out her guest; there is little for her to say to me, otherwise, except to ask after business. Marci is thinking, and is probably too polite to ask, how it can be that I who am old enough to be her mother could have a grandfather the same age as her own. She is not thinking, of course—children rarely do—that her own grandfather is of an age to have been her great-grandfather, possibly her great-great-grandfather. I will leave that to Arlene to try to explain.

I merely nod in response to Arlene's question. "They grew up in Tipeeho," I add.

"Tipeeho?" says Marci. "Where's that?" She gives her question that peculiar adolescent emphasis that suggests she really doesn't believe such a place exists.

"North of Claremore," says David. "Cherokee country, Rogers County."

"When was that?" asks Marci. I am surprised that she is interested.

"Before statehood, I think. I don't recall the details," replies her father. "Father told me little. I really don't remember. Old Levi Murphy founded a dry goods store in Tulsa shortly before statehood, and my father came some years after. He practiced law in St. Louis awhile, I think. The two families have been very close since, though"—he pauses delicately—"there was some falling out between Father and Old Levi after Old Levi, ah . . ." He was trying to be tactful.

"Went peculiar," I said.

"Well, yes," murmured David, "ah, in his last years, senile, I suppose. He developed some, uh, peculiar obsessions, I think, and, uh, became enraged that our law firm could do nothing to help him establish them."

All three of David's children are listening now. There is something about family histories that captivates even the dullest spirits.

It is Marci, however, who demands particulars.

"Well," said David, glancing at Arlene, who is satisfied, her hostess's conversational ploy having been so successful, "it's been a long time; it doesn't matter."

"Oh, it's all right, David," I say and then to Marci I explain, "Old Levi in his last years decided that he was a Jew and he wanted that fact authenticated. He became so obsessed with the idea that we ceased all Christian practices around the house. For several years we didn't even celebrate Christmas, although Levi never actually became a practicing Jew, either. We lived in a religious limbo."

"*Was* he a Jew?" asks Brooke.

"I have no reason to think he was."

"What a peculiar idea. Why did he think he was a Jew?

"I have no idea."

"Murphy isn't even Jewish."

"No, but Levi is."

"Good grief," says Marci, "that's hardly reason to change your religion. Lots of people have Jewish first names. Abraham Lincoln, for instance."

"Isaac Newton," says Brooke.

"Joe DiMaggio," says Danny.

"Joe DiMaggio?" says Marci, and everyone laughs.

"Joseph is an Old Testament name," Danny defends himself.

"Well, so is David," says Marci, "and, for that matter, Daniel."

I am willing to let the conversation degenerate into something else, but Marci comes back to it after mirth has been milked from the Old Testament names.

"I don't really understand," says Marci, "how Grandfather and Old Levi—why was he called *Old* Levi?—could be boyhood friends?"

David glances at his daughter lovingly and patiently. "My father was in his sixties when I was born. He didn't marry until quite late in life. It's simple mathematics, Marci."

"Oh."

I do not bother answering her question about *Old* Levi. It would require explaining about Lee's name change, and that is more involved than one dinner party conversation could reasonably accommodate. She has apparently forgotten her question, which is just as well. I do not care to follow this conversation further, anyway. There are too many questions for which I have no answers.

"Old age is sad," sighs Arlene, rising, signaling the end of that conversation and ordering coffee and dessert in the great room from the ubiquitous black girl who is serving us.

"And ask Miss Cohn to bring Mr. St. Cloud in by the fire if she thinks he's up to it."

Arlene is careful about the *St.* Cloud. Most of the family goes by "Cloud," and indeed the law firm is called Cloud, Cloud, Breckinridge and Tyme. If that firm had not always represented Murphy's Department Stores, Inc., I certainly would have chosen it simply on the strength of such an euphonious name.

We are settled and coffeed by the fire when the nurse wheels Old Daniel into the room and parks him close to the blaze, which is, of course, a gas log, though it looks quite real and is even hickory-scented. Arlene thinks of everything.

The stooped and vacant figure in the wheelchair is little more than skin stretched tight over bone with patches of thin hair at appropriate intervals. Old Daniel has always been a part of my life like the old house, a part of the background, never intruding but always there. My earliest memories, most of my memories of him, as a matter of fact, are ageless. I never thought of him as old so much as eternal. I see him so infrequently now that I am always caught off guard by his aged state. Old Levi never got old; he just died. This is not a new thought; though they get older, the people we are most familiar with, they are not like the aged strangers we encounter, those perpetually aged who were never anything else in our eyes. So it was with Levi. I watched him age and die and yet he was never an old person in the manner of old strangers.

But Daniel—Daniel has become old, so old that I have a hard time recalling that this worn-out piece of human machinery was ever anything else.

"Did you have a good dinner, Father?" asks David cheerfully, as if the dimly sighted form can actually understand him. Old Daniel says nothing. Unhearing, uncomprehending, he stares toward the programmed flames, predictable, never sparking or shooting high or dying low.

"Sometimes," says David to no one in particular, "there is a sign of life. Sometimes he smiles or nods."

"Or talks," says Marci. "I've heard him get started and all excited about something that makes no sense at all. Like a child playing make-believe."

I have a hard time imagining any sound coming from this wrapped and blanketed figure.

This evidence of mortality casts a slight pall, which soon passes. I place the wrapped Christmas package on Old Daniel's lap and he touches it and then looks down but makes no move toward it. I take it and carefully unwrap it. It's a *Pictorial History of Oklahoma*. I'm not sure how well Old Daniel can see, but I hope that he can make out some of the pictures. It doesn't look promising. I open the book to the page I have marked, a picture of Main Street some time around statehood, with a sign prominent in the background: MURPHY'S DRY GOODS, and I hold it toward Old Daniel.

"Can he look at pictures still?" I inquire of no one in particular.

I place the open book on the old man's lap and he hunches briefly over it, staring, and then he looks away. I do not know if he sees or if he comprehends, but he glances back at it several times as the conversation moves on.

"I have another box of papers," I say to David. "Some that Old

Levi tucked away under the stairs. Nanny found them. I don't think they are significant."

"Have you looked at them? I want to get to court before the first of the year, you know."

"I've glanced through them. They seem to be mostly personal things—quite old—some few official-looking documents, family photographs."

"Family photographs?" David is aware that "family" is not a term often used to describe the Murphys. We were always simply "the Murphys of Murphy's Department Stores."

"Old Levi's family, I think," I say. "Old Levi, I do know, was raised by his grandparents and a couple of maiden aunts, I think. I don't know any particulars, only some names. All three women," I say, laughing, "were apparently named Louisa," and I carefully pronounce it "Lou-i-za" in the old-fashioned manner of Levi. "And his grandfather, I know, was Obediah Murphy, O.B. for short." Obediah and three Lou-i-zas, Louisa One, Louisa Two and Louisa Three, Old Levi had called them; these were details that even a bored teenager would remember.

"Ah," says David. Arlene is fidgeting; she wants to change the subject, probably to spring fashions. She often quizzes me on such, reasoning, I suppose, that as a department store head I should also be a fashion expert. I am not. Nor am I a merchandising genius. I am an old-fashioned, hardheaded businessperson. I was taught by Old Levi and Lee and I know what I'm about.

"The Old Bastard!"

We all jump. The words in ringing, clear tones, catching us all so unexpectedly, have come from the frail mound of humanity in the wheelchair. Old Daniel has spoken. Both girls begin to giggle and their mother shushes them; but Old Daniel has no more to say.

"Weird," says Brooke.

"He is upset about something," says Arlene.

And so it seems. Something has stirred the ancient memory, however incoherently, in the old man. Perhaps the picture book.

"How weird," repeats Brooke. I have to agree.

After a pause, when it is obvious that Daniel has resumed his comatose state, the conversation drifts on. A sudden snort from the old man at length startles us again, but he is only asleep and Arlene summons Miss Cohn to take Old Daniel away. The indefinable smells of age—camphor, dentifrice, Lysol or some such mixture—hang on the air, mingling strangely with the artificial hickory smoke and the assortment of bath colognes that David's women wear.

The day eventually wears out, as such days do, and I make my excuses and all rise, including the children, to see me to the door. We stand for a brief moment in the entry hall, making those meaningless little remarks, putting off opening the front door and admitting the winter night, the air of which has suddenly become much more frigid, a blast of wind preceding the oncoming cold front. Miss Cohn appears from the hallway to the wing where Old Daniel is housed.

"Is he still sleeping?" inquires Arlene solicitously.

"No. I'm getting him some Ovaltine."

It is curious that the aged are always offered Ovaltine as the drink of choice, a palliative to put them to sleep, when a hot rum toddy would serve the same function much more agreeably and appropriately, warm milk being the drink of babies, stimulating growth, alcohol a preservative for those that require preserving.

I am almost to make that observation aloud but both word and thought die aborning, victims of the shattering shriek that echos down the hall from Old Daniel's open door.

Such a shriek does not invite polite shuffling down the hall to see what he needs; it demands immediate attention from all who hear it, and we stumble all over one another in our haste to get to Daniel, this shriek most surely signaling his imminent demise.

But he is sitting straight up, staring hard ahead of him, clutching the arms of his chair, his voice strong as it had been earlier before the fire, an unbelievable sound coming from that long, emaciated body.

"God curse you, Levi! God curse you. Oh, God will curse you!"

With that malediction pronounced, the wasted body relaxes against the cushions and pillows that prop it and the old eyes resume their sightless stare. The sigh in the room is almost audible.

"I'll get the Ovaltine," says Miss Cohn.

Ah, the Ovaltine, that ubiquitous palliative, to soothe the ancient nervous system, to coat the aged abdominal tract and so to put to rest whatever terrors precipitated the outburst.

I am relieved to make my way home, driving the black Lincoln through residential streets, unwilling somehow to hit the largely deserted expressways.

Nanny is not yet home and I realize I have once again forgotten to set the electronic burglar alarm. I leave it unset about as often as I remember to set it. The burglar system was David's idea, he being, rightly I suppose, concerned about Nanny and me living by ourselves, unprotected by anything save a few dead bolts and Nanny's all-night television set.

Burglars have not taken advantage of my lapse, however, and things are just as they were when I left, including the aging liquor box at the foot of my bed.

There is no time like the present, I impulsively reason, and I lift the box to the bed and slowly remove the musty papers and faded photographs, spreading them in an orderly manner all over the bed. A disturbed spider ambles across a dusty page and I brush it aside. Many people are afraid of spiders, but they've never bothered me. I stare a moment at the spider and muse that perhaps those people excessively frightened by spiders were flies in an earlier existence.

Spread out around me, the contents of the Seagram Seven carton are vaguely familiar. I have indeed seen them before. There are grim photographs of grim people in grim clothes wearing grim expressions. The names on the back in pencil or faded ink are not decipherable. There are some documents and bills of sale, dated, for the most part, fifty to seventy-five years ago. I stare at one such document—it is, at cursory glance, a note for $600. I can't make out the date but I am arrested at the signature on the document, arrested enough to stare for a long time at the ornate curlicues and elegant flourishes. The first letter finally assumes the shape of an *O*, and it is easy enough to follow the rest of the word to its conclusion. *Obediah. Obediah* something, something *Murphy*. The "something, something" appears to be letters, or perhaps only decorations, but I think that what I am staring at is the lavish signature of the founder of the line, Obediah Murphy.

I flip through the other odds and ends of papers, newspaper clippings, bills of sale. One of the newspaper clippings, I notice, announces the marriage of Levi Murphy to Miss Elizabeth Butler "of this city," although there is no clue as to where "this city" might be located. I ponder briefly having the clipping laminated so I can save it, and then I smile at such uncharacteristic sentiment on my part.

At the bottom of the box is the ringed binder that I recognize as Old Levi's book. The binder, splotched with the faded stains of age and smelling of mildew and dark corners, is undecorated save for the address label—Murphy's Department Stores, the return address, and boldly printed where the addressee's name should go: LEVI'S BOOK. This, then, is the book he read to me so many years ago, keeping me up yawning through the night.

I say "read" me his book, but that's not quite right. For "read" is not what he did; there was hardly enough there for a moderate-sized article, much less a book. He had been waiting for me, pacing and agitated, when I made my unauthorized entry through the window, by way of a sturdy trellis. I thought, of course, that I had been found out and that my late-night dallying on the sandbars of the Arkansas was the reason for his agitation. He did not allude to it. I don't remember how he prefaced his reading. By the time I realized that I was not the cause of his consternation, he had begun his reading. He read from his book and explained and digressed as he went. I remember at first being interested but confused. I didn't think of a tape recorder. There probably wasn't one anyway. He talked and read most of the night away, but by the next day he had apparently forgotten the whole thing. I don't recall that he ever mentioned his book again or that I ever saw it. I wonder if it makes any more sense now than it did then?

But it takes only a glance to convince me that the reading of it will have to wait a more leisurely time. It's late and I'm tired. These papers scattered over my soft pastel comforter are strangely compelling, but everything about them, even their withered odor, distances them. I think that they never could have smelled fresh or new, have been shiny and clean. They have always been old, replicas and debris of a far civilization that never really was. I pick up a group picture, six grim-visaged people.

I stare at the old photograph, not particularly unlike a hundred others of that period that I have seen. The six—three women and three men—had been stylishly posed, the men standing behind the seated women, whose voluminous skirts run together like some strange three-headed creature with an enormous posterior. I adjust my bifocals carefully and six identically suspicious stares glare back at me. Those stares, I wonder: Are they indicative of mean and tight personalities common to that period of history, or do they only indicate an honest apprehension at the photographer's powder flash that reduces every countenance to an unshadowed, expressionless plane?

The photographer's art is amateurish, even, I suspect, for that day, and it is impossible to get any clues as to personalities. The women, I know, are the fabled Louisas—One, Two and Three—and the old man, his hat at a rakish angle, ruffles at his collar and pants unnaturally tight (I wonder how he avoided the baggy pants that seem a natural part of the aging process), looks like some aging Dumas character. The two young men: one, I suppose, is Levi, though I haven't a clue which, both being stern of expression (or frightened) and of about the same height, nor is the old man, Obediah, I suspect, much shorter, though slightly stooped.

I turn the picture over and stare closely again at the faded writing on the back. I can't begin to make it out. Were I interested enough, I might find an expert who could decipher it. But I see nothing in the expressions, washed out by that old photographer's bright flash, that makes me interested in knowing more.

These papers will take more deciphering than I am up to at the moment. I could put all of them away and take them out again, but I decide to leave them spread out for the time being. It will not be the first time I've slept in Lee's single bed because my own large one was covered with papers. Nor am I afraid to sleep in Lee's bed. I do not fear being haunted. Lee had so little spirit that he could not afford to leave any behind; he'll need all he has to relocate on the other side. I do not mean any unkindness; it's merely an observation.

I do not think I would sleep so comfortably in Old Levi's rooms. I am suspicious that he secured them before he left, as if he sometime thought he might come back.

I glance once more at the clutter of papers on the bed and pick up a brittle folded paper, so brittle that I wonder if it might break right in two. It proves to be a curious thing, filled with neat, precise, tiny circles and slashes and x's, all in columns. There is an order here as if they mean something, an ancient hieroglyphic language or a secret code. And still more curious: the thing is attested to by that same ornate antique of a signature, which I take to be Obediah Murphy's.

I let the dry old paper drop and drift back to its fellows on the bed. There is something lonely about these bits and pieces of someone else's memories, dusty and faded, beyond anyone's recall. That is a late-night thought. I try to shake it off. I pass through the papers again and pick up a yellowed newspaper, the Tipeeho *Tribune*, October 12, 1903. I am immediately arrested at the headline: WAR HERO PASSES TO HIS REWARD. It is the obituary of my ancestor Obediah Murphy, an obituary written in that personal, subjective style of old-time newspapers, at once both self-important and gossipy. I cannot contain a startled laugh when I read it.

Colonel Obediah J. M. Murphy of this city was the victim of a dastardly attack from the rear on the 7th day of this month. He did not survive that attack.

Colonel Murphy was set upon by Mr. Tommy T. Timmons of this city who accused the Colonel of unseemly attentions to his wife, Mrs. Timmons. Mr. Timmons then proceeded to fire several shots into the back of Colonel Murphy as he departed the window of the Timmons home. At the time of his demise Colonel Murphy was in his 84th year.

Mr. Timmons in view of his advanced years was not incarcerated but was confined to his home. Mr. Timmons is in his 78th year. Mrs. Timmons who is confined to her bed with gout and rheumatism and other vicissitudes of age did not comment upon the attack.

Colonel Murphy was mourned at services the following day by all who knew him. He had served with honor at Pea Ridge; he had been by turns a farmer in Tennessee and Illinois, probate judge in Missouri and legislator in Arkansas before arriving in our Territory some three years ago.

He was judged to be a man of honor and learning, wise and persevering. He will be sorely missed by this community.

He is survived by his wife Louisa of the home and by two female relatives also called Louisa and a grandson Levi Murphy, a student at the Missouri University for higher education at Columbia, Missouri.

I stare at the yellowed page, then read quickly through the article again. This can't be real, yet it obviously is. The anonymous journalist, if not precise in his details, was at least clear on general events. That old joke. That ancient punch line, shot at eighty-three by a jealous husband.

I want to laugh. Perhaps it is the dusty dignity of the aged photographs and papers that keeps me from it.

I take up Old Levi's book. The beginning sentence is arresting enough. "I am damned. So be it. I have at last shut the door on the Old Bastard and his three Louisas. There will be no more." What follows lapses quickly into an incoherent collection of names, some dates, some towns and copious mention of Obediah, O.B., the Old Bastard, of Louisa and of Daniel, too. When I finish, I have more eyestrain than information.

Is this all there is to it?

TWO

THE PAST

*T*he Old Bastard was dead and we buried him.

"I vould haf a fine, tall stone cut fer him," said Louisa One, my great-grandmother. "I vould haf a fine, big stone." That was the extent of her mourning, though my grandmother, Louisa Two, mourned with enough volume and enthusiasm for both, and perhaps for all three, had my own mother either voice enough or understanding for grief.

It was almost as if Obediah had left not one but three widows, all named Louisa. Mother, daughter, granddaughter, they all seemed of an age and they all likewise orbited as planets that luminous star which was Obediah Murphy, though he was but fumes and flash to their substance.

I, I could not mourn him, ever, though townsfolks, friends or curious onlookers, with doffed hats and bowed heads and clasped hands, seemed genuinely bereft. I could detect, however, that occasional twinkle of an eye or slight grimace of the mouth that marked more the tolerant affection than the grief of those uninterested mourners.

In the late night that followed, I watched the flames as they approached, caressed and then devoured the pages I was feeding singly into the blaze on the small grate, each page an ash before I committed another for incineration, until the entire contents of my journal had been so reduced. No more. I thought, So perhaps it is with the Old Bastard, the eternal fires of hell at this moment enfolding.

I was not comforted at that thought, nor was I distressed. There was in fact an empty space in the hollow of my stomach where feeling ought to have been. More evidence, perhaps, of what my great-grandmother old Louisa One has always called my dark side. "Levi," she is wont to say whenever my actions seem to her inexplicable, "ye haf to you a dark side. An' I don't understood it." I have never been quite sure what she means by "dark side," but if it is a reference to my tendency toward introspection and my rigid guidelines of personal performance and exact thought, then I accept that label; for truly I am as unemotional as the rest of this family is emotional, and I would assuredly remove myself whatever distance, spiritually, is necessary to be as different from Obediah as night is from day.

But Obediah is dead, dead and interred, gone at long last from my life, freeing me to approach without reservation this new century that I am to work with. Alas, he did not go without one last humiliation, shot down as he was by a jealous husband, and that not even in the dignity of drawn weapons at dawn but in a squalid back room by a drunken old sot.

I have read and reread the pages of this journal, begun for my own satisfaction at the very dawn of this century with intent to record the years and the business of them, for I know myself to be able and I view the future as mine for the taking. But these pages, reviewed in the light of the Old Bastard's death, revealed more of myself than I would reveal and more of Obediah than I would want the world to know. Should that day come that I would write of my life and accomplishments, I can return in memory to this time and resurrect those facts which I would have resurrected. And only those.

As it stands, the Old Bastard is dead and I am heir to his fortune and head of the strange combination of personalities that make up my family. Great-grandmother, grandmother, and mother. All named Louisa, for ease of identification often called Louisa One, Louisa Two and Louisa Three. Though with that childhood knack of simplifying and identifying, I early began referring to One as Grandmother, though she was in truth great-grandmother, and Two I have simply called Louisa or Two, for she has always seemed dispossessed somehow, like a maiden aunt. My mother, Three, I call Three or Mother, though in truth, she being mindless and silent, the need to call her anything is rare. And certainly I am fond of these three old women, all so perversely devoted to that old bastard Obediah Murphy. But then, I have never been able to account for womankind, these three no different—for all their peculiarities—in that respect. I am responsible for them and for their welfare now, and for Daniel, too, for he is ever too good-hearted and shallow to be of much consequence on his own; and these responsibilities I take very seriously.

Thus, with the last shriveling page, my journal is gone and so, too, perhaps Obediah, but the memory of both is vivid and shall so remain, the memory of Obediah grown more bitter, if possible, through the general kindly reactions to his humiliating demise, starting with that spurious newspaper eulogy, for such is all it can be called.

Upon reading that account of the Old Bastard's death, I was appalled. I went directly to my great-grandmother to complain of it. She had, of course, already heard it, some helpful soul or other always eager to be involved in such funeral festivities, basking in reflected glory, as it were, if only by providing condolences, food and in this case reading services.

"I tought n'en vas nice, Levi," she said to me in her own quaint argot, the antecedents of which I have never been able to decipher, nor she to explain.

"Nice, Grandmother? Nice? That newspaper fellow made the Old Bastard out to be a hero, a veritable war hero, a man of achievement. When he was none of that. He was a wastrel, evil, a lecher, a fornicator."

"Ah, Levi. I n'en know, how is it that ye must vest Obie vit evil n'en he vas ne'er capable of?"

"Grandmother! He was a liar and a thief to boot."

"Ah, nay, Levi, he vas ne'er a thief. And he vas ne'er a liar. He vas truthful ever to me. Vit his dying breath he said to me, 'Louisa,' he said, 'I should've gone out the front door.' His veriest final vord."

Grandmother, like everyone else, could not take the Old Bastard seriously, even in death. He was the object of gentle merriment, like a wayward child. Passersby on the street tipped their hats and smiled their condolences, and I saw the smile in their eyes, gently chiding a naughty child for having gotten into mischief and so brought about his own demise. I did not understand it. I have never understood it.

I turned my attention once more to the newspaper account of Obediah's accident. The journalist had called upon us the afternoon of the fatal shooting, his hat in his hand, condolences and apologies on his lips. We had sat, the four of us—Louisa One, Two, Three and myself—in the parlor, the work of the undertaker not yet completed, the remains as yet undelivered.

The young journalist's questions were gently probing, I give him that, none of the harsher questions the circumstances might have warranted. Grandmother sat, obviously impressed by her stature as widow of the deceased, her enormous bulk supported by a chair and two canes, one for each hand. I marveled, as I have before, that a woman of her years—for she was older by at least a decade than Obediah, and the newspaper account put him at eighty-three, which was probably more or less accurate—could retain so much bulk, great age as a rule tending to shrink. Two did much of the talking, making but little sense, prattling incessantly, in her dreary, futile, continuing effort to upstage Grandmother. My own mother, Louisa Three, struggled with the buttons on her bodice, Two regularly and gently restraining her from undoing them altogether, for my mother, Louisa Three, has been mad for long before my own birth. Fragile and fading, Three has always seemed to me to be only a presence, a form, from which the person it once housed has long since fled, that form's only contribution the birthing of a male bastard, the son, I'm told, of a passing peddler, by name Mendel the Jew.

I sat among these three, grimly reminded that I was now solely responsible for these three eccentric old women, my mother at once both youngest and oldest, senile and helpless; my great-grandmother, the oldest and yet the youngest, bright, alert, cheerful, as if she would live another ninety or more years.

At length the young reporter asked politely of our various names, particularly as to spelling. "I am Levi Murphy," I said, spelling the last name carefully, reasoning that even a newspaper reporter could manage to position the four letters of my first name in their logical sequence.

"And ve are," said Grandmother, indicating the other two ladies, "Louisa Murphy."

I quickly spelled Louisa for him, for fear that the pronunciation would baffle him. I give the reporter good marks again at least for his tact in not inquiring as to the curiosity of a household of women, all directly descended, all having the same surname. Or perhaps that peculiarity did not capture his notice. The truth is, bastards run in our family.

"Ah," the reporter said, realizing that the peculiarity of the pronunciation did not extend to the spelling. "Lou-i-za?" he carefully enunciated.

"Yes," I said. "They are all three named Louisa. It is a family name, passed down for generations."

"Dey vas named fer me," said Grandmother.

"I was named for you," corrected Two, "and she"—she indicated my mother, at work once again on her buttons—"was named for me."

"I see." I do not think that he did *see*, but he made the best of it. "And is it not difficult to distinguish so many by the same name?" he asked, again with the utmost courtesy.

"Ve are Louisa One, Two and Three," said my grandmother. "I," she said, lest the obvious be missed, "am One."

"I see," he said again, without I suspect, really seeing. "And you"—he looked at Two—"are, I am sure, understandably distressed at the abrupt departure of your father in this most heinous fashion?"

"He was not my father," snapped Two.

"Not?" The journalist was now more perplexed.

"Colonel Murphy," said my grandmother, giving the Old Bastard his spurious title, "vas mine 'nudder man."

"Her second husband," I translated.

"Ah," said the reporter.

He went his way and covered his confusion, I suppose, by making up what pertinent information he felt he had missed. Louisa One and Two were delighted with the obituary as it read, like other nonreaders so impressed by the written word that its very existence, graven as it was before them, gave credence to that which was otherwise incredible. It is a flaw, I realize, not limited to the illiterate.

There had been no mention made of Daniel's rather tenuous place in the family. Had I been he, I would have considered that propitious. Would that I myself could have escaped mention. In truth, I don't suppose it would have mattered that much to Daniel either way, he having no real connection, save legal, with the rest of us. However, he hastened home from St. Louis as soon as he received the telegram and could make arrangements, though it was three days past the Old Bastard's interment that he arrived.

I sought him out with the newspaper clipping, only to find that he had already read it; and not surprisingly, he merely shrugged.

"He does not deserve this. He has been an embarrassment and a fornicator as long as I can remember."

"Which was more serious, Levi?" Daniel smiled. He was ribbing gently, as was his wont.

"Don't make light of it, Daniel. You at least do not have to bear the stigma of his name. He is not really your relative."

"And is he yours?"

Daniel's classes at law in St. Louis, I thought, had made him uncommonly argumentative, pacifism being more his natural inclination. "By definition, by custom, yes. I grew up with him from a babe; I carry his name, as do my mother and both my grandmothers. That he is a stepparent makes little difference. I am more free to detest his memory than you, who are only a ward of the court and are as free to be indifferent if you like."

I thought that sound reasoning on my part, but Daniel only smiled again and drawled, "Let it be. The Old Bastard's death should unburden you. It is customary, Levi, to forgive the dead. Forgive and forget. The one generation forgives and the next forgets."

It has always been easy for me to anticipate Daniel's actions. He is predictable in all things. I could tell that he was about to wax profound, for instance; it was in the stance he took and in the slight sigh before he spoke. It was almost as if he had taken out a pipe and lighted it.

"There is a process of regeneration of the dead that commences almost immediately upon the final breath—when they are no longer things to be feared or dealt with. History, for instance, has always a kind word for all but the most bestial. So let it be with the Old Bastard. That newspaper fellow, he has already begun that process."

There have been times when I have wondered if the law is really where Daniel's talents lie, if he would not perhaps be better suited for the study of philosophy or literature. He takes his profundities so seriously; indeed, those are all that he does take seriously. But it was the Old Bastard who destined him for the law and me for merchandising.

"Ah yes, a lawyer, attorney, solicitor," cried the Old Bastard in his sonorous tones, ever loving of the elegant phrase, the important-sounding term. *Solicitor.* Where had he picked up the word, he who could barely read or write anything beyond his idiotic signature?

"Ah, it's the least ve could do," Louisa One had said, that peculiar comment not being the first reference that had ever been made to some obscure debt relative to Daniel.

"Yes," thundered O.B., himself so hard of hearing he seemed to think that the rest of us were also. "Yes, and the Jew boy he should certainly go into merchandising, be a merchant, as his history dictates. All them kikes are peddlers of one sort or another." And he laughed at his private joke. He always did when he called me "Jew boy." Nor did he seem to realize at all that I might be offended, so casually and naturally did he come out with it.

"Levi must learn merchandising. This"—and he waved his hand in a broad gesture encompassing the wilderness around us—"will one day be large cities and people and shops. This is the beginning, Jew boy, and you will be a part of it."

All of my life, as far back at least as I can remember, as we traveled westward, the Old Bastard always proclaimed each new stop permanent, as the new beginning, the West won. "Here," he would intone, "will I build a city. I will people it from the issue of my loins," as serious as an Old Testament prophet. And in truth, he might well have, had we been able to stay put for any length of time.

But sooner or later, more often sooner than later, circumstances would make it necessary for us to move on, often rapidly and by the dark of night, and we would leave this future Murphysboro or that Murphystown or the other Murphysville, whatever egomaniacal name the Old Bastard had bestowed on that particular outpost.

Until at last we were here, among the Indians and outlaws in the Cherokee Nation of Indian Territory, this town at least more promising than most places we had occupied. But it already had a population, so no need for Grandfather's ambitious loins, and it already had a name, Tipeeho, a more richly deserved Indian name than any Murphystown or Murphyscity or Murphysburg that O.B. might come up with.

"That newspaper fellow was a fool," I replied in answer to Daniel.

"Would you rather he had told the unvarnished truth?"

"Yes," I said, and I meant it. "Everyone in town already knows the unvarnished truth, but posterity, should posterity be at all interested, will be misled."

"Ah," said Daniel, "posterity is always misled. History is an exercise in misleading."

Daniel was being intellectual again, at once his greatest strength and his greatest weakness. He has always been able to think clearly and articulate accurately. It is an aptitude for action that he lacks, which is why I do not fear to let him talk; when it is time for decisions I will make them. It has always been so, even when we were boys.

Daniel is two or three years older than I am, that being the assumption, at least, as there are no records as to his birth. He joined us when I was nearly six years of age; he has been with us since. Though there have been occasional references to an existing family, none has ever come forth; we grew up as brothers. Perhaps it was the sense of insecurity at being deposited abruptly with a strange family that resulted in such tractability. Never mind that he was always older than I—though gangling, still gangling, Lincolnesque perhaps—when there were conflicting decisions, I always prevailed. I still do, and I see no reason to think that it will ever be any different.

I am very fond of Daniel. He is entertaining in his cerebral fashion; but my university experience—now complete, since I must assume command of this strange vessel—only shored up my negative opinion of intellectuals and their effectiveness at anything more than talk.

I have found no great value to rationalizations about the past and the drawing of parallels from art and music and poetry to support varied contentions about that vague phrase "the human condition." Such talk is as cheap as the glass of beer over which it is customarily conducted. I myself drink no spirits of any sort; nor do I ponder the human condition. Life is a ledger that either balances or not. The Old Bastard's did not; it was full of debits and overdrafts and faulty calculations. I would hate to see Daniel's go that same direction. Perhaps the study of law will indeed stay those sad proclivities for thought as a substitute for action.

As to the three aging women I find myself solely responsible for, they are of no serious account. Not that I do not care for them, but they are only women, to be fed, and clothed and directed. That is all.

When my own history is fully run, however, I greatly desire that it include the intelligence that Obediah Jonah Micah Murphy was a bastard, a lecher, a fornicator and a fake. One way or another I shall make it known that being shot in the back by an irate husband was not an arbitrary ending to the Old Bastard's several decades but an end most fitting and just. For fornication was his sole preoccupation.

"If history misleads," I said at last, "then history is not being writ by the proper hand. History is too important, perhaps, to be left in the hands of romantics and intellectuals."

Daniel laughed agreeably, never one to quarrel, and changed the direction of our conversation. I think that he will never make a trial lawyer.

"Will you be returning to Columbia?" he asked directly.

"Not, at least, until I have settled matters here," I hedged, there being no necessity to tell Daniel that I felt that I had got all I needed from university life. "You, of course, must take your law degree," I added.

"Is there money?" He seemed relieved, for I knew that Daniel enjoyed his student days and was only a year or so away from being able to practice law.

"Statehood," I reminded him, "is only a matter of time. We will have need of trained minds. The money? There seems to be sufficient."

Indeed, we have never wanted, have been clothed and educated and generally provided for in a manner that even a successful farmer—for such due at least I grant Obediah—would be hard pressed to secure. The truth is, I had no idea where that apparent wealth originated, and the time had come for me to find out.

To that end I sought out Louisa One with a view toward getting our affairs in some sort of order, nor could I but expect them to be chaotic, given the Old Bastard's lack of both learning and concentration.

I found Louisa One and Louisa Two in the sitting room, One engrossed in needlework, Two pouting and sulking as she did on various occasions.

"I am making mine funeral clothes," One greeted me.

"What, Grandmother," I teased, "going so soon? Why, you just only got here."

"She'll outlive us all," grumbled Two, "just so's she can have the last word."

Louisa One ignored her. "I vill go to mine grave in something new. I vill not get nothing new again, I tink."

"What is this grave business, Grandmother? With Grandfather dead, why, you can go courting again." It was something Daniel might have said, he being more given to flippancy than I.

"I haf been ready. I've been ready a long time, only I could not go before Obediah. I haf that responsibility, ye see. I haf to stay vit him. I haf no intention that he lif vitout me." She shook out the garment she was stitching, eyeing it critically, measuring it perhaps against eternity. "I lif already more than ninety years. Don't nobody need to lif so long, ye tink. But anyvays, I an't going until I'm ready. I'll call the Indian first before."

Ah, that damnable Indian. "Chief Four Lumps," Daniel always called him, because that was how he drank the tea that Grandmother pressed upon him, though "pressed" is hardly a good word, as the Chief would have nothing at all to say to her until she offered tea, and then he would take it, unbearably sweetened by four lumps of sugar (Grandmother ordered lumps from St. Louis, the only sugar lumps in the entire Cherokee Nation, I suspect).

"A fraud," Obediah had maintained cheerfully of the old Indian, the pot maligning the kettle.

Fraud or not, Chief Four Lumps was tedious at least. If not the same age as Grandmother, he was surely not far behind, for he recalled, or claimed to recall, and I have no reason to doubt his veracity, the removal of the Five Civilized Tribes, as they are called, from the southeastern part of the United States. The "Trail of Tears" the

Indians call it. And he claimed to have fought for the Confederacy in the Civil War under the Cherokee General Stand Watie. Again, I have no reason to doubt him. I only tire of hearing his complaints of ill-treatment at the hands of the United States Government, claiming abuse from Andrew Jackson and further abuse from the Reconstruction Congress.

It is similar to the tirade of Reconstruction colored people, bemoaning the years, nay, eons of slavery, as if it were our fault, and claiming restitution for that which most of them never suffered. These red men and black men needs must realize, I think, that until they can lose themselves in the general population they must suffer injustice on account of their heritage, nor can they lose themselves until they have paled themselves to the color of that general population; for their colors give them away. Once having paled and lost themselves, perhaps they would then suffer only those indignities the rest of us suffer, which can truly be at times outrageous.

For such expressed attitude I have been labeled pompous by Daniel, lacking in human warmth by Louisa, and accorded O.B.'s "Maybe, Jew boy. Lookit yer own self, pale and tall, with an Irish name. You've lost your own self in the crowd, now, haven't you, Jew boy?"

My views on the subject, I think, though piously denounced from many quarters, are more generally held than those same quarters would admit.

It was to the old Indian, however, that Grandmother turned for advice, fraudulent or no. She has made up her mind that he, by some ill-defined legerdemain, can foretell the future, or that part of the future as it pertains to her considerable suffering with the vicissitudes of age, particularly in the matter of her stiffening joints.

"He does it vit chicken enters," she confided once.

"Innards. Chicken innards," I corrected. "Ah, Grandmother"—I was as polite as I could be in the face of such rank nonsense—"chicken innards, warm or cold, north-, south-, west- or east-facing, upside down or wrong side to, will not foretell the weather. If the temperature drops and the weather is damp, it is likely your rheumatism will be affected, that's all. That old fake, that conjuring red man, knows no more of weather prognosticating than he does of drinking tea."

"Ah, Levi, ye lack human varmth."

How she equated human warmth and superstition as opposed to cold-heartedness and the scientific method, I did not know. What I did know was that the Cherokees of my acquaintance, red and therefore doomed though they were, were as intelligent and as superstitious and as educated and as ignorant as the population around them, no more and no less. They were not, that is to say, given to sitting cross-legged on the floor, wearing feathers copiously and prognosticating through intelligence gained from fresh chicken innards. Such views, however, seemed to make me suspect in Grandmother's eyes.

"What difference does it make?" Daniel laughed. "Humor her. She's old, and as long as the old fart doesn't spread chicken 'enters' all over the parlor carpet, what's the harm?"

"Ignorance is the harm."

"Pompous ass," Daniel might say, or something like that. I never cared for Daniel's language. He had always been careless of it, from the day he arrived at our house so many years earlier. Two would occasionally reprove him for it, but neither Grandmother nor O.B. seemed to notice. I did then and I continue to do so. Careless language—and that includes the profane—is a sign of a careless mind. And in spite of his intellectualizing and the nearness of his law degree, Daniel's language had got considerably more careless since he had gone away to study.

"I vill not die," Grandmother said, "vitout consulting the Indian. He vill let me to know if I stay do I suffer an easy or a hard vinter," she said, as if in answer to my unspoken question.

"Grandmother," I said as patiently as the circumstances would allow, "before you and Chief Four Lumps make any precipitate decisions, it is necessary that we conduct some business. As head of this household, I need to gather whatever information we have concerning matters business and financial."

She looked surprised. "You," she boomed so abruptly that I started, "head of the household! I am head of the household!"

I had not been as circumspect as I ought. Grandmother was very ticklish on that point, having always claimed seniority over everyone, including, of course, the Old Bastard.

"The voting head," I replied, immediately angered at myself. That had always been O.B.'s winning argument.

"I can vote!" he would shout at the climax of a rare household dispute, which he would otherwise inevitably lose. "I can vote and you cannot!" he would announce triumphantly.

"You can shit!" would be her rejoinder, but it was not enough. She would be stumped. She did not know why he could vote and she could not, only that it was so and that it mattered.

I hurried on before she could shout out an expletive at me. Louisa

One's expletives are rare and therefore uncommonly effective. "Someone besides yourself needs to understand our family situation," I said.

"I suppose," she muttered.

"Someone has to take care of Three," I said, of my mother, "when you are gone. I shall have to do it." I knew that would win her over.

Two was still in the room, and her testy "Humph" made me realize that she had been left out again and that she resented it. All of my life she has angled for position in this group, to little avail; I suppose it has always been thus. She has no position, even less than her own daughter, feebleminded though Three is, and certainly she has no position over me, the heir in this disturbed family.

"Ah yes, yes, of course, yes," murmured Louisa One. "My books, Levi, fetch me books from the secretary," and she motioned toward that ornate piece of furniture that had been with us as long as I could remember, a burden every time we had to move quickly.

"My books are there. Two," she snapped, "fetch me my glasses."

Louisa Two rose slowly and laboriously, her own bulk only slightly less than her mother's and her own joints only slightly less impaired, but it was less her crippled state that she was in no hurry to do as she had been bade than her reluctance to be of any assistance to her mother.

"My glasses!" snapped Louisa One.

"In a minute," said Louisa Two, petulant as a child, as she labored grumbling toward the breakfront across the room, a distance of several feet, and returned with Grandmother's glasses.

Indeed, that is exactly what they were, glasses, opera glasses, ornate, gold-trimmed, inlaid with mother-of-pearl. Grandmother would use none but these, a gift from the Old Bastard from the World's Fair in Chicago. She thought that spectacles made her look old and she liked the elegance of the opera glasses. In truth, they made little difference. It was not often that she had anything to look at save some close needlework, for she could not read a word, nor write one, either. Precisely what she was planning to do with the "glasses" relative to her "books" I could not imagine.

Now, the Old Bastard could at least write a little and make his numbers and sign his ridiculous signature, so I supposed that that was what the books would contain, whatever records the old boy had been able to keep. I only hoped they were sufficient for my purposes.

However, the "books," when opened, proved to be but blank pages, one single long sheet of foolscap, folded in the middle, lying between two blank pages. That sheet of paper only was marked upon.

And those marks were like nothing I had ever seen. They were tidy, symmetrical and totally unintelligible, but, like pagan hieroglyphics, they seemed to mean something. There were lines and triangles and slashes and circles and circled *x*'s and circled slashes and slashed triangles, all in neat columns that apparently led to some conclusion, and at the bottom was the Old Bastard's distinctive signature with its ridiculous flourishes and curlicues, Obediah J. M. Murphy, familiar enough to me who had witnessed it all my life, but difficult, I suspect, for the unwitting to decipher. The Old Bastard was inordinately proud of that signature, as were Louisas One and Two.

Louisa One held her opera glasses to her nose, scanned the mysterious sheet of foolscap and beamed. "An't it pretty, now?"

"What! What, Grandmother, is this?"

"Mine books. Dese are mine books. See." She pointed at the signature at the bottom of the page, as if that signature gave credence to this tidy bit of doodling. Child's play. That's what it reminded me of. Child's play, a child playing at "store" before he had got either numbers or letters, though no such child could ever have been so tidy.

Grandmother took pen in hand and, peering through the gilt opera glasses, went carefully down the columns of figures—for so they would certainly appear to an archaeologist studying the remains of some long-defunct civilization. Grandmother paused, frowned and made a careful slash through a virgin triangle, for all the world as if she knew precisely what she was doing.

"Grandmother," I insisted, "I need figures. I need to know what are our assets, our liabilities. I must get our affairs in order and you present me with a play book of nonsense. This," I said, gesturing toward the sheet of foolscap, "makes no sense whatsoever."

Grandmother looked hurt. "Vy, Levi, of course it makes sense. Vat you mean, makes no sense?"

"Grandmother, perhaps Obediah could make some sense of this. Possibly, though it hardly seems probable, he even knew what he was doing and could have deciphered this code. But Obediah is dead. There is surely something other than this?"

"Vy, Levi, Obediah never done dis. Vat you think? Obie had no head fer figures. I vould never trust him to keep books, no more'n I vould trust him too much vit money. Dese are mine books and I know vat dey say," she said. "An'," she said, patting my hand, for that was all she could reach, "I vill teach you it." And she proceeded to do so.

To my astonishment, she carefully translated the dots and circles and slashes across the first line of columns and announced that Eli

Livingstone owed us $65 on a note, plus $6 in interest, the total sum of which was to be delivered to us no later than the last day of this year. And in that manner she continued down the line of columns. I hastily procured a pen and set about transcribing and within short order had determined that, should these figures be correct, we had not a single liability, but a prodigious number of assets, largely in outstanding loans.

"Grandmother, are you certain of these figures?" I questioned.

"Two!" she snapped. "I need mine box of papers."

Two groaned and grumbled and finally rose and made her way back to the breakfront and returned with a cardboard box that I had long known was there, but had never paid any serious attention to, only to notice that it was filled with papers, papers that proved to be notes, properly made out, each attested to by Louisa One's careful *X* and the Old Bastard's silly signature.

In addition, there were deeds to parcels of land, some quite large, in various states and counties where we had resided, some dated long before my time, as well as an assortment of bonds.

"Ve get the rents from dese," said Grandmother. "And, Levi, dere is gold coin and silver, too. It is beneath mine bed, rolled in a quilt. It is mine mattress money. Obie never knew it vas dere," she said. "He never come to mine bed much."

"Grandmother," I said, "I must sort this out and get it properly banked. It is never wise to keep large sums of cash on the premises."

She only shrugged. "Do vat you haf to. I plan to die. You take care of it. I'm makin' mine funeral clothes. I vant to be planted by the side of Obediah. Dat's all. I vill put the lace from mine vedding collar on mine funeral dress. Obie vould like it, vouldn't he?"

Taken somewhat aback, I could only think to murmur, "I'm sure, Grandmother."

Two rose with more alacrity than I supposed she possessed and muttered a contemptuous "Humph" and waddled out of the room.

"Levi," said my grandmother, lowering her voice to a loud whisper, "ven the time comes, you plant *her*"—and she nodded in the direction Two had gone—"you plant her on the clear udder side of the grafeyard. She gets on my nerfs," she confided, for all the world as if she feared that Louisa Two would continue her irritating ways for eternity were she not banished to the far side of the burying ground. The aged can be strangely irascible.

"Grandmother, there are other facts that I needs must ascertain, lest they be lost with you and Obediah." As delicately as I could, I was questing after my own paternal history and my mother's, too, and, not the least, Daniel's.

"Are there perhaps more papers, perhaps letters and documents that I should know of?" I had approached her and Two before with such requests for information. As a child, I was hardly delicate. "Who am I?" I would cry in a small rage, for I have been obsessed all my life with knowing those facts of which I have been kept ignorant.

"Why, yer a Jew boy." The Old Bastard would laugh and gently ruffle my hair, for he was, scoundrel yes, but always gentle with children. But he would never explain his Jew boy reference further, and I would tease Louisa One or Two to know more.

Two might shrug and One only mutter, "He don' know nothin'."

And what of Daniel? I knew, of course, as early as I could understand such things, that I was a bastard and my mother likewise, and, for all I knew, everyone else in the household. I had always been envious of Daniel's orphaned state, believing that he was not a bastard, but the product of a real family, from which he had been only temporarily separated. As a child, I used to worry that his family would one day find him and take him away, leaving me in my bastardy, alone, forever.

I am now a little more tactful in my questioning, but the response remains vague. I repeated my question. "Are there other personal documents that I should be privy to—perhaps O.B.'s war record and such?"

But Louisa One was not to be outfoxed, though I am certain that she knew what I wanted and that she likewise had the answers that I sought. Quite bluntly, I did not want her to die until I knew for sure, or at least had all the information that she had. I would not remain forever in a genealogical limbo.

"Ah, Levi," said Grandmother, "I am very tired now vit all mine thinking. Tomorrow maybe I'll think some more."

I had been dismissed. Louisa One was through thinking for the day, and I knew her well enough to know that no amount of badgering would change her. Louisa One was a very stubborn woman.

I had thinking of my own enough to make up for the both of us. It was perhaps enough at the moment to try to absorb what I had found out of our financial status. I found Daniel, who was readying for the return trip to St. Louis, as if he feared that his chance might be lost were he to tarry.

I reassured him and told him what I had found out and we both marveled and laughed that Old Louisa should have turned out to have had such a business head.

"We should have known," said Daniel. "It's always been obvious that it was she who ruled the roost."

"If not the rooster."

"Ah, Levi. Remember what I said. Forgive the dead."

We still did not know, of course, where all the money that Louisa One invested had come from in the first place. Given her reluctance to talk, we might never know. But the information that I wanted had little to do with fortune, and I was determined in my quest for it.

"Well, Levi, you're too serious. It gains you nothing to grudge a dead man. The future is all we have," Daniel repeated.

Louisa One had herself said something to that same effect. "It is sinful, Levi, to vorry vit that vich you can ne'er change. Go on about yer life."

I did not speak and Daniel looked for a moment at his shoes and then sighed audibly. It was rare for Daniel to be so serious, without that quip or half-formed grin by which he usually denigrated his own remarks. A tendency to quick retorts and glib quips, I think, denotes either a shallow sensibility or an insecurity of purpose. In Daniel's case I assume it to be the latter.

In many areas Daniel and I are compatible; we have been close for many years, it might seem like brothers, almost but not quite, for there remains that distance between us that only the closest brotherhood might bridge. Still, we balance each other's personalities, I think. I am more serious and given to introspection, traits for which Daniel continually chides me, but from which I think he could profit had he them in like manner. For he is too easy, too glib, too popular among his fellows and certainly among the ladies.

I will give him no edge in good looks, for I am nearly as tall—we are both taller than most, he besting me by perhaps three-quarters of an inch. But he is strung out, while I am compact and carry easily twenty-five pounds more on my frame. But I stand aloof from young women and they in turn give me wide berth. It has not been, I suppose, only my bastard state that makes me reluctant to develop friendships among the fair and comely, for there are several among my acquaintance who do indeed fit that description. As much as anything, I suppose it has been the Old Bastard's reputation as a lecher and fornicator in his advanced years, a reputation that was the object of general mirth, rather than the scorn or detestation that it deserved, that restrained me.

I am yet stung, and possibly always will be stung, by that continual embarrassment. I would do nothing to give the impression that I follow in that venerable tradition. I would remain celibate the rest of my days rather than risk such reputation.

Not so Daniel, who dances with the girls, and, when I am not about, does more even than that, I suspect. For he calls me "stick-in-the-mud" and "damp blanket," yet he will not step out of line in my presence.

It is not that the juices of my own manhood have never been stirred. I have been moved to the point of pain at the vision of a contoured nape of neck or an ankle carelessly exposed or even a glance from sometimes incredibly mystifying blue or brown eyes, though I tend to prefer brown. I have often thought that I would take myself to Kansas City, perhaps even St. Louis, and seek out those houses of bawd that my fellow students often discussed with relish, only I find it distasteful to think of planting my seed in a whore's womb, and then I remember that I am myself the issue of a madwoman and some passing whoremonger and chide myself for such unmerited aloofness, as if I were a crown prince. I am a bastard and I am an anomaly. Bastards beget bastards; yet I remain a virgin in a promiscuous world.

"Does it not bother you yet, Daniel, that we neither of us know aught of our forebears, of our antecedents, you even less than I?" This is not a new trend of thought between us. We have followed this line of conversation many times, always to much the same conclusion: Daniel's shrug.

"Until there is some reason for it, I see no point in worrying it, Levi. 'Stir a turd, and make a stink.' The past has nothing to do with us. We are both grown, nearly educated, and I see no point in moping about after some dreary past experiences, which, after all is said and done, have nothing to do with our lives. Up, up and away, I say," and he sounded a sudden Teddy Roosevelt charge. "We've San Juan Hill to take! No, Levi, we've the world to take, and it is ours!"

Well, he had degenerated again into foolishness and there was no talking to him about it. The time would come, perhaps, when he would be interested.

Daniel left early the next morning, by coach, to Joplin, where he would catch the train to St. Louis and resume his studies. He kissed each Louisa on the cheek and slapped me hard upon the back, admonishing me on the inadvisability of taking wooden nickels. I saw him to the coach and he shook my hand and then enveloped me in a bear hug. This at least I knew to be sincere.

I returned to Obediah's house, that imposing structure in the middle of town. It had been built, rather, assembled piece by piece from a kit ordered out of Chicago, by a wealthy contractor who had then the misfortune to die before he had even moved his family into it. Obediah had bought it then, we being but fresh to the Territory. The deed I had spied among Grandmother's papers had been signed by the worthy, but deceased, gentleman's executor and bore both Obediah's distinctive signature and Louisa One's less than distinctive *X*, which I suspect would never hold up in a court of law, being both *X* and female, but she always insisted on adding her mark to documents.

I was somewhat startled to meet old Chief Four Lumps departing just as I arrived, his dark dignity covered in blankets and feathers. The Indians of my acquaintance did not wear blankets any more than they wore feathers. And I wondered if the old aborigine had been dallying with fresh chicken innards on behalf of Louisa One. Perhaps the blankets and feathers represented his working clothes. I could not entirely suppress a wry grin. I was beginning, I feared, to think like Daniel.

I found Louisa One in place, propped up by chair and canes, in the parlor. Neither Two nor Three was present.

"And what," I asked, "was the Chief about?"

"Ah, he vas not so sure. He needed more chicken enters. I haf to vait." She was quite cheerful for one involved in so intimate a task as deciding her own life or death. I found it hard to imagine that Grandmother would choose to die, anyway, and I sincerely doubted her ability to carry through on it even if she so decided, for she is a survivor. It would take at least a runaway freight train or a tidal wave or a monumental twister or some other unlikely act of God to do her in. She was in quite good health, remarkably good health for someone of her advanced years, her senses all as acute as they needed to be, or as she required them to be, her hearing being bad only when it proved convenient for her to be hard of hearing. But for her rheumatism and her ponderous weight, her health was as stout as, perhaps stouter than, that of many persons half her age.

I wondered if she were up to "thinking" this morning, and with no preliminaries I attacked the question foremost in my mind. "Grandmother, what do you recall of Daniel's first appearance in our family?"

"Nothing," she said.

"But, Grandmother, now that can't be. It's important. What do you remember of his arrival? When was it? Why did he come to us?"

"He vas a babe, a babe in bunting," she said, belying her "nothing" of the moment before. "Obediah found him on our doorstep in a basket," she added, embroidering this trite story.

I wondered if she expected me to believe it. "Now, Grandmother," I sighed, "that just isn't so. You know it isn't. Daniel was near to eight years old when he came to us, far too large for a bunting or a basket."

"Vas he n'en? I told you I don't remember."

"You mean you don't want to remember," I said.

"Vat?" she said, cupping her hand around her ear as one of her sturdy canes, suddenly loosed, clattered to the floor.

She was asserting her aged prerogative to go deaf when such disability might prove advantageous.

"And where is Two?" I asked.

"She got mad at the Indian," my grandmother, her hearing miraculously restored, reported. "She cussed at him and I sent her to her room."

"Well, perhaps she can answer my questions," I said.

"She do," said Louisa One amiably, "and I break her back." She added, "She don' know nothin' about nothin' anyvay."

That may or may not have been true. I did not get a chance to ask, for Louisa Two kept to her room until dinner and then she appeared but as at best taciturn and sullen.

When I have taken the trouble, I have tried to feel sympathy for Two. Nearing seventy herself, she has been, I suppose, deprived of her old age, at least deprived of the proper respect for it, by the existence of her own mother, even though their constant bickering at times has made it difficult to treat either with the respect to which their great ages entitled them.

Two, who is given to more or less constant grumbling and complaining or, when there are guests, simpering and giggling, was this night strangely quiet at dinner. I found it refreshing to finish a meal free of chattering and bickering. I can't speak for Grandmother, for she said little, only commenting in passing on the inability of the old Indian prognosticator to do his job effectively.

As soon as the meal was completed and the dishes were being cleared by the girl—a country girl hired by One and Two for all-purpose cleaning and cooking duties, who held in awe our formal ways, I fear, for we always dressed for dinner—Two again went

directly to her room. She would obviously not be approachable tonight for the kinds of answers that I was seeking. I made up my mind
then that the next day, or as soon as Two's disposition was sufficiently
improved, I would get her aside and do some serious questioning. She
certainly would be able to provide some information.

But that was not to be. The next morning found Two seated in
front of the open grate in the parlor quite as dead as the ashes she
stared at. Grandmother was in a positive rage, for Two clutched to
her bosom in frozen fingers that very piece of lace from Louisa One's
wedding dress with which Grandmother had been planning to festoon
her own funeral garments.

As Grandmother struggled to free the lace thus tightly gripped,
she let fly a string of expletives, a number of which I had not realized
she even knew, most of the invective directed at that malingering
prognosticator old Chief Four Lumps.

"Dat sonovabitchin' fart," she cried. I had eased her away from the
remains of Two and led her to the kitchen and seated her, pointing out
that the lace, old as it was, was quite fragile and further pointing
out as delicately as I could that the undertaker might best be trusted
that duty.

"Dat goddamned rascal Indian. Him and his enters. He fools
around and she beats me. She beats me. Vel, hell vit 'em. I just von't
die. Hell vit 'em."

She might have, had she the necessary equilibrium, stamped her
foot for emphasis, so incensed was she.

"Levi," she said, staring coldly at me, "you go to the grafeyard and
you tell 'em where to dig her hole. Put it in the far corner away from
me and Obediah." Then she brightened. "Maybe dere's anudder
grafeyard, far distant, ve could put her in?" Then, as abruptly, she
reconsidered. "Ah, no, ve couldn't do dat, couldn't do it. She got to lie
vit us—only not so near."

And then Grandmother began to cry, to howl, to wail. Suddenly,
unexpectedly. "She vas mine baby. Mine own baby sucked at mine
breast. Mine last vun, all gone. I never thought she vould grow up and
get old and die. I never thought dat at all."

The girl had run to fetch the undertaker, and that venerable gentleman arrived just in time for the wailing. He consoled Grandmother, his velvety voice gentle, his experience in such matters
putting the right words in his mouth. "We must trust the Lord. The
Lord giveth and the Lord taketh away. Your child is with the Lord

now," he said, as if he were indeed comforting a mother bereaved at the loss of an only and dear small child. "You must trust the Lord."

Mercifully, the undertaker had gone to see to the remains before Grandmother muttered, "Better to trust da Lord dan dat fuckin' Indian faker."

We buried Two the next evening a distance of perhaps twenty-five yards from the Old Bastard's resting place. It was as far as we could get her from that spot, though Louisa One complained of its proximity. But it was a small churchyard and Obediah was buried near to the center, making it impossible to remove Two very far from him and still keep her within the consecrated area.

I did not bother to telegraph Daniel. He, having barely got back to St. Louis, could hardly retrace his steps. I wrote him a lengthy letter and bade him not to worry.

For some weeks thereafter, as my errands carried me through the town, I would be stopped and offered condolences for my double loss, though in truth the major portion of those sympathies were offered in the name of Obediah. Nor was there any of the smirking and giggling one might expect, considering the amount of mirth that the Old Bastard's misadventures had afforded these same people. When they said that they would miss him, perhaps that's what they intended, or that they would miss the pleasure his dallying had afforded them by way of gossip and joke.

I might have been ungenerous to my fellow townsfolks, but I could hardly expect them to wink and chortle over his many peccadilloes to a mourning relative such as I. It's hardly possible that they did not think upon it when they mentioned him, even affectionately, as many did. For he was notorious in his amorousness, in his willingness, yea, even eagerness, to jump between the sheets or at least offer to jump between the sheets with ladies of all ages and persuasions. That he had not gotten shot more often than he did is in itself remarkable. I do think him capable of having mounted up, like a dog, right in the middle of Main Street were he able to find a partner so willing.

In the big house we are down now to One and Three, Two having been deducted from our numbers. And each morning I half expect to find One in the parlor dead as her daughter, but she seems to have decided, as she threatened, not to die at all and she is, if anything, sprightlier than before, though I suspect that she misses Two if only because she has no one with whom she can bicker.

Three has not quite been able to absorb the two losses. She seems to realize that there is something not quite right, for now and again she whimpers quietly and searches through the empty rooms, not unlike a bitch whose pups have been dispatched.

Grandmother will of course not last forever, contrary to her own expectations. She is in truth my last hope, and I have every intention of nagging her until she at least tells me what she knows, even if it be scant.

But when, after a decent interval, I broached the subject again, Grandmother seemed strangely acquiescent.

"I don't know"—the old woman shrugged—"maybe dere is no reason vy not now."

"If you have any information concerning my and Daniel's antecedents, we have the right to them." I was quite firm.

"You have a dark side, Levi," she said inexplicably, nor do I believe that her reference to my "dark side" had anything to do with my heritage. I think she has interpreted my aloof and introspective nature to be "dark" because it is so foreign to all those others around her.

"Maybe. It may be." And she launched abruptly, startlingly so, into her history.

"I'm from Pennsylvania Dutch," she said. "Mine fadder vas a Rippert, Eli Rippert. Mine mudder, I don't remember vat her name, only it vas Martha. Her mother vas Indian, anyvay, only a real Indian, not like dat fake old Indian vit his silly enters." She paused to glare at me, as if the silly Indian and his enters could be ascribed to me.

She continued and I listened as patiently as I could, but at the moment it was not her history but my own about which I was eager to hear.

"I liffed in Philadelphia all mine life, until I vedded Daniel Varner and he brought me to his fadder's farm in Tennessee. I thought I vould die in dose voods, but I learned about farms and voods pretty quick.

"I had a bunch of kids, maybe seven altogether, I kind of fergit; three or four, dey died anyvay. The fever it vas so bad in dem voods, and Daniel Varner himself, he died of it, too.

"Den I married Obie. I had four of Daniel Varner's kids den. Three boys and mine Louisa."

This was news to me. I had no idea that there were any but Louisa. "The three boys," I said, "where are they?"

"Danny and Charlie and Henry. Vell, I don't know. Henry he

died in da var. Dat damned var," she said. The "damned var" of which she spoke was, of course, the War Between the States. Whenever anyone mentions "the war," that is the one they are talking about, as if there had never been any other; though the Spanish conflict was just behind us, it was never given the serious respect accorded "the war." It was the conflict between the Union and the rebels that was branded *the war*, all others from the beginning of time only a prelude to that, and any to follow but a weak imitation.

"Danny, I don' know. Fer a long time I don' know. Charlie, he died a few years back, I heard. He had a bunch of kids. I think about them sometimes. Danny and Charlie, dey never really liked Obie, though." Her look was perplexed, as if she had never been able to comprehend that thought.

I waited a moment before I prompted, "Well?"

"Vell what?"

"What else? What is the rest of the story?"

"Vat you mean? Dat's de story. Vat you vant, 365 days of every year?" she said testily. "Louisa Three, she vas born, and den you, dat's all." And she telescoped those two events as if the one immediately followed the other. Perhaps to her aged mind that was the way it seemed.

"Grandmother," I said as patiently as possible. "For my own peace of mind, I would like to know who I am, what is my heritage. Why did Grandfather continually call me Jew boy, for instance?"

"Oh, don't vorry it. Don't vorry it. He neffer knew. He alvays liked to tease dat you was got by a passing peddler. It vas a joke. I think he finally got to believe it hisself. But he don't know. Your grandfadder, he always liked to joke," she recalled fondly.

I was stung. A passing peddler. The old bastard! "Obediah Murphy, at least, was not my grandfather. I will no longer even dignify him with that honorary title. I suppose," I muttered in some bitterness, "that my natural grandfather was another passing peddler?" For all I knew, all the women in my family had a predilection for peddlers.

"Vat you talkin' about? Of course Obie vas your grandfadder. Don't be silly."

"Grandmother, he was only a step-grandparent, that's what I mean. Remember, I am descended from Daniel Varner. My name quite rightly ought to be Varner, not Murphy. That whom I have reference to is that passing stranger who fathered my mother, Louisa Three, upon Louisa Two." That was as clear as I could state it.

"Faddered Louisa Three? Vy, Obediah vas de fadder of Three. You didn't know, I guess," she said vaguely.

My "enters" suddenly knotted and I fervently wanted to walk from the room, to hear no more. The prattling of the old woman, I sensed, was about to become intolerable. When we were boys, Daniel and I accompanied the Old Bastard to the World's Fair in Chicago, for we lived in the southern part of that state at the time, and O.B. had a passion for fairs, large or small, and took in all that he could. I rode the Ferris wheel, feeling superior to Daniel because he would not. I was only a few moments in the air before I decided that I would rather not continue with the journey I had set out upon. But it was too late. I was committed and could not escape. That same sensation which I had felt then, trapped high above the fairground, was the same sensation that came back to me, waiting for Louisa One to finish what she had started.

"Surely you mean stepparent?" I whispered, for I could not trust my voice not to do me in. My palms were quite wet and I clung to the side of the chair in which I was sitting almost as if I feared slipping from it, so great was my agitation.

"No, no. Obie vas sometimes naughty, you know, fer he vas only a man, and he slept vit Two; she vas a bad girl." Obie was "naughty" but Louisa Two was "bad." "Dey done dat twice, too, only the udder baby he died."

I sat still, clinging to the chair, my vision not quite clear for the throbbing at my temples. I did not think to ask of Daniel, to demand an explanation, to curse the name of Obediah Murphy, even to wonder at Louisa One's equanimity in the face of such a confession.

"Dat's all I know of our history. It an't much," she added cheerfully, "for almost an hundred years, is it?"

I shook my head, for it was the only movement I trusted myself to make. My throat was clogged with emotions I had not yet sorted out.

"And Obie, I dunno"—she shrugged—"about him, about his antecedents. He vas a bastard, you know."

I sat for a long time, she staring benignly ahead as if recalling some pleasant experience, before I groaned and murmured over the agitation in my throat, "Of that much, at least, I am certain."

THREE

THE DISTANT PAST

*I*n the year of our Lord one thousand eight hundred and nineteen Gobiatha Murphy, a maidservant to the wife of Jeremy Caleb Thompson, Esq., of the county of Wise and the state of Virginia, gave birth, in travail, to a healthy nine-pound male bastard. The bastard was named Obediah Jonah Micah Murphy.

There was no particular consternation that Gobiatha should have done such a thing, she being but a maidservant, apple-cheeked and plump; indeed, such event had been predicted openly as her ever rounding form had become abundantly obvious to all.

Nor was there any untoward distress in the fact that the Reverend Robert S. Howell, recently graduated from his divinity studies at the Harvard University in Massachusetts and come into the backwoods of Virginia to spread the Gospel on a circuit and who had found the company of the maiden Gobiatha exceedingly pleasant, would, when he himself noted that same abundant roundness, hear the call of the Lord to carry his teachings farther abroad and remove himself by dark of night from the house of Jeremy Caleb Thompson, Esq., who had given him succor in his ministry.

Gobiatha's labor was hard, given her youth and the boy baby's size, as well as his determination to back into the world both butt and foot breech.

"Sidewise," commented the midwife.

"Oh, gawdammit, merciful Lord!" shrieked the suffering Gobiatha. "Lor's blood, what's keepin' it?"

"B'Glory," marveled the midwife when she finally coaxed feet and butt from the sobbing girl, "'tis a male child, hung with nuts like gourds." She popped loose the head and whistled through her teeth, several of which were conveniently missing and so accommodated a most effective sound. And to prove her point she held the young one, squalling, wiggling, red and waxed, high so the whimpering mother could observe the wonder of such an infant. "Just look to them balls," murmured the midwife, Cousin Jane. "Oh, it's a stout one, lass, a stout'n indeed." Gobiatha hiccuped and turned her face to the pillow.

In pride Cousin Jane showed the healthy boy around, front and rear, and marveled that Gobiatha had survived such a monumental labor, and she confided further that most likely this would be the girl's only child, as she was almost certain to have damaged herself irreparably. "Broke the mold," said Cousin Jane to many agreeing nods.

The news was passed quickly around until at last it reached Jeremy Caleb Thompson, Esq., who upon consideration of all of the details of the situation gave silent thanks, it occurring to him that he had been blessed indeed by the Lord for his willingness to have sheltered the young minister while he preached the Word of God, for which service the Lord had seen fit to leave to him, Jeremy Caleb Thompson, Esq., not only a healthy boy baby who would grow to working size anon, but also a full-blown, not quite virgin maidservant whose mold was broken. He made plans that, after Gobiatha's confinement should be done, he would make it a point to visit often with her in his capacity as household head to advise her on the raising of a boy baby and other pertinent matters.

Nor was Mistress Jeremy Caleb Thompson particularly distressed when her husband made good upon his plans. Good maidservants were hard to find, particularly maidservants no longer likely to take time off to birth bastards. And if Master Jeremy Caleb Thompson chose to spend himself on such a maidservant, it was just that much respite for her, Mistress Thompson reasoned, the women of her acquaintance agreeing all that man's appetites were greater than a single woman ought to have to appease, and the more willing maidservants there were, the less time they themselves would have to spend accommodating those appetites and the fewer births they would suffer as a result. A maidservant both willing and barren was to be considered a household convenience.

However, when Obie, which name had seemed more appropriate for an infant than the cumbersome Obediah Jonah Micah, was nearing four years of age, his mother was persuaded by a neighboring bound servant to accompany him by stealth into the wilderness by way of the Cumberland Gap. The bound servant, Thomas, assured Gobiatha that they would return for Obie "sometime," the vagueness of which promise did not particularly unsettle the young mother, as she had no great desire to walk through the Cumberland Gap with Obie, who was large for his age, on her hip.

Jeremy Caleb Thompson, Esq., properly outraged at the gross lack of gratitude his generosity to the maid had generated, immediately declared Obie deserted, orphaned and a ward of the court. And in short time the boy was bound over to Master Jess Overstreet of the county of Hancock in nearby Tennessee, whose wife had borne him none but daughters and who had need of a strong young male to help with his crops. At four years of age Obie was accepted indifferently into this family of women, fed and clothed until he was six, big as a ten-year-old, and could be introduced to the pair of cows whose needs he met twice a day, except when they were calving.

By the time Obie was eight years old Master and Mistress Jess Overstreet, a kindly couple, had married away six of their daughters; the seventh, Rebecca, being at once the oldest, fattest and most ill-tempered, would have to await, her mother assured her, "a widower, who could nay afford to be picky." In addition, there resided a slave girl, Mattie, about seventeen years of age, though indeed no one was ever certain of slaves' ages, who saw to the scullery and the chamber pots and helped Obie to carry the water and other matters not deemed fit for the mistress or her oldest daughter.

Both Mattie and Obie suffered now and then at the hands of the ill-tempered Rebecca, who, when things did not go to suit her, which was often, would smack either Obie or Mattie wherever it was convenient, usually Obie's rear end or Mattie's face.

"You leave that Nigra be," her mother would remonstrate. "Respectable 'uns don't mistreat their Nigras."

Of Obie's distress Mistress Overstreet generally said nothing, as it was assumed that a growing boy, to prosper, needed the regular administration of justice upon his hindmost parts.

When Obie was nearing the end of his tenth year he accompanied Master Overstreet across the boundary into Virginia, where they visited the Lewisburg Fair. The boy, who had never journeyed so far in his ten years, was impressed and suitably awed by the sights and sounds of the fair, thinking that it must indeed be the most exciting spectacle in the entire universe. There were dancers and musi-

cians and displays of livestock, including cows and sheep and chickens
and some slaves, as well as tables filled with corn and pumpkins and squash and pies, adjudged to be the best that the good people
in and around Lewisburg could produce.

"Why," asked Obie of Master Overstreet, "is this place called
Lewisburg?" Indeed, it amounted to but a few buildings of log and
mud around a flat and open space.

"That is Master Bob Lewis's store. He has named this place for
himself in the hopes that it will one day become a dwelling place
for many families and a credit to his foresight."

It was a long speech for Master Overstreet, who was more given to
listening, having spent so many years living with a wife and seven
daughters.

Obie stood in the midst of the colorful, laughing crowd, jostling,
dancing and occasionally fighting, and thought that he could not
imagine a thing so fine as a fair.

"I must see a kinsman, Obie," said Master Overstreet. "I will meet
you back here anon as soon as I have accomplished my business."

Obie contented himself wandering around eyeing the displays of
wondrous big squash and pumpkins and ears of corn and trying to
look hungry enough that he might be offered some of the pie that the
goodwives stood guard over.

When, some time later, Master Overstreet reappeared, he had
with him a large slave, who, he explained, would accompany them
home, he being pay for the debt that Master Overstreet had hoped to
collect. The slave's name was Benjamin, and Obie was excited at the
prospect of a new slave. It was almost as good as a new kitten.

"Why," objected Mistress Overstreet, when she had inspected
black Benjamin, "do ye need a field Nigra?"

"Ah," replied her husband, "he's a good nigger, it seems, and will
be better kept here than he might otherwise have been; he can teach
what he knows of mule and ox to Obie, and in a year or two, when
Obie is big enough to work the fields, I can sell Benjamin for profit."

Rebecca, in the meantime, stared openly and critically at Benjamin, who was a large and handsome black man, while Mattie, peering
from around the lilac bush at the kitchen door, curled her toes in the
dust at the view of the broad, black, muscled back. The big black
towered over the master, who, it must be admitted, was middling
short at best. Rebecca's glance traveled from the slave's broad, benign
smile to his shoulders, pausing overlong at crotch, and down to his
large flat feet and back up to crotch level before she grunted

"Humph," or something very like that. Mattie's glance traveled the same path, but she reacted with a nervous giggle that brought the black man's attention to her. She retreated quicky behind the lilac bush and smoothed her apron and brushed the crumbs from her mouth.

"Obie"—Mattie grabbed the boy by his elbow—"you go find out what that big niggah's doin' here."

"I already know," said Obie. "He's to work here. He's to teach me everything he knows. He's our new field hand."

"Oh, law, law, law," moaned Mattie and she danced round and round outside the kitchen door.

"Mattie," snapped Rebecca, the expression on her face attesting to a sudden rise of temper, "you get on with your soapin' you don't want to get your ears boxed." And without warning she aimed a cuff at Obie, but, experienced and nimble, the boy ducked it and darted away.

And the slave Benjamin did indeed teach Obie all that he knew of mule and ox and all related subjects of animal husbandry, of which occupation Obie seemed to possess certain natural inclinations, if not so great as the big slave's, at least impressive in a boy. Both the bulky oxen and the recalcitrant jacks moved with unexpected alacrity for both slave and boy, the one because his strength was such that he could, if necessary, outshove either and the other because with word and gesture he could coax activity from them.

"Boy's a wonder," Benjamin would offer to Master Overstreet. "A true wonder. He could talk a squirrel out'n a acorn, Ah do b'lieve."

"Indeed," the old man would murmur upon such occasion, as he had himself been outcharmed by the young rascal enough times to be wary. "I do not worry for Obie in the hereafter; he may well wheedle the sandals right off the Lord's feet."

The boy, endowed with deep dimples, unruly dark curls and wide, ingenuous eyes, had, more by instinct than cunning, for Obie was not a cunning child, developed those assets to his own advantage. In a word, Obie got what he wanted, in return for which he offered nothing but a kind of cheerful greed that adults, for no reasonable purpose, find enchanting in attractive children, that same greed in homely children being decried and treated to proper rehabilitative measures.

"You spoil him," accused fat Rebecca. "You spoil him because he's a male, because he's a pretty bastard."

"Perhaps," replied Mistress Overstreet.

"He's not responsible."

"He's not my child. I'll not worry about him. When he's a man he'll go."

"You treat him like a puppy. What makes you think he'll ever be a man?"

That the ill-tempered Rebecca, who seldom possessed even the most common kinds of judgment, could be so perspicacious in her assessment of Obie Murphy is perhaps one of those wonders about which conjecture is futile. Suffice it that she understood the boy better than few others ever would during his long and colorful life.

At twelve years of age Obie was taller than any of the women in the household and Master Overstreet, too, who, it has already been explained, was middling short for a man. Only the slave stood taller. Benjamin and Obie worked together through the long summer days, and Obie was a good worker, for of the vices that human flesh is subject to, Obediah Jonah Micah Murphy would in his lifetime dabble innocently in all save slovenliness and sloth and prevarication. Obie liked to be neat; he liked to be busy; he would not take the trouble to invent a falsehood. Little more need be offered of Obediah's character; for there was little else to him.

The slave Benjamin, with whom Obie conversed almost constantly, was not, as was to be expected, a worldly man. His expectations rose no higher than those of most slaves, than, indeed, those of most men of whatever persuasion, which is to say that when his craving for physical nourishment was satisfied, his thoughts and conversation turned to subjects of further sustenance of finer appetites and to the maidenhead that provided that sustenance. And Benjamin, in his simple manner, passed on to Obie his personal knowledge of that important subject.

"Hit's like Christmas Day." The big black man waxed poetic.

Now, Obie, who even before Benjamin's arrival had had a basic knowledge of the ins and outs of such matters, had never quite heard this heretofore unexperienced sensation thus described.

He understood Christmas Day, its warmth and security and excitement, when friends and relatives gathered and there was more to eat than was necessary and there were sweets and singing and in the end quiet contentment and blessed sleep. To get that kind of sensation anytime you wanted simply by going inside a woman seemed to Obie reason enough for the excessive interest all men and boys he knew seemed to have in this subject. He longed to try it himself as soon as possible.

"I don't think you ready yet," countered Benjamin. "Le's see what you got. It don't look like dis here, do it?" And the big slave released his large member, which with the conversation had been growing increasingly lengthier and heavier, from its confinements, as did Obie his own. Obie stared at the long black protrusion speculatively; he was reminded of Ned, Master Overstreet's own mount, whose dong was usually tucked neatly up between its hindquarters except when it needed to piss, or inexplicably now and then left hanging, shank length, as if waiting for something. Such was Benjamin's. By comparison, Obie's little prick was a giddy thing. He stared at it, quite disappointed that he couldn't get it to do what Benjamin's was doing or what Ned's would do.

"You jes' ain't ready yet," consoled Benjamin, looking around. Perspiration had unaccountably popped out on the big black's forehead, and he abruptly quitted Obie's presence and made his way into the barn. He was gone some minutes, and when he came back, his member was once again carefully confined and his expression relaxed.

"Like Christmas Day?" asked Obie in wonder.

"Jes' like it."

"And is it like Christmas Day for them, too?"

"Sometimes," sighed the black man. "Sometimes dey moans and tells you, 'Like dat, like dat,' or dey says, 'Oh, yeah, yeah, dat's it, dat's it, oh, yeah, yeah, mo', mo',' and dey pushes dey belly agin yo' belly and dey pushes and moans and laughs."

Obie wanted to ask to see the black man's dong again, to see if it was getting bigger and stiffer again, as the horse's did. But Benjamin went on.

"An' den sometimes dey gets contrary and sassy and tells you you a no-good fuckin' nigger dat doan know how to do it. Dey can be dat contrary, but you got to put up with it, 'cause dey got it an' you got to git it."

Obie considered the whole thing for some length of time and asked finally if he might someday watch the process.

"Hush, yo' mouf, youngin. Dat's turrible."

Obie failed to see what was so terrible about such curiosity. He had upon occasion watched the oxen mount and hump, and likewise the sheep, though not Ned, which poor beast's long dong was oft left dangling to no purpose, as there was no female of his particular persuasion near enough for regular service. If, Obie reasoned, he could watch other beasts mate, what was "turrible" in watching niggers mount? Anyway, the beasts provided no clues to the Christmas Day sensation that he was seeking, for they quickly dispatched their duties and left off to graze or stare into the distance as was their wont.

Obie had little of that cunning and stealth oft associated with voyeurs. Were he to note a female sheep indicating her readiness to be humped, he would but wait until a nearby buck hastened to accommodate her and watch with interest. So it was with Benjamin and Mattie.

Upon an early evening Obie noticed Mattie banging and slamming about the hearth, glancing through the open door toward the barn, her agitation attracting both the attention and the wrath of Rebecca.

"Watch what you're about, slut," cried Rebecca as an iron pan intended for the rack above the hearth clattered to the floor.

Mattie bowed her head, replaced the pan and swept hastily at the ashes scattered on the hearth, with another worried glance toward the distant outbuilding.

Obie sought out Benjamin, splitting wood beyond the woodshed, and found the big black similarly agitated. A glance toward the slave's trousers, where the large member was straining against the fabric, revealed the source of that agitation. Obie sauntered around the building, waited but a moment and dashed toward the barn, entering from the side far to the house, posting himself in a dark corner behind a plow and harrow, and waiting.

It was Mattie who slipped into the darkening gloom first, silhouetted against the open door, the same by which Obie had only just recently admitted himself, her skirts already gathered about her knees, which Obie studied with some interest. Obie had seen knees on young girls, in the main knobby and unattractive, but the only truly feminine knees he had ever observed had been fat Rebecca's when he had peeked at her as she squatted pissing behind the woodshed, and but for the location of her face it would have been difficult to distinguish knees from butt, so enormous were both sets of flesh.

He had come upon her unawares, and as he had had no premeditation in that encounter and as she had placed herself, however unintentionally, upon his path, he quietly and guiltlessly had observed as he might a doe or bunny he had happened upon. Fortunately, fat Rebecca did not know that she was watched.

Mattie moaned softly when Benjamin appeared, unloosing his engorged member as he entered, and they set immediately to their task without preliminary discussion. That Mattie wore no undergarments did not surprise Obie. He wore none himself but in the cold of winter, so he did not note the absence in the slave girl.

There was little that Obie could make out from the dark thrashings on the pile of straw in the far corner, though he sat up on his knees and stretched his neck to observe. But the sounds the thrashing pile made intrigued him. There was something more in the ecstatic moans of the girl than Christmas Day could effect. Mattie, like everyone else, enjoyed the festivities of Christmas, but the same intensity of pleasure that Obie now heard was never apparent on that holiday, nor were the eager groans of the male slave. This was indeed something greater, if possible, than Christmas Day, and Obie reached down to caress his own small member, which tingled but slightly and made only feeble efforts to rise.

Abruptly the black man rose from the girl and tucked his limp member away. And as abruptly he scooted from the barn. Mattie sat a moment and sighed, then, rising, smoothed her clothes and skittered from the barn, leaving Obie to judge what he had seen. But for the sounds of intense pleasure, he could see little difference from what he had observed in the beasts of the field.

Shortly Obie came upon Benjamin currying Ned, whose member was likewise placidly tucked away. The horse was standing against the stiff comb, resting a hind foot. Benjamin was whistling.

In the house Obie found Mattie humming and turning the crock of clabber against the wall, clabber that would on the morrow be ready to hang for cheese. Obie edged close to her and detected an odor foreign, he thought, from that usually associated with the business of kitchen and hearth.

Fat Rebecca came through, passed close upon Mattie, sniffed, Obie thought, glowered and suddenly fetched him an unexpected cuff to the ear.

"Get gone from that clabber," she snapped, making ready to swing again. Obie edged away. He did not think that potential molestation of the clabber had been what had aroused the ire of the woman, for she glared again at Mattie, who had stopped her humming and was vigorously and with great attention stirring the clabber with her wooden spoon. Rebecca sniffed again and with eyes narrowed quitted the room.

It was Mistress Overstreet who first noticed with mild annoyance the sudden expansion of the slight slave girl's waistline, and she mentioned that fact to Master Overstreet in the presence of fat Rebecca and Obie.

"It 'pears that Mattie is with child," she murmured over her darning basket.

"Ah?" inquired the master. He did not seem particularly distressed at that intelligence, but the mistress observed that such expectation would eventually interfere with Mattie's household chores and would of course require some arrangements for the expected infant.

"She is young, I think," observed the mistress in much the same manner in which she might discuss the first calving of a heifer.

"This is outrageous," snapped Rebecca, who from the first mention of the impending confinement had exhibited signs of extreme agitation.

"Will we keep it?" asked Obie.

"Eh?" Master Overstreet was engrossed in his pipe, his stockinged feet turned sole toward the cheerful flames at the hearth.

"The nigger baby? Will we keep it?"

"Ah, the little 'un. Time enough to think on that. Time enough."

"We don't need a nigger brat around here," said Rebecca. "And we needs must get shut of Benjamin or we'll have a yard full of little darkie bastards before we know what's about."

Mattie, who had been resting on her shuck tick close by the pantry, crept to the door and peered in at the conversants. The mistress glanced her way but said no word to her, either to bid her stay or be gone.

"With but the four of us, we hardly have need of three slaves," observed Mistress Overstreet, "and certainly no more than that," she added in reference to her daughter's previous observation.

"Sell Benjamin and the baby," directed Rebecca, "and keep Mattie close by home from now on so she won't have a chance to burden us again!"

"Well," said the master, "I don't know. We have time to think on it, I say. Perhaps after next summer's crops are laid by and the wood cut, I will return Benjamin to Virginia."

"What about the infant?" snapped Rebecca, her high color and shrill voice attesting to her agitation.

"It is naught to get excited about," calmed her mother. "We'll see to it in its proper time." Mattie backed quietly from the door and crept, shivering with more than cold, to her bed, and she pulled the comforter up over her and buried her face in the shuck ticking.

The next afternoon, as Master Overstreet sat by the fire recovering from his dinner, the slave Benjamin came to him, his distress apparent, Mattie standing stiffly some paces behind him.

"Me an' Mattie, we like to marry," said the slave quickly.

A strangled cry came from fat Rebecca, who stood at the far side of the room. Mistress Overstreet looked up from her needlework and even Obie paused in his play to stare at the big black man.

"Well now, Benjamin," the master recovered, "I'm not sure what you mean?" A proper marriage for slaves, of course, being out of the question, they might live together on some plantations and call themselves married and raise families, and perhaps that was what Benjamin had in mind.

"We don' want to get parted," said the slave, beginning to tremble, his resolve deserting him.

Master Overstreet was not an unkindly man, and he noted that the big nigger was distressed and he comforted him as best he could, soothing, "Now, Benjamin, I am not a man of means, and keeping a family of slaves would possibly burden my resources. I must think on it. You go on about your business and I will give you a decision anon."

It was the best that Benjamin could hope for, and he backed bowing and bobbing out of the room.

"Outrageous," screeched Rebecca. "Marriage! Marriage!" cried she, who had yet to taste of nuptial bliss. "Fornicators! They should be flogged and sold. Fornicating under our very noses!"

Obie was quick enough to figure immediately what was meant by fornicating, and he wondered if Rebecca had peeked at the slaves in their passion as he had. He followed the conversation with interest.

"Fornicators!" the righteously indignant Rebecca shrieked again.

"Now, Becky," calmed her father. "Niggers can't fornicate no more'n can the sheep in the field nor the ox in the barn."

Obie felt his small member grow slightly stiff at mention of the barn.

Master Overstreet's point was a theological one, that darkies, having neither soul nor God nor hereafter, were, therefore, incapable of sin, as a bitch in heat was not sinning, nor the dog that humped her. He might have made that point a little clearer to his ruffled daughter, but, in truth, he was not quite certain but that women also fell into that same category, although the question, then, of moral responsibility became at that point so complicated that he gave up the thought completely.

"Well," snapped fat Rebecca, "the ox in the barn and the sheep in the field don't marry neither, nor even live together as they were."

Ah, the master was stuck up in the flypaper of his own analogy, and he remedied that situation as most prudent persons do; he abandoned the analogy altogether and resorted to shouting to make his point most effectively. Now, Master Overstreet was not upon most occasions a shouting man, and thus his startled daughter retreated hastily from her position.

"I am a reasonable man," spoke Master Overstreet shortly. "These creatures have mated and do not want to be parted. As long as there is no purpose to be served in parting them, it shan't be." He glared sternly at his daughter and then, softening, said, "Becky, I shall, however, remove them from this property so as not to add to your distress."

A man of strong resolve, Master Overstreet rose forthwith and sought out black Benjamin, whom he found forlorn, leaning against the wall of the woodshed.

"Benjamin," directed Master Overstreet, "it is not my desire to see you and Mattie parted, if that is your wish. I shall return you, along with Mattie, to Virginia and see that you are settled there as one. Tomorrow we go. I want you to wrap your belongings and be ready, all three of you," he added, apparently forgetting that the baby was not yet an accomplished fact.

Obie was not delighted at this turn of events, as he rightly surmised that much of Benjamin's and Mattie's work would fall to him upon their departure, and, too, he had hoped to solve this Christmas Day riddle, either by further observation or, when the time was ripe, by execution. Mattie, he had thought, would be a satisfactory accomplice in that action. It was with some distress that Obie watched Master Overstreet depart just past dawn astride Ned as the two slaves walked behind, with shoes upon their feet against the cold and their belongings, meager though they were, tied and carried over their arms.

In three days' time Master Overstreet returned from Virginia with the intelligence that he had settled Mattie and Benjamin upon an estate large enough to accommodate all the babies Benjamin could beget. Rebecca remained sullen for several days.

Through the rest of the winter, Obie and Master Overstreet shared Benjamin's chores and Rebecca and Obie shared Mattie's, though in truth the larger portion of Mattie's work fell to Obie's lot. Obie, without meaning to, grew three inches taller and added weight, and the dimensions of both his hands and his feet were such that breakable dishware was not safe around him. His eyes grew darker, or perhaps only seemed to, under the heavy growth of eyebrow that bloomed inexplicably, and he developed, again quite unintentionally, an expression about mouth and eye that suggested that he knew something that he was not willing to tell anyone else. He did not have such private information, of course, being quite willing to tell anyone anything. In the light of day, behind barn or tree where he pissed, he peeked at his private parts and examined them for evidence of impending manhood. At night, resting on the shuck ticking, he stroked into the night that member which was not so small anymore.

He did not avoid fat Rebecca so much, for it seemed to him that she did not strike so often, as if she had lost some of her fight with the departure of the slaves. He was not certain, and, not being of a philosophical turn, he did not speculate upon the reason for this, but bounded cheerfully around kitchen and yard, his ankles being more and more exposed until Mistress Overstreet constructed him two new pair of breeches, long enough to cover the exposed shins. He looked quite grown-up in the new pants.

"Obie," commanded Rebecca one early spring day, "come with me to the barn. I've something I need you to help me with." Obie rose and followed without question.

Once inside the barn, Rebecca stopped short. "Pull down your pants," she commanded. Obie was surprised. "Pull 'em down, I say."

Obie did as he was told. Rebecca stared critically at his member, caught in repose. She reached out and stroke it. Obie felt it stiffen with a pleasurable tingle.

"Ye know what it's for?" asked Rebecca. Obie nodded. "Good," she said.

And she plopped herself down on a pile of straw and drew her great skirts up about her waist, taking pains to retain some under her bare butt, lest the straw prick that tender flesh. Obie stared down at the large, dimpled thighs, parted by a jagged triangle of coarse, dark hair.

"Well?" said Rebecca.

Obie felt his member begin to slacken.

"Get on. We dan't have all day," snapped the woman.

Obie obeyed the command and felt himself sink onto the soft, rolling flesh, like riding a gentle bark onto the rolling waters. But Obie's stubborn member refused to regain its strength, and try as he might, he could not make it navigate the channel as directed, though Rebecca proved an able channel master and tendered instructions and orders and finally threats before she finally took the recalcitrant member in her own fist and used it to suit herself, at last pushing Obie aside and giving him an irritated box to the ear and a lengthy sermon on his uselessness in all things, ending with, "As big a boy ought at least be able to fuck decently." And she left him agitated and disturbed on the pile of straw.

Obie did not speculate upon the maiden Rebecca's expertise in such matters, as he was more highly interested in examining his own contrary member, which was, now that opportunity was past, regaining its strength in a startling and prodigious manner. Obie feared that his new trousers would not be able to contain it, but he found to his great delight that with proper handling the thing could be tamed. Indeed, he found need to tame it several times that day and into the night and again the next day.

And when next the opportunity presented itself, he went to Rebecca and said, "Becky, I do believe that I can now afford ye the relief that ye was seeking a while past."

She thought upon it a moment and, finding her parents otherwise occupied, led the way to the barn, where Obie displayed for her his sturdy part and allowed her to stroke and pet it and finally receive it with much moaning and sighing and undulating of her large soft body. Her big belly and mountainous teats engulfed the boy, and it was, he thought, what riding a wave must be like. Nor was he thinking of Christmas Day but of tumbling waterfalls and flooding waters and crashing waves when he finally released himself to much moaning and petting from his vessel. And later that day, left unattended in the house, the two went forthwith to the floor and repeated the act, and every day thereafter when opportunity presented itself. Behind the woodshed, in the forest, the barn, the wagon, Obie lost himself and his seed in these mountainous folds of female flesh.

It was the first day of May that Master Boise Johnson, whose plantation occupied some three hundred acres in the adjoining county, came to call with a view to securing the favors and the hand of fat Rebecca. His call was not entirely unexpected, as his own wife of fifteen years had in late February died in childbirth, leaving him with six children, the youngest of whom was four years of age, the babe that precipitated its mother's demise having gone to its eternal reward along with her. Those given to finding signs of comfort in the most dismal of situations were wont to view that circumstance as a blessing, it being inconvenient enough leaving a man with six motherless children, without also leaving a helpless infant for him to attend.

There was little question but that the widower would have to seek a wife, in haste, as spring planting was hard upon him and he had neither maiden sister nor cousin to call upon and his three oldest children were boys who were likewise needed in the fields. Master Johnson would, of course, have preferred to have found a widow in similar circumstances, even though it would be an added burden of children, as such widow would needs be grateful and undemanding. But as such was not presently available, he must content himself with a single woman, one not likely marriageable to a single man, her gratitude being tempered slightly by the presence of six children to be tended. And though Master Johnson was aware of fat Rebecca's ill temper, he comforted himself that she would bring to the marriage a good stock and a potential inheritance of property.

And so it was that fat Rebecca became the bride of Boise Johnson and was removed to his farm in the adjoining county. And when, some seven months later, she produced an eight-pound baby girl to make seven Master Johnson's issue, it was her mother, Mistress Overstreet, who shook her head and murmured in some awe that had that baby, which was destined to grow as fat and ungainly as Rebecca, gone full term, it most certainly would have been an infant of monstrous proportions.

But Boise Johnson, who could count and cipher and who had a large measure of common sense, found reason to rejoice in the infant's precipitate appearance. Rebecca had rendered him a great service and resulting debt in his distress by marrying him and becoming stepmother to his large family, while he had, however unwittingly, returned the favor in like measure. They were now even up. He had no need to brook her ill temper, and indeed Rebecca, with the birth of her daughter, established as modest and calm a demeanor as a husband could ask. She would bear Master Johnson four more children while accomplishing her household and wifely duties with efficiency and calm humor.

Obie, who had no notion of counting and who thought little of

either fat Rebecca's departure or her motherhood, only looked with
uninterest upon the ungainly infant that Rebecca had produced and
gave the matter no more thought. The infant was named Rebecca
Jane.

In the fall of the year after fat Rebecca had wedded Boise Johnson,
it was determined by Master Overstreet that Obie should go for a
term of lessons. His bound term very nearly run, the young man
would have some need for reading and ciphering. Mistress Overstreet
nor any of her daughters could write or cipher, and although Master
Overstreet could, to some middling degree, do both, he did not feel
either competent or patient enough to teach Obie. Obie was sent to
lessons at the home of Douglas McAlister, whose wife, Mistress
McAlister, conducted primary lessons for beginning learners of all
ages, for Obie was not the only gangling boy who took his first lesson
as he neared manhood.

The group of boys, ranging from six to nearly eighteen, took their
lessons in letters and numbers in Mistress McAlister's parlor on those
days that were not fit for outside work. At most, Obie Murphy attended those lessons a total of three months and learned to make most
of his letters and all of his numbers and to identify certain common
printed words were they short enough.

As this met Mistress McAlister's requirements, it was determined
that Obie, along with several of his fellows, should travel the following school term to the Olde Maundy Meeting House located on the
eastern side of the county, where the Reverend Joshua Trafalgar Mason conducted more formal lessons for both boys and girls of all
teachable ages, while on Sunday ministering to the souls of all practicing Christians in the area, save Catholic, Quaker, Methodist and
Campbellite.

In truth, Obie did not spend much more time with the Reverend
Joshua Trafalgar Mason than he had with Mistress McAlister and her
charges, but the time so spent would prove to bear heavy account on
future adjustments Obediah Murphy would be called upon to make.

Obie, in what amounted to silent acclamation, was chosen natural
leader of Reverend Mason's male charges, said charges making their
choice with that same attention to detail and perspicacity by which
their elders make such choices. That is to say, the boys looked around
and discovered that Obie was the biggest among them, the strongest
among them, the most agile among them, and he had a look about his
mouth and eyes that suggested that he knew more than he was willing

to tell, which indeed he did, having already tasted copiously of the fruits of manhood that the others as yet only dreamed about.

Obie accepted his role of leader as he had accepted previous gifts accorded him, with cheerful greed and good humor, as if it were simply as it should have been. In return he gave nothing, led neither raids nor revolutions nor forays into the girls' jumping rope or stone rolling, but stood his ground, allowing himself to be generally admired.

In Reverend Mason, Obie found the only force that would ever profoundly shape his life, such influence being threefold. First, the good man wore the cut of his clothing in the manner of the eastern seaboard, in that his shirt—for he had but one, which he assiduously cared for on Saturday so that it would carry him through until the next Saturday—was ruffled at the collar and his trousers and waistcoat were slim, even snug, to his figure, which was as tall as Obie's own. The men and boys of Obie's acquaintance, who wore generally the comfortably baggy breeches and loose collars of the backwoodsmen, paled in their comparison to the handsome minister.

Second, Reverend Mason's cultivated voice rang with sonorous authority through the building and carried beyond the hills, reaching even the most sluggish of schoolboys, encouraging and exhorting and remonstrating. In private, going back and forth to school, or attacking his own daily duties in barn or field, Obie practiced those tones and inflections, his own voice being naturally and prematurely heavy.

And finally, Reverend Joshua Trafalgar Mason possessed a calligraphy, a written hand, particularly in his signature, that captured the boy's imagination. There was in those flourishes and curls a majesty that scorned the signature of an ordinary mortal. It was a signature that commanded respect in and of itself, that could borrow money without shame, attest to marriages and births, yea, even deaths, and inhabit those rituals with a solemn dignity and manifest greatness that ministers of the faith with lesser signatures, particularly were they *X*'s, could never hope to attain; it could, in a word, rise above the signatures of mortal men and assign itself a place in God's ledger.

It was one of the rare occasions in the life of Obediah Jonah Micah Murphy that he would indulge in a premeditated act. He set out to ape the minister-cum-schoolmaster. In a rare self-analysis, he ascertained that he, Obediah, had those natural credentials by which the minister stood apart from the ordinary. He had, to wit, an impressive name, the bastardy of which was not taken much into account in those days, it being a not uncommon circumstance; he had a commanding stature; he had a voice of authority. He had but to cultivate a signature and acquire the clothes and he would be able to stand in the company of such as the Reverend Joshua Trafalgar Mason.

As Obie's intercourse with numbers and letters was limited and would remain limited, his task proved arduous. But with much copying and practicing and experimenting, and with great industry and perseverance, Obie at last perfected that worthy signature that would carry him into debt, turmoil, disgrace and disaster for the better part of another seven decades.

But in attending so assiduously to that one particular of his education, Obie neglected the rest and never learned to read beyond the most basic primer, nor to write to much account, though he could figure by some means in his head, a feat learned from black Benjamin, who lacked also any other scholarly accomplishments.

OBEDIAH J. M. MURPHY he wrote in curlicues and flourishes and was satisfied that the requirements of higher education had been met, and he determined—he did not plan, for Obie was never capable of the foresight required to make plans—that he would be a preacher, rather than a teacher, as a preacher could stand before a crowd and be admired for his figure and his signature and his sonorous exhortations without having to know anything useful.

Upon a fall day Mistress Overstreet called to Obie that she had an errand for him to attend for her.

"Master Varner that lives beyond the lime kiln to the north has fallen by some manner from a high bluff and killed himself and left Mistress Varner a widow. It is a shame," she went on, for all the world as if Obie were actually interested in what she was saying, Mistress Overstreet being of a talkative and gregarious nature and, having no one else around to talk to, often talking with Obie of such things, he listening politely and paying but scant attention.

"It is a shame," she went on, "the old woman left to herself to spend out her last years, her daughters married and but one married son surviving. She has lost now a total of three sons and a husband and perhaps a daughter or two, I do not recall." She paused to let the import of that intelligence settle upon the boy. "The fever in that area north of the lime kiln is fair fierce. I would not live there a moment longer, 'twere me."

Obie waited patiently through this long preface to his errand. He was fairly sure what it would be, as he had several times in the past been sent to carry food and condolences to a grieving family.

"Take Ned, for the master has no need of him today, and carry these loaves to Mistress Varner and recommend to her the sympathy of Master Overstreet and myself and all our daughters." And she gave Obie a parcel wrapped in brown paper, that by the feel and smell of it could be naught but three large loaves of fresh-baked bread.

Obie rode Ned slowly along the path to the lime kiln and stopped there to ask further direction, as he had never been to the Varners' place, nor even, he was certain, ever met any of them.

Several rods beyond the lime kiln hunger overtook the boy. He fought it for a few more rods before he pulled his mount off the trail and in a secluded spot broke open the package and tore off a generous end from one of the loaves and consumed it. Now Obie considered. Two large loaves would surely be enough for the bereaved family, as other neighbors would be likewise sending such to them, and Obie could not very well present the widow Varner with a molested loaf of bread, and in truth, he, Obie, was certain to be hungry on his way home. He tore off a portion of the brown paper wrapping the loaves and wrapped the mutilated loaf securely and tucked it snugly in the high crotch of a tree against his return.

Obie rode on, and in less than an hour he found the Varner plantation, for such was called a large farm in that area of Tennessee in the mid-1830s, and, seeing no one in the front of the house, he dismounted Ned and led him around to the back where a young mother sat on a stoop nourishing her infant at her breast.

"Vat d'ye need, boy?" said the young woman.

Obie was staring at the engorged breast the infant was attacking with such relish, and he quickly held the parcel in front of him lest the sudden rise in his breeches be noted and censured.

"I need Mistress Varner," said Obie.

"I am Mistress Varner," said the woman.

Obie was somewhat startled, as he had envisioned the widow Varner to be old and faded and he was ill prepared to tender sympathies to a young woman, particularly one with a bared breast.

"I am brought ye this, Widow Varner, and sympathies from Master and Mistress Overstreet and all their daughters," said Obie, presenting his careful speech while staring openly and admiringly at the breast thus pummeled by the hungry babe.

"Nor am I the vidow Varner," replied the pretty woman. "I am her daughter-in-law. The vidow Varner is vitin," and she nodded toward the open door.

Obie did not move, being much interested in the large teat and the havoc its sight was causing his irrepressible member. There was nothing unusual, in Obie's experience, in the sight of a feeding infant or the breast upon which it fed, but his own appetites had late become such that they were stirred by sights and even odors that once would have moved him naught. Nor was it the young mother's face, which, though pretty, was roundish and of the sort that would fade anon, that aroused Obie, but her enormous gland, bared to the infant, that sent the juices flooding and startling Obie's private parts to attention. He made no move toward the open door but stared enraptured at the babe thus attached.

The young woman glanced up from her babe to see the boy still staring at her. "B'gone, you naughty boy," she said in some irritation. It was not the first time she had been stared at while nursing one of her children, nor was it the first time that she had felt irritation at a passing male's inability to remain calm in the face of such normal and natural activity. "B'gone!"

"And what is it, Louisa?" came the voice from the kitchen, that voice followed immediately by the figure of an older woman, gray and slightly stooped.

"It is something from the Overstreets."

"I am sent by Mistress Overstreet to tender sympathies," said the boy, his sonorous tones and gangling dignity bringing a slight smile to the widow Varner's lips.

"And indeed," she replied, taking the parcel from Obie, who, thus unencumbered, quickly stuck his hands in his pockets, "please return my thanks to Master and Mistress Overstreet."

"Yes'm," murmured the boy and glanced back at Louisa, in disappointment noting that the infant had finished feeding and Louisa had already managed to cover herself against his impertinent stare. The baby hiccuped and yawned, and then made a fussy sound. "Hush ye now, my tiny Louisa," said the mother.

"Wait, boy," said the widow Varner, "I would that ye fetch something to Mistress Overstreet." And she went back into the kitchen.

Obie waited, slightly uncomfortable in the presence of the young mother, who was now staring openly at him. "Vat is your name, boy?" asked Louisa.

"Obie," he said, "Obediah Murphy." She continued to stare. Uncomfortable, Obie shifted his weight and noted that she had a peculiar accent; it was not of Tennessee or Virginia, nor even Maryland; to that extent Obie was familiar. He had no experience beyond that, nor did he speculate long upon it, not being of a speculative nature.

"Vell, Obediah Murphy," said the young woman, "must nay stare in so brazen a manner at a nursing mudder, as it reflects poor upon your own self. Remember that."

"Yes'm," said Obie.

The widow Varner returned with a wrapped comb of honey and bade him to take it to his mistress, the widow even in her bereavement being determined to match gift for gift.

Obie liked honey from a comb, and he recalled the bread he had left in the tree and immediately forgot Louisa's large teat, and his member slackened accordingly. He felt comfortable enough to mount Ned, which he did, and bidding proper thanks, the boy spurred his mount back toward the lime kiln.

"Right comely youngun," murmured Louisa, but her mother-in-law was thinking of other things.

With the comb of honey secured in one hand, Obie urged Ned forward, reins in the other, his growing boy's hunger urging more speed than Obie might otherwise require, for he loved to ride slowly through the woods and think his boy's thoughts. He had marked well the spot where he needs much leave the path, just to the north of the lime kiln, and he found the tree, the parcel still intact, forthwith, and the sun still being high, he dismounted Ned, letting the beast roam nibbling at grass, while he himself prepared for a leisurely snack of bread and honey.

But before the boy could enjoy his leisurely snack among the still foliage of the forest, he must attend to more pressing needs, and he put the bread and honey aside and, finding a tolerably clean spot, free of high weeds, he pulled his breeches down to relieve himself, squatting at the edge of the clearing. At first straining, he finally felt the matter force its way through his anus, and in some amazement he squatted and strained at such length that it seemed to him that this must be a turd of monumental proportions, so leisurely was its pace— a prize-winning turd, a turd, he marveled, that one might show with pride at the Lewisburg Fair, displayed right there among the pumpkins and gourds and squash and yams. He was still smiling to himself at that idea and pulling his breeches back into place when he spied the Indian maiden watching silently from across the clearing. How long she had been so poised he had no way of knowing.

"H'lo," said the boy. The Indian maiden dipped her head in greeting.

Obie knew that this was an Indian, for she looked like an Indian. But in truth, other than in her color and the form of her features, she was much like any other backwoods girl, as the Indians in Tennessee in that period were much like any other settlers. They wore not feathers or paint or beads or skins like other aborigines, neither lived in tepees, but in log houses, some few quite grand, and cultivated the fields and in general behaved like all other settlers. But their features remained dark and their antecedents aboriginal, which was reason enough for other settlers to begrudge them their land and their property.

All of this Obie understood but vaguely, although he had heard it discussed among elders of his acquaintance, most agreeing that President Jackson's plans to resettle the Indians in the far West had been both just and long overdue. Only the Indians seemed to take issue with that plan, their protests not proving potent enough, however, to prevent their being pushed off their land toward the West.

Obie was surprised to see an Indian at all, as most had already been removed, and in truth the one who confronted him was a slight and undernourished child of perhaps eleven or twelve, whose thin garment ill concealed the slight rises upon her chest that attested to her approaching womanhood.

"Do ye live around here?" Obie asked, making conversation, it being awkward even for children to stand and stare at each other in so isolated a place.

The girl shook her head. Directly she said, "We are traveling. We are going West."

"Ah," said Obie, understanding, and his gaze rested once more on her tender bosom, he finding himself as fascinated by the slightness of that bosom as he had been with the fullness of the younger Mistress Varner's.

"Where're your kin?" he asked, and she nodded back behind her.

"What're ye doing here by yourself?"

"I'm seeking acorns for flour," she said.

"Are ye hungry?" and she nodded, not attempting to explain to the large boy before her the circumstances of her family, which were serious and growing worse, they having been forced from their land in the East and having traveled several weeks toward where they hoped distant kin were encamped on the eastern side of the great river. She had lost already a father and younger sister, and her mother was ill and she and her brother, just a year younger, had the care of the younger brothers and sisters upon their shoulders.

She only nodded that yes, she was hungry.

Obie considered the girl's figure and found himself stirred unaccountably by the very innocence that immature development suggested. He knew much of womanhood full blown but naught of it in the bud. He longed to know first hand what was beneath that illdraped and thin garment, what the budding maiden concealed. He stepped toward her, loaf proffered.

Forthrightly, in deep and mature tones, Obie made an offer: a share of the bread in return for a view of that maiden form. It seemed to him a square offer, but the maiden only stared at him.

"I have likewise a comb of honey," he said, sweetening the offer.

The girl beheld the handsome lad, his offer quite serious, an expression about his mouth and eyes that stirred some feeling in her that was new and alarming, that went beyond the hunger of her belly. They were quite alone, she knew, for she had come circuitously to avoid the settlers' homes, far afield from their meager encampment, searching for a nut tree or an oak or anything that might offer sustenance. Her brother likewise searched the streams for fish or frogs or crawdads. They would rest and eat and store up strength so that they could move on.

The maiden, whose name it had not occurred to Obie to ask, was called Manaseeta, and her forebears had hunted the eastern forests, some said from the beginning of time, but their descendants would forage the distant plains. Manaseeta was wise beyond both her years and her experience. The handsome boy before her was big enough to have his way with her, bread or no. She would not have been the first Indian girl stripped naked for the pleasure of laughing white men. On the other hand, a loaf of bread was a loaf of bread.

Silently she untied the garment at the neck and it slipped from her form to her feet. She wore no undergarment. The bronzed young figure was hard and firm, the bare young breasts hardly larger than his own, the tiny belly sunk in where fat Rebecca's had been pendulous, and where Rebecca had coarse and thick hair, the maiden's was fine and downy. For the first time in his life Obie fell headlong in love, as in love, at least, as his immature experience would allow. Only once again in his lifetime would Obediah fall victim to love's sweet blandishments. His heart pounded and his hands trembled and he longed to touch that perfect body before him.

He tore a chunk of bread from the loaf and held it out.

"The honey," said Manaseeta.

"If you will sit with me, I will spread the honey for you."

Manaseeta sat cross-legged before him, staring at him with unflinching gaze, and Obie bit off a chunk of the honeycomb and mashed it expertly on the bread and offered it to the maiden, and she took it and ate it down directly, carefully licking each finger in turn when she was through. Obie was all but overcome, his member stiff to breaking and his nuts nigh to exploding.

The maiden Manaseeta stared hard at Obie and said, "I would have all the bread." Obie groaned and reached out and stroked her muscled thigh. "And all the honey," she added.

Obie put the bread and honey aside and, reaching for the Indian maiden, gently lowered her form to the ground, and he tasted of the honey on her fingers and thence the honey on her lips and then he touched her tiny breasts, leaving a touch of honey on each, and then he tasted those. The maiden's stiff form began to relax. And when he stroked the soft, brown down below her belly, she started suddenly, but under Obediah's careful handling she relaxed again and with expression considerably softened looked up at the dark-eyed boy and he stroked and petted her until all thoughts save one had departed the maiden. And they dallied away the afternoon and tasted of honey until the shadows lengthened.

And when at last the maiden drew on her thin garment, Obie handed her the loaf and the comb and they touched again fleetingly and she disappeared at once into the forest. Obie was bereft.

He was also hungry and wondered all at once why he had not kept at least a bite of the loaf. But a bargain was a bargain. He mounted Ned and the hungry horse turned toward home, both boy and horse with their members carefully tucked away.

Manaseeta returned the bread and honey to the family that awaited her. At her brother's questioning she said only that a nice boy had given it to her, which was true. But her cheeks were red and her step light, and her brother wondered. However, the honey and the bread went far to allay his suspicions.

When, some months later, beyond the Mississippi on the eastern side of Arkansas, Manaseeta gave birth to a son, she named the child Quewanah, which in her dialect meant "Found in the Forest." Manaseeta's mother died shortly, and she was given in marriage to a widowed warrior and bore him many children, a good and dutiful wife, who only now and then paused to stare into a forest with a gentle smile upon her lips; but Manasquatch, her brother, who had eaten of the bread and honey so dearly bought, raged.

Obediah Murphy, in his nineteenth year and the flower of his young manhood, no longer bound but still abiding with Master and Mistress Overstreet, attended a dance on a Saturday night, likewise attended by Louisa Varner, whose husband lay near to death, a victim of that same fever which had already claimed two of his brothers. It was at the behest of her mother-in-law, the young husband's mother, that Louisa attended the dance, as such events were infrequent, and the young woman had tendered long and devoted hours to the care of her dying husband.

The affair was held at the plantation of Judge and Mistress Bailey, where space beneath the round and bright harvest moon had been swept clean for the dancers, such level and hard ground not easily come by at other times of the year.

Louisa Varner came only to sit in the kitchen and visit quietly with the older women, not to join the revelers in the yard. Nor was there any thought of censure that she might leave her dying husband's bed, as it was understood that she had kept dutiful watch and that she needed the respite. She had with her two of her children, it being not uncommon to bring the children to such events: Louisa, who was six years of age, and Daniel, who was seven. Two younger sons stayed with their father and grandmother.

Among the ladies with whom Louisa visited was Mistress Amy Hardmaster, widowed the year before, but bearing the suckling child her husband had left her. She nursed the babe at her breast and offered advice to Louisa.

"Thou must take thy time in choosing again," she said, for she was Quaker. "Thou wilt have land and property and still thy good looks. Canst have a wide choice. While I," and Mistress Hardmaster sighed, "I shall have to await that widower who will take me, as I have neither property nor looks left." And she was right on both accounts.

Nor did Louisa take amiss such advice as premature. Indeed, she had given it much thought herself, and as she was wise and circumspect by nature she had come to the same conclusion as Mistress

Hardmaster. She stared out at the dancers, circling loudly and bois- terously, the fiddle music all but drowned out. She was watching the tall figure of Obediah Murphy, as she had through the night. The color was high upon his cheeks and the ruffles at his shirt collar bounced as he danced, jigging, arms straight at his side, feet fairly flying in the circle of women and boys. Nor was Louisa unconscious of those heavy thighs and the flat stomach and the mound of masculin- ity held in check by the fabric of the breeches that he wore so tight to his figure. The young man was obviously popular with both boys and girls, bounding easily between the two groups to much giggling and tittering among the girls and much hearty laughter and back-slapping among the boys.

"He cuts a fine figure," observed Louisa of Obediah.

"Aye," nodded the widow Hardmaster, "and he leaves a string of woods colts and broken hearts wher'er he goes."

Louisa said no more and the conversation drifted on. Now, Louisa Varner had from a very young age learned the value of diligent obser- vation. And she kept an eye on the flashing figure in the tight breeches and ruffled shirt, and when, late on in the evening, she noted him edging casually away, as if to relieve himself in the woods, she like- wise noticed that Mistress Bailey's colored kitchen girl, Rachel, ab- sented herself inconspicuously from the back door of the kitchen in that same direction, and that less than half an hour later both reap- peared, the girl at the kitchen door, her eyes shining. Were she of a lighter shade, there would have been roses in her cheeks; as it was, she was breathless and agitated. Obediah had rejoined his fellows, who laughed and slapped his back, and one reached up and brushed a leaf from his hair and they all laughed uproariously again. None of the other women seemed to have noted Rachel's absence and so Louisa said nothing.

It was in the shank end of the evening, while refreshments were being served, that Louisa singled out Obediah and went to him. "I vould dat you vould call upon me tomorrow," she said, "as I haf a matter of some importance to discuss vit you."

Nor did Obie recognize Louisa Varner from a previous encounter, the past being to Obie the same as the future, of no particular significance.

"Between noon and dark, if ye please." And she tendered him directions.

Obediently, if curiously, in the late afternoon Obediah rode into

the Daniel Varner front yard, impressed at once by the large house
and the stable condition of fences and outbuildings, and particularly
by the several ricks of firewood already stacked against the coming
winter. Such industry spoke well, he thought, of the farmer within,
nor did he know that the farmer within had been on his deathbed
these several weeks and that the industry was that of his wife, Louisa,
who had seen to the storing of the firewood as well as all other duties
usually ascribed to the farmer.

"You are truly a wondrous woman," the dying husband had marveled and his mother, Louisa's mother-in-law, had concurred. This
daughter-in-law brought from Philadelphia by her son and speaking a
strange argot that was at first difficult to understand, which was,
though she didn't know it, a combination of that German often called
Pennsylvania Dutch in addition to an Indian dialect passed down
from a grandmother. Louisa had accommodated herself quickly to the
life of both a farmer's wife and a daughter-in-law, and with such
success that she was an object of great admiration, her only critics
noting that she was without humor, which she was, and stubborn,
which she was.

Louisa Varner met Obediah Murphy at the front porch and bade
him follow her to the springhouse, which was some distance from the
house where her husband lay suffering.

Obediah waited patiently, noting in passing that the woman's
bosom was large and well formed. Obie did not always remember
names or even faces, but he rarely forgot a bosom, as his attention was
always drawn to that gland when he was in the company of women.

Louisa was quick to the point. "I am in need of a husband, as mine
own is presently dying."

Obediah, who was not always quick, did not entirely understand
her meaning. She repeated and added, "I vould ved vit you on the
occasion of mine husband's dying."

Obie was startled.

"I haf 360 acres in vood and vater and seed. I haf several milch
cows and flocks of sheep and goose and duck. I haf a fine house and a
vinter's supply of vood. I haf need of a husband."

Obediah, realizing at last that this was a serious proposition,
looked around again at the property upon which he stood, but, never
having given any thought to his future beyond a vague noting that at
some unspecified future date he would acquire a pulpit, nor to a bride,
he had difficulty absorbing the idea. Louisa stood firm before him.

Obie understood, at least, that this woman, though older than he, wanted him, and reached his hand around her waist.

Louisa jerked quickly and sternly away and cast her glance toward the house. "It is indignity enough, this dying. I vill not send mine husband to eternity a cuckold." She added, "Think upon it." And she left him abruptly.

Louisa Varner's husband, however, rallied, faded and lingered, lengthening his stay on earth by several months more than had been anticipated, through the winter. In all that time Louisa neither sought out nor saw Obie. Upon midsummer, Daniel Varner at last gave in to the inevitable, turned his face to the wall and died. Louisa and her children buried and mourned him, and within the month Louisa Varner wed Obediah Murphy. And those who had a month earlier mourned the widow celebrated the bride.

"I trust he has saved enough for his wedding bed," observed one, as Obediah danced among the girls.

"Oh," replied another, "I'm told that his pistol ne'er runs out of shot." And they laughed.

When they sat to sign the wedding registry, Obediah worked long and assiduously on his signature, which was all swirls and curlicues and took up most of the space designated for signatures.

Louisa watched with some interest the construction of that signature—Obediah J. M. Murphy—before she carefully put her own mark underneath it. The clerk was obliged to crowd his own signature witnessing the mark in and around the flourishes that made up Obie's signature.

"Ye've made a poor bargain, I fear," said one of Louisa's former sisters-in-law.

"I've made my choice."

"He'll most like to bankrupt your fortune and break your heart."

"I am smarter by far n'en he. He'll ne'er bankrupt me. N'en my heart, it is encased in tough fiber. It can be reached, but it can't be broken."

In the early evening Obie, awaiting dinner, walked by himself around the acres he had so recently come into, admiring the husbandry, for he knew good husbandry when he saw it. He stepped off the land, measuring it as black Benjamin had taught him years earlier. He marked the fences and the water and at last came back to the house and was seated forthwith at the head of the table and served accordingly, who had so recently sat at the foot and waited as the small children of Louisa now did. And those same children deferred to him and called him "Father" as they had been instructed, the three boys and the girl. Louisa seated herself, and the kitchen girl waited until Obie at last realized that a prayer of grace was expected of him. In deep and sonorous tones he gave thanks to the Lord for the bounty of his table and his land and for the health of his family; indeed, did he express his gratitude at such length that certain of the children began to wonder if it would be possible to starve to death during a blessing.

They were shivareed that night, Obie targeted most by the rowdies, carried aloft and flung into a haystack, pummeled and teased; out of respect for her recent widowhood, perhaps, Louisa was treated more gently.

And in the late evening, when it was finally quiet, they went to their nuptial bed. Obie, lying beside his bride on the soft goose down ticking, was not thinking of the business at hand. He was lost in wonder still at the realization that he was at once a man of means, a gentleman, a head of a household, the husbander of fat sheep and sleek cows, his corncrib full, his wood ricks stacked. He felt a sense of accomplishment, nor did he stop to think upon the fact that he had in no way participated in those singular accomplishments; it was enough that they were done. And for a moment he thought toward the future and anticipated the fullness of a long and prosperous life.

"I would found a line," he cried, rising to one elbow. Louisa stared up at him through the dim light. "I shall have a hundred sons," he cried, his ambition stirred.

Nor did Louisa do aught but blink, she being aware that the likelihood of his getting son or daughter on her was slim at best, she having lain with Daniel Varner for four years without child, and, given the unreliability of her menses, she was certain that her child-bearing days were over.

He was all but wiggling in glee at the thought and his agreeable member was acting accordingly.

"Did you know," asked Louisa, eyeing him curiously, "that Mistress Bailey's black Rachel gave birth three days past?"

"Eh?" and then without apparent interest, he said, "Nay."

"It was male. She named it Noah."

Obie may have heard, but he gave no sign, rather indicating in various manner his interest in approaching his bride for the first time. "I," he announced, "shall fuck many sons out of you."

"Well," grunted Louisa, "get on vit it n'en."

He climbed aboard the undulating vessel that transported him then across seas of pleasure and back again, at last landing him, agreeably spent, flat on his back once more.

As he approached sleep, Obie was once more caught up in his dreams of founding a line and the sons he would beget. At last, before he slipped off into restful sleep, he saw himself, aged but not changed, ruffles at his throat, breeches tight, eyes bright, his descendants spread out about him, honored, the family founder, remembered and revered through the ages. And so he slept, this man of means.

FOUR

A STRING OF LIGHTS

Standing in this cold and windblown burying ground where Lee and Levi will forever remain, I think, "Who was he, that distant unknown ancestor Obediah—the Old Bastard of Levi's book? He who begat Louisa, who begat Levi, who begat Lee, who begat me?"

Nor do I precisely know what has brought me here, to this place I last saw when Lee was planted at the dark end of summer. Now it is late February, the faded side of winter. Winter is clearly defined in Oklahoma. No need to rely on calendars or solstices or migrating fowl even. Winter comes when the grass dies. That's it. The grass of choice if Bermuda, and it goes dormant unto death with the coming of winter, only to be resurrected with the warmth. Such will not be the case for Lee and Levi, however, lying side by side on this slight rise, covered over by dead, brown Bermuda grass.

I shrug. I cannot know where Obediah Murphy is, but I do know where Lee and Levi are and where I will one day also be, I suppose. Perhaps I'll be cremated. Surely it would be more comfortable, resting eternally in a cozy urn rather than stretched out six feet down.

Ostensibly I am here to check Lee's stone, ordered months ago and finally erected. The stonemason called maybe six weeks ago to report that the stone was at last in place and to encourage my inspection of same. He called back last week, anxious for some praise, I guess, for I had already paid his bill. I was calmly courteous, amused at the insistent stonemason as well as surprised at this kind of personal attention.

There I might have left it, but a few nights later I awakened from a troubled sleep with the abrupt and certain feeling that I needed to take a look at, not Lee's, but Levi's stone. It was one of those lucid thoughts that sometimes strike in the middle of the night, like recalling something you had forgotten to do or remembering where you had put something. I might indeed have suspected that it was Old Levi somehow from the grave nudging me to this task; however, I am more inclined to accuse the warm pecan pie, washed down with a large glass of cold milk, of doing me in sleepwise. I have never slept well on a full stomach, and milk has not agreed with me in years. That Old Levi's headstone would be foremost in my consciousness at that moment I cannot, however, ascribe to the pie and milk. I suspect that it had more to do with the fact that both Lee and Levi have been on the outer edges of my subconscious ever since Christmas, when I found the box of relics that Levi had tucked away, like a time capsule, under the stairs.

I am here now because of something vaguely irritating and uncomfortable, like a minor urinary tract infection, that keeps my ancestors present in my consciousness.

The two stones I stare at are identical, except that the one is obviously new, not having suffered the outrages of weather for better than a quarter of a century as the other has. They are both stately—and upright. This is an old cemetery and the plots were bought long ago, and in this section, at least, there are no requirements for flat markers, no one a half century or so ago foreseeing even the possibility of motorized lawn mowers, much less riding mowers, and the difficulty to be encountered trimming around cumbersome stones. We live in more ordered times; the dead must be put away, but conveniently so.

I stare at length at the two stones, standing equally tall and imposing and isolated just as the two men they celebrate stood in life. And then abruptly I notice what it is about the stones that has been bothering me. The sensation is not unlike finding an elusive itch and dispatching it. I am surprised that I hadn't noticed it before, except that I saw Old Levi's stone only once before, and that was when Lee was buried. Under the circumstances, I suppose, I could not be expected to be particularly observant.

The inscription on Levi's tombstone is simple and to the point: *O. L. MURPHY 1878–1956.* No days or months. But it is the *O.L.* that I focus upon. O.L.? To my knowledge Levi had no other name. Why the *O?* What does it stand for? *Obediah Levi?* Possibly. Or simply *Old Levi?* Maybe. I turn my attention to Lee's stone and find it ascribed as I had directed: *LEE MURPHY* and his dates. I sense that same irritated frustration that I often felt for Lee when he was alive. Why did he do that to Old Levi? Why divest him of his name and leave him only with obscure initials, initials by which he never even went when he lived? I played fair with Lee. I thought about returning his original name to him in death, *LEVI MURPHY II*, but I didn't, not knowing that he had played such a trick upon Old Levi.

Lee's terrors even in death apparently were deep. His were spray-painted-swastika fears of Levi's alleged Jewishness, those terrors that led him to shed the Jewish name and, with it, all he feared.

It was just before Pearl Harbor, when Hitler was well into his program of annihilating the Jews, that Old Levi first went peculiar, declared himself a Jew, donned a yarmulke and padded about the house invoking the prophets. At that time he was not really old enough to be declared senile, nor was he wildly insane, simply a little dotty. He did not expose himself thus in public, only at home, to Lee's considerable discomfiture. Lee had no faith in Roosevelt's and Churchill's abilities to hold the Nazis at bay, and when they finally overran the North American continent, as he was sure they eventually would, they would drive all Jews before them, most especially Jewish merchants.

That those terrors would persist until Levi's death, long after the Nazi threat had been laid to rest, to such an extent that Lee would obliterate the offending *LEVI* from even his father's stone, seems neurotic at best, paranoid even.

And is this what awakened me in the middle of the night after dallying with Nanny's pecan pie? Had my subconscious picked up on that fact during Lee's interment, a fact finally dislodged by a bout of gastrointestinal distress? Whatever it is, I am mildly annoyed with Lee, even in death. He had no right to play so cavalier with another's name. And I decide to right that injustice myself. Perhaps that will lay my ghosts to rest, that and avoiding pecan pie and milk at bed-time.

It may require a brand-new stone; I don't know. It is probably not too easy to erase cold marble. Well, so be it. Lee and Levi can start even. Then I am struck by a mean thought. It would serve Lee right if I changed the name on his stone back to the original Levi; but I think, Do I really want to risk being visited in the night by a terrified ghost? I put the idea aside. Perhaps we should forgive the dead; it's easy enough.

I pull my coat tighter around me against the chill wind, that wind that is all but omnipresent in Oklahoma—mild in spring and fall, hot in summer, cold in winter and frequently perpetrating turbulent sneak attacks any and all seasons. The wind in all its vagaries is a fact of life in this part of the country, and on the knoll in the cemetery there is little protection against it.

Oddly, this is the time of year I like best, I think, though a pleasant spring day or a copper and azure fall day is always welcome. Most people are weary enough of winter by the tail end of February, and spring comes quickly this time of year. But it is just this bleakness that I relish. The leafless trees and bushes, exposing what the lush summer foliage hides, are like line drawings. For all its spareness, perhaps because of its spareness, I enjoy the bare-bones look of late winter—especially when I am in my black Lincoln with the heater turned high. And I turn away from the stones and make my way toward where my refuge from the cold is parked.

Once cozy inside the car, its motor going, I sit for a few long moments to contemplate the scene in its quiet privacy. It is a Christian burial ground. We buried Levi as he was born, I suspect, a Christian. As far as I know, he asked no other ritual. Truth is, I don't think he ever actually intended to die. He just did one day.

The colorless stones against the dried grass against the gray backdrop of dormant deciduous trees and the colorless gray of the sky make a study in shadows, I think, shadows that flit and wink, pushed around by fickle wind.

I am not afraid in cemeteries. Of course, I do not now frequent them except in ritual, to put aside some acquaintance or other. But when I was young I spent some considerable time in cemeteries, usually supine in the backseat of a car. In the 1950s and early '60s the back seats of automobiles were more commodious and functional than they are now, even black Lincolns, I think with a smile. Cemeteries then were usually unpatrolled and unvisited after dark, save for the horny young who found lovemaking safe among the dead who would not whisper and gossip and accuse.

But that was long ago, and now I think that most cemeteries, at least big cemeteries, are locked up tight against just such desecrations. And I wonder where the horny young go these days. I suppose the sandbars of the Arkansas, my own personal favorite, are still so utilized.

I make my cozy way back toward my office, lunch forgotten, enjoying the spare and bleak scenery that rapidly gives way to developments and assorted building projects. Tulsa is very busy grow-ing, a forward-looking city with neither time nor inclination for backward glances. I am a part of that, the head of one of the few remaining family-owned retail chains in the country. I suppose it will not be too many years before Murphy's Department Stores joins some retail conglomerate or other, but not at the moment, and I have work to do.

Shirley, my secretary, is waiting with the business at hand when I arrive.

"Nanny has been calling," she says. "It's an emergency. Shall I get her for you?"

Shirley Kline has been with me a dozen or so years. We are not close, but she is very competent. I would have trouble replacing her if I ever lost her. Shirley and Nanny are on a first-name basis, even though the two have never met face to face. Nanny calls here on an average of twice a week with one emergency or another. They rarely are. Shirley knows that. She also knows that Nanny is one of the few people in the world for whom I would drop everything, even though her emergencies usually involve her misplaced glasses or a broken doorbell or a stopped-up sink. She has a complete list of service people to call, but she never does. She calls here and has interrupted untold meetings with complaints that the house is too cold or the postman has been uppity. Shirley knows that; she also knows that she will most likely be called upon to solve Nanny's problem, but only after Nanny has explained it to me in detail.

"No," I say, "not just yet. I have another call I need to make." And I direct Shirley to get me the stonemason whose bill she so recently paid. Shirley is a little startled that I have put Nanny on hold. It doesn't happen often. But this tombstone business is the sort of good intention that can easily get lost in daily routine. I'd best do it while it's on my mind. Nanny's emergency will wait, I'm sure.

I do not really relish a conversation with the stonemason, Mr. Jenks. These demi-artists—the people who reweave fabric or tune pianos or cut stones or make fine picture frames—they are a breed, and usually a garrulous breed at that. Taking justifiable pride in their work, they all seem eager to talk and explain and elicit praise, unlike the mere technicians who fix TV sets and root out water lines and set fence posts, mostly in taciturn silence. Mr. Jenks is old and skilled and garrulous, ready with a lengthy explanation of the proper techniques for carving in cold stone whether you want one or not.

It was he, I discovered when Lee died, who had done Old Levi's stone. He told me so himself, called me on the phone a decent interval after Lee's funeral, explained that he had done Old Levi's stone and why it had been an exceptional job, as opposed to those of lesser artisans whose work would not even survive the end of the century, much less eternity. He expected to perform a like service for Lee. I saw no reason why he should not and directed him to make an identical stone. I should have foreseen what he would say. "Like father, like son," he chuckled and thought so well of what he had said that he repeated it and awaited my answering laugh. I said as cheerfully as I could manage that that was probably right.

Mr. Jenks is appalled at my request for a new stone for Levi. I can hear it in his angry response. There is nothing wrong with that stone, it is a work of art, destined for the ages, never to fade and crumble the way some, he says ominously, that he could name would.

"There's a mistake in the name. That's all. I'm sure it was what Mr. Murphy, my father, requested, but it is not," and here I pause for some delicate way to extricate myself, "it is not genealogically correct. My father"—I put a smile into my voice—"was not always accurate as to details. I would not like for my grandfather to go into eternity bearing the wrong name. I'm sure you understand."

He seems somewhat mollified, but does ask suspiciously about the cost, the artisan in him giving way to the businessman. Do I understand that, after nearly twenty-five years, the price of such a stone is of necessity quite a bit higher? He is prepared, too, with a detailed explanation of the reasons for the price rise. I cut him short.

"I would assume that the cost of the new stone would be the same as that of my father's," I say, indicating that such cost would be satisfactory.

He agrees and then, cheerful once more, says, "That'll make six stones I done for you Murphys. I think that's a record for one family. Six identical stones."

"I beg your pardon?" I have no idea what he is talking about. "What do you mean—six?"

"I done three at one time, years back, a nice order. Didn't you know that? I put three identical stones up in a little graveyard up in Rogers County. They was all Murphys, but I'd have to look up the names. I keep real accurate records, don't you know? Sometimes the Internal Revenue wants to see 'em, but lots a times it's just folks lookin' fer kin or where they're buried." He is on his garrulous way, but I let him talk. "It ain't all that uncommon for people to have a stone made for someone that's been dead a long time, someone they probably never even seen. You'd be surprised the folks that come in here and ask for a stone for someone that's been dead maybe a hundred years. A stone to replace a faded stone or maybe one that's been vandalized or maybe even there never was a real stone, just a wood marker or a rock that's long gone. But most folks order only one, and usually not a very big one. So you can see I'd remember if a body come in here and ordered three big, expensive stones. Took months to get them out. He wanted 'em matched precisely to one already set up there."

"No," I say finally, "I didn't know my grandfather had ordered those stones." I am evasive. "He came from that part of the state originally. I suppose they were his relatives."

"Wadn't yer grandpa done it. Was yer dad. You know, that died last summer. I cut them stone several year after yer grandpa passed away."

I am too thunderstruck to reply.

"I can look it up for you. I got the names and dates. I keep real good records," he repeats.

"No, no, not right now," I say quickly. "Just let me know when you finish my grandfather's stone." I ease off the phone as best I can. He is still talking when I hang up.

Well, I think, the plot thickens.

I ponder this bit of trivia for a long moment. This is definitely out of character for Lee. I cannot believe that he could in any way have had even a passing interest in his ancestors, certainly not enough to warrant setting stones for them. I have no doubt that those stones in the Rogers County cemetery are for the three Louisas and Obediah. But why? Why stones so many years after their deaths? How would Lee even know where to find them, but, even more curious, why would he even bother? Lee, who was so totally one-dimensional, who never swerved, who was predictable unto boredom? Even if he had known those elderly kin, I cannot believe that the thought would ever have occurred to him to mark their graves.

Well, the most ready answer to those questions is that in some way Old Levi requested the act, perhaps a dying wish or maybe in written instructions that Lee carried out. Nanny might be able to shed some light on it, or David. And then I remember David's surprise at the mention of those relatives that I had made on Christmas Day last, the day that Old Daniel went temporarily berserk. David probably knows no more about it than I do. It is really no matter, and no need for me to waste a lot of time considering it.

I am buzzed out of my reverie by Shirley with Nanny on hold. "You'd better talk to her," says Shirley, who is usually a good judge of whom I ought to talk to. "She's in a state."

Well, it is not so unusual for Nanny to be in a state; what is unusual is for Shirley to be concerned about it.

Nanny's first word to me over the long-suffering telephone line is a loud and clearly unmistakable "Assholes!"

"Nanny!"

Nanny is not normally given to either blasphemies or obscenities—dark looks and muttered asides but little profanity. I think, as a matter of fact, that "asshole" is the only word of profanity I ever heard Nanny use, and as a rule she uses it as an impersonal word—quite utilitarian, noun, verb, adjective, adverb, interjection even.

I've heard her yell "Asshole!" upon stubbing her toe or dropping something. The first time I recall noticing her peculiar affinity for the word, she was staring at a clogged-up sink muttering about the asshole sink. Another time she accused a recalcitrant vacuum sweeper of being no asshole good. But she never to my knowledge used it in a personal way. She reserves the word only for extreme displeasure and inanimate objects or ideas. "Fools" she applied to human beings—a word I have always thought better than any other for summing up undesirable qualities in lesser people.

"Those fools come in here and tore up ever'thing! Assholes! They tore up ever'thing!"

"Nanny. What fools? What are you talking about?"

"Somebody come in here and tore up the whole house. They strung ever'thing all over, even my flour from the kitchen. They stopped up the toilets; they tore the curtains down. They," and she pauses ominously, "they peed in my microwave."

"Nanny, are you saying that the house has been vandalized?"

I can imagine Nanny nodding her head vigorously into the telephone. "Something," she says finally. "Something," she adds darkly.

"Have you called the police"

"I ain't called nobody. I don't want nobody to see this mess."

"I'll be right home. Just leave everything the way it is. Don't touch anything."

"I got to clean this up."

"Not until I get there."

Nanny, I remember, has probably spent the morning with her "group" at the rec center, playing dominoes and gossiping, more the latter than the former, I think. Tuesday mornings Nanny plays dominoes with the senior citizen group at the rec center, though she would never admit to being a senior citizen. Wednesday nights she plays bingo at her church. Those two outings, plus regular visits with Charlaine and Leroy, constitute Nanny's social life.

"My house has apparently been broken into," I say to Shirley on my way out.

"Burglars?"

"I don't know," I admit. I had forgotten to ask Nanny if anything is missing, I suppose because there is little of any value there, at least anything that I value. "Call the police for me. Tell them I'll meet them there. Nanny," I add, "is in no condition to talk to them by herself."

By the time I pull into the drive, a policeman is already inside, where it becomes obvious that Nanny has in no way exaggerated the mess. Furniture is upturned, some of it smashed, though most of the massive pieces are impervious to casual vandalism. There is the unmistakable smell of human and, curiously, animal excrement, the source of which is in part that which is smeared all over walls and upholstery. Contents of kitchen canisters—coffee, flour and so forth—have been flung throughout the downstairs, and indeed someone appears to have urinated in the microwave. It looks like the work of a poltergeist. A gang of poltergeists. Hungry poltergeists, however, for mixed in with the debris are wrappers of M&Ms and Snickers bars, wrappers that did not originate in the house.

"Kids," mutters the police officer. "They're out of school this week, bored. They probably sneaked in here without any real idea but looking around, and well, one thing led to another."

He sounds patient. He is already alibi-ing them, I think, even without knowing who they are.

"Is this all?" I ask.

"No," snaps Nanny. "Dat upstairs is just as bad. You ought to see what they done to my bath powder!"

I climb the stairs slowly, loath to view the damage. It is as Nanny said—a mess. Broken mirrors—may those vandals, youthful or not, be visited with seven times seven years' bad luck—smashed bottles of cream and makeup and perfume, clothing strewn around and more excrement. Vicious little bastards, I think to myself.

The Seagram Seven box is overturned and smashed; the papers it contained are gone and the bathroom yields a clue as to their fate: ashes in the shower stall and photographs in the toilet, photographs copiously urinated upon.

The police officer is standing behind me as I view the ravaged bathroom. "You might be able to salvage the pictures," he says in some sympathy, for it's apparent that they are old.

"I don't think I'll bother," I mutter and move on. Lee's room has been equally devastated, in so much as it is possible; for Lee's room is, as it always has been, sparsely furnished, and his clothing and personal effects went to the Salvation Army months ago. But the rug has been defecated upon, with some of the defecation smeared on walls and mirror.

"There certainly were a lot of kids in this house in need of simultaneous bowel movements," I suggest to the ubiquitous police officer.

"And dogs," he says helpfully. "Sure is an awful lot of crap," he adds in something like admiration.

"Bean burritos," mutters Nanny. "They been eatin' bean burritos." She states it as fact, not conjecture.

"What about the third floor? What about Old Levi's rooms?"

"I don' know," says Nanny. "I ain't been up there." It is a steep climb for Nanny. She goes up only about once a month and takes with her only a dustcloth and dust mop. The rooms, like Lee's, remain much the same as they were when Levi occupied them himself.

I go up the stairs myself. In an old and dark house these rooms have always seemed, in spite of the magnificent view from the many windows, older and darker than the rest of the house, and this has not changed. There is something intimidating about the maroon floral strip of carpet on the stairs, faded but hardly worn. The smell at the landing is only of mildew and age; the vandals apparently ran out of excrement before they made it here. The landing is free of damage and the door to Levi's rooms is still secured, not locked, but latched firmly enough to discourage casual entrance. It takes enough tries for me to jar the door that I realize that it has not been recently tampered with, and, peering through the gloom toward the stained and weather-darkened windows, I assure myself that these rooms have not been violated. I am strangely relieved.

I do not come to these rooms often. Even as a child I rarely came up here. It was not that I was forbidden to come or even that I was not welcome. I don't recall that Old Levi ever spoke sharply to me about anything. Even when I complained once about the old laurel in the yard, misshapen and ugly, and suggested that he have it taken out, he only stared at me for a moment and then said, "It is important." That was all. But he said it firmly and in such a way that I knew it *was* important. I suppose he made his point, for I have never had the tree taken out, nor even thought of it again, and should anyone even ask why, all I could say would be that *it is important.*

Sometimes as a child I would rush to Levi's rooms for a view, a grass fire or an upcoming storm. The grass fires, which are a fact of life in Oklahoma when the air is dry and the wind is strong, can be seen for great distances, and the view of such a fire to the west from Levi's rooms was, and is, spectacular, the puffs of smoke rolling across the horizon as casually as puffs of smoke from a nearby cigar. And the thunderclouds with accompanying rumbles and flashes out of either the southwest or the northwest were comfortably ominous in those pre-tornado days when we were assured that tornadoes would never strike the city, that the Creek Indians had understood that the Arkansas River would somehow protect when they chose this spot to settle. That was before Nature sent several quick tornadoes through the city, as if to make up for lost time, and Creek wisdom is not so readily invoked these days.

Still, aside from the weather watching, I rarely came into these rooms. I suppose the steep stairs precluded familiarity, that and Levi's strange ways and the studied "oldness" of the rooms.

And that is a shame. The view is spectacular. I am reminded of Arlene's advice, to glass it in, rip out walls, turn it into an airy studio or penthouse or some such. I wonder idly if I could indeed do that. But it is not just a matter of sending Old Levi tumbling in his grave; it is a matter of erasing those few memories, those presences, those ghosts.

Perhaps I am keeping them prisoner; perhaps they are seeking release. Whoever they are, I am sure they could not live in open spaces, under skylights, surrounded by terraces and deep carpet and modular furniture.

I shudder, pull myself away from the view and examine these aging yet ageless rooms. They are as Levi left them. I close the door carefully.

On the first floor several more policemen have arrived. I find them thumping morosely around, sniffing in distaste and assuring each other, "Kids, rotten kids. Ought to keep 'em in school all the time."

But it is muttered without rancor, as if the damage perpetrated by the underage is not so significant as that same damage perpetrated by those over eighteen.

Perhaps that's the way the law, the courts, view it; but whoever, of whatever age, they have effectively sundered me from what little I had of a past. It might be argued that I am no worse off in that respect now than I was before we found the aging Seagram Seven box with its dubious treasures, clues to an unknown past. It is as if some presence had only wanted me to become aware that it existed, but for whatever devious reason did not want me to know more. Ghosts?

I do not believe in ghosts in any sense of the word, nor do I believe this house to be haunted by or possessed by or even under lease to any kind of spirit. What ghosts there are—and that is the only word I can think of—are the result of my own selective memory or subconscious desires or whatever.

I had a dream once, or a part of a dream. At least, I think I did. I have a *memory* of that dream, though, whether I really dreamed all or part of it or only embellished a fragment I can't say. I mistrust memory. But the dream, real or otherwise, clings. If I did not dream it, I must have wanted to dream it.

I dreamed that I was floating, an astronaut walking in space, a pack on my back, struggling for a foothold where there was none, battling zero gravity, struggling to master that which was not, backpacking endlessly through the universe. It comes back to me, that sense of not fright or panic but frustration, anger, at not being able to touch. Not being buffeted or forced by anything, simply unable to secure myself.

Moody; I am definitely moody. It is a strange way to react to such devastation. I should be shrieking and accusing and threatening. I could at least mutter "Asshole" at regular intervals, as Nanny does. But all I do is react calmly, as if this were just another one of those stages, passing the time in meaningless activity day in day out, moodily, until it's all over.

We methodically go through the stinking rooms once more, trying to decide what, if anything, is missing; I cannot say that anything is gone. It's hard to tell, of course, things are in such disarray, but the vandals seem to have taken nothing with them, certainly nothing of consequence. But the policemen find things that interest them, and they confer and murmur among themselves and do policelike things, at least, what I imagine to be policelike things. And then, after taking statements from Nanny and me, they are gone, fanning out through the neighborhood, questioning passersby and neighbors. We are not particularly neighborly, mainly because most of the houses around us—stately homes dating from the teens and twenties—have been turned into apartments and most of the neighbors are of a transient variety. Ours is no longer a fashionable neighborhood, but it has always been relatively safe.

Nanny has a large trash bag and is moving through the house, muttering, picking at scraps and pieces. Her leathery face is streaked with tears. I don't think I have ever seen Nanny cry. It distresses me.

"Don't bother, Nanny. I'll call a professional cleaning service. You go get some things and I'll drive you to Leroy's. I'll go to a hotel. We won't come back until it's all cleaned up. It was due"—I try to smile—"for a spring cleaning, anyway."

Due, very due, long overdue, as a matter of fact. Nanny's housekeeping abilities are satisfactory. She keeps things tidied and dusted, but a house such as this needs more than just the regular application of Endust. It is definitely run-down around the edges.

Nanny does not argue the point. She drops, rather lets slide, the trash bag she is holding and seats herself, *Thinker*-wise, on a stair step and stares in helpless sadness at the clutter before her. I realize that she is overwhelmed. That bothers me, too. I cannot imagine Nanny being overwhelmed by anything.

I call Shirley and with a brief explanation set her on the track of a good cleaning service. I can count on Shirley, and sure enough, by the time I have got hold of David and the insurance adjuster and they have arrived, David with Arlene in tow, the man from the cleaning service is knocking on the door. One of the advantages of being wealthy is that people tend to move rapidly for you.

The insurance adjuster is businesslike, even bored. "You'd be surprised how often things like this happen," he says.

David is perplexed, Arlene aghast, the cleaning man nothing if not to the point. "Gawdam," he murmurs, shaking his head. "Gawdam. This is goin' to take some time," he drawls at last, "and it's goin' to cost ya. I'm goin' to have to pay a bunch to git anybody to come in here and clean this up. Shee-it," he moans. I assume that to be an expletive rather than a descriptive adjective. "But," he adds cheerfully, "you got insurance." The insurance adjuster pays no attention.

"You want these winders warshed, too?" asks the cleaning man.

The drapes ripped from the window have revealed not only their

own dust-streaked folds, but the dim light that struggles to filter
through a windowpane darkened by untold layers of city silt.

"Elizabeth." Arlene has taken her Mother-knows-best tone; her
arms hanging carefully at her sides might just as well be akimbo. That
Mother-knows-best tone she has used on me as long as I have known
her, and it has never worked. Even so, I know what's coming.
"Elizabeth, this is really a blessing in disguise. Since you're going to
be all torn up anyway, you can redecorate. Really, you know how it
needs it." Enthusiasm is one of Arlene's strongest characteristics. If
you were to try to describe Arlene to someone, you would start with
the word "enthusiastic."

"Just have the whole house *painted*, if nothing else."

At the word "painted" the cleaning man brightens considerably.
"We do painting, too," he says, "on the side. I can give you references."

"Really, dear," Arlene persists, "really, I can get you a good ar-
chitect and interior designer, and within six months this place will be
a *showplace.*" "Showplace" is an important word in Arlene's vocabu-
lary.

The cleaning man persists: "Real good references."

"No," I snap, too abruptly. "No. I don't want it painted. I just
want it cleaned. Yes, do the windows. Clean it thoroughly." I turn to
Arlene. "I'll have someone from the store come out and hang new
drapes." That's all that I grant her.

"Really, Elizabeth, you'd be so much happier if you'd brighten
this place up."

I wonder briefly how Arlene knows what would make me happy.
There's no question that the place would benefit from renovation, but
I am very loath to turn loose of it just the way it is. I hug those forlorn
and dim nooks and crannies to me like a security blanket, I suppose.

We are standing in the dining room, Arlene looking enthusiastic
and everyone else businesslike. The table, too massive to be moved by
poltergeists or at least their miniature agents, remains anchored to the
fading carpet as if bolted there. The chairs are, however, moved and
some upended, and dishes scattered, though mercifully unbroken. I
wonder briefly, Why?

Years ago I told Lee that I remembered my mother, recalled her
standing in the dining room. Lucille. Lucille what? Lucille Murphy is
all I know. Lee contradicted me quietly, without passion. No, he'd

said, no, I did not really remember her. I had been too young when she left, too young to remember her.

I'd insisted; I did too remember. He'd dismissed it with a shrugged, "It was someone else. We had many housekeepers, you know."

But I am still certain, or at least I think I *want* to be certain, that the woman I remember was my mother. I don't know why, for I cannot remember her in detail at all, only that she stood in this room, a presence, and she was my mother. I don't remember how she looked or spoke or smelled or anything else. Only that she was.

As I grew older, I picked up a few details about her, not from Levi or Lee but from those people on the periphery of lives who love to offer such bits of information; call it gossip. All they could tell of, though, was her leaving, which was scandalous. They knew nothing more.

I learned at an early age, I suppose, the futility of asking Lee or Levi about anything but matters of current concern, and those only the material and not the philosophical. They had effectively dissociated themselves from the past, and I knew it. I don't know that, as a child, I accepted that detachment as a fact of life so much perhaps as I feared disturbing it. It was like a warm spot in an otherwise cold bed, if occasionally cramped, at least secure from the cold shock that might await elsewhere. Those two old men apparently succeeded through example or guilt or fear of the unknown in detaching me from my own past as well as theirs.

I remember that, as a child, I made up family to fit my needs or moods: a mother who was romantic, loving, cruel or demanding as needed, using my little friends' experiences as a pattern. In such manner, I imagined an entire extended family: siblings, cousins, grandparents. I knew, of course, that they were fantasies, and I never passed them off as real except on rare occasions when I felt cornered. They were not real. The two old men were. I dared not disturb that reality. It was too fragile.

That same fear must still cling. Like holding my breath for a lifetime, I would not disturb any of the comforting familiarity. Now, however, for whatever reason, accident or intent, it has been disturbed for me. Perhaps Arlene is right; now is the time to make changes. But I only shake my head at her.

Arlene sighs. She is staring right at the arrangement of silk flowers that she gave me for Christmas not recognizing it as such, I'm sure, its limp and defiled presence only a part of the general scene.

We are interrupted by a call from the police station. The voice at the other end is smug. They have found the culprits, and will I come down to press charges. "Bunch a kids," the voice confirms.

David's reaction is predictable. "You don't need to go. I'll send someone from the firm." Some junior associate, I'm sure. This is another advantage of wealth. There is always someone around to send, detaching you for the really important work of being rich.

As a rule I am more than willing to take advantage of that perk, but in this instance I am curious to see those who defiled my house and destroyed my past. I want to make sure that they are real flesh-and-blood characters, not some errant spirits bent on mysterious mischief. I am being melodramatic. Moody, then melodramatic—possibly menopausal?

It is indeed kids, four boys and two girls—and dogs, I am told. They are not juvenile delinquents of the long-haired, leather-jacket variety, none older, I'm sure, than eleven, a couple no more than six or seven. The adults with them are their parents.

The police are proud of their detective work, smug that their skillful sleuthing has solved the case so quickly. In truth, I detect more luck in this solution than skill. An officer stopped to ask one of the neighborhood children if he knew anything about the break-in. He did, had been a party to it, as a matter of fact, and was willing, even eager, to tell all that he knew.

The children are all guiltlessly excited, self-important and interested in all the police business around them. "Did you ever shoot anybody?" asks one of the urchins, eyeing a policeman's gun, hanging conspicuously on his hip.

"Not yet," teases the officer, "but don't you try to escape."

The boy's eyes are round, not with fear, but with excitement.

The parents are another story. Their faces are collectively ashen and their expressions strained. One mother is quietly sniffling and another suddenly insists loudly that her son is a good boy, "gets good grades at school and washes dishes every night. He just got in with bad company, that's all."

The others parents glare at her. She has, I suppose, stolen *the* line, all figuring that it was their children who had fallen in with evil influences.

And I think, quite unaccountably, it's all in your point of view.

The horror of a man-eating fish as opposed to a fish-eating man depends entirely on whether you're fish or man.

I ask a police officer as I am leaving what will happen to those children. For answer, he shrugs. "Not much. Go through the juvenile hearing process, be remanded to their parents' custody. Maybe lose TV privileges or have their bottoms whacked."

"Is that all?" I say it too quickly, without thinking.

The officer's lifted eyebrow tells me more than he does. He is thinking, I'm sure, Well, what do you want, lady? Should we put those kids away at hard labor for the rest of their lives?

What he does say out loud, with a shrug, is, "Their parents are probably liable for the damage. You can sue, I guess." That's little help. These parents are all obviously of modest means. A suit brought against them would only make me the bad guy. I don't want that. Anyway, these people have no way to undo damage that can't be undone. They cannot resurrect the ashes that the contents of the Seagram Seven box have become. It is obvious, as it often is, that there are things for which there is no justice. Anyway, I am putting too much emphasis on those papers and photographs. They were of no importance to me before I knew of their existance; why should their loss be suddenly so profoundly troubling? This ancestor business is all pointless, after all. There is no way I or anyone else can know everything about our ancesters. Why focus on a few as if they were in some way more important than the rest simply because you know of their existence?

That conviction lasts about three days before I call in a professional genealogist. I am even embarrassed enough about it that I tell Shirley when I ask her to get me in touch with a good genealogist that it has to do with estate settling, that I need some information not readily available in existing records.

I do not know what I want exactly. Anything will do, I suppose. Any tangible proof that I am genetically connected with a past. I have been left, for whatever reason, with little but memory to link me to that line which I know by reason has to have existed. Old Levi's book has been consigned to memory by virtue of flames set by those small ones hardly past the age of accountability. I grimace at an urge to characterize them as imps from hell. Still, I cannot help making that analogy, cannot help wondering at whatever presence would sunder me from the past, allowing only frail and fallible memory to link present with past.

Memory is an untrustworthy vehicle at best. I need something more substantial, and that need is perhaps what has been impelling me to search. That need, rather than bad dreams occasioned by over-indulgence at bedtime, might be what drew me to the twin stones of Lee and Levi and then directed me to the garrulous old artisan Jenks and his six identical stones. Beyond those stones are facts, reliable information. I would be anchored to some eternity by more than marble tombstones. I would not be orphaned in the universe.

But such information, if it is to be had, will probably require the services of someone more practiced in digging out minutiae than I am. I am frankly intimidated by modern libraries. I have always found that air of sincere industry which librarians seem to share with dental assistants and political hacks unnerving, but in the past I could at least stride purposefully to the card catalog or reader's guides or reference shelves and look up what I wanted myself. I stopped doing my own research when libraries went to microfilm. I would be at a total loss now that things are stored on computers and cassettes and God knows what else.

The genealogist who arrives to talk with me is a woman, about my own age, but somehow more elderly. I had, for no good reason, expected a male genealogist, and I had expected that he would be helpfully sincere, like a librarian. Phoebe Ruskin is none of that. She is more in the mold of Mr. Jenks the stonemason in her certitude of the importance of her calling to the well-being of the human race. I give Mrs. Ruskin what information I have, precious little actually, for which I find myself apologizing. I even tell her about the three new stones and the stonemason.

"That," Mrs. Ruskin reassures me, "is what makes this so fascinating, this *detective* work. Scraps of information, obscure clues. It is simply fascinating. So exciting that I would almost do it for nothing." I notice that she does stop just short of saying that she *would* do it for nothing.

I tell her that I would be grateful for anything she can find out. Perhaps she might even be able to get copies of the newspaper clippings that I lost, at least.

When Mrs. Ruskin resurfaces several weeks later, she has, unhappily added very little to my store of knowledge, two bits of information to be exact.

Though I am disappointed, she says triumphantly, for all the world as if she had uncovered an unsuspected Indian burial ground or a lost continent, "Do you know what your great-great-grandfather's middle initials stood for?

I don't.

"Jonah Micah," she announces. When I fail to respond, Mrs. Ruskin taps her fingernails on my desk top and, nodding, murmurs, "This *is* significant, you know?"

All I can do is reply with a vague "Oh?"

And Mrs. Ruskin launches into a detailed explanation of this significance. "Obadiah, Jonah, Micah—those are the names of three successive books of the Old Testament—three minor Old Testament prophets. Obadiah," she announces, "is the shortest book in the Bible. One chapter, twenty-one verses." She adds, whispering as if the information should be held in strictest confidence, "The biblical spelling was Obadiah, but such variations are not at all uncommon." I remember this now about researchers in general. They always give you more information than you ever wanted or can use. Besides, I do not entirely trust all the information they give, anyway. I do not say that history lies, exactly, only that it does not tell all it knows and, if anything, only hints at truth.

"Jonah, you remember of course, tells the story of that prophet's being swallowed by the whale?"

Ah, the man-eating fish.

"And Micah foretells the birth of Christ in Bethlehem. And Obadiah foretells the destruction of Edom, which was of course the city of Esau—you remember the tale of Jacob and Esau, of treachery most vile, the theft of Esau's birthright?"

I do, but vaguely.

"It is *significant*"—Mrs. Ruskin is tapping the desk top again—"that your great-great-grandfather should have not one but three Old Testament names. Obviously he came from a deeply religious family—Quaker or Presbyterian, I should surmise."

"A Jew?"

"No, no, I think not. Jews are not given to those particular names, not wanting to be associated with *minor* prophets, I suppose," and she laughs at her own little joke.

I thank Mrs. Ruskin and offer to pay her for her services.

"No, no, no. I'll send a statement. Besides, I'm not through. I have not yet heard from the Mormon archives. There are many other avenues of approach. I only found this information on a deed in Rogers County."

"My great-great-grandfather," I suddenly recall, "was a Civil War veteran, I think, and he held elective office in Missouri and Arkansas, too." These two facts have forced their way from deep in my subconscious, from what source I don't know. They only suddenly surface and I am as surprised as anyone.

"Ah, the National Archives. The Missouri State Historical Society. You see, Miss Murphy, I told you how fascinating such little bits and pieces of evidence can be. And there's still the matter of the Sears, Roebuck house. There is mention made of Obediah Murphy in the state guide to historic buildings. Included among those buildings are existing Sears, Roebuck mail-order houses, one of which apparently was owned by one Obediah Murphy in Tipeeho. It's still standing, or was when this guide was published. Tipeeho, Oklahoma, is little more than a ghost town, but like many others it was a thriving little community at the turn of the century."

I do not know what a Sears, Roebuck house is. Mrs. Ruskin is quick to tell me. In the early part of the century, when mail order was an emerging major merchandising tool, Sears, Roebuck offered a complete house, even to nails and fixtures, for $5,000 shipped anywhere in the United States. Several such houses—we would call them prefabricated these days—were put together in Oklahoma, where experienced builders and architects were few.

"Obediah was not the first owner," Mrs. Ruskin emphasizes, having gotten chummy enough now with my distant ancestor to call him by his first name. "He was, I think, the second owner. There were several other owners of that house listed. The book was published in 1966, so I don't know how up to date it is."

A mail-order house. Old Levi must have lived in that house. The founder of a major high-class merchandising chain got his start in a mail-order house. From my history of merchandising undergraduate course, I remember that early-day mail-order establishments were pariahs in the eyes of traditional merchants. This is one of history's little ironies, that Levi Murphy was reared in a Sears, Roebuck house. But I really don't know that for a fact. Only that perhaps one Obediah Murphy did own such a house.

To buy an entire house mail order. Fantastic. Never mind that such might be easily accomplished nowadays, in this the last quarter of the twentieth century. At that time, before creative merchandising catalogs of Neiman-Marcus and others, it was an absolute coup. Indeed, that was the beginning of the Golden Age of Merchandising, I think. Ah, but Sears is dead, and so are Roebuck and J. C. Penney and Montgomery Ward, and so, too, are Levi Murphy and Son.

It is late evening when I pick up Nanny from Leroy and Charlaine's, where she has gone for dinner. Before I get to the door, I hear Leroy and Charlaine shouting at each other. I have picked up Nanny here at least once a week for twenty-five years, and easily half those times I have entered or left the house to Leroy and Charlaine's shouting at each other. I have often wondered if they ever come to blows.

In the darkened Lincoln, weaving in and out through scanty traffic, I ask Nanny about Leroy and Charlaine's constant fighting. What is it about?

"Oh, you never know," she says. "They fights just to fight, I think. Just to remind one another they're still there, maybe. It's important for 'em to have the othern care enough to fight with 'em. People don't usually fight and shout with people they don't care about's opinion." Her reasoning may be profound. Her syntax isn't.

"I allus thought," Nanny goes on, the anonymity of the darkened automobile perhaps making her bold, "that if you all had a fought more, when you was growin' up, you'd a been happier. All a you." Here is someone else who professes to know what would make me happy.

Abruptly, as we top a slight rise, the road narrows, construction barriers channel four lanes of traffic into two. Ahead, stretching at least a full mile before the road bends out of sight, the lights of the moving cars, like a string of Christmas lights, twinkle and flash at regular intervals. I think: I am a part of this, another bulb on the string, and at the same time an observer of the phenomenon, detached and aloof. Each set of twinkling lights represents at least one person, possibly more, a part of a gigantic human circuit, each involved in his own thought processes, mindless, probably, of his position in the circuit—too involved to be detached.

"Do you believe in ghosts, Nanny?" I ask suddenly.

"Ghosts? Spooks?" Does Nanny wonder if I'm trying to change the subject?

"Spirits. Do you believe in them? Sometimes I think I do. Sometimes I think I believe in ghosts."

"Well, everybody believe in ghosts sometime. It dark enough and spooky enough. And yes, I think maybe there's ghosts, even if dey ain't really dere. But if dey makes you think of them and troubles you, den dey're real, even if dey ain't really."

"I think of my grandfather Levi sometimes as a ghost or spirit or something of that sort. I don't really believe in ghosts; it's just a feeling."

"If ever was somebody could make hisself into a spook, it was your grandpa, I think."

"Do you remember anything about him, about Levi?"

"Only that he was crazy as a cooter bug. But I never held that agin him. I figger anyone dat lives so long in dis wicked world got a right to go crazy."

Nanny enjoys her joke with a sudden chuckle and I let the conversation drop. We lapse once more into silence, the big Lincoln, insulating us even from the sounds without, moving like a large black coffin with the slow traffic.

Silence confounds. A lot of people apparently cannot take large doses of silence. That's why, I suspect, so many people turn themselves into human amplifiers, connecting themselves by headsets and cassettes to the comfort of noise. I have never been troubled by silence. I prefer it to purposeless sound.

Nanny does not. Nanny listens to the radio or the TV. She even has a Sony Walkman that Leroy and Charlaine got her for Christmas, so that even when she is out of reach of the ubiquitous radio or TV, she still has access to sound. The silence in the darkened car, moving slowly and imperceptibly with the slow traffic, does not last long. Nanny breaks it after a moment of fidgeting, returning to her original observation.

"Little bit a fight might a brung some life to your house then." I wonder if Nanny is trying to pick a fight with me. She has done it before. But I don't fight. Fighting is counterproductive. I give orders and expect them to be carried out. I know people who do business by threats, shouts, dickering and bargaining. It is what Old Levi called the "peddler" mentality, and he scorned it. Anyone who deals with me regularly, who dealt with Lee, knows what I expect and what he can expect in return. There are no surprises.

"But all y'all ever said to one another was 'Please' an' 'Thank you' an' 'Pass the butter.' I tried," Nanny continues, "I did try. I told Mr. Lee he ought to spank your bottom when you come in late through the winder. But all he ever said was not fer me to worry about it 'cause it was none of my responsibility. That's all. He never said it mean. Jest tol' me to butt out."

She waits, but I don't say anything. I suppose I should be surprised that she knew of my late-night outings so many years ago. But I am not. Nor am I surprised that Lee was aware of them. At the time I thought I was being clever, but looking back, it would be more surprising if Nanny and Lee and perhaps even Old Levi had been unaware of my comings and goings.

"You'd a thought them men would a wanted to know what a gal like you was up to so late at night. You'd a thought they would."

Indeed you would. But Lee and Levi were detached observers, perhaps not even observers, only detached, unconcerned, I suppose, at my youthful lust.

It is late by the time I retire. Johnny Carson has been replaced by an old movie, but Nanny is oblivious to it all. I've never had trouble sleeping. Nor, I think did Lee, and certainly not Nanny. Old Levi, before he went peculiar, was something of an insomniac, roaming the house, particularly the expanse of porches, while others slept or tried to. As a small child I often recognized his nighttime shadow and was never afraid. Perhaps that's why I am not afraid of the dark now, the dark or much of anything else, for that matter.

After Old Levi went dotty, peculiar, he took to locking himself in his rooms on the third floor at sunset and not reappearing until dawn. "Least," Nanny had observed, "I don' have to worry about where *he* is after dark."

Sleep comes readily enough, but the dreams are troubled, disjointed and confusing, as dreams are. I am no student of dreams. I put no more store in the dream explications of Freud & Co. than I do in witch doctors' and soothsayers' dabblings in fresh chicken innards. As far as I can see, dreams are just the product of errant charges touching upon stored memory banks in random order, recent memories joined with past, producing irrelevant associations.

I awaken from my busy dreams and try with slight success to reconstruct what I was dreaming. It is all a jumble of lust and Sears, Roebuck and Christmas tree lights.

I drift back to sleep. "This is the house that Sears built; this is the house that Sears built," I mutter singsong. Like counting backward for an anesthesiologist, I slip into unconsciousness. "This is the house that Sears built."

FIVE

LEVI'S DESCENT

I sat in that ridiculous mail-order house, that Sears, Roebuck house, for almost three weeks, a prisoner of the cold and steady rain that began to fall almost as soon as the last clod of dirt was dropped on Louisa One's coffin. I could not say that old Louisa actually died; she seemed always impervious to such end. I could only say that we buried her, with due pomp and circumstance, beside the Old Bastard, up the hill from Louisa Two.

She went—left her massive body behind, at any rate—without argument, following by only a matter of weeks the final throes of that fradulent Old Four Lumps, Manasquatch, his tribal name. He went at the beginning of February and she at the end.

It took a full day for the neighboring men to hack six feet through the frozen ground of late February. Dying is the easy part. Putting away the remains is damnably hard. Had Louisa One waited only a few more days, the thaw would have begun as the rain seeped slowly through the frozen ground. But she would not wait and we buried her beneath the dry, brown native grass in funeral garments of her own making, a fistful of wedding lace at her throat, as she had desired.

And so, but for the remaining Louisa, whose secrets were locked in the silence of a damaged mind, my past should have been effectively sundered. But I was held still in hopeless thrall, by my own reckoning through a history too ominous to share. I would that One had gone silent to her grave, leaving me with only questions, for the answer I sought and received served only to unsettle me to the point of deadly distraction. I sorted and sifted the matter, and the more I turned fact and conjecture, the more questions arose, like the plowman going over rocky soil, exposing always more rocks than are covered over. And the Old Bastard, who once only embarrassed, yea, even humiliated, now was destroying me. The adolescent anger I once felt for him had with slow, painful realization changed to an aversion so profound that it all but consumed me and I shut myself away almost completely from social contact; for the inescapable truth that confronted me rendered me, in my own mind at least, pariah to any kind of civilized consort. I ate but little and slept less, my concentration even for slight tasks weakened to the point of debility.

"Levi, Levi," Daniel, home for more obsequies of this wilting branch, chastened me, "you mourn too much. They were all three old, all due, overdue. Such deep grief for the aged is not seemly. Death at so great an age is natural. Put aside your mourning and get on with your life. Marry, raise children, continue the line."

Ah. That I most assuredly could never do, could never continue this line. I was and would be of necessity the end of it. I would go no further. The line of Obediah had come to an end.

"Come. Come back to St. Louis with me. Bring your books; do your paper work there. You're too thin, your eyes are too hollowed, your color too pale. Get away. You need to think of other things but this unnatural grief."

It was not grief I could have told David I felt, except possibly grief for my deadened soul. What I felt was a woe too deep for explication.

"What of my mother?" however, was all I answered Daniel.

"We can get someone to watch her, we can hire a lady or a couple to help the girl Molly with her," he cried eagerly and then winked broadly. "There's great sport to be had in St. Louis on the riverfront in springtime."

The sport of Obediah I presumed him to mean. I had no interest in that. I had but an empty feeling in the hollow where desire ought to rise. My youthful fires were brought low by the intelligence of Louisa One. That ménage à trois that produced Louisa Three had confounded me to the point of utter dismay. But the weeks and months of pondering, sorting clues, of sleepless nights and worried days, left me with suspicions so great as to be absolute certainty, suspicions that emptied my soul and my heart of any feeling save complete, eternal despair.

I tried to comfort myself now and then that perhaps my grandmother did not know, could not be certain of Louisa Three's father's identity, that for some malicious reason of her very own she blamed it on the departed Obediah, that it was not true at all. But that was only a slim hope, gleaned from the depths of desperation. No, Louisa One was not vindictive, hardly interested, casual to the point of boredom in confessing her husband to be father to her granddaughter as if it were of very little consequence to her.

Would that I could have stopped it at that point, that I could have turned my thoughts elsewhere; but I could not. There was, in fact, no passing Jewish peddler. That fiction was so thin as to be totally transparent. I did not—as the Old Bastard was fond of announcing— spring from the loins of Judah. Pondering the situation through endless sleepless nights, from every possible angle, I arrived at last at one absolute truth: I am the son of Obediah Murphy, the product of incest most outrageous, incest committed upon the person of a daughter herself incestuous issue, whose accusations would remain forever locked in her damaged and voiceless memory.

I am at once great-grandson, grandson and son of Obediah Murphy. That my mind is not as damaged as my mother's is testimony only to the perversity of Nature. I am the result of lust so unnatural that it has horrified the hearts of men from the beginning of time. To prolong that invidious line, the line of Obediah, would be the ultimate crime against humanity.

"I am not really up to travel, Daniel," I at last alibied to my old friend. This secret I could not share with Daniel, though since boyhood we have shared much, he admittedly more than I. "I have much to do, but I promise with the coming of spring and the cessation of these damnable rains my humor will perk up. When next you see me, it will be all over." I offered him a weak smile, which he accepted as it was offered.

At that time and even after Daniel had returned to St. Louis, I had suicide in mind as the only reasonable end to the line of Obediah. But slowly, staring out daily at the interminable drizzle, I determined that this ultimate sin of Obediah should not go unanswered. I could not leave this life whimpering, victim yet another time of the Old Bastard's curse. I would in some manner find a way to answer Obediah, even in the grave, in a manner so telling that it would make the very gods tremble!

With that certainty growing, that vague goal so much defined, my humor took a turn for the better and the moroseness that had haunted me subsided. I slept once more and I ate.

And as if strengthened by my resolve, spring, which comes

quickly to this part of the country, began to make itself apparent.

At just this time the girl, Molly, came to me to give her notice, it being her intention, she claimed, to wed a country boy of her acquaintance within a few weeks. I assured her, quite honestly, that that would be fine and that I would seek a replacement as quickly as possible. In truth, I think that the girl had become increasingly unnerved by Louisa Three's constant presence, Molly being then the only female in the house, and Three—that designation, I realized with a bitter pang, was no longer necessary—understandably bereft, like an abandoned pup, having attached herself to the nearest approachable being, I at that point hardly being approachable, even by the feeble of mind. And I determined an older, more motherly sort of woman was needed, even though the cost for such experience might be more dear.

The first such lady to answer my advertisement for a "mature woman to act as housekeeper and companion for a matron incapacitated but not bedridden" filled my needs completely, for in truth I had not given the matter the serious consideration that it merited. Luckily, the choice was fortunate for Mrs. Elizabeth Brady proved immediately to be hardworking, cheerful and sensible, if somewhat garrulous and inquisitive.

"Ah, poor dear," she sighed when she beheld my mother and realized what her infirmity was. "And has she always been this way?"

"I am not sure," I replied tersely, for I could but repeat the story that Louisas One and Two had recounted. "I have been told that her disability was the result of a fever, a brain inflammation when she was young. I only know that she has been this way as long as I have known her."

"Nor can she speak?"

"No. She does not speak." It was just as well.

"Ah, she does not have the manner of a born idiot," Mrs. Brady somewhat tactlessly affirmed. "I'll bet that she was quite pretty when she was young, wasn't she?"

My mother stood very still and stared at this strange lady, her manner suggesting that she was somehow aware that we were talking of her.

"I don't know," I answered Mrs. Brady, not bothering to explain that as an infant I was hardly a reliable judge of such matters.

My mother, whose normal restlessness had been elevated to extreme agitation with the successive loss of three familiar beings, began to relax and smile under the ministrations of the kindly Mrs. Brady. And my own energy, strengthened by my resolve to an as yet unformed plan of vengeance, regained its former strength and I set about diligently getting our house in order, Louisa One's bookkeeping being desperately in need of revision.

I had no immediate plans save for sorting out our wealth and consolidating it in some more efficient manner. The active part of my mind being so engrossed might free the subconscious part of my brain to deal with my more profound ambitions. Truth was, I had no idea whatsoever how I would ultimately beard the Old Bastard, as it were, through eternity. I only knew that somehow it was possible and I would have the last word, the last crushing word, whatever it might be.

I sallied out in the town and made business calls, though I still made no social calls, and I chatted and visited with acquaintances I happened to meet and accepted condolences and sympathies as they were offered. Louisa One's business dealings proved to be more far-reaching than one might reasonably expect of an aged and illiterate woman, any such business dealings being highly uncommon.

It was on just such a foray, coming out of the Bank of Commerce one afternoon, that I was accosted on the street by a boy of middling size who respectfully asked, "Yer Mr. Levi Murphy, ain't ya?"

I affirmed that such was indeed my identity.

"I been sent," the urchin began, and from the shuffling of his feet and the nervous manner of his hands I could tell that he was much embarrassed.

"Yes?" I said as gently as possible.

"My grandma sent me with word that she would like to talk to you. That she needed a word with you," he amended.

"And who are you?" I asked with what I fear was just a trace of mirth at the awkward boy's strange request.

He was embarrassed to have forgotten so important a part of his message and blurted, "Billy. Billy Timmons. It's my grandpa as shot yer grandpa to death, and my grandma is Mrs. Timmons, Alecia Timmons, and she's most anxious to talk to you. She said be it either Mr. Daniel St. Cloud or Mr. Levi Murphy, whichever come handiest."

This intelligence came in such a rush that it was a moment before the import of it washed over me. I was caught immediately in a sense of deep revulsion, revulsion, I might add, that did not extend to the innocent boy before me.

"I'm afraid," I began carefully, keeping my voice low and controlled, "that such a visit might not really be proper under the circumstances."

"But, Mr. Murphy, my grandma is old and sick, very sick, and she said that she must talk with you. She said that I should beg you did I have to." Tears had welled in the boy's eyes, his agitation extreme. I paused for a long moment. "I don't want her to die aburdening," he sniffled suddenly. It was obvious that he was struggling to maintain a manly composure.

Perhaps that was why I agreed to go with him, "but very briefly," I cautioned, "for I am a very busy man." I shuddered myself at the very pomposity of that statement. But the truth was that I did not at all want to go, and yet so mired was I in revulsion of Obediah that I was attracted to any mention of him, as a cyclist, desperately trying to avoid an obstacle, will steer instead steadfastly for it.

"We live," Billy Timmons shamefacedly admitted, "behind the livery," and he pointed the direction.

I did not tell him that I was quite aware of where that wine-soaked old rascal Tommy Timmons lived with his family. Some were surprised that he had escaped with his life, much less his freedom, after the shooting of Obediah. But the judge ruled that his great age and advanced lack of sobriety and the attendant "misapprehension of the situation"—those were the judge's words—merited leniency. And thus he was freed, quite probably never sober enough to realize what had happened in the first place. The boy's shamefacedness had much merit.

Billy and I were met at the door of this hovel by a woman I took to be his mother, though the withered look about her was that same ageless look of many women on the western frontier, overworked and overbred, their youth wasted long before its time.

Her reaction to my presence was abrupt. "We don't care to have ye call, Mr. Murphy. We ain't receivin'."

I stepped back, having no intentions of intruding where I was obviously not wanted.

"But, Mama," cried Billy. "Granny sent me to fetch him, Granny said it was important that she see him."

"Gran ain't right. She's sick. You know that. What right you got runnin' around and inconveniencin' ever'body like this?" She glared at the boy.

"But Granny said."

"Gran's sleepin'. And you don't pay no mind to what she says when she's up. She just goes on about things and it don't make no sense at all. We got enough troubles, Mr. Murphy. We don't need no more. You," she snapped at the boy, "you get inside. I'll tend to you."

I murmured a polite apology, but I was vaguely troubled. The boy had seemed sincere, but he would, I was certain, have his ears boxed, in the very least, for his efforts. It did not seem just. The old lady, the last of Obediah's paramours, most likely had nothing to say of any importance, but, victim of my own obsession, I was willing, I think, to listen to anything pertaining to the Old Bastard.

I pondered the incident through the day and then forgot it. Nor did I think of it again until a few weeks later, when I heard that Mrs. Timmons had passed away. I felt a twinge of pity and of remorse, remorse, I think, less for the loss of Mrs. Timmons than for the fact that I had not heard what it was she had to tell me. Probably Billy Timmons's mother—was she a daughter-in-law or an unmarried daughter?—was right in her assertion that what the elder Mrs. Timmons had to say was of no consequence, merely the ramblings of an aged and troubled mind. But another link with Obediah was sundered.

It was later that same day that Mrs. Brady came to me with a request. "My niece," she said, "my brother's daughter, I would like to have her come to stay the summer. She's been ill and can't take the hard life of the ranch."

I was aware that what Mrs. Brady called a ranch was most likely forty acres with a sod house, but I heard her through.

"She would be a help and no trouble. Her father, my brother," she apologized, "is a good man, but he don't understand about bein' sick. He ain't never been and he ain't patient with someone who is. She wouldn't be no trouble, I assure you, and she could help with the needlework, she's most good with a needle, and help with entertaining of Mrs. Murphy," Mrs. Brady rambled disjointedly on, giving my mother a title that she did not deserve (or perhaps did). "It would cost ye nothin', of course, but a little board and room, and I promise you'd not know she was on the place and it'd relieve my mind greatly to have her here so I could keep a eye on her."

Mrs. Brady would undoubtedly have gone on in that manner for the rest of the day had I not put a stop to it. "I really don't care, Mrs. Brady. If, as you say, she will be no trouble, I cannot object to your having such company. We have ample room, and I plan to spend the summer in my study with my accounts. Just let me know when to expect her."

"Tomorrow," said Mrs. Brady.

I could not refrain from smiling. So the arrangements had been let before my permission had even been secured. I was not surprised. Mrs. Brady and I got on well, if only because she did her work and, but for a little unnecessary chatter, kept out of my way and entertained Louisa Three in a most satisfactory manner.

I was myself completely occupied with sorting through Louisa One's accounts, which for all her tidy, if nearly indecipherable, accounting were in a more confused state than I realized. For in her last years she had obviously not been as sound of mind as I had supposed, and there was much repetition of accounts that would require some amount of detective work on my part to sort out.

I had come to the conclusion by then that the proper settling of the estate would necessitate at least a trip to Fort Smith, if not to St. Louis. Much of my correspondence concerning matters of mortgages and property had remained unanswered, due in part, I suppose, to the unreliability of the post to this sparsely settled frontier and partly to the natural recalcitrance of people owing to respond to those owed.

My great-grandmother had of course died without a proper will, as had Obediah and Louisa Two, One's only testament oral, a vague "you remember to take care of Baby Louisa and Daniel ven I go," spoken at a time when I suspect she had no intention whatsoever of going anywhere.

Those dictates I honored, insomuch as I cared tenderly for my mother and I was generous, generous to a fault perhaps, with Daniel, though I hesitated making a permanent settlement upon him, at least until I was certain of the extent of my holdings. I had, of course, every intention of seeing Daniel through law school, even though he seemed to be delaying that process, for what reason I could not determine, except a simple reluctance to leave the confines of the university and face the world at point-blank range.

The diligence of my endeavors indeed gave me some respite from the recent agonies of my personal discoveries, though in those early hours of the day when sleep outruns light, my ghosts would now and then descend upon me with the weight of a thousand anvils and I would shiver and suffer under the blankets of my own terrors. At such moments I would realize that the only salvation for me lay in confronting, if not the ghost, at least the spirit of the wicked ancestor Obediah and I doubted not my capacity to overcome, for in my veins ran the blood of that same evil at least twice over and, ominously, perhaps more. So tainted was my blood, as a matter of fact, that I was surprised that it ran red as other people's instead of black or yellow or some other color abhorrent to God's plan.

Such a sleepless night I had spent when over breakfast, as I was seeking to recover my composture, Mrs. Brady reminded me of the arrival of her guest and hurried to explain once more that the child would be in no way troublesome to me.

I only nodded, hardly conscious of what she was talking about, and retreated to my study, where work on my accounts soon revived me. I had begun to find an interest that I hardly knew existed in these books and in the transport of business that they represented. It was not, I think, so much the accounting of my own wealth that so fascinated me; it was rather the total experience of dealing in the intangibles represented by the curious graphics of my deceased great-grandmother Louisa One.

When I emerged from my lair late in the morning, I confronted Mrs. Brady ushering a young woman visitor into the entry. It was a moment before my mind grasped the import of this situation and noted the valise Mrs. Brady struggled with and realized that the child I had expected in the form of Mrs. Brady's niece was indeed this comely young woman, though the bonnet she wore, in the manner of country ladies, shadowed her face and precluded a careful examination of her features.

"And this is my niece, Mr. Murphy, that I told you about. Elizabeth Butler, Betty, we call her, but she was named for me," said Mrs. Brady proudly.

The girl, who inclined her head shyly in my direction, was above eighteen years of age, I was sure, and though taller by some than the average, she was slight in build, almost frail.

"Welcome, Miss Butler," I said, for want of anything else to fill the gap in the conversation; "I hope that you had a pleasant trip?"

"Thank you, Mr. Murphy," the girl replied in a voice so soft, or was it deep, that I strained to hear. "The trip was some warm and dusty, I'm afraid. I came by wagon and am not as fresh as I wish I were." There was, apparently, no dissembling about this young woman. I had asked a question and she had answered it, without resort to the tittering platitudes about a pleasant journey that I might have expected of one so young and so apparently inexperienced.

"And are you tired?"

"Yes," she murmured.

"Ah, now, Betty dear, let me have your bonnet and I will put it

away and show you where you may wash and rest before dinner."
Mrs. Brady held to the country way of designating the noon meal
"dinner," and I had myself over the past few months got used to that
designation.

The girl reached for the bonnet to comply with her aunt's request
and shook it loose from her head. With the removal of the bonnet I
was surprised to note that the girl had no hair, or at least, very little
hair. What there was, however, was thick and dark and showed promise of future luxurious growth and curls.

"I have suffered from the typhoid fever, Mr. Murphy," said Betty,
aware that I was staring at her uncovered head. "I lost all of my hair to
it and very nearly my life as well. My hair is returning, and with it, I
hope, my strength."

"She's cured now, of course, Mr. Murphy," said Mrs. Brady hur-
riedly. "She's no danger at all. The doctor confirmed it; it's only rest
that she needs to be good as new."

I had the feeling that Mrs. Brady had not intended for me to find
that intelligence out for fear that I would not allow one so infected on
the premises.

"Like Samson, perhaps." I smiled at the girl, making light of the
situation in mention of that Old Testament character.

"Perhaps." She smiled back. It was a pleasant if weary smile,
close-lipped, disclosing no teeth, but uncovering a small dimple at the
corner of the mouth. The girl's eyes were a deep blue, made bluer,
perhaps, by like-colored circles beneath them. I have always been
attracted by women's eyes. They touch me as ankle or walk or elbow
touches other men. But it is difficult to stare at someone's eyes as one
might covertly ogle an ankle or departing fanny. I turned away.

My mother was standing in the doorway, her bodice carelessly
buttoned and her bun, which had been neat at the nape of her neck
earlier, askew, dangling gray-streaked curls down her back. Thus my
mother often was. She was given to unbuttoning herself and then
struggling, usually with little success, to rematch button and but-
tonhole. She could occupy herself by the hour, buttoning and unbuttoning. It was always necessary to check her condition relative to her
buttons before we allowed her to see visitors. We had this day neglected that duty, and she presented a disheveled appearance to our
guest.

But Betty Butler only smiled. It was a gentle smile and this time
uncovered strong white teeth, straight and unmarked by the stain or

decay that often characterizes the smiles of working-class or country people. She had, I was certain, been forewarned of my mother's condition, for her expression registered neither surprise nor distress. She nodded and spoke softly to Louisa Three, who responded with a timid moan, for moaning was all the sound that she ever made. She moaned in either pain, fear, hunger or pleasure. It took but little experience to recognize the source of her moan, and the moan she greeted Betty Butler with was one of pleasure.

"Come, dear," Mrs. Brady repeated. "I'll show you your room and you can freshen yourself and we'll have dinner."

Mrs. Brady ushered Betty down the hall toward the kitchen and the room beyond that would serve as her quarters for the summer, as it was screened and cool of the evening. The room had always functioned as servants' quarters, though in the summer it was by far the most habitable room in the house. It might not have been a part of the original Sears, Roebuck house. I did not know the history of the dwelling to that extent. However, it would serve our guest quite nicely, behind the kitchen or no.

My mother padded silently after the other two women and I remained for a time in the same spot, uncertain about proceeding to the dining room to wait for the promised meal or returning to my accounts.

Instead I took my hat and left the house and proceeded to the post office to procure what mail might have collected there. That chore would certainly use up enough time for Mrs. Brady to have gotten her niece comfortably settled and perhaps a meal prepared, too. I was unaccountably hungry.

The mail produced, besides the newspaper that I had been awaiting, a few circulars and a letter from the Fort Smith attorney One had engaged some years ago, apologizing for "unforeseen delays." I was reminded again that these matters of probate would not be satisfactorily accomplished until I personally traveled to Fort Smith to see to them. It was a trip I had postponed too long.

But with each passing day I found it more and more difficult to tear myself away in order to make that necessary journey. And being as perspicacious about my own motives as I was about the motives of others, I knew that the main reason for my hesitation lay in the charming person of my summer guest, whose cheerful presence at least partly lifted the gloom from my house and the agony from my soul.

As Betty's strength returned, her bright laugh filled the house at regular intervals and her short, dark curls, growing daily more abundant, gave her a pert and fresh air. I found myself eagerly awaiting the meals that we all shared and the dark evenings when we sat on the porch against the stifling heat of the indoors. I had not felt so unburdened, I thought, since childhood. The past was gone and the future of no account. All of the women of my house, who once more numbered three, seemed likewise relaxed and content, most especially Mrs. Brady, whose relief at her niece's progress made that amiable lady even more anxious to please. Like one occupying a warm sleeping spot on a cold winter night, I was loath to do anything that might disturb the comfort of this situation.

August, which brought its normal heat and drought, also brought Daniel. Unexpectedly, he breezed into the house, screen door clattering behind him, with a boisterous "Hi-de-ho there, old man," and flung the automobile driver's hat that he had been affecting for some time across the room and collapsed on the sofa before I had time to rise from my desk and proffer my hand.

"I'm tired, Levi," he said, "and I'm hungry and I'm practically a lawyer. How about that, now? When do we eat?"

"Practically a lawyer?" That information seemed to me more important than the state of either his appetite or his energy.

"I will go back in three weeks and commence studying for my examinations, take them in October and, ergo, *summa cum shyster.*"

I had to smile. Daniel could take nothing seriously. He had a flippancy for every occasion. Had life dealt him the blows that it had dealt me, would he then be so flip? Probably he would, his shallowness his protection. At that moment I genuinely envied him.

"When do we eat?" he repeated.

"Ah, I'll alert Mrs. Brady to set another place—a large one," I said, smiling.

"Mrs. Brady?"

"The housekeeper I hired when Molly left. I know I wrote you. She and her niece manage things quite nicely, and I'm sure you'll find Mrs. Brady's culinary capacities to your liking." I glossed over "Mrs. Brady's niece," not anxious to have Daniel attach too great an import to her presence. I even felt a moment's apprehension, for what I could not tell. I had no clear idea, of course, of my own intentions toward the maiden, only that her presence filled me with comfort and even a kind of joy. I was, as I have said, loath to disturb any of that.

"Well, tell Mrs. Brady that I'm ready to put her to the test immediately."

Daniel's facile tongue was momentarily stilled when I introduced him to Betty and Mrs. Brady. I could tell that it was not Mrs. Brady's presence that he found awesome, and I felt a twinge at the glance that passed between the two young people, remembering that it had always been Daniel who was the charmer of women.

My own mother, Louisa Three, glowed at the sight of Daniel's familiar face, and true to form, he had exercised his charm on all three women before the meal was half finished.

"Lovely, lovely, lovely," murmured Daniel later as we smoked in the study. "You didn't tell me about *that*, old man. Shame, shame." Daniel had taken to calling me "old man." I was not overly pleased with the appellation. "It suits you, old man. You're so deadly serious."

"And you're the charmer still, aren't you? Charm the ladies?"

"Ah"—he winked—"I charm the pants off them."

I did not care for his quip, and so I changed the subject. We spoke of business and of the future, neither of us able yet to confess any concrete ambitions.

"Perhaps I'll stay in Missouri and practice awhile. An apprenticeship in an old-established firm would, I suppose, profit me." We both know, of course, that nothing about Indian Territory was either old or established except the tall prairie grass and the motionless stone that lay close to the surface of this lovely but occasionally barren land.

As a rule, it was pleasant to have Daniel around. We had shared much together and could thus reminisce. But not even taking that fact into consideration, Daniel was still a pleasant companion, one welcome everywhere for his easygoing charm and his lanky good looks, those same good looks which, it became increasingly apparent, were not lost on Miss Betty Butler, nor her pert sweetness on him.

He was given to teasing her, as indeed he was all women, including Mrs. Brady and Louisa Three, though the latter ever so gently. "Ah," he would say to Betty, "now tell me about your hair. No, let me guess. You washed it and it shrunk?"

"Wrong. I am actually a boy in disguise—Samson," she cried, stealing my own feeble joke, "and when my hair all grows out, I shall pull this house down around the lot of you!"

And so it went, the lighthearted bantering among them, Mrs. Brady a bemused onlooker, who now and then let me have a wink as if to say, "Now, is this not a suitable couple?" in the manner of middle-aged ladies, anxious, I expect, to relive their own romances vicariously.

Daniel might abruptly reach out and run his hand through the girl's stubby curls and leave them tousled, she laughing, for she was never one to giggle, and shaking them out again. I could at such times but stand in pained silence, incapable ever of touching her person myself, much less in so rowdy a fashion, and I felt myself growing eager for Daniel's return to his studies, about which I questioned him with increasing urgency.

"It's no matter, old man; I do not worry about the examinations. I'm quite confident, you know." And he delayed his departure time by yet another week.

And as the late August evenings began to hint of fall, Mrs. Brady, Louisa Three and I were left more and more on our own on the porch as Daniel and Betty disappeared on long walks, strolling close together, Daniel's tall form inclined toward the girl, she staring adoringly up at him. The gloom that had absented itself from my heart for a time returned as I realized that Daniel only, not I, was free to declare himself to the maiden, for I was held in check by my own awful secret.

It was well into September before Daniel managed to pull himself away for the return to St. Louis, and he had become all at once more grave about his prospects, saying that he must now apply himself with due diligence, for he had tarried too long. I agreed.

"I am eager now," he said, and the expression of concern on his face confirmed it, "to finish my degree and to pass my examinations and get started on this law business." I feared that I understood all too well the motive behind his sudden determination of purpose.

The morning he left, he and Betty took an overlong farewell, standing at a distance from the house, engrossed in serious conversation, and Mrs. Brady, simpering and chuckling, peered out the window at them. The older woman's hopes were high, I could tell, and it dawned on me that her motive for having brought Betty to convalesce in this house might have been more devious than I had imagined, her plan, however, more likely directed at me. I'm sure, however, that she considered Daniel more than suitable as a replacement.

Daniel and I shook hands gravely, and I noticed for the first time that he had got himself proper headgear and was without that ridiculous driving cap he had earlier sported.

"Take good care of her, old man," he said to me, and though he had declared no intentions regarding this girl to me, none but the dullest simpleton could have escaped his meaning. My heart was all but stone as I nodded my acquiescence.

"And I shall be back for good before the snow flies," he cried loudly, more like himself than he had been for many a day.

"I'm counting on you, old man," he murmured again, as the wagon he rode pulled slowly away.

Later that same morning, as I made my way to my study, I overheard Mrs. Brady from the kitchen consoling her niece.

"Ah, now, dear, don't fret. The time will pass so quick you'll hardly know it and he'll be back to stay. Besides, we've got so much to do, the sewing alone should occupy you enough."

The meaning I thought clear: Mrs. Brady, at least, was making wedding plans. I did not know if Betty and Daniel were privy to those same plans, but my heavy heart suspected that they were.

All that day I struggled to keep my mind on the work before me, but the traitorous thing would have none of it and slipped back at any small opportunity to the memory of Daniel and Betty. I could not go on this way; I could not last through two or three months under such strain. It was more than mortal man should have to suffer. It was as if the Old Bastard were reaching out from the grave, taunting me yet.

My first thought was to suggest to Mrs. Brady that Betty, having sufficiently recuperated, should return once again to her father's house. I would do it as kindly as possible, but firmly, for it was my only salvation. But I could not. The thought of the maiden's absence was more awful even than her continued presence to my suffering soul.

I avoided the women as much as possible and kept to my study, though my concentration was not such that I accomplished much of worth. Mrs. Brady began to chide me.

"Now, Mr. Murphy, you don't eat enough or rest. You'll be sick."

Perhaps she feared that I might indeed pick up that same infection which had felled her niece in the first place. I reassured her with the explanation that I had neglected my work during Daniel's visit and now that neglect had caught up with me and a few weeks' concentrated effort was necessary. She seemed satisfied with the explanation.

Increasingly I found myself too restless to sleep and took to prowling around the premises in the late hours, careful not to disturb anyone else. Not surprisingly, my nocturnal forays brought me more often than not close to the back screened room where the object of my distress lay pillowed upon a goose down comforter, a comforter from the skilled needle of Louisa One. I dared not creep too close to that hallowed spot, but stood some distance and waited, I know not for what.

Until, late one evening, my faltering step took me directly to the foundation of that room, close enough that I could make out the form of the sleeper within, not in detail, but enough to unsettle my suffering parts; for I was as human as any man, and indeed the blood of Obediah flowing copiously through my veins rendered me more manly in that respect than many others less endowed, I thought.

The beloved form tossed restlessly, turned once and brushed at her face, as if to brush away an errant curl from her lips, those curls now long enough to cause such a discomfort. I stood staring in at that which I had no right to stare at, my fists clenching and my forehead sweating. I held my breath, for it was coming in such broken gasps that I was sure it would awaken the sleeper within, and my anguish took form in a knot of pain, like hunger pangs, though not so easily assuaged.

For a brief moment I thought the unthinkable: the declaration of my passion and the relief of my agony. But only for a moment, for I was nothing if not self-controlled: the power of my will over the power of my lust was all that kept me towering above the sinful and hateful Obediah; consciousness had final power over flesh. I retreated and paced the night away in restless and feverish agony. By morning my strength was spent, but the lust of my heritage had been broken.

"Mrs. Brady," I said at breakfast, "I find that I shall have to travel to Fort Smith to talk with my attorneys there and to settle a large number of transactions. I want you to see to my dress shirts, for I will leave this afternoon a-horseback."

"Ah, Mr. Murphy, and can't you wait until tomorrow and take the coach?" for such was the euphemism we affected for the horse and wagon that made the run between our part of the Territory and Fort Smith with mail and passengers three times each week. "You really do look weary, and I think you ought to rest before you go."

"I appreciate your concern, Mrs. Brady, but these are matters that have become quite urgent, as I have been dilatory in settling them. I am quite at fault, but I'm confident that with some expedition I can still successfully accomplish my needs."

The situation sounded, I knew, critical; and so I intended it to sound.

"I do not know how long I will be gone, but I am sure that you and

Miss Butler will be able to manage things satisfactorily in my absence."

I closeted myself in my study until Mrs. Brady had done with my shirts, which I took to my room and carefully packed, along with certain of the papers that I needed for the conduct of business and also some changes of socks and underwear, for I needs must go lighter on horseback than I might have by coach.

Still all too disturbed by the presence of Mrs. Brady's niece, I succeeded in my efforts to avoid her and only tenderly kissed my mother's cheek and bade Mrs. Brady take good care of her and repeated that I did not know when I would return. And that was true, for at that moment I truly thought that I might never return, might wander, like the forlorn lover in a bad novel, throughout the world seeking release from the tortures of love lost.

My trip was uneventful and my suspicions concerning the aptitude of the solicitors (for such was what they called themselves, written across their window: SOLICITORS AT LAW, Mr. Helms and Mr. Driver) that I had inherited were confirmed. The two gentlemen proved largely incapable of any significant legal acts beyond notary services, the one approaching senility and the other confused by too long an association with strong drink. Why Obediah or Louisa One had secured the services of this particular firm, if that's what it might be called, I could not imagine.

I was not totally unfamiliar with Fort Smith, for this was where Obediah had made his last stand, so to speak, before embarking west into the Territory. We had lived for a few months in this city preparatory to our final westward journey. I did not know the circumstances that started us to Indian Territory; I only knew that, whatever they were, they were precipitate.

I realized immediately that the lawyers I was depending on were not of first quality if only because their offices lay in one of the more dissolute areas of what was a frontier town, dissolute in and of that fact, notwithstanding the ominous judicial presence of Hanging Judge Parker.

After meeting with these two worthy gentlemen for the better part of an afternoon, I determined that much of what I had entrusted to them I could accomplish on my own with both greater speed and greater efficiency, and that the rest most assuredly ought to be entrusted to attorneys of more ability than these two solicitors exhibited.

I thought of Daniel, soon to be a licensed attorney. Nor did I doubt his abilities, sight unseen; for I knew him to be, when it was necessary, intelligent and capable of energetic application to a given task. But the thought of Daniel disturbed me and I was sunk immediately into gloom again. Daniel, one day perhaps, would act as my attorney; we had always planned that at least, even when we were unaware of the amount of wealth I would come into. But for the time I needed to distance myself from thoughts of Daniel, thoughts that only precipitated memories of Betty Butler. I would inquire and find the best law firm in town and transfer my business there.

Standing at the curb considering all of this, I had been but dimly aware of the female figure hovering, for that was what it seemed, in the background, and I was truly startled when she accosted me. I had been so accosted on other occasions, for ladies of the night were prevalent around the university, though officials and elders would have denied it. I had ignored them then, for I had found them to be unattractive and dirty and ascertained them no pleasure to be with.

My first inclination was of course to turn my back on this creature sidling up to me, hunkering like a bitch in heat, but there was something about her (or was it about myself?) that arrested me. She was clean at least, or seemed to be, but though she wore the requisite amount of color on her face and beads around her neck to denote her status as working whore, she exhibited more polish in her approach, the mark, I supposed, of a true professionalism.

She did not address me as "sweetie" or "sport," nor did she make any lewd suggestion, but only noted that I seemed lonely and that it was a shame in so handsome a young man and could she help? At this suggestion she ducked her head slightly and lowered her eyes almost demurely, fingering the locket at her throat and then the topmost button on her bodice.

I was struck once again by some memory that would not quite come clear, as if I had been at that same spot some earlier time. And then, inexplicably, desire struck, rose from the source I had thought dead and spread lapping at my nerve ends like a smoldering grass fire at tufts of dry grass. It was both inconvenient and embarrassing; I stood, I thought, like a giant sore thumb on a public street corner lusting after a common whore. That same whore recognized my symptoms, for that, of course, was part and parcel of her stock-in-trade, and she edged near me, looked up and touched my arm, her pale gray eyes totally unsettling me, forcing my breath to struggle through clenched teeth.

This was a temptation that I would overcome. I would battle the lust of my heritage to a standstill. And then she murmured, "Come," and eased me by the elbow toward the doorway whence she had originally materialized and I found myself stepping along beside her. The lust of Obediah. So be it! That, I thought, was all I could do to best the Old Bastard, spread his ubiquitous seed from whore to whore; whoremonger that he had been, I would be also and ensure a succession of whore's sons to spread thin his line and destroy his name.

The whore, who offered no name, ushered me into a small but tidy room, dominated by the largest bed I had ever seen. I did not know, my experience being so limited, if I was in an actual bawdy house or if this particular whore worked by herself. I only knew that the sight of the willing woman and the large, commodious bed, the scene, I was sure, of many hours of like sport, had all but undone me and I was ready to rip off my restraining clothing and accost the woman at once. But she turned, again demurely, aside, cast her eyes down and whispered something I could not make out. It made no difference; the blood that was pounding in my ears would have rendered unintelligible anyway anything save a loud shout, and my trembling hands hardly knew what to do with themselves. I did not know if the common procedure called for me to help with her garments, or merely to divest myself of my own. It hardly mattered; so great was my agitation that I would have taken her to the floor if need be. It was the lust of Obediah coursing through my veins!

She looked up and smiled and then with more seriousness looked down at her bodice and I was struck again by that chord of familiarity. And then she began with due seriousness to work at her buttons, which were tiny and, I thought, unsuited for one who had to undo them many times a day.

Suddenly the familiar became recognizable. The tilt of her face as she worked with her buttons, the angle of her head, the pale gray of the eyes and the loosened hair falling from the bun at the nape of her neck. It was Louisa Three that I was seeing, fumbling seriously with her buttons, for all the world as if that were all that mattered. Louisa Three. My own mother! With shattering clarity I saw her in this shabby whore whose person I desired, lusted after. I gasped, and the whore looked up, pausing mid-button, and with a great intake of air and with figure rigid and fists clenched, I was spent before I began.

"Ah," said the whore sympathetically. "Ah, that's all right now.

Don't worry about it." She looked at me and, perhaps noting my extreme agitation, took it for embarrassment, not the horror that it actually was. "Don't worry. It happens. It happens. Sooner or later it happens to everybody. Of course," she added in true business fashion, "I am still owed, you understand."

I could but nod dumbly, for it did not matter at all to me. I only needed to flee her presence, for I was torn with so hideous a terror that I feared I might collapse entirely. I handed over a bill to her and turned abruptly to go, realizing that I had said not one word to the woman through the entire experience.

"Now, don't worry, dearie," she said again in a motherly tone. "You come and see me again and we'll just make sure that don't happen. I'll make it worth your while," she promised with a wink. She reached to touch me, but I was by then backing out the door, flushed and trembling, and I all but tumbled down the stairs and strode, nearly running, the entire distance to my lodging house.

I suffered, agonized, through much of the night, striding across the bare boards of the tiny room, until someone below me pounded on his ceiling and cursed my sleeplessness. I lay then on my bed too wrought up to sleep, to even think coherently. This was where it had brought me, the precipice that I had nearly overstepped, the incestuous line of Obediah, that stud bull who screwed mother, daughter, granddaughter at whim, leaving madness in his lustful wake. I was, I was certain, as mad as my mother, in my own way. It would rise one day, take some form. How very nearly that madness had this day undone me. And I sobbed and cursed, loudly, I suppose, for the neighbor below sent another string of epithets in my direction.

At some point during the night, I finally slept and awakened groggy and unrested, but calmer. The first image to cross my consciousness was the pert and beautiful face of Betty Butler, that which had been placed forever out of my reach; for even without Daniel, I could never offer her myself. Mine was the seed of madmen and I was doomed to celibacy for all of my life. In that way only could I kill out the tainted line of Obediah. I could not visit upon his memory the line of bastards I had briefly envisioned, for even bastards, the sons of whores, have the right not to be born mad.

I hastened to finish my business in Fort Smith. I gathered all my documents and without apology discharged my solicitors there and paid my debt to them and shipped the major portion of documents to myself. And early the next morning I recovered my horse and hastened toward home. I had no immediate plans save to attain the security of my study and of familiar surroundings. I felt fevered and ill and I wanted to be home. Home in my Sears, Roebuck house. Ha!

Mrs. Brady's concern at the sight of me was real. "Now, look at you, Mr. Murphy, you went off like that exhausted from overwork and not taking care of yourself, and you've come down with it, too."

"With what?" I inquired but vaguely of her.

"Well, I guess maybe whatever it is that Betty's got; for she's ailin', too. She's been abed these last two days. Both of you in such weakened conditions, it's no tellin' what you've picked up."

I could tell, however, by the tone of her voice, the worry in it, that she likely feared that we both had come down with typhoid or something like it. And I reassured her as best I could that I was suffering only from exhaustion and would be fine when rested.

"And where is Betty?" I managed to ask.

"She's still abed. She usually feels some better in the afternoons and comes down. But she's been most peaked."

In one respect I was correct. I was tired, tired enough from lost sleep that I slept soundly, my recent terrors briefly abated. I slept through the afternoon and the night without rising and felt relatively rested, if sorely depressed, on rising the following day.

I breakfasted, and still Betty was nowhere in sight. Lassitude all but overtook me again, but I summoned the strength to get my hat and walk to the post office to see if my shipment of papers had arrived. They had not, but there was an accumulation of letters and newspapers, most of the letters dealing with business matters, and one letter from Daniel.

Dearest Levi [he wrote],

I am unhappy, very unhappy to have to report that my examinations have been set back by another six weeks for official reasons that I will not go into here. Suffice it to say that I shall be delayed by that long in returning home.

I would very much like to shuck it all and come on anyway, for I sorely miss all of you. [Homesickness, I noted to myself, had never before been a problem with Daniel.] However, if I am to be successful in these examinations, I must apply myself. I'm sure all of you will understand that.

I will notify you as soon as possible when to expect me. I have enclosed a note to Betty that I ask you please to deliver for me. Take good care of yourselfs. [Ah, Daniel's spelling would never do for a licensed attorney, I thought.] I remain your friend faithful and true, Daniel St. Cloud.

I handled the enclosed note and stared hard at it. It was sealed securely. I held it to the light and was immediately ashamed. Finally I tossed it, rather, flung it on the desk before me and read again Daniel's brief letter. Delayed, was he? So, too, then was my torment, I supposed, and I sat brooding over my fate for the better part of the afternoon. Only when Mrs. Brady called "Supper" did I look up from my folded arms and finally rise, stiffly and uncertainly, and run my hand through my already tousled hair. Such appearance would not do, and I focused on the small mirror atop a bookcase and pushed a pocket comb through my hair and struggled to make myself presentable, expecting Betty at the supper table.

For a long moment I glared at the note, precisely folded and intended for her eyes only, and then I pocketed it and joined the ladies in the dining room. Betty was indeed present, her face pale and the dark circles, which had largely disappeared over the summer, once more prominent beneath her eyes.

We made idle talk of my trip and Betty noted that, having come this far north, she was as far from home as she had ever been in her life, her aunt's rejoinder to that being that all might soon change.

I felt the press of the letter in my pocket and suddenly heard myself saying casually, "I had a letter from Daniel today." At that both ladies looked up sharply and eagerly. "He says that his examinations have been delayed. He does not know when he might visit again." At that, silence enshrouded the room, preceded by a gasp from Mrs. Brady. Perversely, I went no further. Betty's complexion, pale enough, had gone quite white.

"Is that all?" asked Betty.

"All? Why, yes. Daniel's that way, you know. You can never quite be certain of his plans. He flits so from project to project." I said it quite casually, yet all the while covertly eyeing the girl's reaction. She was plainly distressed and excused herself early.

The next morning early she knocked and came into my study bearing an envelope. It was a letter to Mr. St. Cloud, she said, and would I be kind enough to address and mail it for her. It was, she assured me, quite urgent. She held the thing toward me with trembling hands, and I could tell from the flushed and feverish expression that it was more than nervous distress that prompted the trembling. The girl was not well.

As if to prove me correct, she slid at that moment into a nearby chair and held her face in her hands for a moment.

"Betty? Are you all right?"

"Yes. No. Actually, I'm simply a little ill. I've picked up some infection, I think. Probably I'm coming down with a cold. I'll be all right." She smiled weakly. "It just takes me longer to cast these things off than it did before I had typhoid."

"Yes," I said.

"And you will mail my letter today, won't you? I hate to ask, but I'm not up to a walk to the post office."

I assured her that I would mail the letter and she made her way slowly out of the study, turning down my proffered aid. I held the small envelope, sealed tightly, and stared hungrily at it. I had always been a perspicacious individual and certain suspicions were beginning to rise, and with those same suspicions, the germ of a plan, more hopelessly devious than any I had ever thought myself capable of. I paced the room and shoved my hands in my pockets as if to make one last effort at self-control, like a boy eyeing a forbidden plate of sweets. I knew then that I would have those sweets for myself, and in the doing, if my suspicions proved correct, have answer for the line of Obediah Murphy!

At last I tore open the small envelope. The note was brief, written carefully in a schoolbook hand that suggested the girl ill at ease with pen and paper. The rounded letters were spread like teardrops across the page.

Dear Daniel,

I hear that you do not plan to come back soon. It is very important for me to see you. It is very important for us to wed as soon as possible. Please come home as soon as you get this letter. We can marry and then you can return for your examinations. There is no time to spare.

The last was copiously underlined and the girl's name signed to it. I placed it thus opened next to the letter that Daniel had sent. I had not opened that. I saw no need. I had all the information that I needed. I closed and locked the drawer, that same desk drawer in which I had locked my youthful journal—and was youth so far gone? I was briefly grateful that those labored pages had been consigned to the flames, for would I have felt constrained for history's sake to list my own villainies or would I have but chosen and picked among the facts? And is thus history writ—in bits and pieces of selected fact?

When later that day Betty asked if I had mailed her letter, I confirmed that I had.

"And how long do you suppose that it will take to get to St. Louis?" she asked anxiously.

"Ah, I can't say, but I think that the post to St. Louis is somewhat more reliable than it is to lesser localities. Possibly three to four days."

"Then I could expect an answer in a week, perhaps?"

"Perhaps."

Two weeks passed with no answer, and then a third, and the girl grew more agitated. Finally she came to me again and asked if I had had word from Daniel. She was by that time in an almost frenzied state. I answered her negatively and then a few days later went to her and told her that I had had a brief note from Daniel. She started.

"He wrote that he was thinking of putting off his examinations until next summer, as a friend and he had been making plans to leave for the West Coast and catch a freighter to Panama, where they are digging the transcontinental canal."

"What!"

"That's Daniel," I sighed. "He claims that he does not want to settle down and pass his examinations until he has had some adventure, as he put it. He wrote me, of course," I added in the tone of a long-suffering parent, "because he needs money for this excursion." And then I sighed.

Betty had fought her way to a chair and was struggling to hold back tears. If ever there was a time to withdraw and to scuttle my plans, it would have been then. But I held my ground, oblivious to the fact that she was shaking uncontrollably.

"Are you well? I'll get you water," I said and quickly left the room. By the time I returned, she had regained some control of herself.

"Mr. Murphy," she said, stiffly reverting to a formal salutation, "I have overstayed your hospitality, I think. It's coming on winter and I think it best that I return to my father's ranch."

"But, Betty!" I cried.

"It would be best."

My time had come, the ultimate test of my plans. "Betty, dear Betty," I said, kneeling in classic manner and taking her hand. "You cannot leave me. I have refrained from declaring myself because of your weakened condition, but the truth is I love you. I love you and I want to marry you."

I thought my dissembling so transparent that a child could have seen through it, but she did not, whether because of her confused state of mind or her fear or her natural suspicion that she had been taken advantage of. Whatever the reason, she took my declaration at face value.

"But, Mr. Murphy, Levi, I, I don't know what to say."

"Will you be my wife?" I said simply.

I was absolutely clear-headed, cold and calculating perhaps; but I could almost follow her thought processes as if they were being printed by teletypewriter. Her integrity was insisting she confess her condition, her fear was arguing against it. This girl, I knew, was not one to dissemble.

"Levi," she said, "I must consider your offer seriously, but first there are some things about me that you ought to know."

I pressed my palm to her lips and shushed her as if she were a fretful child. "No, no, my love, just say that you will marry me. I don't want to know anything else. You are all I want, right now, as you are this moment." She folded limply into my arms with something like a sob, her integrity giving ground to her fear.

At some future date, should she ever accuse me, I would have her own deceit as my defense.

Betty Butler was carrying a bastard, Daniel's bastard, but a bastard nonetheless, a bastard who would bear the name Murphy. This would be justice. I would found a line of true bastards, all bearing the name Murphy but none the tainted Murphy blood. So be it.

I had only the slightest guilt concerning Daniel. He was a shallow sort, who would, when he discovered that he had been jilted, quickly find someone else. He would not suffer.

But I, I would have my cake and eat it, too. I would, in the act, best the old lecher in his grave. The House of Murphy was as damned and doomed as ever the House of Atreus.

SIX

LOUISA DOES BATTLE

"**W**ell," said Nancy Hawkins, haisting her hindmost skirts to the fire in order to warm her backside, "I wish ye ever such happiness, Louisa," her tone suggesting that she did not believe that such would be the case, however. "I wish ye happiness and hope that ye'll ne'er live to regret yer choice."

"I thank ye fer dat," murmured Louisa. She sat in the armless rocker, a comforter spread across her lap, awaiting her turn at the fire, which, though it blazed and sputtered bravely, like a Campbellite preacher, affected only those nearest to it and that only so long as they did not move away. And the candles that lined the room produced feeble shadows that only emphasized the dismal air which hovered over the deathbed of the widow Varner, that dying soul being the third party present in the room and the only one truly warm, for though she rested under a pile of comforters, the circulation was quite gone from her lower extremities anyway and rendered unnecessary that burden of blankets.

"If ye ever," continued Louisa's former sister-in-law, bending her backside nearer the blaze, "find need of having him whipped or tarred an' feathered, why, Todd Hawkins will be right proud to come to yer service." The lady made this generous offer amiably and let down her skirts to more savor the heat that now lay under them.

"An' vy, Nan Hawkins, vould I vant fer Obediah to be whipped or feddered?" was Louisa's reasonable rejoinder.

"I dunno. Just might be someday."

"He's not a bad man, my Nancy."

"Well, I've only heard stories, you know, mostly of his ways with ladies. But yer the judge, I'm sure, of whether he's a good man or nay."

"I never said he vas good, Nan. I just said that he vas not bad."

Nancy Hawkins stood in silence for a few moments and, ascertaining that her legs were no longer safe from the chill, haisted her skirts and exposed her backside again to the fire. "Ye might a made a better choice, Louisa. Ye have the means and the looks to a selected a far better helpmate."

"Possibly," said Louisa. She tucked the comforter around her small feet and rocked slowly to the sound of the hissing and sputtering flames. The form on the bed coughed once, and both Nancy and Louisa looked over at it. The widow Varner, however, still slept; at least, her eyes were closed and her breathing was regular. She might go this night; she might not. But she would most certainly not last until spring. Late February was, Louisa thought, an inconvenient time to die, but better perhaps than spring anyway, when the time the men spent digging her hole might be more profitably spent in preparing the ground for seed.

There was no necessity in trying to explain to Nancy or anyone else why she had chosen Obediah Murphy over many other potential suitors, had made that choice before any other had noticed that she would shortly be available for courtship. There were many who would have come courting, and Louisa had known it, her most fetching attribute being her better than three hundred acres of choice, well-tended land. Had she been tooth-gapped and teat-withered even, she would have been so courted, but she was none of that, and as she likewise had only four dependent children, Louisa reasoned, she most likely would have had to fend off potential suitors with a stick of firewood.

Louisa Varner was of a reasonable and practical turn of mind, the greatest dower her Pennsylvania Dutch parents had given, and it was that same reasonableness and practicality that led her to choose Obediah Murphy over more reasonable and practical men. She reasoned that, as she was a wealthy woman and as she could take care of herself and her own and as she had no need of anyone to help her, she could thus afford the luxury of marrying whom she wanted, with no need to expect from him any of the necessities that most women require of a husband.

"Then why marry at all?" she might have been asked.

"Vy," she might then have answered with all due reasonableness, "a voman's either vidder or vife." Spinster did not count. Widow counted somewhat better, but it was wife that counted most. A woman did not live without a man if she could help it, the laws of nature and reason so argued, and Louisa Varner would go against the laws of neither.

But Louisa could afford the man she wanted. She did not have to be obliged to settle for a man who would expect to make decisions and to give orders and, in short, to be a household head. She could choose a husband who would be like a rocking chair, to comfort her when she was tired, or like a pet dog, to play with her when she was playful, or like a good goose down comforter, to warm her when she was cold, or like a pair of fine silver candlesticks, to make certain good wives envious when they saw what she had acquired.

"And where is all the light? I need a candle," came the sudden querulous cry from the mound of comforters on the bed.

Louisa and Nan looked at each other and each secured a candle and went and stood by the bed with it. They stood for some moments in silence. In a little bit the querulous cry came again. "Louisa. Nancy. Fetch a candle, I say." Louisa and Nan glanced at each other again, recognizing that the solemn moment of passing was approaching, for the light had gone out of the old woman's eyes as the feeling had gone from her extremities. Her life was drifting away in small bits.

"It is nigh to morning, Mother Varner," said Louisa. "No need to light more candles now, for it vould be a vaste."

And then the old woman understood and she sighed. It was a lonely sigh. She settled her hands carefully on top the topmost comforter and stared at a far corner with perplexed and sightless stare. Perhaps she was thinking that it was so strange that an entire life could be so short, encompassed almost in a few hours. She had been a girl, jumping rope and running through the woods, and she had married and birthed babies and buried children and husband and all in just a few minutes. Surely God allowed more time. He ought to. Someone, she might be thinking, ought to approach Him on that matter and suggest to Him that life is really too short, that He has made it pass too quickly.

Or perhaps she only wanted a drink of water.

But neither Nan nor Louisa ever knew, for she closed her eyes and sighed again and so died. Louisa and Nan put aside their candles and knelt on each side of the bed with clasped hands and sent prayers racing after the departing soul. They did not cry, for the old woman had lived a long, long time and death for the aged is natural, merciful and just.

Louisa Varner Murphy watched Obie from the porch. Bared to the waist, he swung the chopping ax through the air, striking a firm blow to the already felled log with each swing, for he was an accomplished axman. It was niggers' work, Louisa knew; and in truth Obie worked like a nigger, the strong muscles of his back working, it almost seemed, at cross purposes to one another, but, shiny with sweat, each muscle contributed to the motion as a whole, with fluid and graceful ease. All of her life Louisa had casually observed those same motions in the muscled backs of slaves, plowing, sawing, chopping or lifting; she could not recall ever noticing before the muscles on a white man's back so dancing to the rhythm of work. She supposed they did. Daniel Varner had been a willing worker, but, she recalled, he never worked with bared back. Maybe that was the difference. Louisa knew that she should go to Obediah and ask him to clothe himself, as the ladies would begin shortly to arrive and it was not meet that the master of the house should be found not only occupying his efforts in slaves' work, but doing that same work bare of shoulder. But Louisa made no move toward Obie, only stood with arms folded across her bosom, hugging herself and watching the muscled back in bemused fashion.

Obie was not aware that he was watched. He would not have cared, in any event, for he was enjoying himself. Obie liked to split wood. Black Benjamin had taught him to do so with speed and economy of effort. "You just aims and da ax do da work," black Benjamin had counseled. "All you got to do is make sure dat da blade hits da spot. You do what you 'sposed to and den da wood do what it 'sposed to. You miss a lick an' den doan nothin' do what hit 'sposed to."

Now, in Obediah Murphy's philosophy, it was very necessary for everything to work as it was supposed to, as it had been in black Benjamin's philosophy; for there was no provision in either philosophy for dealing with any situation that fell outside the natural order of things. For that reason, Obie enjoyed splitting wood, just as he enjoyed his routine early-morning movement and likewise enjoyed the way his curls fell back into their prescribed positions with the application of brush and comb. He paused only in his work to wipe the sweat (which he also liked) from his eyes or to lift a dipper full of water from the wooden bucket a few paces from his chopping block. Later, he would sort and stack the wood in tidy ricks, and with the coming of winter, each rick would be as carefully unstacked, rick by rick, and such were Obie's energies that there would be sufficient wood to carry over until the following summer, allowing even for routine cooking and boiling of clothes on washday. Had someone suggested to Obie that he could have others do the chopping for him, freeing him to make plans and settle accounts and discuss weighty matters with like-minded landholders or take part in the activities at the cockpit or the race path or the marble ground, he would not have understood.

Louisa's guests would spend the day; for she had pieced together a patchwork to be quilted and had likewise a pair of down comforters, long in the making—such comforters being tedious for both goose and wife—that needed to be knotted, the latter easily enough accomplished, the former more time- and gossip-consuming. An early spring day, warm and still, was perfect for those activities, the frame set up out of doors where the light was good and the space sufficient to accommodate a large group of seamstresses. The quilt would be an accomplished fact before sundown.

Louisa Varner Murphy was not often given to such social intercourse, finding her own swift and skilled needle sufficient for her purposes as she stitched through a long winter her own quilts and comforters. And in truth, her need was not great at this moment; but she might have insisted that the inspiration for such socializing was in her newly married state and her desire to begin all things afresh with a new husband. Or she might have said bluntly, for bluntness was often her wont, that it was necessary for the wives of the neighborhood to view her wedded bliss and so still the ever present rumors of unfaithfulness on her groom's part. Or yet again, she might have confessed a certain eagerness to watch the expressions of envy that would most certainly cross the faces of certain goodwives at the view of her handsome, friendly and industrious man.

She might have affirmed any of those motives. She might have, but she did not, to anyone or to herself even, though any one and indeed all three were in part true. Nor would Louisa admit to the glow of satisfaction that it happened that Mistress Bailey's eldest daughter, Madge O'Keeth, who arrived on foot, was the first guest, standing for a long, unguarded moment on the porch staring at the glistening and busy muscles of Obediah before Louisa greeted her with a carefully patient sign, "An' please, Madge, must forgive mine

Obediah. I sent him his shirt immediate. He's dat contrary. He must have his exercise. My. An' he is so strong an' da shirt so contraints him. My." And she hugged herself and glanced with brief longing toward that handsome figure, so that there could be no mistaking on Madge's part Obediah's impressive strength and that she, Louisa, certainly had experience of that strength. Nor was Louisa disappointed in her guest's reaction.

"Humph. Niggers' work", said Mistress O'Keeth.

"Oh, my yes. It's just terrible, an't it?" sighed Louisa with another glance of tender longing. It was common knowledge that Lem O'Keeth was so dilatory and lacking in industry that he not only did not keep his own woodpile but did not make the effort to get the slaves to do it, either, so that Madge O'Keeth on more than one occasion had recourse to removing the topmost rail from the fence nearest the house and sticking one end into the fireplace to keep the fire going, shoving it farther in with her foot as it burned, while Master O'Keeth occupied his time in important converse at the marble ground or perhaps the cockpit.

"Danny," called Louisa to her eldest son, who was playing at the kitchen steps. "Run fetch yer fadder his shirt, vich lies across mine fedder ticking."

And when Obediah had got the shirt he looked at the women who were gathering on the porch and he waved and grinned without self-consciousness. Nor did he tuck his shirt in, but left the tails to flap and the ruffled collar unbuttoned.

"And how do ye ever keep them ruffles starched?" asked Madge O'Keeth irritably, for her own husband wore naught but the loose blouse and baggy breeches of a countryman.

"It is a vorry," sighed Louisa with another tender glance, "it is an everlasting vorry, dem ruffles and dem breeches. But he vill vear no udder. Dat man. Dat man." And though her words were rebuking, her tone was not.

Rumor and gossip to the contrary, Obediah Murphy comported himself with all due dignity, for he did not in his own mind think himself either lecher or fornicator, and remained true and faithful to his bride, if one did not of course count Mistress Bailey's Rachel, whose black eyes and saucy ways lured him to visit with her now and then in the hollow below Judge Bailey's farthest outhouse; or provided one did not note the lame widow Slade, whose horse he unmired from a muddy hedgerow, for which service the widow offered the handsome young husband cakes and tea and other sweets left unnamed; or if one did not take into account the lonely young wife at whose cabin he stopped for direction early on a winter's eve when he had lost his way coming from the county seat, where he had gone to set his signature to certain papers that Louisa required, that lonely wife being quite free with both her directions and her favors and thereby presenting her husband a precise number of months later with a pretty girl baby, whom the happy father called Patty after his own mother.

Nor would Obie have expected to be called to account for certain actions with Mistress Lake's brother's daughter from Virginia, sent to reside with her aunt because her parents feared that she was getting altogether too thick with a young man of her own county. It was that niece, Peg, round on top, slim in the middle and round on the bottom, whom Obie encountered as she picked blackberries for her aunt on a warm July afternoon. She was of a right saucy disposition and offered to let Obie taste the sweetest berries would he stay and help her fill her bucket. And so Obie stayed and filled the bucket and tasted blackberries of such sweetness that he was reminded of honey, which in turn reminded him of a like chance encounter in his boyhood, and he was moved, as was the girl, and they pleasured themselves until the light began to fail.

"I got lost," said Obie to Louisa, who but nodded and warned that, he being so ill directed, she was going to send Danny or Charlie along with him ere he rode out on a distant errand again. Obie only smiled and looked beyond her, a gentle distant glance whose meaning Louisa would learn to decipher anon.

Peg returned at the end of the summer to her home in Virginia, and when later in the fall her alarmed mother noted an added burden around the girl's waist, she carried the news to the father, who went out forthwith and accosted young Nathan Beck with that intelligence, and that perplexed young man found himself by turns groom and father. Philosophically he shrugged, named the infant after himself and set about assiduously adding to that line which someone had so kindly started for him.

"It is simple lust," Louisa Varner Murphy answered those critics who hastened to her with various reports and tales. "It an't so evil as some things I could mention." And she was thinking of the sloth of Lem O'Keeth and the drunkenness of Rance Stout and the ill temper of Troy Gibbons. "It is natural lust, like a young colt's. It vill abate. I am patient. I vill outlast dose randy vays." If it takes a hundred years, she thought but did not say. Out loud she would affirm his attributes. "He is a good vorker." He was. "He is a good fadder." He was. "An' he makes us happy." He did.

Only Danny, the oldest son of Louisa and Daniel Varner, could find fault with his stepfather; for he was old enough to hear and to understand the rumors and criticisms of Obediah's behavior, such criticisms occasioning certain bouts of fisticuffs, which Danny, despite being tall for his age, usually lost. At such times Obediah's favor diminished in the boy's eyes and Danny complained to his mother, who only shushed him with something like, "Dey spread dem rumors because dey're jealous dat mine husband is handsome and dat he is rich." Louisa understood that either one of those conditions solely would occasion resentment in certain individuals and that both together would drive the truly envious distract. That explanation satisfied Louisa. She wanted no other.

But she felt obliged to occasionally pass such rumors on to Obediah, who, when he heard them, was confused and perplexed. He did not understand why such casual abuse was directed toward him. He was not lustful and lecherous. True, he was friendly and neighborly and obliging. He could not bear to turn anyone down. That was as true of a neighbor borrowing a stud oxen as it was of a woman needing serving. And in truth Obediah did never institute most seductions. He would never have thought of such a thing. He was a husband and a father and a man of means. Such seductions came to him. It seemed that women just needed fucking. And he was of an obliging temperament.

But for occasional gossip, Obediah and his new family led a pleasant and happy existence. Obediah was good at games, and in warm weather he tussled and wrestled with the boys and played at tops and moon spinner and marbles with them. And in the winter they sat by the fire with checkerboard or dominoes and passed the hours, Obie more often than not the winner, for he did not think it moral to cheat in favor of the children, a fact that Danny, who liked to win, noted against his stepfather.

Or in the darkened kitchen, lighted only by the flames from the hearth, for the tallow candles Louisa carefully saved against times of greater need, the children might beg that Obediah tell them again the wonders of the Lewisburg Fair.

And Obediah would lean back in his chair, his boyhood memory coloring the Lewisburg Fair in hues that were never there. Louisa, who had never been to the Lewisburg Fair, but who seriously doubted the potential of Lewisburg (the few times she had been there, a collection of cabins and a pair of stores and a smith) to produce on an annual basis so great a spectacle as Obediah described. But the children so loved his description that Louisa let it pass without comment. In truth, it was the fact that the Lewisburg Fair grew in glory with each telling that made the children so eager to hear Obediah tell of it and to discover what might have been added with each new telling.

"An' will ye take us there?" cried Henry Varner, the youngest son of Louisa and Daniel Varner.

"Most certainly, most certainly," cried Obediah, every bit as eager to return to this wondrous scene from boyhood's memory as ever the children were.

"An' when will't be?" asked Charlie, the second son.

"Oh, soon, soon. I must find when it is held, of course, and then we'll all pack up; we'll load the wagon, for the Lewisburg Fair lasts for weeks and weeks, an' we'll drive the oxen and we'll have us a most merry time." By this time Obediah's eyes would be shining and he might be so eager that he would rise and pace the floor.

Danny at such times said little. In temperament much like his mother, he had his own doubts about the Lewisburg Fair, though he would indeed have liked for everything that Obediah claimed to be true.

Often through the long winter, when there was little to do, little Louisa would crawl upon Obediah's lap when he sat by the fire and curl against him and beg a story. Now Obediah, who knew no stories, or who at least could never recall the details of a story to its conclusion, would at such times instead whistle her a merry tune, for Obie was a much accomplished whistler, so much so that he could veritably challenge the songbirds of spring and come away winner, or at least, so thought Louisa, his wife. And at those times that Obediah would fill the winter-darkened house with spring, all would pause to listen, even Danny, who was generally impatient to get on with a game.

"And when I grow up," little Louisa snug upon his lap would demand with a willful toss of her head toward her mother, "will ye marry *me* and be *my* husband?" And obligingly Obediah would assert that he would most certainly do that, and Louisa would smile tenderly upon her husband and daughter. It was she knew the nature of little girls to plan marriage with their fathers, though in truth little Louisa was not so little, she being of heavy frame and hearty appetite; and she was probably older than most girls are when they court their own fathers, little Louisa being near to ten years old by then.

There was little in life to distress Obediah Jonah Micah Murphy. He ate well and slept well and started each day as if there had been no other. It was only once in a rare while that he would stop to reflect, for reflection was not ordinarily in his nature, that he might frown and wonder to himself why it was that he had fathered no children. Louisa had four and so had proved herself, but he stood as yet without issue, and at such times he might stare critically at Louisa, whose waist perversely refused to thicken, though he himself could in no way be faulted for not trying. But on the whole, like a dumb animal not being uncomfortable, Obediah did not speculate upon what made that lack of discomfort so.

Louisa, in return, required only of Obediah that he make her happy, and her children, and that he vote and set his signature for her when it was necessary, though inwardly she always bridled that it was he rather than she who had the vote. In her mind, not only was she better equipped to think things through and so to make more careful decisions than Obediah, but so likewise were most wives over their husbands, though they might not themselves have realized it. The men being taken up in fighting and in expanding their holdings and in disputing those concerns over which they in actuality had no control (as to the fortunes of France without Napoleon or as to the state of taxation under Master Van Buren or as to the necessary fate of the native red men) were ill equipped to make intelligent decisions on the matter of schools and roads. It was a sore point with Louisa, but one about which she could do naught but send Obediah to do her bidding, which he did, having neither experience nor interest in such matters.

Obediah did love to dress for such occasions, his ruffles starched stiff, and to speak before the assemblage, his deep and resonant voice clear even to those dozing in the back, for his commanding tones brought thunder to a room as his delicate whistling could bring spring to it. But it was Louisa who schooled him in what to say, and so effective was he that he was oft called upon to speak. Obie, though not wise, was also not altogether foolish; he knew when he was prepared to speak and when he was not. And at those times that he was not prepared to speak, he would only wave petitioners off with a promise to "study upon the matter," which gave added weight to his growing reputation as a wise, thoughtful and perspicacious speaker. There were those who predicted that the young man would go far, perhaps as far as Washington, D.C. There were others who would as cheerfully have seen him hang, they being largely of an envious temperament and, seeing Obediah already handsome, wealthy and successful with the ladies, loath to see him also wise and respected. A man ought to take care not to seem too gifted, as it breeds suspicion and envy in those lesser endowed.

But if Louisa could control what Obediah said relative to weighty matters, she could not always control what Obediah set his signature to, for he was inordinately proud of the hand he wrote and could on most any occasion be persuaded to use it. It was much to Louisa's distress that she learned that Obie's signature was to be found on a petition to license a bordello in Lewisburg or to impeach this or that government official on flimsy pretext or even to tar and feather any and all suspected Mormons, Methodists, Campbellites and assorted freethinkers.

Obie was always sorry when Louisa pointed out the error of his ways. "Must not sign anything, Obediah." And then, as if to protect his dignity: "Ye know how dese people are, dese unscrupulous people, dese lawyers and clergymen, dey're so shrewd dat dey make dere case to sound so true. Must take yer time and discuss vid me before ye arrive at a conclusion. Protect yer signature, Obediah." And Obediah would swear to himself that his wife was right and no more would he be inveigled to set his signature to anything, no matter how vital it sounded, that resolution lasting only until someone produced quill and paper, for Obie could not resist setting down his swirls and curlicues for all to admire. It was something he could do that Louisa could not. He might not be able to father a child, but he could set as fine a signature as ever anyone had set, including those who had signed the Declaration of Independence.

"Obie," said Louisa one evening after she had spent the day in converse with other ladies over a quilt at Mistress Hastings' house, "our neighbor Hastings has plans to require that the surveyors plot the new road that they are now surveying so that it runs along his own property lines and in front of his own house and so to Lewisburg."

"Ah. So? Let him eat the dust of the horses and wagons, then." Obie was not seriously concerned, so that Louisa had to explain carefully to him how this gave advantage to Master Hastings over not only Obediah, but other neighbors farther to the south, who would be driven either over high country to market or roundabout by way of Master Hastings' farm. It was to Louisa's mind neither fair nor expedient.

"Master Hastings has called a meeting so to convince everybody to approve his plans. Must go tomorrow night to dat meetinghouse and speak out agin it, Obediah. Ye know," she added, "dat neighbor Hastings, he left off inviting you to attend on purpose, for he fears da power of yer tongue." At that Obediah was mildly incensed and agreed that he should appear and so testify against neighbor Hastings' plans. And what, he wanted to know, was he to say regarding those plans? And so Louisa schooled him carefully and Obediah dutifully rehearsed as the children sat forming audience for him.

If Master Simon Hastings was much put out when he saw Obediah enter the meetinghouse, those several other husbandmen were not and bethought themselves that, with the arrival of Obediah Murphy, the proceedings had themselves risen in stature.

"And now, Master Murphy," said neighbor Hastings, "we are just ready to vote. It is too bad that ye've come so late."

"And what is it that ye've discussed?" asked Obediah.

"Why, only routine matters that would just bore ye," said Master Hastings. "If ye'll just seat yerself, we will vote and then we'll pass around the cider and the ale." That last promise Master Hastings hoped would serve to hasten the proceedings.

"Why, I have come to speak," said Obediah, "for I understand that ye've discussed the platting of the new road to market."

"Aye," said Judge Bailey. Judge Bailey, being one of the few opponents of Simon Hastings' plan, now sensed an ally of great effectiveness in Obediah Murphy; for Judge Bailey was no fool, and he recognized the good sense and careful reason of Louisa Varner in her husband's speeches. "Simon Hastings has here convinced the assemblage of the reasonableness of detouring the present plans for the path of the road and so sending it instead around his own property line, as being smoother, less likely to rut, more easily traveled, if a trifle out of the way for our neighbors to the south. What think ye, Obediah, or have ye thought on this matter?"

And indeed Judge Bailey was most certain that, though Obediah might not have thought on the matter, his wife Louisa had, and he was certain that Louisa's practical mind had seen through Simon Hastings' careful stratagem.

"Aye, I have thought on it and I would speak."

"The period for speaking is passed, Master Murphy," Simon Hastings ruled quickly. "It is now only time to vote lest," and here he winked, "the ale go flat and the cider go stale."

"No," objected Judge Bailey, "let Obediah speak; we would like to hear what Obediah has to say, for we recognize that his comments on a subject are always valid and sage. What say ye, folk, would ye hear from Obediah Murphy?" Nor was Judge Bailey disappointed in the response, for almost to a man the assemblage assented by voice or nod or wave.

Bitterly Simon Hastings recognized his defeat and yielded the floor to Obediah Murphy, and Obediah recited those simple and blunt and altogether reasonable objections that Louisa, his wife, had set forth. To them he added only subordinating expressions and parallel constructions and lofty language and weighty pauses, such as he had learned at the feet of Schoolmaster the Reverend Joshua Trafalgar Mason, not so many years earlier. Those reasoned arguments, delivered in lofty language and sonorous tones, were enough to defeat Master Hastings' proposal, and that good man did, after the vote, gavel the meeting closed and leave posthaste, carrying with him both the ale and the cider, to the considerable distress of many of those who had just voted him down.

Now, Simon Hastings, like many others who fall short in their plans to misuse others, felt misused. And he brooded over many a month about it and avoided converse with old acquaintances, nursing his wounded pride well into summer. But with the coming of the summer busy season, he might well have forgotten the matter altogether or at least shrugged it off had it not been for an untimely suggestion on the part of his wife, Mistress Hastings, who was near to blessing Master Hastings with a thirteenth mouth to feed. That goodwife suggested to her husband that she had settled on the name Obediah should the issue be male, as she had already birthed seven boys and was running low on names.

In truth, the good woman was quite innocent of the travail that suggestion wrought in her husband's breast, that name Obediah having been her mother's oldest brother's name and Mistress Hastings giving no other thought to whom else that name might apply. But the seeds of suspicion, thus sown, had fallen on fertile ground and Master Hastings, distraught, convinced himself that he had been cuckolded, indignity enough without the insult of having to feed and clothe Obediah Murphy's bastard to adulthood.

Nor did Mistress Hastings, weary enough already with too much birthing and too many children, even notice that Master Hastings, her husband, kept to himself and avoided conversation with her. Nor did Simon Hastings object to the name she had chosen though it proved of no account, anyway, as Mistress Hastings gave birth to a small girl who was puny from birth and who did not survive a week. Saddened but relieved, Mistress Hastings put the dead baby away and in her heart hoped that that would be the last of it. Master Hastings could keep to himself until she had safely passed childbearing years for all she cared.

Now, Simon Hastings' hatred of Obediah Murphy was set in cold stone, but he was a slight man and the father of near-grown children; he would in no way be a match for Obediah Murphy should he be so foolish as to accost him physically. But accost him he would, and through the long winter he harbored his resentments and plotted his vengeance, harkening to the biblical injunction "An eye for an eye, and a tooth for a tooth." The punishment should match the offense.

And as Master Hastings brooded over his wrong and kept himself apart from Mistress Hastings, which distancing did aught to improve his temper, his brooding brought him at last to reason that he surely could not be the only man so wronged, that Obediah, being known for his proclivity to bed at will with loose or stray females, had certainly made cuckold of others besides himself. Master Hastings began to examine the smaller children of his neighbors and to note which of his neighbors' goodwives were heavy with child, such condition being fairly common among those wives of childbearing years, most either having just or about to or in the process of, for there were few who were not almost constantly in some process of the childbearing state, those few who held their issue to one, two or three being secretly envied by those wives who bore near regularly in the twelve month.

In his unsettled state, Simon Hastings began to detect the visage or form of Obediah Murphy in any and all children he met. "Now, Master Harris, and that pretty little lady does have uncommon wide and clear eyes. They most remind me of those eyes of Obediah Murphy, do they not ye?" Or he might confide, "Ah, neighbor Rutherford, that's a right lank lad ye've got, bound to grow tall, an't he? And you and the mistress being so slight, it'll be a blessing. Why, he might grow so tall as our neighbor Murphy."

And thus were the seeds so casually sown. "And have ye seen to Mistress Howell's baby son and the thick black curls he's already got? Curls as thick, I declare, as Obie Murphy's."

All the while, Obediah and Louisa, unaware of Simon Hastings' spite, led a busy and productive life. Nor did Obediah break faith with his wife, but for a time or two, which were of no serious account, anyway. With the spring he kept busy with getting in the wood and helping to ready the ground for seed and mending the fences with rail or stone, whichever was needed, for Obediah was ever of an industrious turn and he whistled while he worked and the slaves paused to listen and to smile at the sounds of springtime that came from the master's pursed lips.

Louisa, who could neither read nor write nor cipher, had, because her boy husband could do those things, turned the matter of keeping the accounts over to Obediah, as Daniel Varner in his lifetime had kept them. It proved an unwise decision, annoying to Louisa because she was not given to unwise decisions. It had become quickly evident that Obediah could only tangle their business, and she had quickly taken back her accounts, but not quickly enough to avoid costly entanglements.

Josiah Watkins of Washington County had ridden a day and a night to settle accounts with the widow of Daniel Varner, only to find that the note he owed had been misplaced and that Obediah had no notion of what was owed or when; and though Master Watkins did know this, he wondered did this young man, who had such a reputation for wisdom, intend in some way to try to collect twice on that debt? He went away mollified only after Obediah had writ a receipt for him, dictated by his wife, that absolved him of the debt, for Mistress Varner Murphy had stored dates and amounts in her head.

Master Will Garner arrived at Obediah's doorstep bearing the deed for property that Obediah had set his signature to, which deed being short by half a section. Master Garner accosted Obediah and threatened to take him to court or at least to punch him in the nose. Nor did Louisa point out that, though the former was possible, the latter would not be in the best interests of Master Garner's physical well-being, for he was shorter by a head than Obediah Murphy and too stout around the middle to give out what he promised. She had the deed read to her and recognized that the error was not Obediah's but the county clerk's, Obediah's only fault being in setting his signature to something he had not read, nor would have understood if he had read it. It was Louisa who directed that the deed be correctly drawn.

Nor did the entanglements stop there. Lem O'Keeth complained that Obediah had tried to collect twenty-two dollars more than was justly owed him, and Miller Hightower claimed that Obediah had sought payment for more grain that he had actually brought in.

Through it all, Obediah had stood perplexed at each accusation, for he was an honest man and had no intent to cheat his neighbors, nor did he understand that the most even-tempered of men will become churlish and suspicious in business transactions. Louisa only sighed and determined that, if her husband could not be trusted to keep the accounts, she must needs do it herself, though the keeping of so much information in her head would eventually become trying.

Now, Louisa had upon occasion tried her hand at ciphering, but she was put off by the numerals with which she had to work. She found those symbols uncommonly vague, endless squiggles on a page, most not even closed but let ramble open-ended. In Louisa's tidy and precise view, such symbols could have no meaning and she could not master them. It was not for lack of a strong hand that she could not master the numerals, for in her years of stitching she had proved a precise and careful seamstress; she who had mastery over so tiny a thing as a needle pulling thread would hardly be defeated by so great a thing as a quill. No, it was the imprecision of the figures she had to work with that put her off, so that she stubbornly refused to recognize them as adequate for her business.

What she appreciated was the geometries of a patchwork, the triangles that formed a star of Bethlehem, the overlapping circles of a double wedding ring, the tiny blocks that, put together, pieced out a pattern in triangles and circles and squares and rectangles. These amounted to something, each piece a self-contained symbol but a part of the whole. Such symbols, she reasoned, made better sense than the ill-formed numerals others used. And so Louisa kept her accounts thus, in completed circles and squares and triangles, slashing or circling or *x*-ing to determine amounts and dates. On a sheet of foolscap, with a large quill, she drew her accounts at the beginning of each month. And when after several months she had completely filled a sheet of foolscap, she held it up and admired its regularity, as she might a completed quilt top.

And then one day, staring at a completed sheet of accounts, it struck her that it formed a pleasing design, and then it further struck her that, a sheet of foolscap being of so fragile a nature and easily lost or destroyed or withered with age and damp, she could as easily set that pattern in a quilt block, with accounts receivable in red, perhaps, and mortgages in blue and deeds in green and debts (there were ever few) a touch of pink to brighten the top. And so as each sheet of foolscap was completed, Louisa set it in a quilt block, embroidering *x*'s and slashes as needed, before she stored the foolscap away in her books. Nor did she explain to anyone what she was piecing; it was a permanent record, for her only who could not write, of her business transactions, as other quilts she had put together were records of births and marriages, a scrap here or a piece there refreshing her memories of the trivial as well as the momentous. Louisa, as the years passed, would be able to read her history in quilt blocks as others might theirs in journal or diary. It was a history as accurate as memory and as private.

Now there commenced to be heard murmurings against Obediah Murphy among those who had so lately nothing but praise for him. Nor were such murmurings at first loud, nor were they sudden; but nevertheless the general attitude of approbation, which had already conceded Obediah Murphy governorship eventually or even senatorship if he wanted, began to change.

"Well," someone might say, "that Obediah Murphy is for sure and certain wise and well spoke. But"—and his listener might begin to nod agreement even before the qualifying "but" would be finished.

"Aye, 'tis possible to be too glib a tongue," another might say.

"And have ye looked to neighbor Howell's young son and those dark curls he's got, and neighbor Howell and his wife both so fair? Peculiar enough, an't it?" The questioner, not being quite so bold as to name Master Howell a cuckold or Mistress Howell of loose virtue, only pronounced the phenomenon "peculiar."

And in another conversation the conversants might take note of neighbor Rutherford's lanky son, without accusation, but nonetheless each mentally measuring his own youngest child or noting that child's color and contours. And thus was many a goodwife maligned without knowledge of it.

Master Rutherford was heard to report that Master Murphy had "near skinned Lem O'Keeth of a sum of money, an honest debt."

"Several hundred dollars, I heard," affirmed one or another of the conversants.

As the months passed, the rumors grew. "I'm told that Master Wilkins of Washington County did have the law on Obediah Murphy, which law Obediah, being wealthy, was able to buy off."

"I've said it and said it," maintained one, "ye cannot trust a wealthy man; wealth breeds greed." And it sounded so wise to the speaker that he repeated that aphorism and all nodded around. Then he went home and repeated his sage remark to his wife, who likewise thought well of her husband's perspicacity and repeated his remark at meeting Sunday next, which remark was widely circulated and improved upon.

"A handsome and wealthy man has to be carefully watched, they say."

"Especially be he a clever speaker, for he can talk a man out of his wealth and a wife out of her honor."

No one was quite sure who it was who first mentioned tar and feathers, but it was Nancy Hawkins who brought Louisa that intelligence.

"Mine Obediah? Vatever fer?" Louisa was piecing a quilt block while Nancy sat opposite knitting on a sock.

"Well, I dunno that it's planned, only that Todd Hawkins brought word of it some days past."

"Well."

"Obie is too free with the ladies, Louisa, is what it boils down to, though it's Todd Hawkins' contention that he gets more credit in such matters than he deserves."

"Well," said Louisa again. "At least Todd Hawkins is more carefully thought than most of our neighbors hereabouts." But she sighed anyway, for Louisa, who was ignorant of letters and numbers, nor could read them or cipher them, could read Obediah as easily as she read her quilt pieces and knew that he was not altogether faithful as he ought to be, though, she reasoned, it also was not entirely his fault, for he did not actively seek such favors, only accepted them as offered.

"And that's a right pretty pattern yer makin', Louisa. I don't mind seeing it before. What do ye call it?"

"Oh, it's nothing really. It's just a pattern of mine own making and has no name."

"Well, it's pretty, though I believe it would benefit a little more pink here and there."

"No. I don't like pink. I avoid pink and only use it ven I haf to," said Louisa. "An' tell me vat particulars Todd Hawkins brought ye concerning mine Obie," she added.

And so Nancy Hawkins repeated what she had heard from her husband, Todd Hawkins, as well as various rumors that she had over the past several months been privy to. Louisa listened, rocking in her chair as she slowly stitched tiny pieces of cloth together. When Nan was finished with her recitation Louisa said, "Vell!" And that was all. And long after Nan Hawkins had taken her leave, Louisa rocked and stitched and frowned until at last she put aside her quilt pieces and rose, her strategy complete.

The next morning she requested that Obediah saddle her a mount, which one she did not care, for she was not ordinarily a rider, nor was she comfortable a-horseback. She would have preferred to go on foot to work her plan, but she needed, she felt, to go in state. Hence the horse.

"I must call on Mistress Hastings, for I hear that she is not well. She has not regained her strength, they say, from the loss of dat last babe."

It was, of course, not Mistress Hastings that Louisa planned to visit, but with her husband, Master Hastings, for Louisa was nothing if not to the point, and it was clear to her as Nan had recited the case against Obediah where that case had originated and why. Never mind that Louisa Varner Murphy had never studied the strategies of war or even understood the intricacies of chess; she knew instinctively that in offense lay her only defense. Louisa set out to do battle.

She stood before Simon Hastings, declining his offer of a chair and Mistress Hastings' offer of tea.

"Mine Obediah," she said to the point, "is right angry. He is dat furious, I tell ye, dat someone has been spreading poison rumors against him. And so I haf restrained him from coming here and have come myself, for to deliver a warning to ye, Simon Hastings, for I vould not yer blood on mine Obediah's head. Ye risk limb, Master Hastings, if not life, do ye pursue such slanderous course." Louisa waved aside Master Hastings' protestations of innocence. "Neffer mind how I know or where it come from; only know ye furder, Simon Hastings, mine own fadder's brother, Leviticus Rippert, is a lawyer from Philadelphia, a Philadelphia lawyer," she repeated, lest the import of that be lost on Simon Hastings, "and he vill not look kindly upon such slander. Ye haf yer choice, Simon Hastings, to leave off slandering Obediah Murphy and to help restore his name or to be called out on the field of honor by mine Obediah (vich I vould not like, as I said. I do not vant yer blood on mine Obediah) or mine uncle, Leviticus Rippert, the Philadelphia lawyer, vill take by suit a just amount to restore mine Obediah. Good day, Master and Mistress!" And Louisa whirled away, remounted her own horse, which was held by the slave that had trotted after her the whole distance from her plantation to this, and rode uncomfortably, back stiff and straight, the slave trotting behind, whence she had come, leaving a stricken Simon Hastings behind.

And thus the rumors, of which Obediah remained largely ignorant, abated and eventually died, for Simon Hastings in no way wished to be called to account by Obediah Murphy or his uncle-in-law the Philadelphia lawyer, Leviticus Rippert.

Louisa, however, remained unsettled and spent many hours pondering her situation, wondering how often in her marriage she would have to fight such a battle.

It was on a Midsummer Eve when Obie came in from the back field wearing the faraway glint in his eyes that Louisa had learned to read, that Louisa made her decision.

"I haf decided, Obie," said Louisa, "dat it is time fer us to leave."

"Leave?"

"To move, to go, to migrate Vest. Vest, ye know, dat is vere de future lies. I haf heard dat and I believe it. Ve can grow no more in dis place, neither crops nor spirits. Ve should go vere de land is new, and de opportunities. Vere ye could rise to yer gifts."

Obie was moved to speak. "An' do ye think I could found a city in the wilderness?" He was thinking how Bob Lewis had founded Lewisburg and how nice it would be to found a Murphysburg and perhaps to institute a fair that would outshine the Lewisburg Fair. Given a promise, he ran with it like a playful kitten with a skein of yarn.

"Perhaps," said Louisa. "Yes, perhaps." And she sighed. For what had been to her a hard decision came down to a lark for her husband. And she wondered if it would ever be so.

SEVEN

THE THEYS HAVE IT

I am greeted by cheerful whistling coming from the open door to my house. Charlaine is here helping Nanny. I know, of course, that she is here, because I have just parked my shiny Lincoln next to her pockmarked Chevy. And I know that she is working because she is whistling. Charlaine always whistles when she works; the harder she works, the more she whistles. It is an unusual talent for a woman, I suppose, but I reflect that black people seem to have this great affinity for music, any kind of music, even, I suppose, the quick chirps and trills of a whistled tune.

I have just come from an afternoon of golf, a game which I took up under protest, but which I now find very relaxing. It seemed to me, when David and Arlene first broached the idea several years ago, that golf—at least the kind of golf played at our club—was the pastime of the ambitious, those making business deals or struggling up the social ladder. I did not feel that I fit either category. I am rich enough to occupy any rung of the social ladder I choose and I am not particularly ambitious in business, either, being rather the caretaker of someone else's earlier ambitions.

But Arlene prevailed—something she does not often do—and I took up golf, a game I found I had an easy affinity for. "Women are natural golfers," the pro explained. "They're born with the right kind of swing." I think he meant it as a joke.

I play with groups, one or another, because that's the way to play, but in the main I think I would prefer to play by myself. I am not competitive as a golfer. I like to shoot a low score only because it tells me that I have hit the ball well, which is, I think, what attracts me to that activity. I like the sense of well-being, call it accomplishment, that I get when I hit the ball, follow through and watch it in its flight. It is nice to hit the ball correctly, and it is satisfying to have the ball then do what it's supposed to do. It's all a matter of applied physics, I suppose. Maybe that's all any sport is, applied physics: motion, reaction and the attendant results.

Charlaine and Nanny will have moved all the furniture and polished everything within polishing distance. A few times every year, Nanny calls in Charlaine to help with the heavy work. In the past they confined their efforts largely to moving furniture and dusting under things, but since the professional cleaners went through the house and washed down everything, even the windows, I sense that Nanny feels it her duty to prove herself as good as they. She and Charlaine have all the drapes open, obviously polishing the windows again, so that sunlight, once a suppliant to this household, now barges in like a near-relative.

Charlaine, I think, does the yeoman's share of the heavy work, Nanny being more gifted at giving instructions than in lifting furniture. Besides, Charlaine is a big woman, not fat but tall and strong and handsome, too, several shades lighter in color than either Nanny or Leroy, and her children are mostly of shades somewhere between the parents' colors. Taken as a whole, they are a handsome family, high-cheeked and bright-eyed. There may be some truth in Nanny's claim of Indian blood.

And while Charlaine works, she whistles, a cheerful and energetic tune. Nanny likes country-Western and so wears her Sony headset. The arrangement seems to work.

Charlaine greets me as I enter, and I wait patiently for Nanny to notice me and unplug herself from those timeless refrains that make up most of country-Western music. It is a moment before she notices me, in some surprise, and I am moved to wonder if that's how it is to be deaf, forever startled by sight unaccompanied by sound. In a sense deafness is what this headset represents, ignorance at least of any sound save that being insinuated into your ears. Nanny stares at me blankly for a long moment, waiting, I think, for a song to come to its conclusion before she reluctantly disengages herself from that private world of personal noise.

"An' don' it look nice now, dese here winders cleaned an' da shades open and light comin' in? Don' it make you want to git it all painted?"

There's another one after me to paint my life. Granted, the bright light doesn't do anything for the condition of the walls, but I hesitate to take that step, for the one improvement makes everything else look shabby, like a perfectly respectable pair of shoes, worn but serviceable, in a shoe store look instead like orphaned children. I bought new drapes; that should be enough.

"Close the drapes and you won't notice the walls," I suggest. "I don't like the smell of fresh paint," I add in defense.

"Well, I don' lak the smell of what dem kids smeared all over dese walls." Nanny insists that she can still smell that, though it was cleaned off and disinfected months ago.

"Now," Arlene had said then, "you must look at this as a blessing in disguise, just what you need to prod you into doing something about this . . ." Arlene paused for a word. Perhaps "hovel" or "hole" came to mind, but what she finally settled on was "gloomy place." It is interesting that it is usually someone else's misfortune that appears as a disguised blessing to interested onlookers. Those suffering the misfortune usually fail to recognize the blessing so visited upon them. I had failed, certainly, to feel blessed by excrement on my walls and heirlooms in my toilet. I knew what Arlene meant. Ultimately she wanted more than new drapes and a coat or two of paint; she wanted walls removed and windows replaced and ceilings lowered. My stubborn streak prevailed. I would not even have accepted new drapes but for the fact that the old ones were not salvageable; but I picked out something as close to the others as I could.

"We even been up topside," says Charlaine, with an unexpected nautical term.

"Topside?"

"The third floor."

Ah, Old Levi's floor. "Whatever for?" I mutter in some apprehension.

"We warshed winders," says Nanny, "an' opened 'em up to air and we put bakin' soder all over de place."

"Baking soda?"

"It absorbs odors," says Charlaine. "That place is musty as all get out. Baking soda really does work; it'll clear a lot of those old odors away and maybe the rest of the house will smell better."

Old houses, I think but do not say for fear of hurting these two energetic women's feelings, are supposed to smell old. And *old* is a comfortable smell besides. All I actually say is a sort of noncommittal

"Ummm," and I head for my own rooms and the comfort of my tub and hot water.

But I pause on the landing and stare up the steep stairs at the unaccustomed light filtering down from "topside." Without thinking, I continue up the stairs and through the open door to Old Levi's rooms. As advertised, there are open boxes of baking soda all over the room and the windows are swung wide, admitting the warm and fresh early summer breeze.

Leaning out the window, I can almost touch the old laurel. Has it grown shorter? Probably not. Memory has given it a stature it probably never had. And the old rock beneath it, too. David and I used to play there as children—among the boughs and around the boulder. It seemed an exciting place then. Now it only seems forlorn. I glance back at the rooms, newly dusted (do I detect the odor of Endust?). They are much as I remember them. Only the light has indeed replaced some of the gloom. The bureau liner is freshly laundered and the doilies starched; even the old comforter folded neatly across the foot of the bed seems freshly shaken and plumped. It is an old down comforter, an antique, I suspect, for it was old and musty when I was young and Old Levi on cold mornings would throw it around his shoulders and wear it, like a hair shirt, through most of the day, padding from room to room and heater to heater. That was before Lee had the central heat and air conditioning installed.

I close the windows and draw the blinds. There is no need for someone to have to make another trip up these stairs tonight. I don't know about the baking soda. I leave the boxes as they are; it probably takes a long time for the baking soda to work its magic.

I stood thus in these rooms, how many years ago would it have been, the day that Old Daniel came with David to take me to the fair, and Levi and Daniel quarreled? Not fiercely, of course, but it was unusual enough to hear any disagreement in this house that I was awed, not frightened, simply impressed. I could not, I'm sure, have been over eight or nine years old, and David was about the same.

"Fairs are frivolous," Levi had complained, "frivolous and shoddy, with shabby people."

"Ah, not for children, Levi, not for children." Daniel had prevailed and we had gone to the fair. The Tulsa State Fair was a monumental community event then, and it still is. But I had never been, nor had David. I suppose we had begged, for the schools let out and the schoolchildren were given free tickets to go. David and I were always put off by not-nows and some-other-times. So it was with some surprise and delight that we greeted Old Daniel when he came into the room where we were playing and announced without preface that he would take us to the fair if we wanted.

David was as startled as I, for his father took him on no more excursions than my father took me. Just why this tall and stately old gentleman, who looked so out of place on the midway in his dark suit and square hat, impulsively took us to the fair that afternoon I'll never know, I suppose. It was my first visit and the last until I was old enough to go by myself, by which time I was easily bored, as I had set my sights on more worldly goals than the make-believe of the fair.

But when you're eight or nine years old, I wonder if there is anything more exciting than the fair. Old Daniel, a child clasped firmly in each hand, took us through the exhibition buildings and the barns. We viewed the livestock and watched chickens being hatched in an incubator. "Now, isn't that something?" murmured Old Daniel. "Isn't that something? You know, in all my life on a farm I don't think I ever saw that. Those old broody hens, you know, they always hid out with their eggs." He seemed quite as excited as we were. He talked for a long time, while David and I fidgeted, with the ranger at the conservation booth, and then he dragged us through the exhibits of quilts and jams and baked goods and prize watermelons. David and I wanted to see the industrial exhibits, the boats and cars and trailers, but Daniel was not interested; instead he paused overlong at the homemade quilts and the 4-H tables. Eventually we found the hot dogs and the lemonade and the games of chance and the rides that David and I longed for.

I would have ridden everything, even those rides that I couldn't qualify for, though I stood on tiptoe beside the sign that said that you must be at least so tall to ride a given ride. I did ride the Ferris wheel and the tilt-a-whirl and the bumper cars and the merry-go-round. David was more timid than I and clung to his father's hand and watched while I indulged in the more exciting rides.

"I went to the biggest fair there ever was," said Daniel at one point. "When I was your age, no, actually quite a bit older, I guess."

"Where was that?" asked David, who like me, I suppose, could not imagine any fair any greater than this one.

"The World's Fair in Chicago in '93. Ah, now that was a fair. The biggest Ferris wheel that ever was made. But I didn't ride it. I wish I had," he said with a trace of sadness. "I wish I could tell you that I was not afraid and I rode it. But I didn't. Ah, but Levi did. Your grandfather did, Elizabeth. But I was too fearful. I was fearful of high places. I still am, you know."

Excitement eventually gave way to weariness and we went home. Neither Lee nor Levi asked about the fair and I don't recall that Daniel ever took us, or even offered to take us, on any other outing. Thelma, his wife, sometimes took us to the movies and to Sunday school, but that was all.

I have not been to a fair for years. I don't remember the last time I went. Possibly I will never go to another fair. I see no reason to go.

"Charlaine's leavin'," calls Nanny from downstairs. Like an imperious dowager empress, she is ordering me to come and say goodbye to Charlaine. And like a dutiful subject I do, poking my head over the banister with good wishes and thank yous.

I make my way back to the sanctuary of my own rooms and the comfort they afford. The broken mirror has been replaced and I have a new line of designer bedding. Otherwise, things are as they have always been.

Violence has touched my life but briefly and mindlessly in the form of innocent children. It is ironic, I think. There is violence all around. I read about it in the newspaper and see it on television, and yet I personally am insulated from it. I never got very excited about Vietnam or Afghanistan or Beirut. Those atrocities had nothing to do with me. And closer to home, even, I am not touched by the casual violence of this small city. I read in the newspaper almost daily about this or that body, found by hunters in a shallow grave or no grave at all or sprawled between parked cars in a shopping center parking lot or floating in a creek, often unidentified or unidentifiable, sparrows fallen from the sky and let lie. Now and then there is some really dramatic act of violence that catches attention, for a day or two, before that, too, passes.

I know that these things happen. I know that there are people who deal routinely in violence and murder, those perpetrating the violence and those cleaning up after it. But it's not my job. I am not a part of it. I am sealed away in my black Lincoln or my paneled offices or my gloomy mansion. And it is ironic that the only violence that reaches me comes at the hands of small innocents, who, having viewed movies about poltergeists and assorted houses gone berserk, see the vandalizing of a spooky-looking old house as only a lark, the consequences of which will pass with the first commercial break.

I have seen one or two of those small hoodlums in the neighborhood and they have waved in a kind of camaraderie, as if we share some important experience. If there is any guilt, it doesn't show.

I have another appointment with Phoebe Ruskin, the genealogist, and I wonder bemusedly about this interest I seem to have developed (or is it Mrs. Ruskin who has developed it?) to delve into my history, to touch the past, when I am so out of touch with the present. Perhaps it is just that distancing that fascinates me, or perhaps it is only Mrs. Ruskin, who can be very forceful in matters genealogical.

I think, though, that in the main I view life as from a control booth, events going on all around me to which I contribute nothing. It is a sad thought for such a cheerful day.

When I was young, college age, I tried inexpertly to find the living and join them. That was what led me out the window after dark in my *Barefoot Contessa* period, when I fancied that I looked like Ava Gardner and brushed my eyebrows in a high arch and wore my peasant blouses down over my shoulders and a gardenia in my hair.

It was also that desire, to find a direction, that led me in college to the liberal arts crowd, particularly the English majors and the drama students whose lassitude I took for world-weariness and whose misdirection I read as despair. With the natural perversity of the young, I shunned those with whom I would eventually have the most in common—the business majors and the merchandising students and economics majors. It was the day of the coffeehouses and the Beatniks, and though I was never so young as to take either too seriously in the scheme of things, I did fall brief prey to the casual ennui and postured hopelessness of that crowd.

And it was Bradley, he of the disheveled long blond curls, lanky cynicism and weary slouch, whose lack of direction I mistook for sensitivity, who led me to his poets as the only salvation and to his bed as the only meaning. It was heady stuff for an eighteen-year-old heiress. Bradley never knew I was an heiress; I was not entirely foolish. If he had known, he probably would have stuck around longer than he did. I never really kept up with Bradley after we parted, only I know that he went from writing poetry to writing novels, thence to graduate school, and the last word I had of him he was an admissions officer in a small southern college.

In his one-room apartment, amid paperbacks and Modern Library editions, we consumed large quantities of cheap beer while he read me his poets. He barely tolerated my Edna St. Vincent Millay but led me instead to his Robinson Jeffers, whose blunt, sonorous and lengthy family sagas of violence and lust and incest were better suited to Bradley's dramatic flair than Millay's sonnetry, and seemed to lead, too, more readily to his couch, for at that point I began to abandon my *Barefoot Contessa* posture in favor of Jeffers's Loving Shepherdess, that dotty dame willing to lose her life for the relief of mankind's suffering sexuality.

Nor did Bradley ever realize, I think, that I came to him already deflowered, my promiscuity a secret, for some feminine instinct told me that these sensitive poets require the regular sacrifice of a virgin for the sustenance of their sensibilities. And it was indeed Bradley's requirement for virgins that led to the break when I was obviously no longer certifiably so. That was my only broken heart, and it mended quickly. I transferred to a college closer to home and finished out my degree among my peers in the business department.

Amid my designer bedding, I sit propped by pillows, struggling to keep my mind on the business at hand that these musings keep interrupting. I glare through my granny glasses at a distant mirror and see only a blurred picture. I cannot get used to these glasses; I cannot remember to look over them at distances. They irritate me. The whole idea irritates me, that my eyes should so suddenly give way on me. It is a natural consequence of having lived over four decades, I know. Lee wore his glasses on a chain and plunked them on his nose as needed, and Old Levi wore dime store glasses that he was forever putting on and taking off, pretending he didn't really need them. After he went peculiar, he sometimes affected an antique pair of opera glasses, particularly when he was going over business figures. I wonder where those glasses are?

My musings are again getting in the way of my work. I might as well put it away and take it back to the office, where I might be able to concentrate. This tendency to wander aimlessly down Memory Lane seems to be growing. It must have something to do with my advancing years. Sometimes I think it would be nice to have someone to discuss things with. But sharing my secrets has never been my inclination. I suppose I am a loner at best, secretive at worst. I have kept to myself, even with Dr. Harvey, that shrink of my adolescence.

It occurs to me that the only ones I might even consider talking to would be Nanny, who would likely prescribe Epsom salts or something similar for what was ailing me; or to Arlene, who would undoubtedly suggest a seminar on the middle years or a self-help group or would pull out this month's book on crises of the mid-years. What I probably need is a vacation.

When I appear at the office, Shirley is already at her desk. I am not late, nor is Shirley early. We have this arrangement perfectly timed, so that there is about five minutes between our arrivals.

"Shirley," I say, hardly pausing as I pass her desk on the way to my office, "I think I need a vacation. Hilton Head perhaps."

She will know what to do. She will check my calendar for the next few weeks, pick a convenient time, call my travel agent and let me know when I'm leaving and how long I'm staying.

In among the usual meetings and appointments, I am scheduled this morning to talk with David's Marci and I have an appointment with Mrs. Ruskin, the genealogist. Marci is after an interview for a paper she's writing for a class; I have the vague impression that it is some sort of women's studies course. I told her that I would be happy to be interviewed at home or over lunch or some such, but she insisted that she wanted to get the "feel" of my position. I take it that this is to be a very businesslike interview. I sigh. I have been so interviewed before. The newspapers, one or the other, every few years like to do a profile on the successful businesswoman. I think in all those inter-views—there must have been a dozen over the years—only one ever made it to the business page. The rest were featured for the women's pages or the Sunday magazine, among the articles about trained dogs and Houses of the Month.

Marci, as I greet her, I remember is a cute girl, taller than average, with her mother's brown eyes and David's pointed chin. Her person-ality did not come from either of those sources, I think. When last I saw her at Christmas dinner, she was dressed in a collegiate cliché. Today she is dressed in a businesswoman's cliché, blazer, skirt, shirt buttoned to the top and tied off with a small ribbon. She is "dressed for success." I think I like her better in jeans.

Today Marci is all business. Seated on the edge of a chair, she dispenses quickly with the small talk and gets right to the questions. Education, years in business, title. I notice that she does not ask age, and I ask her about it, anxious to be helpful. I am not sensitive about my age, I assure her.

"That's not it," says Marci. "That question is discriminatory, like religion or sex or race."

I notice a discrepancy but keep it to myself. Once she committed herself to write about a woman's success in a man's world, are not the discriminatory lines then moot? I do not press the issue.

Among the questions Marci asks, "Is there any single thing that a woman can do to rise to this management level?" It is a predictable question that requires a predictable answer, but I cannot help myself.

"The single most important step would be to inherit a department store."

Marci does not laugh.

"I mean," she says, "you certainly must have had to struggle, to battle the male establishment at some point?"

"Marci"—I am patient—"I have never battled for anything except, occasionally, my virginity." Again she fails to see the humor or at least ignores it.

"Well, you can't simply step into a top management position like this without encountering some difficulties, even if you did inherit the business."

I think Marci may be getting annoyed at my casual attitude toward her questions. At last I say, "In all seriousness, dear, I have fought no sexist battles. My father was a good manager, an excellent manager," I hear myself saying and am surprised to realize that it is true. "His father before him was an excellent manager. And I only just took full control of the business five years ago, when Lee retired. At that time I had been in the business a long time and I knew what I was doing. I was never hassled because: one, I was effective, and two, I was the boss's daughter. I have been immune, if sympathetic, to the plight of women in business."

"If you had married"—Marci tries a different tack—"would your husband then be the head of the business?"

"Ah, Marci, *if* is not relevant. It has no substantive meaning. What is substantive is that I am the head of this business and I make the decisions. Right now I am struggling to decide whether or not to close the business in downtown Shreveport and, if so, whether to move it to a shopping center and, if so, which one, or do I just junk the whole operation, which of late has been marginal at best? I will read reports and listen to counsel. I will order that studies be made and I will be advised on advisabilities, but in the end I will make that decision. And do you know how I'll make my decision?"

She does not.

"I will shake my head, frown and say something like, 'Oh, what the hell, I never did like Shreveport anyway: Let's pull out.' And before you decide that it's management by whim, let me hasten to tell you that it is not; it is management by training and instinct for business that I inherited from my father and grandfather, an instinct that my peers and my managers recognize and respect. I earned that respect, but not by doing sexist battle. I have been totally isolated from that struggle. I am, if you wish, asexual."

Marci looks vaguely troubled and I hastily ask, "You do have other women to interview, others who have had to struggle?"

She looks at her paper and goes through a list of names, a judge, a school administrator, a real estate broker, all names that I recognize and respect. I nod.

"I don't want to disappoint you, Marci, but the occupancy of this office has nothing to do with sex. It has to do with money. Money is the great equalizer, after all."

"Surely," says Marci with a determined and sincere wrinkle between her eyes, "you've had to do some battle, you've had to fight for what you wanted?"

I take the question as seriously as it is intended. To tell the truth, it's not something that I have ever thought about, at least on a conscious level. "No, Marci, I don't fight, I don't 'do battle.' I overcome a certain number of obstacles, but they are hardly battles."

"I don't understand."

"Unlike a battle, the outcome of one of my struggles is never in doubt. I will not lose. I will not lose because I do not go into confrontations. When I face a struggle, I find out what it will mean to the business, what I will need to get around the obstacle. I never go into that kind of situation unless I, one, know that I need to, and two, know that I can win. The cards are stacked in my favor. In a word, I do not fight for principles. In business such fights are usually not cost-efficient. If I face a corrupt building code, for instance, I must weigh my need against the cost involved. It's simply business."

"Do you ever"—and here Marci looks uncomfortable and slightly embarrassed—"battle for *anything?*" she asks at last. We have, I am sure, gone far afield from her original list of questions.

"I don't know, dear. I can't remember anything that I've actually 'done battle' over. Maybe your father and I, when we were small, probably we fought over toys. I'm sure we did, because we played together a lot."

"Don't you think that . . ." Here Marci sort of swallows her question, its only vestiges a concerned frown and a distant look in her brown eyes. I'm sure she had on the tip of her tongue some feminist question or other concerning my lack of commitment and then thought better of it. Good manners? Or perhaps the feeling that those clichés would ring uncomfortably hollow in these paneled and imposing rooms? Whatever her reason, I think well of her. Behind the youthful clichés that she affects is, I think, a bright and determined young person. I try to recall and then merely hope that she is the child of David and Arlene that I am godparent to.

"What do you plan to do with your life, Marci? Are you going to be a lawyer?" I am thinking of Old Daniel and David and thinking Marci perhaps more suited for following that tradition than Danny, her brother, who is only a vague memory of sweater and chinos and styled hair.

"Oh no. That's already a cliché. Women lawyers, they're so common. Every third woman in college plans to be a lawyer. I'm going into urban planning. That's the challenge of the future. Before I die I am convinced that we will have left traditional cities behind, that the megalopolis will be fact."

"And have you never thought of going into retailing? In a store like this, perhaps?"

Her tone is apologetic. "No, Elizabeth. This store isn't really"— here she pauses—"relevant, you know."

I didn't, I admit.

"I mean, it is not relevant to *need*. You deal in what people want, not what they need. You sell no necessities here. I want to deal in what people need, whether they know it or not."

The child has brought me up quite short. I think I ought to congratulate her, but I do not. I simply nod thoughtfully and she proceeds with her questions, predictably, and I, I answer them predictably. Then I do congratulate her for the thoroughness of her research. And she is pleased, I think, but more awkward and insecure than she thought she would be. We conclude the interview with small talk. I inquire after her family, her brother and her sister. They are well and busy, I am assured. Danny will be entering law school in the fall.

"And your sister"—I struggle for the name that escapes me for a brief moment—"Brooke. What are her plans?"

Marci only smiles and all but dismisses the question with a wave of her hand. "Brooke will be a sorority girl. A sorority girl forever."

"I didn't know that was possible."

"You didn't? Just look at my mother. What do you think she is? No, Brooke found her life's commitment when she pledged. She will spend her life planning pledge parties, attending alumnae functions, serving on boards, raising funds. In between she'll probably marry and raise a family. But mainly she'll just be a sorority sister. Now and forever, amen."

I laugh. Marci has suddenly relaxed, her blazer and tie giving way to jeans and shirt. I see her depart reluctantly. We have probably reached a point of communication, but time has run out and Shirley is buzzing me for Mrs. Ruskin, whom I have kept waiting as it is. I am going, I think, from the sublime to the ridiculous. That is an unkind thought, and then I remember that I am not held responsible for what I think, only for what I do or (I think of Marci) what I don't do.

Phoebe Ruskin, too, is all business, but she is not dressed in trendy blazer and tie but in a polyester pants suit, circa 1974, I think. My trained retailer's eye takes in that information almost unconsciously. The pants suit is a trifle small on Mrs. Ruskin, whether the fault of the woman or the suit I can only guess. "Stretch fabric does not shrink," a buyer told me once. "It just gets tighter when you wash it."

There is a fervor of mission about Mrs. Ruskin, that same fervor that I detected briefly in Marci. Mrs. Ruskin has accomplished something and she thinks it is important and she is anxious to get on with it.

"Your great-great-grandfather, Obediah Jonah Micah Murphy," she announces proudly, "was court-martialed during the Civil War." I am not exactly bowled over by this intelligence.

"Ah, that is good news," I say.

In her excitement Mrs. Ruskin misses the sarcasm. "He was not convicted," she adds in a tone of voice that suggests that there could be no doubt of that worthy's innocence, for Obediah has become a friend to her, he who is still only a nodding acquaintance to me.

"Why was he court-martialed?"

Mrs. Ruskin has been waiting for that. "Murder," she announces triumphantly.

"Well." I am a little startled. This is definitely not what one hires a genealogist to find out. The idea of Levi's grandfather being so accused gives sudden interest in what Mrs. Ruskin has to add.

"He was acquitted of that charge. I have this from the National

Archives. But all the information that I have is that one Obediah Murphy, Colonel with the 36th Illinois at Pea Ridge, was acquitted of murder, it being noted that the killing was accidental."

"Well." So the Old Bastard of Levi's history had killed someone. I try to focus on that ancestor; but all I come up with is a mental image of Old Levi himself in full uniform directing a slaughter as casually as he might have directed the placement of new merchandise. Without passion. A lack of passion seems to run in the family.

"That's the only information I got from the National Archives, that and the fact that Obediah was pensioned until 1903, the date of his death. I have written for War Department records, if they exist. The War Department, you know, was what is now the Defense Department." This I presume to be a trifle of information that I won't have to pay for. "As to his commission, there seems to be no record of it. I also," she adds with a smug smile, a little too casually, "have here a copy of his obituary I thought you might like to have."

I am pleasantly surprised and take what she offers eagerly, but it is only a photocopy. I am faintly disappointed. One can hardly laminate a photocopy; that would be redundant almost.

"And," says Mrs. Ruskin in a triumphant saving-the-best-for-the-last voice, "I have found *the old home place.*"

Home place? Mrs. Ruskin is beginning to sound like a distant relative.

"The Sears, Roebuck house. I swung through Tipeeho recently. I was in the vicinity, you see." How does anyone get in the vicinity of Tipeeho on purpose? It is nowhere—nor on the road to anywhere. "The house is unoccupied and has been let to run down something terrible. It is a shame. It's one of the few of its kind in the whole Southwest. I really think, Ms. Murphy, you ought to see if you can persuade the historical society to do something about it. They"—and here she paused to draw herself up and point an accusing finger at the offending, if absent, "they"—"are always eager to add something to *their* list without doing anything to see that the property is properly kept up."

Mrs. Ruskin, I already know from previous conversation, conducts a continuous campaign against the "theys" of this world, "theys" who refuse to fulfill obligations and are the single most common cause of the world's ills. "They" is a paranoid pronoun that serves a useful function, like a semicolon, keeping the accusations flowing without actually pressing charges. Without "theys" I fear that violence would be greater than it is. It is a safety valve that allows those disinclined to violence to vent their anger without fear of retaliation. Who, after all, is going to admit to being a "they"?

Mrs. Ruskin is obviously awaiting my comment. "Well, it is too bad, I suppose, but it really isn't possible to restore every old building. They—I use the term advisedly—do the best they can."

"Perhaps. I also," says Mrs. Ruskin, abruptly shifting conversational gears, "located the old graveyard and the four stones you spoke of." She pauses to await my reaction, which is a noncommittal "Oh." "It is one of those small cemeteries, plunked down in the middle of a field, still occasionally used. Some of them are well kept, some are not. Yours"—I smile at the "yours"—"is very well kept and the four stones are imposing, against the other stones especially. Most, I'm sure you know, are quite modest."

I do not know what to say, so I say nothing. I have not been in business these many years without learning something about people's actions. I know that Phoebe Ruskin has a pitch of some sort. I can tell it in the sudden hesitancy and the overlong pause.

Finally she says, "I am becoming quite fascinated, Ms. Murphy, with your history. I sincerely believe that we are going to unearth enough information here that we could do a full-length history."

"Oh?"

"What I have in mind is a book-length biography, history really, of the Murphys of Oklahoma, tying your family progress to the progress of the state. I have," she adds quickly, "a nephew who is a writer. With my research I believe he could put together a very readable book."

Phoebe Ruskin has blind-sided me. I am at a real loss. "I don't know, Mrs. Ruskin. It's not something that I have ever thought much about."

"Please. Just think about it. It's only an idea." She smiles, as if relieved to have got it said. "Give it some thought and we can talk about it another time."

The rest of my day's business is routine and only now and then do I give any thought to my two interviews, feeling quietly proud of pretty Marci's determination to save the world through urban planning and curiously interested in Phoebe Ruskin's surprising proposal. I find the idea more appealing than I would ever have thought, had I, of course, thought. Even so, I do not see success in such an enterprise. I do not think that, talented though Mrs. Ruskin is genealogically, there is enough information available. And there are certainly no photographs, those few having been lost to posterity more ignominiously than I would ever like to have to admit, much less to publish. And what is a history without dim and dreary pictures of stern-faced forebears?

It is, however, unsettling to think that though the Murphys have been an important part of Oklahoma history, certainly merchandising history, there is practically nothing, save a few legal documents, to base a biography on.

Perhaps it is such unsettling thoughts that encourage me to slip a cassette, Mozart, into the cassette player on the dashboard of the Lincoln on the way home. I only play music (or the radio or the television, for that matter) when I actually want to listen, not as a background for my routine activities. I find it difficult to concentrate when there is background noise. On this afternoon, with the temperature soaring as only it can in summertime Oklahoma, I am in the mood to absorb some Mozart. That's all. It is soothing to be isolated in my air-conditioned automobile, insulated from every sound save the Mozart.

I drift along the crowded Broken Arrow Expressway, oblivious of impatient and disgruntled fellow travelers, sweating and cursing in the slowed traffic. The cause of the slowdown, as expected, is an accident, a fender-bender from the looks of it, and though the two cars are off to the side of the expressway the traffic has slowed because everyone who passes wants to look.

The participants in this small drama look properly grim and angry. A young woman leans wearily against a fender of a small car, whose other fender has obviously been dislocated by the white Buick parked just ahead of it. Just which was at fault I could not say, but both drivers are arguing their cases vehemently to the patrolman on the scene. The pickup ahead of me slows almost to a stop, and one of the three bearded men in it leans out the window and yells something at the group, laughs and slaps the side of the pickup. Briefly the two drivers, for such I judge them to be anyway, glare at the pickup and one of them, young and shirtless, lifts his middle finger in salute at the departing pickup. The traffic in my lane picks up just as it slows abruptly in the next lane and the driver next to me, in an old-model Volkswagen, leans out the window to yell something angrily.

It is fascinating to watch. Though I am witness to the confusion and frustration, all I can hear are the comforting notes of an eighteenth-century musical genius. I can close my eyes and leave the rush-hour traffic of the Broken Arrow Expressway for the salon of the Archbishop of Salzburg. But not for long, lest I find myself bending a fender.

The trip home is slower than usual. Had I been listening to the radio, the ubiquitous helicopter traffic man might have been saying, "Traffic is backed up northbound on the Broken Arrow all the way from the on ramp at Sheridan to the Yale exit." It does not bother me, for I am in no hurry and I have lots of Mozart to keep me company.

The only problem I find with air conditioning is in getting from one air-conditioned spot to the next in the summertime. The walk from the garage to the house, a few short steps, is wilting, and the cool air rushing through the opened front door, welcome.

"Dat you, Elizabeth?"

I am taken with sudden apprehension. Nanny rarely calls me anything. Never has. She always called Lee "Mr. Murphy" and Old Levi "Old Mr. Murphy," but the only time she calls me anything is when she is angry or upset, and then she calls me by my first name with the accent on the last syllable as if those other syllables are only a prelude to the important part of the name.

"Yes, Nanny?"

Nanny appears from the back of the house. Her expression is angry. And like a guilty child I immediately wonder what I've done wrong. You never know how Nanny will react when she's angry. Sometimes she sulks and sometimes she shouts. But when she says "Elizabeth" I know she's not sulking. I brace myself.

"Dey're goin to take Leroy and Charlaine's house away from 'em. It ain't fair. Dey do just what dey wants. It ain't fair. Leroy and Charlaine, dey worked hard for dat house. Dey take good care of it. Dey ain't got no right to take it, but dey don' care, dey're goin' to do it anyhow."

"Wait a minute, Nanny. What are you talking about? Leroy's house is paid for. It belongs to him."

"I know it. But dey're goin' to take it anyhow."

"Who, Nanny? Who?"

"I don' know. Dem. De city, de state, de county, de Republicans. I don' know just who. Dey're goin to make it into a freeway."

Ah. That ubiquitous "they" again. I never cease to wonder at all the trouble "they" cause. "You mean Leroy's property is being condemned for an expressway?"

"Yeah, an' you got to do somethin' about it. You got to get it stopped 'cause Leroy, he say he goin' to shoot de first sonovabitch dat tries to take his property. Us colored people don' have a chance. Dey're always after us. Leroy took good care of dat property. You know he does. How come dey can take it away from him?"

"Nanny, slow down. When did you hear about this?"

"Jes' today Leroy got a letter. It said he had to go to a hearing about it. Said dat his property was part of de right-of-way for de proposed expressway. Dey're goin to take his house away from him. Elizabeth, how come progress always goes right through colored town? Goes right through but don' never stop?"

Succinctly put, Nanny, succinctly put, I think. What I say is "Take it easy, Nanny. I'll look into it. Remember, these things take years and often as not fall through, anyway. There are always condemnation proceedings. It's routine. But I'll have Mr. St. Cloud look into it."

"Well, you better hurry, 'cause Leroy, he shootin' mad."

"Ah, Nanny, Nanny, patience. Call Leroy and tell him to calm down and be patient."

"Patient! Ha! Patient! Patient is what people in hospitals is. Patient and sick. Patient won't do nothin' but bury you dead in the ground."

"Now, Nanny—"

"Patient, Elizabeth. You ain't patient. That's not what you is. You just takes your time, 'cause you got nothin' to lose. Dat ain't patient, dat's cunning. Us coloreds ain't got no time. Patient is what de Lord meant when He said dat de meek would 'herit de earth. You what earth He meant? He meant de earth dat you buried in and rot in, dat's what!"

Nanny storms from the room. She is a very wise old woman. She knows that it's always best to quit an argument when you have made your most telling point. "Colored." It is an archaic term, an unpopular term, yet Nanny sticks with it. Not because of habit, but to say "black" would negate her red blood. She says colored because she claims two colors, not one.

Well, between the heat and Nanny's tantrum, my Mozart has been lost. And before I have any peace I will have to settle with Nanny. I put in a call to David, who is still in his office. It does not surprise me. David routinely goes to work early and stays late.

David tells me pretty much what I expected him to. He does not exactly sigh out loud, but his overlong pause when I tell him the problem suggests that he wonders why I bother him with such a matter, why I bother myself with it. Nothing, he assures me, is likely to come of it. It is like a summons to jury duty. Hardly more serious.

That expressway has been on the drawing board for years, a part of the city's master plan, but though some right-of-way has been acquired for it, the chances of its ever being completed are slim at best. Leroy, he assures me, has nothing but time on his side. He counsels patience. I do not tell him that that suggestion has already not been favorably received, and I thank him and suggest that if he gets a chance he might look further into the matter. We leave it there, with a few pleasantries. For some reason I do not tell him about the visit I had with his older daughter earlier. I consider Marci's urban planning and briefly wonder if that kind of progress is the kind that Nanny had reference to, the kind that runs right through colored town without ever stopping.

Driving along the expressway, just Mozart and me, I had visions of a refreshing long-stemmed glass of white wine at journey's end, wine and more Mozart. That tranquillity now shattered, my expectations are more modest. I go in search of a bottle of beer. There is usually beer around the house. Nanny drinks it, and so does Leroy when he's around.

I find Nanny in the kitchen, staring morosely out the window in the breakfast nook. Before I can pass on David's counsel, she turns toward me and says wearily, "I worry about dat boy, Elizabeth. He got a temper, you know dat." I recall Leroy and Charlaine's frequent battles. "He start fightin' or shootin' dem government people, no tellin' what happen."

"Now, Nan—"

"He minds me so much of my cousin Joab. An' you remember what dey done to him?" I do, but that doesn't keep Nanny from telling me again. "Dey taken him out and shot him. Shot him an' den burned him up. Dat's what dey done."

It had been during the race riot of 1921 that unfortunate young Joab had been killed. Those riots, sparked by a minor incident, as such things so often are, a black man accused of getting fresh with a white woman in an elevator, is a fading scar across the history of this young city. The subject used to come up with some regularity, but I have not heard anything about that event in quite a while, now that I think of it. Perhaps that hair shirt has worn thin.

After three days of rioting, looting and burning, "colored" town was leveled and the dead and missing numbered in the hundreds, among them Nanny's cousin Joab.

"He jis' wen' off to work one day an' he never come back. He was a good boy. He laughed and he joked and I guess dat was his fault, I don' know, dat he never knowed when to keep his mouth shut. But he wen' off an' we never heard from him to dis day. But dey tol' us dat three white men grabbed him up an' taken him out an' shot him an' den dey dumped him in a house an' piled mattresses on top an' set dem a-far like dey done so many of our houses dat week. Dey tol' us dat. My mama and her sister, my Aint Clarice, dey wen' out lookin' fer him, wasn't safe fer dem but it was a sight safer fer two old wemin dan fer de men to go. But dey never found a trace a him. Dey tol' my Aint Rachel, Joab's mama, dat he got away, dat he run away down to Muskogee like a lots a folks done. An' den dey tol' her dat he been seen in Kansas City an' dat he was comin' home when it was safe. She knowed better, a course. She knowed. But she pretended she believed 'em. An' so we all lied to one another about it. Aint Rachel and Mama and Aint Clarice, dey all went to dere graves storyin' like dat. I think maybe dey tol' it so often dey 'mos believe it."

"Now, Nanny, don't worry. This isn't 1921 and nothing like that is going to happen again."

"It ain't, Elizabeth! It ain't! What's wrong with you, girl? Don' talk Martin Luther King to me. Don' talk civil rights to me. I know. I know. It might be nice and smooth on de top but dere's terror down underneath. Dere's still terror dere, an' when it goes off, it ain't goin to be smooth on top no more!"

I know what Nanny means. The potential is still there. It probably always will be, in one form or another, race or religion or nationality or whatever difference demagoguery can accuse. It will not happen? What I mean is that it has never happened to me. I have no experience of it. I don't ever expect to have any experience of bareboned violence. Consequently I don't expect it to happen to anyone I know.

"An' Leroy, he 'minds me so much of Joab."

I have heard Nanny's story three or four times before, but this is the first mention I have heard of any resemblance in any way between Joab and Leroy. It is a resemblance, I think, that Nanny wants to draw. Memory, I think, is unreliable at best; at worst, it is as two-faced as a nosy neighbor.

I am insulated from race riots as I am from all other violence; it has not touched me. Nor, apparently, did it touch Levi and Lee, though they lived through the same period as Nanny.

I asked Lee about the riots of 1921 one time after Nanny had been talking of them. I asked him what he remembered of them. He only looked vague. "There was some such disturbance, I think, sometime after the First World War. *They* fought, the Negroes and the whites. I don't remember it much. I was not involved."

Old Levi said much the same thing when I asked him once; I was in elementary school doing a report about the Glenn Pool, that monumental oil strike which brought instant wealth to this territory. "Yes," he said, "*they* brought it in quietly, without fanfare. I was not involved." And I asked him about statehood and the ensuing celebration and he murmured distractedly, "Yes, I suppose, yes, I think *they* made quite a todo over it. I don't recall the details."

Is the vote in? And do the I's have it? Probably not. It looks more like the Theys have it.

It is later that night, Nanny retired to commune with NBC, that I sit at my tiny secretary—it is far too dainty and delicate a thing for serious use, but it has been in the family a long time, I've been told— and compose a letter. I write it by hand on stationery I generally reserve for notes of congratulation or bereavement. I address it to the State Historical Society in Oklahoma City and I begin:

> Dear Sirs,
> It has come to my attention that a landmark on your 1966 list of historical old homes has fallen into serious disrepair and . . .

EIGHT

LEVI'S FALL

*T*he letter that I wrote to Daniel informing him of my marriage was a masterwork of dissembling made simple because he had never actually informed me of the seriousness of his intentions toward Betty, which name I had replaced with *Elizabeth*, the better to distance her from her previous history. Had I been able to name her entirely anew I would have done that. She would have become my Daphne, my Penelope, my Ophelia, detached completely from past or future.

Had Daniel previously declared his intentions to me concerning the maiden, I would have stood accused, guilty of bad faith at the least, treachery at the worst. But he had not, and so I could write innocently, "I was ever so relieved to find that you and Elizabeth had no understanding, for I postponed my own suit because I feared that such was the case. You afforded me quite some agitation upon the matter, old man. For shame!"

What perversity caused me to add that last, that subordinating appellation, "old man," I could not say. Daniel had been severely injured by my deceit already; there was no call for insult to be added to it. I would like to say that I was shamed at my own actions; but the truth was that I was not. I posted the letter light of heart and without afterthought. It was accomplished and my grief and my agony and my suffering quitted me, as the fog the low-lying areas with the coming of the morning sun.

Elizabeth and I were married in a brief ceremony attended only by the minister and his wife, who presided over the organ, and by Mrs. Brady and Louisa Three, carefully buttoned and brushed for the affair. And thus the Sears, Roebuck house, which had already witnessed three funerals, was privy to its first wedding, and I assumed, in short order, its first birth.

Elizabeth did not invite her family, which consisted of two older sisters, both married, and three brothers, as well as her father. She later wrote them only that she had married "of late," but as her health remained fragile, she would put off the introduction of the groom until spring. Mercifully, Mrs. Brady could not write but sent her best wishes by Elizabeth, and by the time the lady realized just what her niece's symptoms were prelude to, that good soul would most likely abet any necessary dissembling. So common, indeed, was that occurrence on the frontier that there was a saying to match it, that "the first baby can come anytime, but all the others take nine months." Besides, though she might be confused by it, and possibly uncertain of the event's propriety, Mrs. Brady had at last all that she wanted: her beloved niece would not be forced to return to the hard life of the country, to be prematurely aged by too much work and too many births.

Since Mrs. Brady was now classified as a relative, it became necessary that I secure the services of another woman for the more taxing of household chores, freeing my newly acquired aunt to be companion to my mother and, though she did not yet know it, to function as nurse for the infant that Elizabeth would too soon deliver.

Daniel eventually returned my letter with only feeble wishes of "felicity" for my newly married state and best wishes to my bride. He wrote at length about his examinations, which by then he had passed, and informed me that he had accepted a quite promising position with a law firm in St. Louis and that he would no longer need the moneys that I regularly sent him and would, indeed, be in position shortly to begin repaying those advances I had heretofore made him. He would not, he wrote, have the necessary time to visit with us at Christmas, as he had planned, and hoped that we would have a happy one without him. His letter was signed simply, Daniel Cloud. He seemed to have lost his "St."

I was not in the least hesitant in claiming my husband's prerogatives, nor my bride in affording them. Indeed, she acquiesced readily, even eagerly, to my attentions, and my own instincts in such matters proved sound. It would be hard to imagine any man ever so content as I was. I realized that my bride's responsiveness to my caresses might amount to still more dissembling on her part, an anxiety to assuage any suspicions I might later entertain when her condition became apparent or even an imagining in the dark under the gentle pressure of my body that she was being ridden into ecstasy not by a hastily acquired husband but by the lover of her dreams. It did not matter. I had my prize and I would not damage it with second guesses.

The first frost was upon us and we lay warm each night making love beneath a goose down comforter from Old Louisa's needle, the last, indeed, that ever she made. She had been talented with her needle and with the plucking of down and had made several such comforters, though this was smaller than most, as she had run out of down and patience at about the same time and had pronounced it done and herself through with the making of comforters. In truth it was the rheumatic condition of her fingers that ended any serious needlework, though she would never admit to it, only declaring abruptly that down comforters were both tedious for the seamstress and an imposition for the goose.

It did not matter. I would have been comfortable had the comforter been twice again as small, for I was warmed to overheating by the frail form that lay beneath my searching caress fluttering like a bird held in the palm, feathers no longer disguising its fragile and delicate substance. So was my beauty, and I held her, stroking, caressing, searching, discovering minute by minute, even, the secrets of that other sex, secrets that hold men in such splendid thrall. And I imagined with each passing day that I could detect the swell of those tiny breasts, they that grew hard to my touch, hardly when I had first beheld them more than twin rises on an otherwise flat and barren landscape.

That that perfect form would soon swell with another man's bastard and that my own days of manly pleasure were so numbered only added intensity to my desires. I did not look down that distant road; I did not think, consider, what would happen once that babe was born and my love would again be receptive to seed, my own tainted seed. If I thought at all, it was only a vague and distant dream of barrenness on her part, if not extended celibacy on my own part. As it was, I took what was mine, what deceit and treachery had bought, without remorse or apprehension.

The bastard who would carry Obediah Murphy's name into the ages would not carry his blood. And in my own mind the end truly justified the means. *The bastard is dead! Long live the bastard!* Ha! Nor did it matter one whit that only I was privy to this plot and that only I would ever know that it had been accomplished. It was enough. I had the will, and that will would lift the burden of my dark heritage from me.

It was shortly before Christmas that we became aware that something was amiss with Louisa Three, that she was failing in some inexplicable way. That the confusion of a confused mind can grow more so had hardly entered our minds, so that Louisa had become quite distracted before the realization struck us that something was more profoundly wrong than was usual. She paused confused in mid-step, looking bewildered, as though she did not know where she was or where she was going, or wandered out the door and down the road without coat or bonnet, on her way to some unrealized destination. She stared straight ahead for hours and forgot the struggle with her buttons.

It was Mrs. Brady who at last approached me with the suggestion that something was definitely wrong with my mother, that her weight was down alarmingly, and her manner most profoundly disturbed, though "disturbed" hardly seemed the proper word for one whose movement had slowed by then to almost none.

Seated at the table, Louisa might stare all but unseeing at her plate of food, until Mrs. Brady gently lifted her fork for her, and finally spoon-fed her like a baby, urging her to chew and to swallow, a time-consuming process that only seemed to befuddle her.

The doctor we called in to examine her at last only shook his head and murmured, "Too bad, too bad. She is," he explained, putting away what few instruments of his trade he had used, "forgetting."

"Forgetting?"

"Her entire disease has been, I think, a kind of forgetting. The first shock, probably when she was quite young and due to a sudden illness, was a trauma of forgetting, forgetting on a conscious level, speech and concentration and learning abilities. She has deteriorated, slowly I'm sure, so slowly that no one was really aware of it, losing first subconscious memory and finally motor memory. She is forgetting everything, even basic reflexes. She is forgetting how to eat, to swallow, and eventually, if some infection does not take her first, she will simply forget to breathe. It is," he added, "not a common disorder, but neither is it entirely unknown."

It is perhaps merciful that such an infection did indeed take the third Louisa before her suffering, as well as our own, could become acute. She contracted a fever, which rose alarmingly, and Mrs. Brady put her to bed and watched over her with as much solicitude as if she were her own child. Louisa clung to life for several days, and that dear soul Mrs. Brady hardly left her bedside, comforting, soothing, wiping her heated forehead and coaxing broth through reluctant lips; and through each night Mrs. Brady, Elizabeth and I shared the watch, though it was Mrs. Brady who insisted upon those long and tedious hours from midnight to dawn. Waking and dozing, she kept that lonely vigil until one morning she started awake to find that Louisa's spirit had slipped away, freed at last from the useless prison that an accident of nature had condemned it to.

We buried my mother a day later in the small graveyard that housed Obediah and the other two Louisas. And so the Old Bastard had gathered at last all his women to this forlorn seraglio.

Elizabeth, my wife, stood beside me, her hand resting lightly on my arm. "I'm so sorry, dear Levi," she said.

"If there is earthly entrance to hell," I murmured, "it is surely on this plot of ground."

"Shush, my dear," she whispered, "shush," mistaking my meaning, I'm sure, for grief rather than for the rage it was. I paused briefly at each grave and introduced my Elizabeth to my forebears.

"We are a family of bastards," I announced abruptly to my wife, and indeed I'm sure that she had already ascertained that intelligence at least to some degree, for all she said was "And then you do not know your own father, he who fathered you?"

I explained briefly that I had been got upon Louisa Three sometime after the onset of her disability, the offspring, my grandfather had insisted, of a passing Jew peddler. That was all I would tell. No more.

Elizabeth was, of course, properly incensed. "That anyone would so abuse someone in her condition," she began, but I stopped her with a smile.

"Had he not, I suppose, I should not myself be here at this moment, nor should I ever have known the pleasure that the last few months have afforded me." And I truly meant it. Though there had been a time that I would gladly have ceased my existence, been happy indeed, to have never existed at all, these few months of stolen pleasure I would never willingly give up. The irony of it was that I had not a venal passing peddler to thank but the wicked Obediah.

We rode the buggy home over the roads rutted from freezing and thawing, but mercifully dry. The horse stepped carefully, for he was well trained and knew his business, but even so the vehicle jarred and bumped and I was concerned for the fragile one at my side and for the burden she carried. And I pondered again, as I had of late, that perhaps I might look into the purchase of a horseless vehicle one day, a vehicle that might move with less disaffection over these rutted roads than the horse-drawn carriage did.

We sat, the two of us, before the small fire on the hearth in that lonely silence that any death begets, she resting quietly within the circle of my arm. "My own mother died," Elizabeth said at last, "when I was small, so small that I hardly remember. My two sisters by turns raised me, and my father. My father is a good man, but stern. But when I lay ill with the fever he sat every night beside my bed, and when I would wake in the night I would see him there, watching or sometimes dozing, until at last I began to mend. His patience"—she smiled—"would hardly go further. He did not understand convalescence and pronounced me 'spoiled.'"

Such obtuseness I found difficult to understand, for if there was anything that my love was not, it was spoiled. Nor, by contrast, was she in any way obsequious. Excluding that one moment of weakness, bred by anxiety and rejection, she had been nothing if not straightforward and honest in her dealings with me.

"My father," she repeated, "is a good man, an honorable man, and thus I was raised. 'A man,' he said, 'must always do what he is supposed to do the way he is supposed to do it; neither more nor less. Any debt,' he would say, 'is an honest debt to be repaid with interest.' It is how I was taught and it is what I respect." She said the last without self-consciousness, and if she were thinking of her own debt to me, I could not tell. I was certain, however, even if affection should not grow and take its side next to respect, she would still not consider her debt to me discharged during her lifetime.

And myself, I even began to consider such attitude on her part justified. Perversely, I congratulated myself on my own nobility in taking on another's bastard to raise, quite ignoring my own deceit in the matter.

Elizabeth took on the management of the household cheerfully and competently, insomuch as her health permitted, for she was still weak, weaker than most women approaching confinement, I thought. And as her condition had got beyond the stage of conjecture, she and Mrs. Brady began making overt plans for the coming event. Nor did Elizabeth exhibit any of the simpering and giddishness that one associates with primigravidas but came to me and announced abruptly that she was with child. I myself feigned surprise and delight at the coming event, which she and Mrs. Brady had set at late summer, I myself assuming late spring to be more accurate. It was a disparity that we could discharge, I was certain, after the fact.

As days and weeks went by, I began to detect a certain change in Elizabeth, as if a weight had been lifted, a lightening of her spirit and a more playful attitude, more resembling her attitude toward Daniel months earlier. It was when she spoke, as she did with more intimate frequency, of the coming of her child, almost as if she had come to believe herself that it was I, not Daniel, who had fathered the child. And, indeed, my anticipation of that blessed event began to be such that I myself almost believed it, believed that I had in some miraculous way fathered the child, without passing to it any of the dark blood that was Obediah's.

It was a curious sort of euphoria, for I knew in my mind that it was not so, but my heart rejected that intelligence. I was as happy as any man ever was in anticipating the birth of his first child, and our household, though nominally in mourning, became ever more cheerful as February gave way to March and spring and winter commingled as they do in that month, winter, of course, eventually succumbing to the blandishments of spring.

As such is often the case, with the coming of spring I shucked off the comfortable winter lassitude in the face of new resolve. Nor was it a new thought to me that spring is more the time of resolution than the first day of January that we traditionally set aside for that purpose. Indeed, I had pondered on other such occasions that New Year's Day and April Fools' Day might most reasonably be exchanged, the bitterness of January more appropriate for fools than the freshness of April.

My own new resolve came slowly, that I, having a family now to provide for, had best consolidate my holdings at last and set a course for the future. Nor did I see that this small community would serve that future. When Obediah Murphy first settled, he had proclaimed it the New Jerusalem (for Obediah was nothing if not expansive). But the New Jerusalem was fading fast and cracking at the mortar. What had been a few years earlier a promising metropolis was suffering from competition from cities to the south, particularly Tulsa, Red Fork, Sapulpa, adjacent communities that straddled Creek, Cherokee and Osage nations and sat upon the banks of a great waterway, or at least the greatest that this territory could provide.

I spoke to Elizabeth, consulting with her about my thoughts, for I had found her instincts in such matters fine and her questions (for questions were all she had, she being both young and inexperienced) probing and to the point. She was hesitant concerning any great change of situation, which was of course understandable.

"But, Levi," she said, "it certainly won't hurt for you to investigate. I know nothing of business matters, but I am willing to learn and I certainly trust your judgment in these things. Do make some inquiries and then let us discuss it further." I could not have made a wiser disposition of argument myself.

It was on the strength of these discussions that I sent out such letters of inquiry, to Tulsa, to Guthrie, to Kansas City and even to Chicago. There was no need for haste, and I felt any substantial change would needs be leisurely.

And then Mrs. Brady died.

Elizabeth came to me midmorning one day in late March and said that her aunt was not feeling well and had lain down and probably would not join us for dinner. We had no way of knowing that indeed that dear lady already lay dead in her room, the victim of that sudden death which now and then so unexpectedly takes people yet in their prime. So it was with Elizabeth Brady. She had apparently closed her eyes to rest and so was gone. And mourning, like a vindictive storm, struck once more the house that Sears, Roebuck built.

"I do not believe," I told Elizabeth after we had at last laid Mrs. Brady to final rest, "that we should say in this house any longer than necessary. I think it bodes ill and that our future lies elsewhere."

"Ah, Levi," she smiled, gently chiding, "and do you believe, then, in spirits?"

I thought about it for a minute. "Perhaps. Ghosts? Yes, perhaps. Not substantial ghosts, those that rattle chains and cast ghastly light in the dark. But the ghosts of memory, those spirits that rise out of one's own darkness, they are very real, real at least in their ability to unsettle. I would not, in a word, be comfortable in a place which housed so many of those kinds of memories."

She nodded slightly and lowered herself into a chair. I noted that there were puffy circles beneath her eyes and that she breathed hard at slight exertion. Motherhood compounded by grief, I supposed. That she were not bedridden was amazing, for she had indeed absorbed a great many shocks in the past several months.

I had already made up my mind to travel to Tulsa, my inquiries having substantiated my belief in the potential of that location. I had made several contacts of a business nature and was beginning to be excited at the prospects.

And so I left Elizabeth in the care of Inez, the black woman who had joined the household when Mrs. Brady had been elevated to in-law and who now bore the burden for most of the household chores, and I set out for Tulsa, driving my carriage, with a view toward spending several days and possibly a week or two scouting around that city in search of a favorable business climate. Though I was not normally precipitate of nature, I had very nearly made up my mind to move my small family, or what would soon be my small family, and this ambitious young city seemed promising indeed for such a venture.

I registered myself for lodgings at the Brady Hotel, one of the several new buildings in this small city, growing awkwardly and rapidly as a gangling boy; and though the Brady was not so commodious as those hotels I had visited in Chicago and St. Louis and Kansas City, it was certainly some improvement over what had been here the past few times that I had visited. This sleepy village had come suddenly to life with the bringing in of a substantial oil deposit on Dr. Bland's farm near Red Fork, and the ensuing publicity had brought fortune hunters aplenty from all over the world, much as the announcement of gold in the Klondike had done for the far North some years back.

It was this precipitateness that mainly bothered me in my search for a settling place; for I did not want to be a part of a stampede that would pass anon, rendering all else transient as well. I would have serious discussions with the men of prominence here, and I would have figures, not boosterism, for this small city boasted a booster club quite out of proportion to its size and wealth. Indeed a booster train, coaches and freight, was already planned for a trip across half the continent eastward to bring news of this city to that crowded and jaded area and urge the settlement of business and industry in the new West. That booster trip had already been much publicized and substantial plans for its implementation had been made. And that was all to the good and showed a certain determination on the part of the city fathers; still I needed more than unsubstantiated promises to lure me here.

After my evening meal, I took myself around the community to pass the time until dark, for I was not a tippler, nor did I enjoy the boisterous and smoky confusion of the hotel lobby after dinner, though I had been informed that it was in such places that the real business of the oil boom was conducted. My pilgrimage took me down new streets, dusty and unpaved, but with new buildings of all sorts springing up. The orchards and gardens that had once made the distance between dwellings and businesses seem great were mostly gone, and the population, which had swelled to nearly five times what it was before the oil well in Red Fork, was set at something over six thousand souls, an immense growth in four or five years, it seemed to me. And though I had doubted it some when the desk clerk at the Brady had bragged of it, I found it easier to believe as I walked the streets and noted the people still abroad after the dinner hour.

There were, the desk clerk had informed me, serious plans afoot for paving of the main streets, though the management of the Brady would settle for simply oiling the dusty street in front of the establishment; and in addition, I was informed, a bridge had opened the year before, the first bridge across the Arkansas River, linking the oil fields (for such was called that still largely undeveloped but promising area) on the western side of the river to the city on the eastern side. As I had strolled quite far to the south, by the time I started north again it was growing dark and I hurried some, for I did not want to find myself too far abroad after dark, for a city that booms has generally more than a fair share of unsavory denizens.

On approaching the center of the city I was startled by a sudden rush of flame leaping skyward in a jet. I thought at first that some great fire had broken out, but quickly realized that the flame in question was somehow controlled, as if it had been turned on. And as I rounded a corner, I saw that that was indeed the case, that a natural gas well stood on the outskirts of the business area and it had been lighted and was being tended by a jovial group of men. It was an impressive sight, the flames shooting skyward, held in check only by their own consuming greed, greed which devoured that very fuel which would propel them farther. It is difficult not to be awed by natural forces, floods and flames and great winds, to be mesmerized by their very ferocity and the potential destruction that they represent; and so one might stand for hours staring at rolling floodwaters, entranced by the power of nature gone berserk. So I stood staring at that great flame clawing at the sky, and I knew that, given its head, such flame wanted nothing more than to devour everything, even itself, in its own greed. I was not of a philosophical bent, however, and I let the thought pass.

In its place a memory grew, uncomfortable as an elusive itch, until at last it came to me: the great fair in Chicago in '93. The World's Fair that the Old Bastard had taken us to, Daniel and me, had insisted in the face of One's reluctance and Two's open hostility to the idea, had insisted that it was his duty to see us to that fair, there probably never being another so grand in our lifetimes. And thus we journeyed to Chicago. As we were living at that time in the southern part of the state of Illinois, it was not a difficult train trip on the Illinois Central. Such a flame had greeted our first view of that event, a torch they called it. I had been both awed and frightened by the magnitude of such display, and Obediah, too, for he removed his hat as if in the presence of flag or death. Daniel did not seem so overwhelmed but complained only that he was hungry and he wanted spun sugar and lemonade.

As the memory faded, so, too, did the flame, for the group of men, who had apparently been charged with its maintenance, shut the thing down. I could not but wonder if it were symbolic of the transitory nature of this community as that other flame had been of the great exposition of '93. It was a thought that carried me back to the Brady and so to sleep.

The next morning after breakfast I took myself to the Bank of Commerce to meet with a Mr. Tremble, with whom I had had some correspondence. I was met very cordially by that man, affable yet intense in his desire to persuade me of the merits of locating in this young community. He, of course, knew that I was a man of some means and that I wanted long-term investments, that I was not, as many of the city's newcomers were, interested in a rainbow's pot that they saw in the coming oil boom. And it was with such long-term goals that Mr. Tremble regaled me, the promise of a great city and the advantages of being a founder of that city.

"It is rare indeed, Mr. Murphy," he said, "that a man has the opportunity to found a city, and rarer still to found a city based on a new industry, unknown in all history, and that in a new century and in a new state."

I nodded my agreement, thinking that though his point might not necessarily be sound business, it was certainly sound metaphor.

"Oil," he went on, "will be the basis of this new century, as well as natural gas and electricity. Fortunes have already been made and more are to be made, you may be sure, in oil and in the maintenance of that oil economy. It will not be like silver and gold strikes, spectacular for a few months at best, until the easy money has all been got. Getting oil from the ground is hard work, long and tedious work, and not a pastime for amateurs but for professionals who know their business. And those professionals say that the oil is here and will be many years in the exploring and developing. I will," he said, "introduce you to other businessmen, members of the Commercial Club, those who have made long-term investments in the future of this city. We do not"—he smiled and rapped his knuckles against the desk—"intend to see our investments vanish."

"I would not think so," I murmured.

"You have heard of the booster trip planned for this spring?" he asked, and I nodded. Indeed, that trip had been greatly publicized. "That is just one of our projects; we have many more—hotels in particular, transportation, paved streets and motor cars, many, many more motor cars, for oil represents an inexpensive fuel for those contraptions," he said, "and our future is directly linked with them. But we need other industry. No matter how powerful, a single industry can never be the basis of the thriving metropolis that we envision.

"And so, Mr. Murphy, the choice is yours. There's real estate or livestock to invest in, or business, retail, wholesale, insurance, transportation. You may even invest in oil. Eventually most everyone does to some greater or lesser degree. It is a candy store with all bins wide open. You have but to select."

Mr. Tremble was a persuasive gentleman. He truly believed, I was certain, everything he was telling me, and as we walked to our noon meal he paused here and there to point out a new building, a proposed expansion, to extoll the virtues of the new station house and note the substantial nature of the buildings in progress, also to introduce me to various business and professional men on our route. I was greeted by those with great courtesy and genuine enthusiasm when Mr. Tremble would remark in one way or another that "Mr. Murphy is interested in investing in the future of our town." I could not fail to be impressed by the excitement projected, to a man, in that "future" to which Mr. Tremble was fond of referring.

After we had eaten and Mr. Tremble had talked on and on of the merits of this location and its exciting future, we returned once again to his bank, a new and substantial building in its own right, and there Mr. Tremble turned me over to a young man, Otis Wheeler by name, for a further reconnaissance.

"I am not," apologized Mr. Tremble, "I fear, up to the kind of expedition that is necessary. Otis will have to function as my legs for me, and he is very astute as to real estate, Mr. Murphy. He won't lead you astray."

The young man in question (in truth, I think, not younger than myself by many years, though my seriousness of purpose made me seem older by decades next to his affable and buoyant spirit) was ruddy and round-faced and had the look of a farm boy even in his high collar and vested suit.

He affirmed that impression by admitting, "I am a native, Mr. Murphy. I know this land well. I was raised south of here in a sod hut, and not many can make that claim this day and age. Except for the red men, almost everyone here comes from somewhere else, most hoping for easy money in oil. I am," he said, turning a serious and somewhat pompous visage toward me, "in real estate myself. Mr. Tremble and his directors, they rely on my advice. Real estate is where the wise will invest, Mr. Murphy. With no land, you know, you get no oil."

Otis, whose legs were as strong as promised, led me on a circuitous route about the city, dropping anecdotes as he went. "A cowboy come in here from Wyoming. Got off the train and saw a hack awaiting. The sign on the hack said: 'Fifty cents for any part of town.' Said the cowboy, 'Well now, that's a bargain I cain't hardly to pass up.' And he pulled out a four-bit piece and said, 'I'll take the northwest part.'" Otis laughed out loud and, hardly waiting for any expression of mirth on my part, went on, "That was his mistake, you know. It's the southeast that's to grow, I think."

"Over there," said Otis, as we passed a building of brick and mortar under construction, "over there, that lot, a feller paid twenty-five dollars for it just a few years back. And within the year he sold it for fifty dollars and bragged all over town about the killin' he made. That lot, now, even without the buildin' you couldn't have for a hundred times that amount. I wonder what that feller thinks of his killin' now?"

Such were Otis Wheeler's anecdotes, amusing for the most part, and informative. "Over there, that white house, that's where Damon Courtwrite lives. He's got three marriageable daughters, all pretty as can be. I got my eyes on the middle one, Lucinda Ann, but the other two are free, as far as I know, if you're interested."

"I am a married man," I said.

"Ah. Well, that's too bad."

I do not think Otis meant any offense, and I took none. The

Courtwrite sisters would, I was sure, find grooms aplenty without me.

Otis secured a carriage and we drove north beyond the outskirts of town, through gently rolling hills that became ever steeper. It was a pleasant drive in early spring, and though the landscape of the Indian Territory generally lacked that luxurious growth that I had known as a child east of the Mississippi and even through Arkansas and Missouri, it had nonetheless a spare kind of beauty to be appreciated. There were trees enough, but in the main not tall and crowded, for the rock that lay close to the surface of the land precluded the searching roots necessary for lush growth of deciduous trees. The grass was tall and thick, like prairie grass, among the outcropping of giant shelves of rocks along with the aged and worn boulders that lay like shattered prehistoric eggs, petrified and calcified. The view from these hills was only more hills and higher, until we reached an overlook, obviously popular, littered as it was with the debris of a careless civilization. From that vantage point we could see beyond the hills to the horizon, with the river bottom lying below, the meandering stream making its lazy way eastward, its lassitude soon to be broken by the spring rains that would fill its banks and rush it frenetically toward the Mississippi, where it would join with others for the final trip to the waters of the Gulf and the endless tides beyond.

I was entranced by the view and gazed silently for a long moment, apprehended by the thought that I was not only an observer of this panorama, but likewise a part of it. I turned to Otis and abruptly inquired of him, "If you were to plan to build a home in Tulsa, where would you put it?" I knew, of course, that the spot on which we stood would be in no way suitable for a permanent dwelling, but it had been this view which inspired my sudden interest in building a home.

"Ah," he pondered, "there are many spots. Would you want to be close to your neighbors or far, on a main street or removed, near the river or back?"

"Near the river and with a view of it."

"Well," he considered, the salesman in him making itself known, "let me show you some ground, most of which I know to be obtainable at a reasonable rate."

By the time we reached Tulsa, it was growing late. Otis stopped the carriage at the edge of town and gestured southward toward the west. "Yonder is Turkey Mountain on the far side of the river. Opposite on the high bank are, I know, some lots of ground to be de-

veloped. The price of those lots once the development begins will
jump skyward. Tomorrow I'll take you over there and we can scout
them on foot. It is too late tonight. But I have lots of time. How about
you?"

I nodded. I thought of home and of Elizabeth, but this growing,
burgeoning place with its attendant enthusiasm and excitement had
reached me. Formless plans were beginning to spill out of my subconscious as floodwaters over an ill-kept levee. I had planned to spend
some time here, and so I would.

I had Otis deliver me to the Brady, declining his offer of supper.
My head was filled with undefined dreams and I wanted time and
space for the sorting of them. I did not have the inclination for idle
chatter with Otis Wheeler. I dined alone that night and eagerly
penned figures and plans, my excitement growing. Excitement of any
sort was quite unlike me, particularly excitement engendered by no
special thing, only vague dreams. After my meal, again uncharacteristically, I sat in the lobby of that hotel and watched men of all kinds,
obviously consorting and plotting and dickering amid heavy smoke
and hale laughter and shouted oaths of all manner. It was a boisterous
and exciting scene and I felt like a bystander at an acutely contested
horse race, joining the excitement of the thing as if I had been participant and not spectator.

Seated in a far corner, I thought myself quite unobtrusive, but
such was not the case. I might have suspected that word of an investor
in town might have gotten around and my presence have been duly
noted.

The man who joined me strode deliberately to where I sat, offered
me first a cigar, which I refused, and then introductions, which I
accepted.

"I am Booth Copeland," he said, sticking out a hand, which I rose
to accept. "I am an oilman—a wildcatter, if you like—and I am looking for investors in my enterprise." He was nothing if not to the point.
Still, I was about to send him quickly on his way but he said, "I have
already spoke with Tremble over at the Commerce Bank and he assured me that he'd recommend my enterprise to you, as he said you
was interested in investments. I have oil leases aplenty and equipment
and know-how. I am going to make a strike, soon or late, I don't
know. But I do know that I am certain to make a strike. I have need
only of more capital."

It was said without braggadocio, as a matter of fact and not merely conjecture or wishful thinking. I could not keep from being impressed by the gangling man before and his simple insistence on his certain success. He was older than I by perhaps a decade, but he was not yet gray, only weathered.

"I do have some faith in Mr. Tremble's recommendations," I said to this man Copeland. "Only I am not given to spur-of-the-moment decisions on the making of investments. Though I am still young, I have had some experience in business investments and I like to make such decisions based on facts and figures, rather than on the strength of recommendations." I felt vaguely pompous as I issued that pronouncement, but still it was true.

"And I'd say that speaks well of yer business sense," said Copeland. And then, abruptly, he motioned me to take my seat and he procured a straight-backed armless chair behind him, swung it around before me and sat backward in it, hands clasped before him.

"I am not asking much," he said. "I want ten investors with five thousand dollars each. For that five thousand each investor will buy five percent of the profits. It's that simple."

"Indeed it is. But what exactly is five percent of a dry hole, Mr. Copeland?" I had already picked up some of the oil field jargon. It was in the air and quite impossible not to acquire. Nor was I averse to using it.

"Not much, Mr. Murphy," he said, laughing, "not much. And be assured, sir, that there will be dry holes. But just as certain as ye can drive a hole far enough and eventually pull water, so, too, can ye drive a hole into them Osage Hills and pull oil. In a week, maybe, in six months, in a year. But eventually it will happen. But," he added with something of a sidelong glance toward the boisterous assemblage around us, "this business an't fer the impatient. They're better off panning fer nuggets in mountain streams. The investment's not so great."

"So what you want is a patient man with five thousand dollars?"

"What I want is ten patient men with five thousand each."

"And do you think you'll find them?"

"Yes."

That was very much the substance of our conversation. After a few pleasantries and my assurances that I would seriously discuss the matter with Mr. Tremble, he excused himself and drifted away. I watched him go and marveled that a single man could generate so much self-confidence.

Mr. Copeland was, of course, not the only oil prospector who was
aware of my presence, and as the evening wore on, I was approached
by several more with very similar suits to Mr. Copeland's. Whether
because Booth Copeland was more persuasive or whether because his
manner was more direct and less insinuating or whether simply because he had come first, I found myself comparing those other sup-
pliants much less favorably to him. I put them off quickly by asserting
that I was not interested in oil investments but only in, possibly, real
estate or perhaps retail or wholesale enterprises. I would, I told each
one carefully, leave the oil business to those more practiced in speculation. But, to be truthful, I found all the attention to be exhilarating.

Otis Wheeler was prompt the next morning and picked me up
right after breakfast in his rented carriage, and we stirred our way
down the dusty streets toward the river. Passing the Courtwrite
house, Otis eagerly brought up the subject of Damon Courtwrite's
middle daughter. I glanced toward that house thoughtlessly, and my
attention was caught by a small but graceful evergreen tree planted on
the protected side of the house. Not normally given to noticing such
things, I could not say what there was about the little tree that attracted me, perhaps its graceful boughs or the very fact that it looked
so out of place in a countryside given over to persimmon trees, river
birches and rough cedar.

"Whatever kind of tree is that?" I inquired of Otis. He glanced in
the direction I was pointing and shrugged.

"Mrs. Courtwrite is big in the garden club. She's got a lot of
peculiar plants and stuff. I could find out fer you," he added eagerly
and winked. "It'd give me excuse to call, you know?"

"If you like." I laughed.

The lots to which Otis Wheeler directed me were situated on a
gently sloping hillside, not so steep but that a house could not be
easily built there, or several houses, as was the plan. We strolled over
that hillside, faintly colored with the greening of the native grass. I
strode to the highest point on the hill and looked out across the river,
but my view was blocked by a bluff on the west side of that river.

"Wait here and hold my hat and coat, Otis," I directed. "I intend
to shinny up that tree and see what's to be seen."

"Well then, I'd say that you are indeed a thorough man," replied
Otis.

I went up the tree and was some pleased to note that that largely
unused skill of boyhood had not deserted me. I went as high as I safely

could and balanced myself in the junction of two branches and looked about me. The bluff still blocked the view to the southwest, but to the northwest the view went as far as the horizon, the river, like a molting snake, leaving a careless trail over the terrain. And on the horizon there was smoke, not tiny puffs as from a chimney or campfire, but as from a major conflagration. I stood a long while glancing around over the view and then like an early-day explorer I claimed that view as my own. I would have it. It would be a gift from me to my beloved wife. And so I shinnied carefully down, remarking on the ground as to the condition of my trousers and noting also that I had seen great clouds of smoke and wondered what it might amount to. Perhaps I was thinking of those tales of savage Indian raids on westward settlers that I had heard of.

But Otis only smiled and muttered, "Grass fire. This time of year the grass gets to burnin' and, fanned by the wind, it burns itself all the way to some natural barrier. That fire's a long ways off, too. Were it close, you could already get a whiff of it on the wind. Got quite a view up there, didn't you? What you seen was maybe forty or fifty mile away."

Otis drove me back to town and I stopped in to talk with Mr. Tremble. I asked him first about Booth Copeland and his enterprise.

"All I can say, Mr. Murphy, is that I have myself been persuaded to invest with Mr. Copeland. I have thoroughly checked his facts and his credentials, and both I find to be sound. I have likewise checked your own credentials, sir, which is why I recommended you to Booth. I suspect that an investment of five thousand dollars would deplete your reserve by but little, and the potential reward is, I am certain, great." At which point Mr. Tremble pulled down a map on his wall and with pointing stick, much like a schoolmaster, he explained as simply as possible the process of oil exploration. I was quite impressed, yea, even excited.

By the time I left Mr. Tremble's office in the late afternoon I had signed contracts for the lot that I had visited that morning and I had agreed to an investment with Mr. Copeland. I was in the process of establishing myself and with a precipitateness quite foreign to my nature. My usual caution seemed somehow dated in this exciting and feverish climate.

In addition to all that, Mr. Tremble had given me the name of a building contractor whom he proclaimed a veritable artist. But once more it was too late in the afternoon to undertake serious business, and so I spent the evening in my room, making plans and drawing diagrams. I would, I decided, begin the building of this house with the idea that Elizabeth, when her health permitted, could oversee the finishing of it. All at once I was feverish in my anxiety to be moved and settled. I had risen in a few brief months from deepest despair to the greatest exhilaration. And though I was never a drinking man, I thought that I could feel what it must be like to be lifted, mind out of body, by spirits. The excitement I was beginning to feel could, I was certain, be likened unto a drunken euphoria.

I was all morning in Dewey Lane's cramped quarters the next day, conferring with that craftsman on the construction of the house I planned. He looked at my simple drawings and shook his head. "That's quite a house," he said. "I doubt that you goin' to want anything like that overlookin' the river. Ought to go closter to town."

"I want it by the river."

"You don't want all them winders neither. You only goin' to git the sun in the summer and the wind in the winter with all that glass facin' northwest. House's too tall, anyway. Cyclone'd take the top story off about ever' fifth spring." All of this counsel he offered without ever having set foot on the plot I had chosen.

It was apparent that Dewey Lane was one of those garrulous and opinionated artisans whose skill, though highly prized, must be dearly bought at the price of continued argument over what should or should not be done. It is a characteristic shared by the very skilled, those who appreciate their own work and feel more competent to advise than to be advised. A project undertaken with such a one could degenerate into a contest of wills or rise to a successful partnership. I understood that (and so, too, perhaps did Dewey Lane) and I was willing to join in that struggle of wills for the sake of the monument to love and to the future that I had planned. A lesser, more agreeable builder would not do.

Dewey joined me at my projected building site in the afternoon and began immediately finding fault. I think that I would have been disappointed had he not.

"That rock 'ere? What you aim to do with't?"

He was pointing to one of those ancient boulders that I had found so fascinating about this area. A rock large enough for three or four small children to play on, or for a courting couple to lean against, a landmark washed smooth by timeless elements, and faintly pock-marked, like an aging maiden lady.

"Hit'll be hell to move," observed Dewey.

"I do not want it moved," I said in sudden inspiration. "It will be the center of my garden. I'll plant a tree beside it to shade it and I'll have roses and peonies, daisies and nasturtiums all about, flowers for my wife, and a beehive, perhaps, and shelter for the birds."

Dewey gave only a forlorn look, the look, I thought, of a misplaced pup. "Wal," he drawled at last, "ladies do set a store, I guess, by pretty flowers; but me, I call it waste to set flowers where corn and squash could grow."

In spite of muttered misgivings on Dewey's part, we struck a contract for the building of the house and he promised detailed plans in short order. "But hit's too tall a house, Mr. Murphy," he grumbled. "I tell ye hit's too tall."

The house I had proposed was three stories tall, with the top story given over to a large room with a panoramic view from a line of windows, that room, I thought, to be used by the children and I envisioned them spilling about on the floor in merry games or reading, perhaps singing around the piano I would purchase. I made a note to myself that we must be sure that those windows would securely lock, lest we lose a child or two out of them, and I chuckled at that thought. Dewey Lane gave me a curious look but said nothing. I was thinking of all those children, nor did I have any idea where I thought they might have come from, only that they were mine. I think that the shadow of Obediah must have completely faded in the sunlight of this new resolve and this new enterprise. I was already in mind's eye a happy and contented father and husband, founder of family and of business, yea, even of a new city.

Elizabeth and I would occupy the second floor, which would boast sitting room, bath, sun-room, porch and commodious bedchamber, with the first floor given over to dining, entertaining, music room and library. I planted my feet on that barren piece of real estate and stared northward. But for Dewey's presence I would have shucked coat and hat and shinnied up the tree to absorb my view once more. I restrained myself, however, lest that unimaginative sort think that I had let go my reason entirely.

Seated in the Bank of Commerce with Mr. Tremble and Otis Wheeler, I felt myself altogether a comrade, an accomplice, though I had been in this city just under a week.

"I have thought considerable on your situation, Mr. Murphy," Mr. Tremble was saying, after a preface of general remarks and pleasantries, "and I think I have found a further investment for you. There is a retail store on Main Street, stocking fine merchandise—too fine, perhaps, but that is not the point. It was established by Mr. D. W. Phelps and Mrs. Phelps. They arrived here last year by train from Ohio with a view toward establishing a fine retail outlet, one that does not do business in hardware, but only in fine dry goods. Alas, Mrs. Phelps has decided that she does not care to continue here, as she finds it dusty and altogether too rugged for her tastes, and she has, I have heard so at least, made life quite uncomfortable for Mr. Phelps on account of it. At any rate, he is eager to find a buyer for this enterprise, which has living quarters attached. He will even"—Mr. Tremble smiled—"throw in his Packard automobile, which he had shipped direct from his home in Cincinnati. I think that that automobile has been used but little, as Mrs. Phelps found the existing roadways too rough for her comfort."

"I take it," I said, returning the smile, "that you are in favor of my buying this property?"

Mr. Tremble shrugged. "It is a sound investment, even if you never run it as a store yourself. It is a good building, well stocked, and its value will do naught but rise. If," he smiled, "you do not want the Packard, I'm sure that Mr. Phelps can find an independent buyer for it. It is quite an object of interest and curiosity around here as it is."

I did not tell Mr. Tremble that it was his mention of the automobile that had indeed caught my attention, that my interest in a horseless vehicle had been piqued since long before I had come to this place. Unaccountably I thought of Daniel's jaunty riding cap, with its flaps and the dark goggles that he had affected even though he had no automobile.

"Well," I murmured, "I'll think on it. Otis and I are to look at some rural property this afternoon. A leisurely ride through the country will give me time to consider. You seem bent, Mr. Tremble," I said with a laugh, "on getting all of my money invested in your city."

"That is indeed my intent." He smiled back.

As we drove through the countryside, I lost in thought, Otis said suddenly, "I found your tree for you."

"What?"

"That tree that you asked after. Mrs. Courtwrite's tree. I called on the Courtwrites and she told me it's a laurel, not native at all, but grows lots in the Pacific Northwest. I can tell you," he said with a rueful grimace, "more about that damned tree than ever you'll want to know, as Mrs. Courtwrite, finding me interested, bent my ear about forty-five minutes on the subject. But it was worth it. That is the most courteous the old woman has been to me since I started calling on Lucinda Ann, and after that chat we was allowed to sit late on the porch swing without interruption. I thank you for the suggestion," he added and we both laughed.

A laurel? So that was what that graceful tree was, so delicate and out of place in this tempestuous land. Ah. That was my Elizabeth. Yes indeed, I would plant such a tree for her, beside the large boulder, all surrounded by flowers and shade. A bower of love. I was forced into a wry smile; I had become a woeful romantic in a matter of months.

By the next evening I had not only made contract to the farmland that Otis and I had surveyed, but had also bought, lock, stock, barrel and Pacakard, all of Mr. D. W. Phelps's worldly goods, and that grateful gentleman and his wife were making plans for a hasty retreat from their western adventure.

Had at that moment the earth rolled and trembled and cracks opened wide and smoke and steam escaped them, I would never have ascribed that phenomenon to a natural movement of the earth, a quake, as others might. I would have known it for what it was: Louisa One rolling and tumbling in consternation from her grave, over such hasty and perhaps unwise disposition of her wealth. So be it. I had done with the Old Bastard and all his Louisas, anyway. I was a new man in a new world.

How eager I was, how eager to begin my new life, and I chafed to return to Elizabeth, to share with her this excitement, more excitement than any I had ever experienced, I thought. But I still had much to see to. I must get Dewey Lane started on his project, and I must master the Packard, the latter, I suspected, more easily accomplished than the former.

Otis Wheeler was a most willing accomplice in my suit to master the vehicle, and, like boys on a holiday, we participated in high-spirited driving over the countryside on road or trail, wherever we could encourage the machine to go. We drove, turned, backed, started and stopped and occasionally pushed or pulled as was needed. It was altogether a lark and I felt younger, I think, than I had ever felt, and freer, too, and Otis Wheeler was my comrade, my buddy, my friend, I knew, for life.

With Dewey Lane, however, I returned quickly to maturity. I

would be certain that he would do what I wanted done the way I wanted it done before I would trust him alone with the project. And after a while I settled that point with him: it was not he whose money was building the house, nor was it he who would live in the house. At length he understood, agreeing to build what I wanted, comforting himself with only occasional grumbling.

"Watch out for that rock 'ere," he cautioned. "Snake at the foot of it."

I stepped quickly backward and Dewey tossed a small stone toward the boulder. I saw wiggling of the grass and then a lazy movement, and the reptile made its way around the rock on the the other side. "I'd sure move that 'ere rock, I was you. Copperheads dearly love 'em. You'll have a nest of copperheads in your backyard every summer."

"I will take my chances with the copperheads, Mr. Lane," I said.

"They're cranky in the spring; just woke, you see. They like to lay in the sun around rocks. Always look out for snakes in the spring around rocks. Hit's a good rule." He gave the information as if I wanted it. I simply nodded.

"I'd sure move that rock. Matter of fact, I don't think I'd even build here. Bad sign. Copperhead. Bad sign." The sigh I returned that commentary was so profound that Dewey said no more.

By the time I had mastered the automobile and resolved all of my new business deals, Mr. Lane had staked out the building and had begun digging of the cellar. All of this I had accomplished without once consulting Elizabeth. I could not be sure how she would react to it, but I was certain enough in my own mind of the rightness of the course I had set that I was sure I could persuade her had she any misgivings.

I set out in my newly mastered machine with what can only be described as a light heart, leaving my horse and carriage liveried. I was not far gone on my journey, however, before I realized just how great had been my dependence on that horse, whose instincts and judgments I trusted and could so concentrate on other matters. The machine, I discovered, had no such instincts, nor any judgment whatsoever. I was completely in charge, and if I was to reach my destination, I would need to pay close attention, for what passed as roads in the Territory required sound navigation and steering.

In spite of dust, noise and breeze generated by the machine, I was aware that the weather about me was becoming suspect. For in the

Territory, when spring weather turns suddenly damp and still, the air heavy and fetid, a prudent man's thoughts turn toward cyclones, which have in the past passed with great regularity through this part of the country in the spring. And though I had never been party to one personally, I had seen the devastation such winds could wreak. When I felt it safe to lift my eyes from the road, I scanned the horizon suspiciously, but the clouds, though they gathered ominously, only flashed occasional lightning that spoke more of rain than of wind. Still, even rain would not be welcome. I would as lief not have had to handle the machine in wet and muddy conditions.

I remarked to myself that perversity of nature which seemed so to grudge the life-giving moisture and so often sent it washing and blowing, destroying as well as maintaining life. There was, of course, no explanation for the antics of the atmosphere, which could on the one hand send gentle soaking rain or soft snows and on the other hand raging storms and ferocious blizzards and devastating winds, like an unjust monarch providing what must be provided but at a terrible cost.

Even over the noise of the machine, I could sense the stillness, as if all nature held its breath as the clouds warred with one another, all the while moving steadily ahead like a vanquishing army. And had I not already been overeager to arrive at my destination, such ominous natural activity would have spurred me on, and I did not tarry, though the bumping machine and the gritty wind that struck my face gave me cause to wonder at the wisdom of my choice of transportation. That which had seemed like a toy now seemed a perverse and demanding piece of equipment, and the running of it work, not play.

I arrived at my destination just ahead of the rain and I angled the automobile into the empty carriage house. The noise we generated in so doing brought both Elizabeth and Inez hurrying to the porch, and I waved jauntily, turning the motor of the contraption off in great relief. Inez bolted across the yard and, breathless, arrived at the Packard almost before I had managed to untangle myself and release my stiff limbs from the position in which they had been so long imprisoned.

"Is dat yours, Mr. Murphy? Law, law, law. Looky dere at dat? Looky dere. What you do wit da horse?" Inez's questions piled up faster than I could answer them, and I merely chuckled an affirmative to the first one.

Elizabeth stood on the porch, quite still and unsmiling. I ran toward her, hurrying with Inez right behind me, for the wind had come up in a sudden damp gust and the drops had begun to splat the dusty soil.

"Elizabeth, my dear," I called, but she did not answer, only stood and waited.

"She not been well last couple a days," Inez whispered behind me. I could tell then that she was indeed pale, dark circles shadowing her eyes, her posture profoundly weary. I hushed my own concern with the observation to myself that such would certainly be the case with one so near to birthing a child. One could hardly expect her to be jumping up and down in excitement. Worry was a burden I refused to bear, for things had gone so well with me that I could not imagine their ever going otherwise, as, on a bright and sunny day, it is quite impossible to imagine the weather being other than eternally perfect.

By the time we reached the porch the blowing rain had driven Elizabeth back into the house, and Inez and I both stamped and dripped our way into the entry, not soaking wet but not quite dry either. Elizabeth greeted me but unenthusiastically, I thought, considering how long I had been away and the nature of my business. But then, she obviously was not well.

"Law, law, Mrs. Murphy, you got to go down dere an' look at dat machine soon's it stop rainin'. I ain't never seen nothin' lak it."

"Ah, my dearest," I said, "it is but the first of many surprises I have for you." And I went on to outline briefly my adventures, topping the whole dissertation with the news of the house I was having built for her. "We will fill it with young ones, Elizabeth, and they'll know naught but love."

But what greeted this exclamation was something like a sigh. "I don't know, Levi, it seems like a great deal to think about. I don't feel quite able to comprehend it all now."

I was disappointed. It was not the scene of excitement that I had planned. Only Inez's black eyes seemed to grow large with the telling, and she murmured over and over, "Law, law."

And then Elizabeth quitted us abruptly, hurrying up the stairs toward our bedchamber. I started to follow but thought better of it. She needed rest and time to absorb all that I had told her. It was perhaps too much at a time; I should have held off some of the information until she was better. I had been thoughtless, I chastised myself.

The bundle of documents that I had carried in from the automobile was still tucked under my arm, and I asked Inez to look in upon the mistress in a while and ascertain if she would be up to sharing our evening meal, for I was myself quite hungry and I took the papers I held into my study and closed the door behind me. I would sort through them and file them this very evening, I decided, before I went to the post office to collect what I was certain would be a quantity of mail stacked up in my absence.

I put the papers down and immediately noted a pair of letters neatly placed side by side in the middle of the desk. Just as the body sends forth warning juices against sudden attack, so, too, I'm sure, does the brain. My sudden apprehension and attendant fluttering pulse and respiration could have been no greater had those letters been instead a deadly snake coiled for attack, and I was as loath to touch them. I only stared at the pair for a long moment, caught my breath in a lengthy sigh, turned away and strode to the window and stared out at the rain, which had settled into a steady and gloomy drizzle.

And so I had come full circle. My world had once more crumbled against a backdrop of dismal rain. I cursed myself for a fool. Why had I not destroyed those letters long before, committed them to flame? That oversight I knew to be my undoing. Why Elizabeth had been rummaging through my desk I could not say, only that she had been, I was certain, and had found those missives so carelessly stored in a desk drawer. I turned back to the desk, determined to at last right that error. I snapped a lucifer between my fingers and held the two offending pieces of literature aloft with a view toward destroying them and letting the devil then have the hindmost.

"One of those letters belongs to me, thank you," said Elizabeth from the doorway at my back. I stood briefly, then blew the lucifer out and held it smoking, as the gun of a murderer does. I waited.

"I have worried and worried these past several days on how I would confront you with this evidence of your treachery and deceit," she said, the gentleness of her tone rendering her words all that much more unbearable.

"I loved you, Elizabeth," was my explanation. I congratulated myself that I did not mention fairness in relation to love and war. I only said it abjectly, beseechingly.

"That is hard to believe. To so treat one you love. It is hard to believe."

"And tell me, Elizabeth," I said, resorting to my only defense, "did you not likewise deceive me and take me for a husband when you sorely needed one?"

"I did," she said simply.

"And are we even?"

"I don't know. I really do not know either what to do or what to think, Levi. Only that I would like to go home, to visit my family, to bear my child at my father's house and so to think and work things out. I need some peace, and everywhere I turn in this house I am undone by memories and accusations and fears. I would like for you to take me home for an extended stay. That's all that I can say at the moment." And with that she left me. I looked down and discovered I was still holding the dead lucifer in my fingers and I flipped it away, mindless of where it fell.

Elizabeth did not come down for supper and my own appetite, once so demanding, was quite absent. I toyed with my food, to Inez's consternation, and left the table quickly, retiring to my study with a pot of tea. There I spent a sleepless night, tossing on the couch and pacing the floor, my demons my only companions. It was that old lecher come back, he who had been absent from my dreams and my terrors the last few happy months. Had he escaped from hell to torment me, or only from my own tortured, dark interior soul? The peace I had believed was mine was not to be, and I knew only I could never possess my love again, I who had only the seed of madmen to offer her. What foolish optimism had led me to delude myself that anything else was possible but wretched celibacy? By morning I was hollow-eyed but calm, and the pot of tea, untouched, sat cold upon the desk.

Elizabeth and I met at the breakfast table, she more wan, if possible, than she had been the day before.

"I would go to my father, Levi, and I've packed some things in boxes. Will you take me or shall I hire a wagon?"

I did not try to talk her out of it. Perhaps distancing ourselves from this place might well be wise. "I will take you," I said. "The trip can be accomplished fairly speedily by automobile. We shall go in my new machine." I knew that the road west that we would travel for the greatest part of the distance was well traveled, smooth and passable in most weathers. It would indeed be a more comfortable trip by automobile. Nor did she protest that decision, and I hoped that perhaps her curiosity about auto travel might be piqued. I was not thinking beyond the moment. All that I knew was that I could not, I would not live without her.

It was the next morning that we set out, with a lunch provided by Inez, who was clearly worried.

"Now, you all be keerful," she cautioned, and I reassured her.

"Don't worry, Inez, we'll have a fine trip. And when I return I promise I'll give you a ride to wherever you want to go."

Elizabeth sat apprehensively as I cranked up the machine. At the last moment I had procured a lap robe for her, the best I could do, Louisa One's last down comforter. It turned out to be about the right size. And so we set off, the trip too noisy for any but shouted conversation. There was nothing to do but think our own thoughts. We paused for lunch and rest a few miles before we were due to turn south again and off the better roadway. There was little sign of recent rain this far west, and so I hoped we might find conditions on the ancillary roads acceptable.

Elizabeth said but little, only noting that her back hurt from so long sitting, and I helped her up from the rock upon which she had been resting. We drove on, lost in our own thoughts, and with direction from a farm boy found the road we needed to go south. The road we found ourselves on was better than some I had traveled but was still much more rutted than the one we had just quitted. Elizabeth clutched at the door, trying to settle herself, and at one point reached over to touch my arm, but when I looked her way, she only shrugged and turned away. I noticed, however, that her expression was strained and her countenance moist. In some anxiety I speeded up.

The rock that the wheel of the Packard hit, which threw it askew and into the ditch, my horse would have avoided. With instinct and skill he would have guided the carriage around the obstacle without mishap, and so, too, would I, had I been paying closer attention. That says, perhaps, that of the two of us the horse was the smarter, or at least the more experienced in roadwork. We bounced to a stop, nosed into the soft embankment. Elizabeth clutched the door with both hands, her face quite pale.

I got out and surveyed the situation, but it was not promising. I could see no way out of the predicament without help, though I gave the machine a tentative push or two.

"I shall have to walk for help, my dear," I said. "I'm sorry," I added. I scanned the horizon for signs of civilization, but found none. I knew what was behind—very little and that a far distance. I decided to go forward. But Elizabeth stopped me.

"Levi, please don't go yet. I am"—here she paused and struggled to get the words said—"I am not well; I am in pain," at last she gasped. "I'm afraid. Don't leave me alone. Not yet." And she groaned. "I don't think it will be long, Levi," she said at last.

The sensations of fear and helplessness commingling were among the least pleasant that I had ever experienced. "You need someone better equipped than I, Elizabeth. I will run for help. Surely there is someone nearabouts. There has to be!" I fairly shouted that last.

"No, Levi, Levi," she cried, "don't go, don't go. I don't know what to do. I am so tired."

I composed myself and surveyed the situation. Cursing myself for being a careless fool was no help. I did what I could to see to Elizabeth's comfort. I helped her into the backseat of the Packard, for it was resting under the only shade at all near; the early leaves, still pale, gave some shade and promised more. Her skirts, I noted as I helped her with them, were soaked and stained, from what I did not know, and she seemed hardly able to lift herself as I settled her onto the seat. There was nothing else that I could do but clench my fists with each succeeding groan, they coming closer, it seemed to me. I supposed I would be called when I was needed.

I took note of a tall tree some hundred yards up on a slight rise, and in inspiration I darted toward it and, grasping a low branch, hoisted myself up and climbed as high as I could. The only thing to be seen was a puff of smoke to the south, smoke that I was certain came from either a house or a campfire. That would be the direction to go for help. And I climbed down.

I heard Elizabeth cry out just as I hit the ground, and I dashed back to the machine.

"Oh, God, my God. Help me, help me!" she cried. "Daniel, my darling, help me!"

I know that it is not physiologically possible, but at that moment my heart ceased to beat and I stood as stone ere it started again, and with the rushing of the blood to my temples came the greatest pain I have ever known, pain and the darkest despair as the woman who was my wife called in travail another man's name. She had not called out my name, but his.

"Ah," she sobbed and I think mercifully fainted. I knelt and within a moment lifted up that small bundle of humanity, wrapped in nature's own package, ugly and beautiful at once, and not knowing what procedure to follow, I shook it slightly as if to wake it. The loud sound surprised me, but color began to course at once through its body and I was eye to eye with Daniel's bastard child. It was Daniel's, not mine, a healthy male child from the look of it, the love child of two others, not mine.

There is a primordial evil, more hateful than deceit or treachery, that can rise suddenly, uncontrollably, in some men, cold and inhuman. And it was with such evil that I viewed the bastard son that I had thought to take as my own. It stood between me and any joy that I could ever find. Better madmen, I thought, than bastards!

I found Louisa One's down comforter and wrapped it around the infant, who had quieted by then, and I held it stiffly, with no feeling at all save revulsion.

"Levi," whispered Elizabeth. "And it's all over? Levi, my baby, what is it, how is it? Give me it."

"It's dead," I said.

"Levi?"

"It was born dead. It is better you don't see it." I wanted to see the pain course across her face as the pain had coursed through my heart. I was not disappointed, as she tried to struggle up on one arm and finally, failing that, fell back limp, her face turned away, and sobbed.

I carried the wrapped bundle a distance away. I had no plans. Everything I had done and said had been impulse, and I would rely on impulse to carry me through. I did not know how easily babies died of neglect, but she would not have Daniel's bastard if I had to strangle it myself.

When I returned to Elizabeth she had stopped crying and she was staring ahead, her face ghastly pale and her breathing shallow. "I am bleeding, Levi. It does not seem to want to shut off. I am going to die, Levi. That's all. And it does not matter. All I had is dead. Daniel's child is dead, and I am shackled in marriage to one I cannot love. I do not care to live, Levi." She said it with a sigh and carefully composed her hands.

Ah, the pain again. The hateful pain, and she would have the last word, for I knew her to be right. She was too pale, her eyes too glazed. Without attention, she would surely die. She would leave me alone, unmanned, and I hated her for it. I hated her for having Daniel's bastard, unreasoning hatred, and for then leaving me as only an honest wife can leave, in death. God Almighty only knows how much I hated her!

"I am going for help," I said. She did not answer.

I walked over to where the infant still lay covered with the down ticking, which would muffle any cry, I thought. I picked it up and held it. It was a warm little bundle, sleeping perhaps, resting after its arduous journey into existence. Damn her! She could die if she wanted. With her gone, I could have my bastard and no one the wiser.

I could yet beard that old incestuous fornicator and carry the final joke into eternity.

I called out again, "I'm going for help. I will return."

"Levi," I heard her faint call. "Levi, tell me, please, was it a boy or a girl? That much, Levi. That much only. I beseech you. Let me know my babe that I can name it and so join it in the hereafter. . . ." Her voice faded and I did not answer. The babe will be named Levi, I thought. Levi Murphy, the bastard son of a bastard son.

I turned and walked with the baby in my arms. I did not walk south toward the smoke I had seen, but I walked back in the direction we had come, certain that any help in that direction lay quite far away.

NINE

OBEDIAH COMES TO GRIEF

*T*he letter that Nancy Hawkins received in the spring of 1859 from Louisa Varner Murphy portended, she knew, another address change, for then only did Louisa write, it being somehow important for her to keep her former sister-in-law informed.

> Dear Nancy Hawkins and Todd Hawkins her husband,
> I take my pen in hand in hopes that you are all well and to assure you that we here are not suffering.

In such manner did Louisa's letters always begin, and those that Nancy Hawkins returned her, though neither actually did take pen in hand, nor even read the letters themselves, as neither had ever mastered those arts and they were dependent on friends or professional scribes for the writing and reading of letters.

And such letters Nancy always heard with interest, though neither the form nor the style nor the dialect were those of her former sister-in-law, and thus did Nancy have to strain to make out the voice of that loved one whom she had not seen in many years.

> We have had no infirmities, nor serious illness to strike us since last I sent you word; and my daughter Louisa's baby girl has been walking some months past and speaks with great fluency for one so young.

This Nancy Hawkins pondered, remarking to herself the fact that Louisa had never mentioned any husband for the younger Louisa, and so she noted to Todd Hawkins, who only observed, "Maybe there an't none."

That babe [continued the voice from the letter] is likewise named Louisa, which is a pretty name for such a pretty babe, though mine Obediah [Ah ha. Here the scribe had failed to correct the pronunciation, much to Nancy Hawkins' delight, as that touch of authenticity gave credence to the entire letter, which without Louisa Varner's curious inflections seemed almost a forgery] does complain at so many in the household with like names.

And Nancy Hawkins observed to Todd Hawkins, her husband, that it did indeed seem peculiar to carry that name through so many consecutive generations.

But Todd Hawkins only remarked, "Well, you know Louisa, strong woman that she is, she gave her name to be carried by her daughter and that being something of a failure mayhap decided her to try once more."

"And what kind of thing is that to say?" chided his wife.

Todd Hawkins only shrugged, remembering the second Louisa as the girl he had last seen, even then ill tempered and oversized, "fourteen stone or a barrel," as the saying went.

Obediah's enterprises have prospered and he has settled us now on the western edge of Kentucky near to the small village of Taylortown. Danny has stayed behind in middle Tennessee and refuses to follow, though Charlie and Henry both still reside with us; but it is my hope and that of my husband that each will find him a wife soon, as it is time they settled themselves.

"I should think," said Nan Hawkins, nodding, at that, knowing that all three of her nephews were nearing thirty and beyond.

I have no more to say at the present and send hopes again that you and all of yours are well and instruct that you give my best respects to all inquiring friends.

Indeed, the mystery of Louisa the younger's baby girl was a long time in being solved. Louisa Varner Murphy had become enraged when it became apparent that her daughter was with child and without husband, though the baby was very nearly an accomplished fact before her presence became obvious, as Louisa the younger had fulfilled her girlhood promise and had become increasingly stout, "fourteen stone, if she's a pound." The girl's equanimity in the face of impending motherhood might have been admirable had it risen from some more respectable source. She fanned herself, for it was a moderately hot summer, and rested her swollen ankles on a chair and smiled considerably to herself as in great satisfaction for some accomplishment.

When her condition could no longer be concealed, she only smiled placidly at her raging mother.

"I vant to know who he vas dat faddered dis child," shouted Louisa. "I vant to know who dat rascal is, dat scoundrel, dat reprobate is; I vould haf him fer mine son-in-law."

But Louisa either smiled or did not, but she never answered, and her mother raged on, slamming dishes and pans, exhorting the merciful Lord to smite every one of them dead and in His infinite mercy to reduce the fornicator and adulterer to everlasting ashes.

At such times Obediah, who was never happy in an angry atmosphere, absented himself, and he being neither a drinking man nor a gambling man, sought out what other entertainment was afforded. And it is possible, though not recorded, that at least three more births were the eventual outcome of Louisa's anger.

But Louisa the younger was not talking, and her mother was reduced to eyeing suspiciously any male who had in the past been seen in the vicinity, from the circuit-riding Methodist to the senile old woodsman who scouted imaginary savages in the hills and woods nearby. But to no avail, and Louisa's baby was born a bastard.

And Obediah, who was generally partial to children anyway, became immediately enamored of this tiny creature, the surprising product of her oversized mother.

It was the birth of the third Louisa that precipitated the further westward movement of Obediah Murphy's family, for Louisa reasoned that in a new locale the baby need not be labeled a bastard, nor her daughter a woman of loose and questionable morals. It was another of many removes. They had moved several times in Tennessee, each move a little more westerly, inspired sometimes by suspicions of Obediah by either Louisa or her neighbors or sometimes by the profit that Louisa could realize in selling her land and removing to a farther plot.

Over the years and through the many moves, Louisa's needle had been busy, and she had pieced together quite a number of quilt blocks, the pink of the earlier blocks now quite gone.

With the birth of Louisa's baby girl, Louisa the elder sent Obediah scouting for a place to remove to, with speed rather than profit being the primary motive, and it was Obediah who determined to go north

into Kentucky, and it was he who found the small community of
Taylortown, on the northern border not far from Illinois.

Taylortown boasted a few cabins, a smith and a store, and it was
of the storekeeper that Obediah inquired, "Why is this placed named
as it is?"

"Taylortown?"

"Yes."

"Why," said the old man proudly, "it is named for me, for I am
Taylor and I come here right behind the Indians as they crossed
toward their western lands."

"Ah," said Obediah.

"But I fear," said Old Taylor, "that when I go, the name will go
with me. And that is sad. I have no issue, you see, and my wife is long
gone." He did not say that she was dead, but Obediah presumed that
to be the case. "I think that no one will care to keep the name of a dead
man on this place. An' don't you think that is sad?" Obediah nodded.
He thought that indeed it was sad. "It will probably be called
Springfield, for every nameless place is always called Springfield, I've
noted. It is sad," Old Taylor repeated.

Now, Obediah thought that since the old man had all but relin-
quished claim to the name of the town with his eventual passing (and
Obediah noted that the old man was indeed quite frail), then the
naming of the town would be up for grabs.

So it was that Obediah Murphy contracted for an agreeable tract
of land near to Taylortown, and within a month returned there with
his wife and family, two sons, a daughter and a pretty baby.

But Danny Varner declined to accompany his mother and
brothers to Kentucky. "It is too far north," he said. "It is practically in
Illinois. I am a southern man. I will not leave the South. When the
war comes, as it certainly will, I'll be close to where I have to be."

"What war?" asked Obediah.

It took Obediah but a few months to improve upon the small cabin
already built on the land he had purchased, and by cold weather they
were all secure in commodious lodgings. And through the winter
Obediah made plans for spring planting, played with the baby and
whistled the eternal tunes of spring, all the while keeping watch on
the health of Old Taylor the storekeepr.

It was midway through the third Louisa's second year that the
mystery of her birth was solved and her male parent identified. In the
following manner did Louisa Varner Murphy make such discovery.

In the early afternoon of a bright spring day, having brushed the ground outside the kitchen thoroughly with her broom, Louisa determined that, it being a nice day, and still, she would do the same for the far outbuildings where the chickens were locked up at night against various night-prowling varmints, both human and animal. Such brushing down of the ground around her house was not particularly peculiar, it being instinct bred into her from her long line of Pennsylvania Dutch forebears. On the way to accomplish her task, however, she was arrested by noises coming from behind the straw stack kept close by the house for the goats and the milch cow.

The sounds Louisa heard were the sounds of lust in progress. She knew them well. The giggles and groans and rustling were too familiar. She had not been twice wed and burdened by seven births without having considerable experience of those noises. And the feminine giggles she identified immediately as belonging to her daughter, Louisa, whose giggles were highly individual as well as a little irritating, for she tittered and squealed and punctuated them with nasal snorts that most people found disconcerting at best.

The fornicator was back! Louisa was never slow to do battle, and she determined instantly that she would disabuse him of any notion of ever returning. She would make crow's bait of his balls and drive his divining rod clean up into his tonsils, and she stormed around the straw stack brandishing the only weapon at hand, her broom, but as it was fresh pulled and tied, the broom proved to be a weapon of considerable persuasion and Louisa smote the bared male backside, hardly wide enough to disguise the voluminous folds of flesh that made up her daughter, Louisa, beneath.

That the bared backside belonged to her husband, Obediah, was apparent to Louisa immediately upon rounding the straw stack, but that intelligence stayed her hand not one whit. Would he be a fornicator, he would feel the wrath of her broom for it. Nor was Obediah able to defend himself, for he had reached that pitch of passion from which there is no returning, and all his strength and concentration and attention must be directed to the completion of that act.

Louisa the daughter was, however, not so intent upon her business and commenced to squall and struggle against the blows that rained down upon them, for though Obediah's person might protect part of her, her mother, Louisa, was finding unprotected spots and was striking from the side and the top and poking from underneath to dislodge the two. Louisa the daughter struggled wildly, heaving and rolling and squalling, prolonging Obediah's painful pleasure by that much. Louisa wanted nothing more than up, for she had experienced her mother's broom on other occasions and had found the experience to be both enlightening and persuasive.

"Fornicator, fornicator, son of a whore, daughter of a bitch!" cried Louisa Varner Murphy, her anger and rage leaving her somewhat less than rational in the matter of epithets. "Whore! Whore!" she screeched, and she struck Obediah once more on his bare bottom, such a blow that Obediah first gave off a sigh of sweet release, immediately followed by a yelp of pain as he perceived the stinging blow directed at his bare flesh. He rolled over on his back and quickly realized that it had not been a wise decision and rolled once more atop the struggling Louisa, who had not managed to free herself enough to rise to a protected position.

"Whore's-son-slut, whore's-son-slut!" chanted Louisa Varner Murphy, swinging the broom in rhythm, as methodically as a housewife beating rugs. And such was how Henry Varner found his mother, stepfather and sister. Attracted by the noise, he rounded the straw stack and stared wide-eyed and embarrassed and backed quickly away to find his brother Charlie, who was on a back forty plowing against the spring planting.

The two brothers cursed and conferred and at last strode back to the house, where Charlie procured a whip and a gun and Henry a rope, and they joined the family behind the straw stack.

"And, Mother, now, should we whip him or shoot him or hang him?" inquired Charlie, who most favored whipping because he was uncommon skilled and accurate with his bullwhip.

Louisa Varner Murphy stood panting, arms akimbo, while her daughter and Obediah sat on the ground, having covered themselves, but unable to rise out of fear of the broom, which Louisa kept cocked and ready to go.

"And what shall it be, Mother?" asked Henry politely.

Louisa glared at her two sons and then suddenly let fly with the broom in their direction. "Hung or vipped or shot! Vat you mean? You get your ass out of here, both of you, hear? Get back to your work, I neffer heard no such nonsense before! Get!"

Wisely the two brothers backed away and returned their equipment whence it had come and went back toward the fields muttering and cursing softly to each other.

"You," shouted Louisa to her daughter, "you get to dat house and tend your infant. It needs feeding. Get!"

And as Louisa struggled to her feet and scurried, panting, across the yard toward the house, her mother marched behind, calling out as if to some unseen presence, "Whores and bastards and bitches and asses, dat's vat I got to contend vit. Lord, Gawd, it an't enough I got a fool fer a daughter, but I got to get a fornicator fer a husband!"

Now Obediah sat for a long time behind the straw stack and considered the situation. At first he worried that he had distressed his wife and was vaguely ashamed at the manner in which he had done it. After a time he began to think that, no, it was he, Obediah, who had been ill treated. For had he not been doing a favor? Had he not pleasured a woman who would otherwise get no pleasure, she being of a large frame and evil disposition? And though Obediah did not actually recall the similar pleasuring of fat Rebecca that many years earlier, the sensation had been much the same, of newly lost innocence and newfound manhood.

But though he, Obediah, had in truth realized a goodly amount of pleasure from his encounters with the daughter of his wife, didn't he dearly adore that small daughter he had got on her, he and all who saw that baby, and wasn't that a great thing that he had done to have presented the family with that babe, a babe which the ill-tempered Louisa probably never would have had without him, and didn't he deserve praise rather than censure? Should he be blamed for fathering a child, anyway, on the daughter when the mother perversely refused to bear?

Such was the reasoning of Obediah until, by the time he had sat and considered for a long time, he at last began to feel himself ill used and not nearly sufficiently appreciated.

Such reasoning, too, followed Louisa the daughter as she sulked in the house, seated rocking her baby, that baby contentedly attached to the enormous gland her mother presented her. Had she not, thought Louisa, been able to do for Obediah what her mother had not? She had presented him with a pretty baby and Louisa her mother had never, nor would she ever. Were Obediah to have issue, he certainly would have to go further than her mother's bed, and it was not right that Obediah should be deprived of heirs because her mother was old and barren while she was young and fruitful. And, indeed, did her mother not adore to distraction the sweet baby girl that was hers and Obediah's, and should not her mother thank her rather than chastise her? And thus the young woman comforted herself and looked forward to the time that she would be with Obediah again.

Louisa Varner Murphy speculated also upon the situation. And once her wrath had run its course, she began to find excuses for her husband, Obediah. Was he not victim of the juices that run rampant through a man's veins and the blandishments of a seductress, for such was how she saw her fat daughter? And knowing that Obediah always needed controlling, for he lacked any control of self, had she herself not been negligent in allowing the situation to come to fruition? It was not Obediah's fault that her daughter was a slut. And so reasoning, Louisa determined that she would set a course that would preclude any more such dallying and keep Obediah firmly in line.

But Louisa waited several weeks before she called the family together, including Charlie and Henry, and apprised them of her decision.

"Dis nonsense it haf gone fer enough," she said without preface. "If ever Obediah and Louisa mine daughter should have concourse again"—this was Louisa's word, and though it might be employed in an unusual manner, all who heard it understood—"do dey ever haf concourse vunce more," she repeated, "den dey shall leave mine house and Obediah he can provide fer Louisa and her baby and Louisa she can cook fer him and starch his collars fer him. I vould haf none of it."

Now, as both Obediah and the younger Louisa knew that Louisa Varner Murphy was a woman of her word and having made such declaration would stick to it, and as Obediah had little interest in being forced to provide for a family and as Louisa the daughter had even less interest in cooking meals and starching collars, they both acceded hastily to the conditions Louisa had set, with only one minor abridgment.

"It's possible," admitted Louisa the younger, "that I might be once more with child. But it an't my fault," she added peevishly.

"An' who's fault vould it be, pray?" snapped her mother.

"Well," amended the girl sullenly, "what I mean is that it was not from something we done recently."

Louisa glared hard at her daughter and Obediah fidgeted and wondered to himself if it would help the situation did he begin to whistle a merry little tune. But he thought better of it.

Louisa at last merely sighed and said, "Ve vill attend to dat in its time." And thus were they dismissed.

Obediah, relieved to be free and having nothing seriously to occupy himself with, as the wood was ricked high and the corn laid by, took himself to Old Taylor the storekeeper, upon whom he had been wont to look in regularly with a view to ascertaining the state of the old man's health.

Old Taylor, though he looked frailer with each visit, seemed determined to go like an old building left to sag slowly into ruin rather than falling like an old tree uprooted suddenly in a windstorm. Obediah found it all disappointing, though he did like Old Taylor and found him entertaining and informative company. But Obediah was in a haste to get on with the renaming of the hamlet, which had already added a trader's cabin and two more residents. He had about determined that Murphystown was his best bet, as there was already a Murfreesboro in Tennessee and he would not like to be thought to be naming his town after that one. But Old Taylor remained stubbornly alive and seemed to grow perversely prouder all the time of his part in naming the place, which precluded Obediah's going to the old gentleman and politely asking to go ahead and (with his approval, of course) rename the town, as he had once considered doing.

Old Taylor, who took delivery of supplies of staples from wagons passing through, likewise got some newspapers and also reports from the drivers; such reports did he pass on to those of his customers who happened in. The news was all of the impending war, a possibility of which Obediah was only remotely aware and Louisa his wife dismissed with "It von't happen." Obediah trusted Louisa's judgment and so paid but little heed to rumors of war.

"Well, they say," said Old Taylor to the several men who sat around his small store, as Obediah likewise, between summer harvest and fall harvest, and with nothing much better to entertain themselves, "that we all will have soon to declare ourselves, that here on the border as we are there will be no rail straddling."

The ensuing conversation was only as wise as most such conversations, each man defending the position he held, brooking no argument no matter how sound that argument, though in truth most of the argument supported the position of Jefferson Davis and his government insomuch as the debaters understood that position.

"And what think ye, Obediah?" asked one, for Obediah, wherever he went, managed to retain that reputation for thoughtful persuasion and perspicacity that he had early on earned.

Obediah answered as he was accustomed to answer questions upon which he had no opinion, and they were many, that he had as yet not studied all the various arguments and was still pondering, though (and here he wisely sided with the majority) it seemed to him that the position of the Southern statesmen had at least the same merit as that of the federal government and perhaps more. And those who heard him went away in the certitude of Obediah Murphy's wisdom and of his eventual upholding of their own honorable positions.

Obediah went home to Louisa and asked her opinion.

"It won't happen," she reiterated.

"But if it should?" Obediah was concerned, and though he trusted his wife's judgment in most matters, it came to him that she had not been privy to all the information that he had and that it was possible that she refused to recognize the possibility of such a confrontation because she didn't want it to happen.

Louisa only shrugged. "Should dat happen, ve vould attend to it. But so far it an't happen, so ve don't need to attend to it. Dey're an't nothin' ve could do no vise," she added quite reasonably. "I haf mine own things to attend, anyvay."

Obediah did not pursue the subject, for Louisa's temper was short, shorter than usual. Louisa the younger, far enough gone with child that she knew herself to be safe from her mother's broom, had gotten rebellious herself, and that was rebellion enough, in Louisa's view, without troubling herself over that possible larger one.

Louisa the younger had grown increasingly demanding and disrespectful. Like a favored concubine, she lorded it over her mother. Only once did she come close to losing that sanctuary that her condition afforded her. "I think," she said one day, "that I should be Obediah's wife as I am the mother of his children. You look too old, anyway, to be wed to him." Though that last observation was true, it also was not wise, for Louisa the elder got into such a rage that the frightened daughter waddled hastily from her presence and stayed carefully out of sight for several hours. And it was many weeks before she regained her superior self-confidence and returned to her demanding ways.

"Ma," complained Henry, "can't you do something with her? She thinks she's a queen."

"Ne'er fret, Henry, ven vunce she's got two young ones pulling at her and two shitty bottoms to see to, she an't goin' to feel like no princess fer long." Louisa fully intended that, once the second baby was born, her daughter would take full responsibility for both babies. There was nothing, she reasoned, like squalling babes to put a woman in her place. Though, indeed, Louisa the younger had been quite spoiled in that matter, as everyone had been anxious to help in caring for the third Louisa, a pretty, bright and thoroughly adorable little girl, whose sweet disposition, pretty expression and uncommon good sense did her grandmother proud, and Louisa the elder was pleased enough that she had insisted on passing that name on one more time, this time much more satisfactorily.

By the time the fall harvest was complete and the pumpkins pulled and the sweet potatoes stored, Louisa the younger had gotten immense, swollen from her toes to her bloated face. She was no longer snippy and demanding, only angry and uncomfortable and sick, blaming her condition on anyone within blaming distance, except of course Obediah, he who most deserved the blame. She scolded her mother for keeping the room too cold and her brothers for making too much noise and her little daughter for prattling. She blamed God for the fact that the winter was coming, and she blamed the natural order of things for slowing down and prolonging her considerable discomfort.

Obediah she blamed for nothing, but he, being uncomfortable in the face of ill temper of any sort, found himself increasingly passing time at Old Taylor's store and marveling that that old fellow could remain upright and completely coherent when he should have given up the ghost years before. The talk there was still of the seriousness of the breech between the Northern states and the Southern states, which talk made Obediah uncomfortable, although he had joined some time earlier his fellows in condemning the North, having no other choice, as Louisa adamantly refused to take a position.

When the younger Louisa's time finally came, it was early of a frosty morning and lasted through that whole day and another night. Her mother, sensing early that this would be a difficult birth, sent Charlie through Taylortown to the north for Mistress Higgins, who midwived regularly the wives about the countryside, and she came in haste. Through the long day Louisa the younger moaned and cried out and cursed and vomited and screamed. The two older women conferred.

"Them pains are too close fer too long," said Louisa Varner Murphy.

"Aye. An' her color's not good and she's too swolled. I don't like the look of it. The babe might be breech and it might be sickly." She did not say "dead," though both women thought that, too, possible.

Obediah, disconcerted by Louisa's screaming, had taken baby Louisa and had gone to converse at Old Taylor's store, where all who came by stopped to admire the little girl. And Obediah explained happily that her little brother was involved in making his entry into the world.

"An' yer sure," someone teased, "that it'll be a boy?"

"Oh, of certainty, of certainty," cried Obediah. "We already got a girl." It was reasonable.

Nor did any of the listeners remark upon the absence of the babe's father, no one being quite certain as to his whereabouts, though vague rumor had it that he had been killed or destroyed by illness or some such, after having got his wife with her second child. No one was certain enough of dates and ages to be able to calculate any more reliable information than that.

Little Louisa charmed all who met her, and she chatted and laughed and confirmed that she would soon have a baby brother and that she was much excited, having no playmate close by her own age.

As Obediah and little Louisa strolled home they discussed the event in progress.

"And what," asked Obediah seriously, "should we name our little brother?"

Louisa gave it the serious consideration she thought it merited and at last answered, "I would call him Obediah, I think. Yes, Obediah would be a good name."

"Indeed," said Obediah, "I had thought that myself." And he picked the little girl up and hoisted her to his shoulder.

Obediah was inordinately proud of his little girl, she being both pretty and uncommonly bright and articulate for one so young, but he longed for a son. From the earliest days of his marriage he had planned for a son, a son to bear his name and carry on his but vaguely realized work, a son to help him found his dynasty. But none had been forthcoming, and though he had not worried greatly over the matter, for he was not a worrying kind, it did concern him some that he did not seem to be able to get a child, either male or female, so that when Louisa was born, though he had the wisdom not to proclaim her as his own, he was proud and some relieved. Now he was to be blessed with a son to carry on his line. Was never a man so content as Obediah Murphy.

But when they got home at last in the late afternoon, he was greeted by the stern expressions and tight lips of the two older women attending the birth.

"It's an uncommon hard birth," Louisa the elder said to him. And that was all.

Well, Obediah thought to himself, that's too bad. But as Louisa is a large woman, she should have the strength to survive it. He did not give any thought to his infant son, as it did not occur to him that the babe might be in danger.

The boy baby that was eventually born was large, which had been part of the problem. With relief Louisa the elder took the sticky creature that Mistress Higgins handed over to her. He was indeed too large, more swollen than fat, and the color that should have coursed through his body failed to come. He was too pale. He made but a feeble cry, which brought Obediah poking his head into the room.

"A boy," murmured Mistress Higgins and a joyous smile danced across Obediah's face, only to be replaced by one of grief and despair with Mistress Higgins' abrupt "I fear, though, he won't live. I observe him to be birth-poisoned throughout. The mother," she concluded, "I think will live, though she'll be right sick and birth no more babies. I seen this to happen too many times."

And so, too, had Louisa Varner Murphy. The death of a newborn babe, and of older babes, too, as well as their mothers, was not at all uncommon, and indeed almost all families had experienced at least one such loss and often more.

Louisa the elder held the hastily wrapped little bundle and heard another faint cry from his bluish lips and felt the rattle of his body as it tried to absorb lifegiving elements. And she looked up at Obediah, her husband, and saw the stricken look on his face, pale as the babe's, pitiful as a whipped dog, pleading soundlessly with her to do something, to save this small creature, his only son.

"He vill not die if ever I could help it," snapped the baby's grandmother. And Louisa Varner Murphy locked her will with the will of the natural order of things. She quickly wiped the baby clean and wrapped him in warm swaddling and soaked a rag with camphor and held it near, and he coughed, a strange little hacking noise that racked his small body. Louisa could still hear the rattle from his lungs and only occasionally a feeble cry. She sat down abruptly by the hearth and ordered the fire built high and the tallow candles that she saved against times of need lighted to give the room as much light as possible, lest the babe still think himself in the darkened womb. She rocked hard and sang to the little one, and the smell of camphor hung heavy in the room. At last Louisa began to talk to the babe, explaining to him the necessity of living.

"Must live and grow and be big. Must be a boy first, to play and run and throw rocks into the brook and chase the squirrels up the tree and eat vit both hands at vunce and tease your sister. Must be a man and love a women and marry and bring children into the vorld and so to be old and a grandfadder. Must not die before ye see the geese headed toward the sunset or the snow upon the ground or the clouds of thunder yonder banked. Must gather up all yer strength, small babe, and push toward life, fer it's pain ye know now and sickness, too, but t'won't last, and ye'll grow and love and be loved and it's vorth all the pain that is."

And Louisa rocked the babe fiercely, the cabin lighted up like day, Henry and Charlie stoking the fireplace and Obediah replacing the tallow candles. But the small babe did not seem to think it worth the effort after all, and before morning even Louisa, his grandmother, had to recognize the rattle in his small chest for what it was. She held him tighter still, his own mother, struggling herself with the same fluids that had poisoned him, far too ill to hold him. Louisa rocked him and crooned a low and wordless tune of the sort that nurses have crooned their babes since ever time began, assuring the babe that he would be prized and protected ere he was to manhood grown.

Obediah sat across from Louisa, holding his hands clasped in wordless misery, until at last with the early rays the babe gave up the effort and so died. And Obediah Jonah Micah Murphy knew true grief for the first time in his life, for he had never lost anything he prized or failed anything important. Nor did he understand how so profound a loss of something he had never really had could be.

But Louisa his wife knew, she being experienced in the loss of babes, for though it happened often and to all families alike, the pain of each such loss was as new as if it had never before been.

Henry and Charlie found a spot on the side of a hill, shaded by a big tree in the summer and protected in the winter, and, grieving for the child that neither had ever held, dug a safe place for him to rest eternally.

When little Louisa rose the next morning and inquired after her brother, she was met with dry-eyed silence. Obediah only turned away.

"He is gone," Louisa said at last.

"Where did he go?" asked the little girl.

There was a lengthy silence as each person pondered the proper answer. It was Mistress Higgins who at last said gently, "Jesus came and took him away."

The little girl frowned at that intelligence but asked no more. All through the rest of the morning she was seen to be considering and thinking and pondering and sneaking sidewise looks at the grieving elders. At last she came to her grandmother, Louisa, and touching that woman upon the hand, she said, "Grandmother, I would as lief that Jesus not call on us no more."

"N'en I, child, n'en I," said Louisa.

Grief is hardest borne in the wintertime, when death lies all about, anyway, and there is little to occupy time or hands or mind. Who would spare the hardest grief to loved ones would take care to die in early spring, when life is growing from the ground and there is work anon to blunt sorrow's edge until time and memory can permanently soften it.

And so it was that Obediah quitted the grieving household, which grief was often edged with harsh words, and passed his time at Old Taylor's store. And when the Southern states seceded from the Union and formed the Confederate States of America, word came first to Old Taylor, and Obediah carried that word to Louisa his wife, she only pausing and then without comment shaking her head. And when war actually broke out between the Northern and Southern factions, word came again to Louisa from Old Taylor by way of Obediah. Louisa greeted that news with a prolonged sigh and then sat with a thump, for she was grown portly with age, on the step outside the cabin and rested her chin upon her fist and frowned.

Both Charlie and Henry, however, were more vocal in their reactions. "We must join up," cried Henry, and Charlie nodded, both being excited at the prospect of an adventure, as prospects for adventure were few in that sparsely settled area where there were neither wild savages to track nor marriageable maidens enough for all prospective suitors. A war happened into their lives at precisely the time that they needed something like that, just before each settled into stodgy, permanent bachelorhood.

"We shall to Paducah and enlist in the Confederate cause," cried Henry.

"No, no," amended his brother, "not to Paducah. We'll to Orleans and join up."

Henry immediately approved the wisdom of his brother, who was older and therefore had seen that Orleans, being far from potential shooting and a fine city with many pretty girls to admire a smartly uniformed soldier, was indeed the wisest choice for enlistments.

"We'll to Orleans!"

"What about the crops," asked Obediah, for spring planting was nigh.

"Oh, bother the crops," cried the young men in boyish glee. "There's a war to be fought!"

Up to this point Louisa their mother had said naught. At last she rose slowly and stiffly and announced, "Ve vill move north, to Illinois, to Cairo. But before ve go, Obediah, mine husband, ve must collect all our rents, sell all our properties and call in all our notes, though ve take loss on all dem, fer ven dis var be done, dey vill be no moneys at all in dese Southern states to collect."

"Mother! North?" cried Charlie.

"North. Dat is vat I say. I haf thought on it and thought on it dese many months dat dis var has hovered, and dere vas much to consider both vays. But at last it come down to dis: mine uncle Leviticus Rippert, the Philadelphia lawyer, he fought in dat udder var dat built dis Union togedder, dat var vit George Vashington and dem udders. He was proud of dat, vas mine uncle. Ve vill not help to tear dat Union down. And dat's all it is."

The declaration thus made, Louisa went into the house and left Charlie and Henry to ponder in disappointment, for it did not enter their heads to argue with her, particularly when she invoked the name of Leviticus Rippert, the Philadelphia lawyer, for that name was all but sacred in that household.

It was Henry who brightened suddenly. "We'll go to St. Louis!" he cried, and Charlie recognized his younger brother's brilliance immediately, for though St. Louis might not have the French-speaking maids of Orleans, it, too, was a fine city, with fine ladies to admire dashing war heroes. And, after all, North or South, it was the same war anyway.

"Obediah," said Louisa as he prepared to depart for a morning of conversation at Old Taylor's store, "tell dat old man Taylor dat ven dat circuit rider passes by, I vould see him, as I must send a message to mine son Danny Varner to get up here and to join us in our move."

Louisa had learned long before not to trust Obediah with any writing assignment other than his signature, and that only when it was closely monitored. She had found that, for notary purposes, a circuit-riding preacher was often as good as any, though not always, for some of those men of the cloth, though sincere, only pretended to read from the Bibles they held, having memorized sufficient passages to support whatever doctrine each espoused, though not always carefully enough to avoid certain disagreements and varied interpretations, which did not bother Louisa at all, though she recognized such discrepancies, having been well taught from the Bible when she was a girl. Her main interest in the occasional meetings such preachers held were social in nature, and she cared not at all for doctrine, no matter whose.

In due course the circuit rider appeared and was able with some skill to take down Louisa's message in all its particulars, even to duplicating her own style.

> Mine son Danny Varner,
>> I vould haf you join us as ve vill flee north and take vit us all our capital. I vould not be a part in the sundering of dis Union, vich von't vork anyvay. Make haste, fer our delay makes the departing only harder.
>> I remain yer respecful and loving mudder Louisa Rippert Varner Murphy.

Louisa sealed the letter carefully and paid a handsome sum to a local youth to ride nonstop until he had delivered it into Danny Varner's hands in Tennessee, and he was instructed to return any message.

The letter that the messenger returned did not surprise Louisa so much, for she expected it.

> My dear and respected mother and her husband,
>> I grieve your decision and I would change it if I could. But I know that that is probably not possible. I am a man of the South and a believer in the Southern cause. I cannot desert that cause. I remain your affectionate son, Danny Varner.

So be it, thought Louisa and made no further mention of her oldest son, though his two younger brothers muttered some that he was allowed to stay and fight for the South, but they having considered both sides and having weighed the heat of New Orleans against the cold of St. Louis, decided it was a toss-up and so joined the removal plans cheerfully enough.

Quietly Louisa called in her notes and sold such properties as she could, both near and distant, and through it all dispatched Charlie and Henry and Obediah stealthily across the border into Illinois with various goods and livestock and moneys to be deposited. And Obediah heeded her instructions carefully until all was accomplished that could safely be accomplished. Some lands and moneys she would have to leave in Tennessee and Kentucky and hope for the best. It had become dangerous to linger, as daily the murmurings grew that Henry and Charley had not yet enlisted in the Southern cause, though both insisted that they were making plans to enlist.

Leaving all furnishings save Louisa's secretary, which was carefully concealed, and pleading a business trip to Paducah and enlistment for the young men, the family pulled out of Taylortown by wagon, but not before Obediah made one last call upon Old Taylor.

Old Taylor was not there, but only a small group of serious-faced men. The old feller, they explained to Obediah, had fallen into a coughing fit from which he did not recover and so had dropped dead. There being no heirs, the gentlemen were occupied in the business of deciding what to do with the old man's property and had about concluded to divide that property among themselves, and did Obediah, whom they knew to be a man of means, want to buy that property from them?

"He was my friend," sighed Obediah, genuinely bereft.

The gentlemen nodded solemnly.

And would he be interested in such a bargain? repeated one after a decent interval.

"Yes," said Obediah, "yes indeed I would. I will buy all of this property." He paused. "After I return from where I am going," he added.

It was with a very heavy heart that Obediah departed old dead Taylor's town.

They settled on a section of land near Mount Vernon, Illinois, far enough removed from the Mississippi River and the Southern borders that Louisa felt reasonably secure from the strife, yet not so far removed from the land and neighbors they had just quitted.

"Dat var might be over someday," she declared, "an' ve might vant to go back."

The section of land that Louisa bought was fertile and well watered and boasted a finer house than ever they had lived in before, it having belonged to a Southern sympathizer who had found it expedient to remove himself, precipitately, leaving behind most furniture and some clothing. As it was heavily mortgaged anyway, the bank reclaimed the farm and put it up for sale. Obediah paid for it with gold coins, which so impressed the bank officers that word of the Murphy wealth got around quickly.

In a matter of days, Obediah was called upon by a gentleman of the county, one Adam Springer, with a business proposition that he assured Obediah would both benefit the Northern war effort and make rich those who had participated in it.

Obediah quickly shepherded Adam Springer into Louisa's kitchen, where she, up to her elbows in flour, was making dumplings to go with the fat hen stewing on the hearth. Now, Louisa Varner Murphy's talents for successful business dealings included an uncanny ability to correctly size up those with whom she dealt and the judgment to know whether serious, intelligent, trustworthy. That had always been the basis of her success in business, and she employed that talent as she listened to Mr. Springer's proposition.

"I have access," he said, "to several loads of cotton bales, already paid for and on the river north when war was declared. They are being held ransom just below Cairo, and for five thousand dollars in gold they will be delivered into my hands. But I have not got five thousand dollars in gold." Mr. Springer addressed those remarks to Louisa, realizing immediately that that was where the decision lay.

"I do not like ransoms," said Louisa.

"Let me just say, then, that such duty paid will ensure the safe delivery of that merchandise, which has already quadrupled in value since it first was set afloat. And should we keep it a few months in storage, it will go even higher."

Louisa eyed the petitioner for a long moment before she said, "Mine Uncle Leviticus Rippert, the Philadelphia lawyer, he taught me business a long time ago and he taught me the value of an honest bargain. Mine Obediah vill deliver to ye a strongbox vit five thousand dollars gold at the place and time of yer choosing. I vill expect the return of dat five thousand, plus half the profits realized on dis venture. I vould haf a strict account, too. Mine husband, Obediah," she added with a narrowed look at Adam Springer, "he is very strong and some ruthless."

Adam Springer looked at Obediah Murphy, standing fully six inches above him, and he could tell that Obediah was indeed strong, and perhaps ruthless; of that last he could not be sure, as Obediah was not following the conversation but was instead watching a cow in the barnyard who was making overtures to a large bull.

That veiled threat was not really necessary, either, for Louisa had yet to misjudge any man in a business dealing. She did not ask particulars upon how Mr. Springer intended to carry out his part of the bargain, nor did she ask for papers or notes, it not being the sort of thing that she could carry to the courts anyway. Nor did she bother herself over any legal aspects of the matter, only to congratulate herself that she could help in the effort to hold the Union together and realize a profit at the same time. Without handshake and with none but a friendly nod, Adam Springer departed, having given careful directions on the time and place of delivery of the strongbox filled with gold.

As both Charlie and Henry were anxious to volunteer for the war, Louisa finally acquiesced. Obediah she appointed to accompany the two to St. Louis and so to see to their needs and bring back what information he could. But it was with a heavy heart that Louisa watched her sons ride merrily off to war as if to some frolic or dalliance that they fully expected to discharge by suppertime.

Now, neither Obediah nor either of his stepsons was wise in the way of large cities. They had been to no larger place than Chattanooga in their lifetimes and so were most considerably impressed by the size and bustle of this busy city, filled as it was to overflowing with soldiers and would-be soldiers. Indeed, finding a place to enlist proved easier than finding a place to tie their mounts. And so as Obediah stood holding the horses, Henry and Charlie were signed up and sworn into the Army of the Potomac and issued orders in that short space of time.

"They have told us to report to the 36th Illinois," said Charlie in some vexation, for he had planned to spend the war dallying about this grand city, and now it looked seriously as if they might expect him to fight.

Obediah was as sympathetic to their plight as he could be, but he was in truth quite fascinated at the sight of the Union officers, scurrying impressively around in their dark blue coats and striped breeches and wide-brimmed hats. The one who had sworn in Henry and Charlie in particular, with gold epaulets on his shoulders and sword hanging at his side, caught Obediah's fancy, and he thought that surely that officer was at least a general, if not greater.

Obediah stared at the officer's gold buttons as if in a trance and slowly raised his eyes from them at last to find that worthy staring at him.

Indeed, Obediah had no way of knowing that the officer in question, a lieutenant in his dress uniform charged with the business of recruiting and enlisting, was thinking what a boon would such a figure of a handsome man be were he dressed in Union blue, for every recruiter knows that it is the sight of that uniform modeled for them that elicits enlistments from civilians as much as ever does patriotism or defense of cause.

"And are ye, sir," asked the young officer, "come to enlist this day?"

"What? Enlist? I? No."

"No?" And the young lieutenant's expression took on so sorrowful a cast that Obediah felt it incumbent upon him to explain his business.

"I accompanied my sons," he said, and added proudly, "They have both enlisted just now. But I have never fought a war. I know nothing of it. I am too old," he said quite honestly, for he was never vain of his age. And he truly thought that wars (when he thought about wars at all, which was seldom) were the sport of the very young, like tag and blindman's buff.

"Old, sir? Old? Why, never. Nary was a war ever won without the advice of the elders and their sage wisdom. You, sir, are a man of presence. In this uniform"—and the young man tapped himself upon the chest—"in this uniform, carrying vital information to the generals, bearing maps and battle plans . . . why, sir!" And the lieutenant, who was skilled in his occupation, let Obediah's imagination finish out the thought.

Obediah stared hard at that uniform, for the lieutenant had doffed his hat and bowed with a flourish and had come up holding a quill, which he offered to Obediah. "Just set your signature, or your mark, to these papers and you will be issued a uniform and sent to a command."

Obediah touched the ruffles at his throat and took the quill, frowning all the while. Now, it has been previously recorded that Obediah Jonah Micah Murphy was not to be trusted with a quill, and when the lieutenant asked, "Do you write or shall I find a witness for your mark?" Obediah boomed, "Why, sir, indeed I do write!"

And with much flourish and many starts and overlong pauses, Obediah commenced to set his signature to the paper as the lieutenant watched in fascination the construction of that mighty signature.

"Ah," he said and motioned others standing nearby to come witness the execution of this signature, the lieutenant thinking that he at least had enlisted a schoolmaster, if not a lawyer or perhaps a college president, so elegant was the name being set so assiduously.

With a final flourish, Obediah looked up in triumph and the

lieutenant beamed. "Congratulations. You have enlisted in the United States Army!"

And so it was that Obediah went to war with his stepsons. Louisa his wife and Louisa the mother of his child mourned as if he were already killed, though Louisa the elder did observe that Obie was more like to come home safe from the war than were her sons, nor did she explain what made her sense that, that her sons were somehow less safe and more mortal than her husband, Obediah.

"I haf sent four men to var," said Louisa, "and I ask the good Lord dat I get dose four back again safe." She included her oldest son, Danny Varner, in that count, for she was certain that he fought, though he fought on the side opposite his brothers and stepfather. It was, in Louisa's thinking, a crazy war that set brother against brother. But, in Louisa's thinking, it was a crazy war that set any man against any other man.

"I am going to go with him," cried Louisa the younger, "for he will need me."

"He vill need you the same as he needs a goose tied around each foot; now get in the house and tend yer child. She needs you." The younger Louisa did not mention going to war anymore, though she did sulk the better part of that day away.

Obediah, along with Henry, Charlie and many other recruits, most quite a bit younger than Obediah, were sent with little preparation south to Lebanon in Missouri, just to the northeast of Springfield ("Ah, another nameless town," thought Obie), which city was held by the Confederates under General Price, they having defeated the Union troops at the Battle of Wilson's Creek near Springfield.

At Lebanon, General Sam Curtis was gathering together the Army of the Southwest, his intent to drive the Confederates from Missouri and to secure that unsteady state for the Union.

Obediah Murphy and his sons hardly understood that greater plan, however, and as long as the weather remained warm, the food plentiful and the company merry, they all thought war to be indeed a pleasant exercise, although Obediah did frown at the weapon he was issued. He was not a hunter, nor did it ever occur to him that he might shoot a man. He put the rifle aside and wished that he might have a nice sword to brandish.

By the time fall had slipped into winter, most of the chickens and geese and pigs of the neighborhood had already given their lives for the Union cause and the men were left to grumble over their rations of sweet potatoes and wild squirrel or rabbit, when that could be found. And the drills and games of warfare, which had seemed a lark in the balmy days before Thanksgiving, by New Year's were dreary at best, and often torturous.

"An d'ye think the Rebels're goin' to wait until yer feet are toasty warm and yer bellies passin' filled and yer body nicely rested before they attack?" yelled the drill sergeant to his complaining troops.

General Curtis, passing quietly among his troops, noted the grumbling.

"A man needs a horse," complained a footsore soldier. "A man needs to feel the power between his legs, whether it be on a horse or on a woman!"

"I think I'd ruther ride a horse to battle than a woman," joked another.

"Oh, I don't know," rejoined another. "Lonesome as I are right now, I think I'd ride a woman right to the feet of Lee hisself."

"I come to fight a war," complained a mountain man. "If we an't goin' to fight, then I say we might as well go home. I don't cotton to settin' on my ass in the snow."

General Curtis, standing outside the light from the campfire, listened.

"Aye," said another, "an' I don't know that we can win a fight, anyway. Lookit what the Rebs done to us at Wilson's Creek an' us outnumberin' by thousands."

The silence from the group gathered around the fire assented to the seriousness of that observation.

"Ah no," came the deep and quiet rejoinder of Obediah Murphy, standing tall and silhouetted by the fire, erect and straight as the flagpole itself. "Ah," he said, "that will not be. We will win because the Union must endure." He said it as if he believed it. And indeed he did, because Louisa his wife had told him so and he knew her to be right. "It will not be an easy battle, nor an easy war," he went on, warming to his topic as if he stood, not before a campfire in the January of a great war, but rather in the lantern light of a meeting-house somewhere or other, expounding the views of Louisa Varner, making her plain and honest sentiments profound, "and much will be lost in life, in fortune, in courage. But we shall win; we shall endure and we shall overcome!"

There was a perceptible brightening of spirits at that, for Obediah had impressed the recruits already with his strength and agility, with his willingness to work and with the soundness of his reasoning and the depth of his wisdom.

"Ah," moaned one young recruit, "but it's cold and we're hungry and tired. This dreary winter will surely drive us all distract."

"Aye," said the mountain man, "would that it were spring and that we could fight. Then we'd all feel better fer it."

At that Obediah commenced to whistle softly, and as the men turned his way he picked up the tempo and he whistled up spring, and then he whistled up battle and marching and fighting and the men could not but clap their hands in time with his music, and by the time he was finished, all felt refreshed as if they had actually marched safely through battle themselves, and their talk turned to sport and horses and crops and women, the things that men most concern themselves with.

"Who is that man?" asked General Curtis of his aide, who did not know but promised to find out. And within the hour he brought the general information on Obediah. The general by then sat in his tent and listened.

"He is Obediah Murphy, enlisted with his two sons in St. Louis. He is said to be fearless in battle, stronger than two grown men and quicker than an Indian on live coals. It is thought that he is a doctor or a lawyer or college professor, for he writes a fine hand and he speaks with wisdom and polish."

The general thought about that information for a long time and at last he said, "Bring Obediah Murphy to me first thing in the morning. I am going to make an officer of him."

General Curtis had thought to make Obediah a captain, perhaps, for he had the power to sway men and to lead them, and when troop morale began to fail, such leaders were indispensable. General Sam Curtis was a simple man who understood soldiering best, and upon questioning Obediah Murphy at length, he realized that one thing this learned and profound man did not understand was soldiering. He might be wise and he might be agile and strong and brave, but he did not know a left flank from a right flank. Pity. The general determined at last that Obediah's greatest usefulness would be as a figurehead. Therefore he made him a colonel, as colonels were only passing useful in fighting wars anyway.

On the spot, Obediah Jonah Micah Murphy was commissioned a colonel of the Army of the Potomac and properly outfitted as such with broad-brimmed hat, sword and gauntlets. And General Curtis himself had to admire the figure that strode away from him clad in Union blue, tall and erect, exacting admiring glances and straightening recruits to attention. General Curtis only noted to himself that he must be careful that Colonel Murphy never be put in a position where a sound military decision would be important.

"Colonel Murphy's chief function in this army," General Curtis announced to his staff, "is as liaison to the troops. He is to listen to their problems and their grievances and he is to advise them. Choose for him a handful of seasoned fighting men to act as aides."

And so Obediah became "the Colonel," reputed to be both a wise statesman and a fierce fighting man, for the aides who accompanied him were known for their own courageous ferocity in battle; among them were Eli Case, former Indian scout, purported to be possessed of a few scalps of his own; Tom Timmons, hard-drinking and hard-riding companion to Sam Curtis himself; and Irish Malone, a refugee of the potato famine and said to be tough enough to survive on goat dung and Rebel blood. In the midst of that group towered Obediah Jonah Micah Murphy, whistling up spring and eyeing camp maidens and farm girls alike.

In February of 1862 General Curtis's troops moved against Springfield, and the Confederates under General Sterling Price quickly fell back, as Price received no aid from his fellow general Ben McCullough, as expected. Through February, the Confederates retreated south, fighting rearguard actions and burning anything that the advancing Union troops might find useful. Among those advancing troops were the 36th Illinois, and on March 7 a major confrontation of those two opposing armies occurred near Pea Ridge in Arkansas.

It was General Sam Curtis himself who issued orders concerning the deployment of Obediah Murphy during that savage battle, the general's purpose relative to Obediah having been successfully realized; for Obediah, wherever he went, inspired awe and admiration among the troops and a legend of magnificent proportions had grown up about him. General Curtis recognized the value of such legends and instructed Colonel Murphy's aides, "Move him strategically, but keep him safe. Defend him with your lives if needs be, but keep him close to battle and move among all the troops so that each group of fighting men might feel that he is one of them." So instructed, Eli Case, Tom Timmons and Irish Malone nodded their understanding.

"An' d'ye know, General Curtis, sir," said Eli Case, "that the Rebs has brought upwards a thousand a them red savages from the Territory to fight?"

Curtis nodded.

"We'll be leavin' here with fewer scalps 'en we come with. But then," he added with a sly grin, "so will the Rebs. I know them savage bustards fer what they are. Watch the trees, General, watch the trees, fer they'll ne'er come out a hidin'."

"I will watch the trees; you watch Colonel Murphy. The Rebels may have their Indians, but we have our Colonel Murphy. Mount him on a white horse and guard him well!"

And so it was that Obediah Jonah Micah Murphy fought the Battle of Pea Ridge, mounted upon a pure white horse, brandishing his sword high, surrounded by ferocious protectors, riding pell-mell through fire and smoke, charging and laughing and exhorting, so that indeed each group of fighting men that he happened upon was right cheered and relieved to know that they were being led by such a man and that as a result no harm could befall them.

Obediah enjoyed it all immensely, for he moved too fast through the smoke and confusion to note the carnage all about, to see the bloody dead being casually wrapped in the dried leaves and grass of the battlefield, nature's impersonal winding sheet. He did not pause at medical stations, nor see the stacks of amputated limbs, with stockings lovingly hand-knit and garters still clinging to some, nor hear the groans and curses of the wounded and dying. He never saw the scalped men left bleeding and sightless, for they avoided the trees where most of those lay, and though a flint-tipped arrow or two passed close by, Obediah did not notice, but Irish Malone did take one in the thigh, and only tore it out himself with a curse and flung it whence it had come. Not once did Obediah notice a squealing horse, its rider gone, its body bloody from its own wounds, nor smell the burning flesh of a cannon-struck youngster. Nor did he know (until much later) that Henry Varner had been wounded and captured almost upon the first volley of shot. Through the veil of smoke that hid the agonies of war from him, Obediah rode singing and whistling and calling out encouragement, praising God, the flag, President Lincoln and whatever generals' names he could remember; as saints of war he exhorted the foot soldiers to victory in their names.

Obediah rested but little through two days of fiercest fighting, and changed his mount to a fresher one on two occasions, so that he was as muddy and stained as if he had fought the oncoming army toe to toe and those who saw him remarked to themselves that the Colonel had certainly dispatched countless Rebs to their rewards and the story passed down the line that the Colonel had already two mounts shot out from under him and had personally bested General McCullough in hand-to-hand combat and left that general dead upon the battlefield; though the latter was indeed true, the former was not. The general was dead, but it had been a foot soldier of the 36th Illinois who got him, and not Obediah Murphy. The only blood upon Obediah's sword was his own, as he had managed to nick himself upon the cheek in brandishing his sword in greater enthusiasm than was necessary. That wound was, however, noted and quickly ascribed by the adoring troops to a confrontation with a scalp-taking savage, that savage now himself bereft of scalp.

And so the legend grew, with the considerable aid of Obediah's cohorts Eli Case, Tom Timmons and Irish Malone, for while he was brandishing and exhorting, those other three warriors gave the ghost to many of the enemy, particularly those savages upon whom they chanced, most particularly Eli Case, the Indian scout, for there was little mercy in that man, and none at all toward the Indians to whom he had the natural antipathy of one who had spent a lifetime wronging them.

Eventually the battle abated in favor of the Union Army, which, though outnumbered by several thousands, had carried the day, those troops boasting that they could have won against twice the odds, for did they not ride behind the banner of the invincible Colonel Murphy?

But Colonel Murphy was by that time quite tired, and he and his aides rested off away from the battlefield. Obediah lay on his back and stared at the clouds and thought what an exciting and tiring experience a war was. Irish Malone examined his wounded thigh and plugged the hole with a wad of chewed tobacco, while Tom Timmons drank from a bottle he had unearthed and hummed to himself.

Only Eli Case, the Indian scout, frowned. He stared into the distance and the frown deepened. With a slow intake of breath he hissed, "Hark, look to yer scalp. There's a Indian about. I kin smell it." He rose to one knee and listened intently as the others held their breath and peered carefully around.

"It an't but one," said the seasoned scout, "an it's over that rise." He rose and stepped cautiously in the direction he had pointed, as did the others, though Irish Malone groaned at the pain the effort cost him. At the top of the rise they peered into the distance, just in time, indeed, to see a lone Indian warrior covered with dirt and blood and war paint leap out suddenly upon an unsuspecting farm girl gathering in her milch cow, pull her down, tear her skirts away and begin to use her for the satisfaction of his lust.

"Ahhhhh!" The sound that Eli Case let out was not loud, but it was such a sound that stood the very hackles at the back of the neck to attention. And before anyone else could move, Eli Case was darting soundlessly down the side of the hill where the Indian and the maiden struggled. Close behind him came Obediah Murphy, for he was quicker on foot than the other two, the one being under the influence of drink and the other being wounded.

Nor did Eli Case slow down but charged the mating pair, knife upraised, and with a sweep reached down and grabbed the Indian by the hair, raising his head and encountering his surprised stare, all soundless save the screaming and sobbing of the girl; and Eli Case with his knife cut clean through the savage's neck and pulled his severed head away from his body and held it aloft, at which the maiden fainted dead away, the warrior's seed spilling into her as his blood spilled over her.

The girl never did regain her senses. (Obediah, telling Louisa about the incident much later, affirmed that she had gone quite mad as a result of the Indian seed, it being incompatible with a white woman's constitution. "White women raped by a Indian always go mad, ye see. It has to do with the seed." "I vould think," suggested Louisa, "dat it vould haf to do vit finding yerself fucked by a headless corpse.") But the girl bore, the proper number of months later, a son more white than red, who was named Curtis McCullough by the girl's bitter kin, halfheartedly raised by them until he was old enough to be shoved off on his own, he being eventually hanged as an outlaw in the wilds of the Territory.

Obediah had never seen a man killed; though he had ridden through a fierce and savage battle, he had not consciously witnessed the massacres that are common occurrence in such situations. He stood horrified at the sight of his aide gleefully holding the trophy aloft. He was shaken, unnerved, unable to think, and instinctively he pulled his sword, for no further purpose, perhaps, than to have something to hold on to.

What Eli Case was thinking no one would ever know. He might have been crazed by the bloody act or startled at the sight of the extended sword or perhaps simply unaware that it was there. Whatever the case, he turned with a shriek, lunged or fell but in some manner impaled himself on the sword that Obediah held instinctively in front of him. And that was how Tom Timmons and Irish Malone found them: the unconscious maiden, the decapitated Indian and the dead Indian scout, run through with Obediah's sword, still clinging to his grizzly trophy with one fist.

"Crise sake," murmured Tom Timmons, "what the hell you done, Colonel?"

"Lor gawdamighty," moaned Irish Malone, beginning to suffer those pains of infection that eventually took his life ere he rode again into battle.

"Crise sake," repeated Tom Timmons. "Here, grab yer sword. We got to make like him an' that Indian done each other in. Hurry up."

The two aides rushed Obediah back to his horse and left the scene as it lay. But Obediah, giving the situation all due consideration, after a time went to General Curtis and told him the story, for Obediah did not know how to lie.

The general listened patiently, clasped his hands and sighed and wondered not for the first time if the actual fighting of a battle were not the easiest part of being a commanding officer. Tom Timmons and Irish Malone had done the smart thing and let the dead lie dead, but Obediah, now having opened the can of worms, would have to be attended to.

"I have no choice but to hold you for court-martial," sighed the general. "Please don't leave the camp." And he dismissed Obediah, who wondered what the general had meant. Why would he leave camp and where would he go anyway? Obediah sat in his tent for a long time pondering it all and wishing that he had Louisa to guide him, for she would surely make it simple and he could understand it. She would know what to do; he did not, only that he would wait and do as General Curtis told him.

Later he strolled from his tent and walked slowly through the camp, being hailed by all those he met, some of them perplexed, for the rumor had spread that the Colonel was to be court-martialed for the killing of an Indian who was raping a white girl. The troops could hardly understand that. Nor did any even ask after Eli Case, he presumably killed by that same Indian.

General Curtis had cause to sigh once again when he heard the rumor that was being spread among his troops. "People never get anything right," he noted. "History itself is, I suspect, little more than a compilation of misinformation."

Obediah, lost in thought, strolled far through the camp, nodding and saluting courteously those who spoke to him until he became aware all at once that his walk had indeed carried him far afield and he found himself in the vicinity of a crowd around a wagon. At the edge of the crowd stood a small group of Indians, women and old men, and though the soldiers called out insults to them the Indians stood in proud though mournful dignity.

"Hey, an' there he is," cried out a soldier, "there's Colonel Murphy that kilt this red savage." And the soldiers laughed and shouted at Obediah.

An Indian man, probably not so much older than Obediah, but grayer and more lined, stepped forward and addressed him. "And are you the Blue Coat who slew Quewanah?" It was a respectful question, for in battle one warrior has the right to kill another. It is indeed expected. Without that, there would be no point to war.

Obediah realized that he had happened onto the wagon bearing the remains of the dead Indian warrior and Eli Case, lying side by side in the brotherhood of death.

"I did not kill the Indian," said Obediah with his customary honesty. "My aide killed the Indian and I killed my aide." Those nearby who heard were startled, considered for a moment and, deciding that they had not heard what they thought they heard, forgot it. But the old Indian looked at Obediah and saw an honest man and he believed.

"I am Manasquatch and Quewanah is the son of Manaseeta my sister." He nodded toward the group of Indian women, and a woman, younger probably than she looked, worn and grieving but altogether sturdy, stepped forward. "She begs the return of her firstborn," he said with dignity, and then added, "He was the son of a white man, but he is all Indian, for the white father never claimed him."

"Shit, get out a here," called out a soldier, safe in the midst of the crowd, "we goin' to use that savage fer fish bait."

"No," said Obediah, his voice summoning up thunder, "let the woman have her son. I, too, have lost my own son and I know the pain. Let her take her son." The woman bowed her head and the crowd went silent, adding to Obediah's legend that he was not only strong, brave, agile and wise, but also compassionate and generous in victory, and they knew themselves lesser men for being in the presence of one greater.

"Thank you," said the woman, who was not confined to her native tongue. Her voice was deep and soft as a distant river, and some far memory like an autumn wind in the drying leaves stirred Obediah and then left. The soldiers fell away as the Indians slid the wrapped corpse from the wagon, shouldered it and carried it in dignity, followed by the Indian women.

Manaseeta stopped before Obediah and said again, "Thank you," and thought how tall and noble this white man was. Then she turned and joined the grim procession.

As Obediah watched the procession out of sight he thought to himself how strange it was, this killing of one another over the fucking of a woman, so insignificant a thing and so natural, like going to war over a pissing spot.

In haste General Curtis called a court-martial for Obediah. Story topped story and rumor countermanded rumor until no one had any notion what was going on, only that it was muttered among the troops that the general, being jealous of the stature of Obediah Murphy, was out to get him. And General Curtis, having made a mountain out of a molehill, was now forced to live with it.

A battlefield court-martial must of necessity be speedy, and so was Obediah's, and he was as speedily acquitted of murder by reason of his own testimony. He told the truth; for he did not know how to tell anything else. If the judges believed him or not is of little consequence. Had he confessed to most wanton murder, he likely would not have been found guilty, for the general and his staff did not want to face the consequences of such a decision.

It was determined that Obediah, because of the seriousness of the wound upon his cheek and because of having lost one of his sons in battle, should be given indefinite leave to return home and attend to himself and to the boy's mother.

Obediah went home to Louisa his wife and Louisa his lover and Louisa his daughter. He carried the news that Henry Varner had been captured at the Battle of Pea Ridge. He did not say that Henry had been wounded and captured, for he did not know that for certainty; it had only been reported so.

"He vas mine baby son," was all that Louisa said.

"Ah. He will be safe now. They will not harm him. They will not harm a prisoner. And this war, why it won't last another month, I'm sure of it."

But Louisa was wiser than Obediah and she knew better, though she did not argue the point.

"I am cold," announced Obediah suddenly, though the weather was warm and fair. "Why am I cold?" And he sat shivering in the sun and Louisa eyed him with real concern.

By nightfall Obediah was ill. Nor had he ever been ill in his life, no more at any rate than slightly. His fever rose alarmingly and his throat swelled and his eyes glazed and both Louisa the elder and Louisa the younger ministered to him. By morning his mind was confused and he called out exhortations to his troops and he alternately sweated and shivered, Louisa rolling down the comforters from him for the former and piling them up for the latter.

"I cannot swaller," he cried at one point. And for three nights and days the two Louisas tended him, both alarmed at this strange battlefield fever that swelled and puffed his face and left him crying in pain. "I hurt. I hurt from my brains to my balls and back again," he moaned. "Oh, Lord God, d'ye curse me yet fer a murderer?"

But by the fourth day the fever subsided, though the pain and swelling did not, and though he complained and grumbled incessantly, Obediah was mending, though he could not know that the fever would leave its mark upon his life forever.

It was then that little Louisa came down with the fever, though it affected her differently. She lay pale and still for several days, seemed to mend, and suddenly with a great strangling cry began to tear at her throat. Rolling and tossing and screaming through the night, her fever shooting high, the little girl cried out for her mother and her grandmother and bade them help her, only to fall all at once silent and then comatose. And she lay thus for days, her breathing a rattle in her chest.

"My God, Louisa, she will die. We have lost too much. We cannot let her go!" cried Obediah from his own sickbed.

"I vill not let dis vun go," announced Louisa Varner, and she rolled up her sleeves and for sleepless days and nights she battled, setting her will once more against the natural order of things. She wetted the little girl with wet cloths, first hot and then cold, steamed her and forced thin gruel down her throat, talking constantly to her, though she did not respond. With the stubbornness of her Pennsylvania Dutch forebears, Louisa Varner held the little girl to her and bade the Angel of Death keep his distance. It was a battle that Louisa won, but it was a battle better lost. For the child that returned from the edge of death to them was not the child that had gone there. What they got back was a pretty shell of a little girl, one that could no longer talk or think and who stared perplexed for several days as if she were trying to remember something important, and then gave it up and so sank into a private world from which she never returned.

Obediah went out one day several weeks after and found Louisa his wife standing forlorn and weeping at the edge of the creek that fed both house and barn. He waited a long time for her to speak, but she did not, only stared beyond where he could see. At last he sat down and waited. After a time Louisa sank slowly as her balky joints would allow until she sat beside him and so laid her head upon his lap and wept. Nor did Obediah know what to do, for never had he seen Louisa weep.

In a while came Louisa the younger, carrying the little girl, and she joined them, settling her bulk beside Obediah, and he took the little girl and set her upon his lap and Louisa the younger leaned against him and the little girl smiled a pleased but vague little smile and addressed herself to the buttons on her garments, twiddling them between her fingers as if she would know what they were for.

They sat for some quiet moments that way and then Obediah began to whistle softly and the little girl settled quietly against him and he whistled spring and war and grief and the sounds he made rose and floated into the trees, diminishing in the distance, the sounds of love and pain.

And Louisa wept no more, but only listened.

TEN

VIRGIE'S PLACE

I do not view the seasons of the year the way most people do. I am a retailer, and as such I am usually a season or so ahead of nature. Though both calendar and foliage proclaim fall, my calendar is set on spring, having already dispatched winter, and looking forward to summer. I dealt with fall and Halloween six months ago. I miss out on a lot of seasons that way, which is why I am caught up short, I suppose, when an existing season calls attention to itself.

It is impossible on a leisurely drive through the hills of northeastern Oklahoma not to realize that it is October. Even if the azure skies and turning foliage do not forewarn you, the gaily carved pumpkins and limp scarecrows and black cats with arched backs in passed picture windows will. I notice these things in some surprise, for I have strolled for several weeks through my store with its trendy scarecrows and designer witches on broomsticks all but unseeing, my mind already passing judgment on the coming summer's swimsuit display.

It is definitely fall and it is definitely October. The good-natured skeleton hanging full length on a front door tells me that. I suppose there was a time that Halloween celebrations, in dim prehistory, served the useful function of exorcising terrors, giving subconscious horrors body and a night of their very own so that they would lie in peace for the rest of the year. But that was long ago and now our terrors are made cutesy and trendy. Most of the jack-o'-lanterns are smily faces, except for an occasional disgruntled one with downturned mouth, and we tell the children that there are no horrors, that all the spooks are really good guys, if somewhat mischievous.

Ah, but the terrors are underneath. And the little children last year wandered from house to house examining their goodies for razor blades and singsonging, "Trick or cyanide." The horrors are not cutesy, only trendy.

Such a gloomy thought, however, does not survive long in the bright light of an October day, and I think to myself that I ought to do this more often, that it is refreshing out in the countryside. My routine carries me from home to office to airport and only occasionally to Hilton Head for golf and recreation. I think in amusement that I ought to tell Shirley to book me a leisurely drive through the country every four months or so.

It is perhaps the impulsiveness of the drive, though, that makes it so refreshing. The letter from the historical society bothered me: ". . . appreciate your interest," it said, ". . . house in great disrepair . . . other better-kept examples including both a Sears, Roebuck house and a Montgomery Ward house." (Ah, I didn't know that. But I should have guessed. Keeping up with the competition. I wonder which company started it?) "We regret that we do not have the means to restore more historical spots."

And thus are all my Louisas and my Obediah dismissed. I think of Phoebe Ruskin's proposed biography. Her enthusiasm has hardly waned, though the sources of information seem to have all but dried up. "I cannot understand," she said the last time I talked with her, getting directions by phone for the ancestral catalog house, "how there could be so little information about so prominent a family? Your grandfather was apparently little more than a recluse and your father, too!" She said it as if it were my fault and something shameful to boot. I could have told her that, of course, indeed had tried to, but she would not believe that anyone so successful in business would not serve on any committees or boards or endow something at the university or attend galas and balls. Something to get their names in the newspapers, at least.

Now the historical society has dismissed my relatives. History seems determined to forget us. Well, the historical society may not have the means, but I have, and I am curious to see this house. I cannot say exactly why I am all at once eager to touch my history, only that I am. Nor am I sure exactly why I am making this trip. Is it possible that I might have the old place restored? What would Arlene say, should I suddenly decide on a full-scale renovation of an old, unoccupied house, when I won't even have the interior of my own painted? What would Nanny say, as a matter of fact?

I am cheered by that thought to the little town of Hubbard, the

community I must pass through before I make a right, as directed, at
the four-way stop to Tipeeho. Hubbard, to my way of thinking,
might well qualify itself as a ghost town, and I wonder how Tipeeho
could be any ghostilier. Ah well, I relent, there are several busineses
on the main street—a gas station with the original Phillips 66 sign
weathered seriously and ill disguised by another fading sign, E-CON-
O-GAS, a combination beauty-barbershop with no distinguishing features, a church (All Souls Baptist. I wonder if it knows how close it is
to Episcopalian?). And Virgie's Café sits adjacent to Pete's Family
Entertainment and Car Wash. The entertainment seems to consist of a
pool table and the car wash of coin-activated hoses. There are a few
houses, but getting through the main part of town is a matter of
seconds, even if you stop at the four-way stop. I will probably have to
go all the way back to Claremore for lunch, for though Virgie's is
respectable enough looking, there is nothing about it to appeal to a
passing stranger. Poor Virgie. And I think: Virgie probably does a
booming business in black coffee and chicken-fried steak and greasy
hamburgers. Ah, I'm being judgmental. Might be that Virgie's hamburgers are a specialty, old-fashioned hamburgers wrapped in thin
greasy paper aglow with ball-park mustard. Might be I will stop by
Virgie's on the way back and order a cup of black coffee and a greasy
hamburger on the off chance that I might make a gastronomical find.
The spirit of adventure is upon me.

Such a hamburger calls up memories of those pre-fast-food days
when a hamburger took some time to put together and came with
potato chips or equally greasy french fries. That was back in those
days when I slipped out of Old Levi's mansion wearing my peasant
blouse and skirt, a flower behind my ear, and caught a bus to that side
of town where there was no chance that I would be recognized, my
lust fired by that first encounter with the acne-scarred teenaged lad
who sat down beside me in the movie where I had gone innocently
enough to see a movie that I had liked and wanted to see again.

He sat beside me and in short order took my hand and, when I did
not object, draped his arm casually around my shoulder, letting his
fingers stray along the bare skin of my shoulders and thence inside my
elasticized blouse. Rather than being alarmed, I was quite interested
in the procedure, as if I were observer instead of participant, and I
wondered just how far he would go, left to his own devices. And so
we dallied two complete features away, his hand at last up under my
skirt and inside my panties, and my hand stroking the member he had

released for that purpose. When the picture ended and the lights went up, I turned my back on him and went out one aisle while he went out the other. I never saw him again, at least not to recognize.

But the experience stayed with me for several weeks until one Saturday night I again caught the bus for a distant part of town, picked up an acne-marked young man, whose awkwardness testified to his virginity, and led him to a deserted building where I shared my own marred virginity with him.

He was excited, enthralled and I suppose in love, and wanted to see me again, a request that I answered with a dramatic "sometime, somewhere" before I disappeared onto a bus again. That was the first of a long line of such encounters, always with the same kind of kid, inexperienced, unattractive, eager and, I'm sure, virginal. I wonder if any of them still remembers his own encounter with dazed amazement, wondering what he had done to have his adolescent longing so perfectly fulfilled, for in those days I was quite pretty, slim and dark and tall—if a little overly dramatic.

I had been on just such an adventure the night Old Levi waited for me with his book, later than usual because the young man I was with proved not only experienced but effective and energetic. But he was the last of a line, for I went away to college shortly and fell under Bradley's spell. But that was another life ago.

I am hardly out of Hubbard on my way to Tipeeho before I am passed on the highway by a pair of motorcycles, one followed by the other, obviously together. They seem out of place in this bucolic setting. But if those motorcycles seem out of place to me, I muse, I suppose the big Lincoln probably seems out of place to the cyclists. This is the land of pickup trucks and slow-moving old-model cars.

The cyclists are traveling fast and they disappear over a rise. I wonder what it is about a noisy motorcycle that inspires a certain macho type of young man, the kind who rides pell-mell in all kinds of weather, helmetless (for there are minimal helmet laws in Oklahoma, the right to bash one's head open on the pavement considered one of those sacred freedoms, like the right to bear arms). I think it must have something to do with having power between their legs, as if balls are not enough.

The community of Tipeeho is larger than I expected. There is, of all things, a drive-in restaurant, plus a couple of churches, a gas station and a grain mill among deserted old buildings that testify to the thriving cattle community this was three quarters of a century ago. My directions from Phoebe Ruskin are explicit. "When you get to Tipeeho, ask somebody." The somebody I ask is in charge of the gas station. He is younger than one might expect to find running a business in this antique of a town, and his hair is thick and touches his collar, as if that's the way he wants it, and he sports a scrubby mustache, that on purpose, too, presumably.

"That old place?" he asks. I nod. I do not see any need to explain my mission further.

"It's a mess out there," he complains, obviously hoping for a clue as to my business there. "You know, run-down and all, overrun with snakes and varmints." Is his expression inhospitable or is it my imagination? He is eyeing the Lincoln. It is not uncommon for people to be suspicious of expensive automobiles. I relent.

"I'm from the historical society," I lie. It is only a little fib, inconsequential; my motives are indeed historical, and semiofficial credentials might make my missiom seem more plausible, and my car. The young man says nothing and I realize that he has not yet answered my question.

"That old house is on a list of historic homes in this area," I add.

"Um." It is more a grunt than anything else.

"Can you direct me to it?"

The directions he gives seem grudging, but he does give them at last, still staring at the Lincoln. I sense a vague antagonism that I attribute to the automobile.

I am somehow surprised to find that the house is actually about a quarter of a mile outside of town. In my mind's eye I think I had pictured it sitting in the middle of town, perhaps across the street from a town square park, with stately trees and an old-fashioned bandstand. It is a standard picture of an old small town, like a town in Kansas, a small town in Kansas being in my mind the quintessential small town.

The house of my ancestors, the house that Sears, Roebuck built, is a sagging, forlorn memory of better days, the grounds around it grown up with weeds, all windows paneless, but for those covered with boards. At some point in its more recent history it has been partially sided with asbestos shingles, once a spring green, now a faded and surly gray on three sides, the back side covered with the black tarpaper of the unfinished project.

This house of Murphy is a crumbling relic, its decline accentuated in the bright October sunlight, and I understand the State Historical Society's reluctance to talk about it. I struggle to put it in perspective, to see it as it once must have been. The evidences of grandeur are few, beyond the architecture itself, late Victorian, gabled on four sides, two-story, a large porch running across the front with bits and pieces of elaborate decorative molding, hanging like torn bits of lace on a worn petticoat, all around the roof line.

The front steps are broken-down, but I don't think I would want to venture in, anyway, mindful of the gas station attendant's threat of snakes and varmints. I wander around the grounds. Not surprisingly, the yard of this sagging relic is littered with the debris of a passing civilization, the beer cans, wine bottles—I laugh out loud at the discarded Perrier bottle. A mixed metaphor. I am a little surprised at the number of condoms, obviously used, that are flung randomly about, like Easter eggs, partially hidden or in plain view.

I thought that, in this day of the Pill and vasectomies and abortions on demand, the condom would be itself an antique relic. The condom was standard equipment in my youth; I carried a package with me wherever I went lest I run into an eager but ill-prepared young man (a precaution that failed me at least twice). I rarely did, for no matter how virginal, in that day and time no boy much past puberty ever left home without a condom or two hopefully secreted in his billfold. It is apparently still the protection of choice in some quarters.

I am filled with a feeling of sadness, mild grief perhaps, that there are no ghosts here for me. The place is leeched of all spirit; the ghosts have fled. There is no history here; I cannot call up any of the Louisas or Obediah. I cannot ask them what it is that I would know of them. They can never answer the questions that I have not yet even been able to frame.

I wander on around the building and stare for a while at the cattle grazing in the field beyond, fenced off from this place—for their own protection, perhaps. It is less littered than the rest of the yard, and there is even some fairly recently loosened soil close by the foundation of the carriage house. The soil is weathered enough that it has obviously been that way for some time, but the slight growth proves that it has been disturbed at least since the grasses began to go dormant. Treasure hunters, I wonder? I think of the intent souls I see strolling around public places and deserted buildings, metal detectors extended like blind men's canes. Or kids playing perhaps? Or maybe a neighbor planning a spring garden? Odd. But the spaded plot is big enough for that.

I am staring at that bare soil as if everything depends upon it. Like the poet and his red wheelbarrow beside the white chickens. And that thought takes me back to golden Bradley, and I cannot contain a nostalgic smile. That smile stuck to my face, I am aware of a spot of color in the loosened soil beneath the drip line of the roof like cheap turquoise, a bit of robin's egg perhaps. I stare at it for a long time, wide-eyed and unblinking, and I turn away with a sigh of disappointment that my trip has netted me nothing, less than nothing. I turn back again, once more arrested by the turquoise blue, and I bend over it to inspect it, casually, uninterestedly.

It is a piece of cheap turquoise, a ring. Shiny enough that someone has recently lost it, I think, and I reach to pick it up. It is stuck to something and I give it a slight tug and instantly recoil in horror. The ring is attached to a finger, the remains of a finger. I gasp. No. Ridiculous. A twig or stick or something. My imagination overrunneth. With the toe of my shoe I kick at the ring and whatever it is attached to. My toe lifts it up and there is no mistaking this time. The ring is attached to a finger and the finger to a hand. Resting across the toe of my Anne Klein shoes, the remains of a hand, bone and withered flesh and cheap turquoise. And the hand is attached to what? I don't know and I am afraid to look. I am even afraid to move, almost in fear that the hand so leisurely resting across my foot will reach out to restrain me. It is a Halloween joke. Someone getting ready for an elaborate prank. That's all. But I back away, slowly, and the hand slides off my shoe and settles to the ground, the shriveled fingers almost clutching, as if they might suddenly gather a clod of dirt to fling. I walk quickly back to my car.

Once there, I stop to consider. Have I seen what I think I have? Have I somehow stumbled, almost literally, upon one of those casually disposed-of bodies usually found by hunters or children playing? Or is this some prank, someone's idea of a seasonal joke? I am not easily startled and never hysterical. There is no danger that I will go screeching in terror back into town. And I think of the service station attendant's mild antagonism.

My first impulse is simply to leave, as if I had seen nothing, and let someone else discover whatever there is to discover. Yet I hesitate to do that. At the same time I am not at all interested in going back there to make sure that my eyes have not deceived me. I solve this dilemma at last by waving down a passing pickup.

"Car trouble?" the affable farmer inquires, and I find myself at a sudden loss, wondering how one mentions the possibility of a corpse.

"No. No car trouble." I pause and then pass on my information as casually as possible. "Back there, behind that garage. There is either a dead body or a bad joke." He turns his head toward me, cocking it as a bird might searching out a worm. "I don't know quite what to do," I add. The farmer is staring at me in my designer clothes leaning against my black Lincoln. If he wonders what I am doing in so unlikely a place, he does not ask.

"Wal now, les' take a look," is all that he says, and he leads the way. I lengthen my stride to match his.

The turquoise-decorated hand is as I left it, grasping, nails, rotted flesh, bone. I stare at it more in curiosity than anything else. Knowing what to expect, I am not startled at the sight of it. It is real. Of that I'm sure.

"Wal," says my companion. And, "Wal," again. "Looks like we found sumpin' here, don't it?" He bends and brushes lightly at the dirt around the hand and uncovers muddy fabric. A sleeve, I'm sure. He mutters something and, standing, finds a stick, bends over again and gently pries under the fabric and dislodges the remains of the arm it covers.

"Wal now," he repeats, "I guess we have found us sumpin' fer shure. We better call the sheriff first thing." I cannot keep from noticing that he has included himself as part discoverer. Fair enough. I do not begrudge him that notoriety. I can even probably move quietly out of the picture and leave him all that credit for himself. But I know I won't. I am, I fear, as morbidly curious as anyone. I want to know what is attached to that arm.

"You stay here whilst I go into town and call the sheriff in Claremore. He won't be long gettin' here's my guess." I'm not sure, but I think he chuckles.

I unlock the car, which I automatically lock no matter where I go, and ease in under the wheel and wonder again if I might not be better off simply driving away. "The body was found by an unidentified woman," the newspaper would say.

The car is hot from having sat out in the bright sunlight. I turn the ignition and switch on the air conditioner. It does not occur to me to roll down the windows, for the only times I ever activate them are when I have business with such people as gas station attendants or toll booth personnel. Fresh air and the dust and noise and pollution it carries with it are not welcome in my car.

My wait is not long, for my colleague in the grisly discovery wheels his pickup in behind my Lincoln and is trailed in short order by a pair of like pickups, carrying a total of five passengers.

"Now, don' touch nothin'," those five are admonished. "The sheriff said, 'Fer crise sake don' touch nothin'." They hardly slow their steps, striding back behind the building and stopping abruptly to stare at our find. My friend presides, proudly explaining with tour guide authority how I had waved him down and how he had wiped the dirt away from the muddy sleeve, thus revealing the decomposing arm.

"Reckon hit's one a them Stoples," says one of the group. It is not a question but a statement, as if he knows for sure. There is some nodding and murmuring. What is missing is alarm, even curiosity.

"Might be, probably is," agrees another. "Bct you one thing, though, they ain't goin' to know fer shure until they roust up a dentist." There are grim smiles at that.

I stand at the corner of the building and listen to these speculations, uncertain about my own part in it, loath to leave yet hesitant to stay.

It is not until the sheriff with several others arrives that I am noticed at all. "You hang around, Ma'am," he says courteously. "I'll want to take a statement soon's we figger out what's happened."

"Hit's one a them Stoples, Sheriff. Bet you money it is."

I would like to know what a Stople is but I do not ask. I am out of my element, a position I do not often occupy, and silence seems the wisest course.

"One a them Stoples fer shure."

The sheriff only grunts as he eyes the situation. Finally he says, "Well, git the shovel and let's git this done."

"That ring looks like a woman's ring," observes my colleague. "That Stople woman mebbe?" My friend—they call him Greer, whether first or last name I don't know—turns to me and, motivated by responsibility or perhaps simple courtesy, explains. "Them Stoples, they was three of 'em, two brothers and one of em's wife, they disappeared sudden about six or seven weeks ago. No question but foul play. Not that they'd be particularly missed. They was pretty trashy people, supposed to be mixed up in drugs and all. Come in here year or so ago from up in Kansas somewhere."

The sheriff only glances up at Greer's rambling lecture. Two of his men, deputies, I suppose, are at work with spades, carefully easing their way around, searching out the contours of the body, if indeed there is one. It is possible, I think, that this might simply be an unattached arm, but it is not; for the gentle probing of the spaces soon unearths a human form. I am impressed at the precision with which the sheriff's men work. Pictures are snapped, measurements taken, and I am reminded of nothing so much as an archaeological dig. I am struck also by the dispassionate attitude of both workers and observers. There seems to be nothing but mild curiosity. The sense of horror that I would have expected is not present. Not even in myself. And I stare as curiously as the next one at the remains in the neat rectangle the men have worked around it. There is little to mark it as human, not hair, clothes or flesh, all of which have been muddied to approximately the same color, the hair curiously matted across the forehead, blood perhaps, and a deathly sneer where the mouth should have been.

"That's what ye call one a them shaller graves, ain't it?" jokes a bystander. "He shore didn't put out much sweat gettin' that 'un covered up. Ye reckon there's more?" he adds with just a trace of eagerness. I notice that the deputies are carefully going over the spaded area; one of them has a metal detector and I am again reminded of a blind man's cane or, better yet, a giant seeing eye. The metal detector's hum rises and falls in an irregular pattern.

"Somethin' here," a deputy murmurs, and the spades are brought into play again, carefully and efficiently. I shudder involuntarily as one of the spades lifts something, part of a leg, I think.

"Why didn't they hide them deeper?" I say to no one in particular and immediately wonder why I have said *hide* instead of *bury*.

"Killin's the easy part," says the sheriff, morosely staring at the work in progress. "It's gettin' rid of the body that's damned hard work. He had a good night's work just to get 'em that far under. In this part of the country we ain't got no landfills or oceans to dump bodies in. You kill someone around here and want to get rid of it, you just got to bury it or throw it in a creek and hope for the best. This feller done more than most. He at least tried to give 'em a burial. He could a just left 'em in the woods."

I can't help noticing that the sheriff has reduced my plural *they* to a singular *he*.

The body count stops at three, three neat, plastic-wrapped parcels, hoisted by stretcher into an ambulance. They would have traveled as easily, I am sure, in the bed of one of the pickup trucks, but that is not the way it's done. The dead, even the trashy dead, are transported in a splendor denied most of the living.

The corpses are identified officially as two males and a female, but unofficially they are the missing Stoples. I ask Greer about them and about his allegations of drugs. It does not seem consistent somehow. Drugs and drug-war deaths are big-city matters. This is not something you expect to find in a peaceful rural setting. I remember the motorcyclists I had seen. Guilty by association.

"Oh no," says Greer, "there's a lot of drug problem around here. Not big, real big, I suppose, a little grass and hash mainly." He flings those terms around with elan. "Word is that marijuana"—he pronounces it *mary-wanna*—"growed around here and over in south Missouri is some of the best there is. Anyhow, hit's a good crash crop." He laughs. "But these punks ain't big-time, you know. They fight over a few thousand dollars' worth of grass like hit was a billion-dollar deal. An' fer my money they can kill each other off an hit won't be nothin' but good riddance."

"Will they find out who did it?" I ask. It seems a silly question, but I am interested.

Greer nods his head, pursing his lips as if to say that the answer to that is foregone. "They already got Earl McCullough in jail, just waitin' fer the corpus delicti to surface."

I seem to have stepped into the middle of an ongoing situation. Instead of being responsible, I am only one more bit of evidence. I think I am a little disappointed. Maybe it's the same kind of disappointment people feel when a great blaze has at last been brought under control and fizzles down, like that old Peggy Lee line, "Is That All There Is?"

The sheriff takes my name and my statement. I explain without his asking that the old house had been in my family when my grandfather was young and I was curious about it. He seems to accept that, nor does he seem to associate me with the department stores of the same name. Murphy is a common enough name. And that's all.

Will I be needed again? Perhaps to testify? He does not think so. That's all. I stare at the old house, deserted again after all that activity, the pickups gone, even my friend Greer's, and I realize with just a slight pang that Greer will stay here among his own and get all the credit for the discovery. I am not interested in notoriety, but I think I am not quite ready to go back to my own world, which is secure but predictable. But I am not a part of this world; Greer is. And his world is, too, secure and predictable. This is just an aberration.

It is perhaps that thought that makes me pull impulsively off the road as I pass through Hubbard and park my Lincoln in front of Virgie's Café. I am not hungry, but I think I would linger in this suddenly more fascinating world a while longer. I am thinking of Arlene by now. How would she have reacted to this situation? And I have to admit it would not have fazed her. She would have chattered all the way through it, her feet a comfortable eighteen inches off the ground at all times.

"I help you?" asks the large woman with the beehive hairdo and the cellulite hips packaged in a polyster uniform, doubtless from one of those ubiquitous uniform shops that inhabit every shopping mall. This must be Virgie. Virgie, I think, is a cliché, and Virgie's Café is a like cliché. It is bigger than it seems from the outside; the large dining room, boothed on one side, with several tables scattered about, is still uncluttered. I expect a china mug for my coffee and that's what I get, set before me on the polished Formica surface. Virgie's is clean, the napkin holders filled and ketchup bottles, sugar and salt and pepper containers wiped clean. I would not be afraid to eat anything here. It has all the warmth of someone's grandmother's kitchen. Someone's, not mine.

There is someone cooking in the back, for I can hear Virgie talking. Otherwise the place is deserted. The coffee is good, soothing after my morning's adventure. I realize that morning has drifted on to midafternoon, and although I am not particularly hungry, I order a hamburger from Virgie. I have a great anxiety about that hamburger, which Virgie delivers shortly. Virgie is not friendly, but neither is she unfriendly, and the hamburger, while no gastronomical find, is no great disappointment either, and it smells secure, which I observe to myself is the way for a hamburger to smell.

I think that I could sit there all afternoon absorbing the events of the day under the comfortable smell of cooking food. Virgie, beyond inquiring if I need coffee creamer, has said nothing more and stands behind the counter polishing glasses. Virgie is a good name for her; she looks like a Virgie. Did her mother have the unusual good sense to give her a name that suited her, or did she just grow into it? My speculations are brought to an abrupt end with the banging of the front door and the entry of a work-clothed farmer.

"Hey, Vonda, where's Virgie?"

"Ain't here, George."

So, All my speculations are for naught. This is not Virgie, after all, but Vonda. It reminds me of the opening for that old radio show—"Archie's Tavern, where the elite meet to eat. Archie ain't here." Virgie's Café. Virgie ain't here.

"You heard they found them Stoples?"

"That a fact? When?"

"This mornin'. Virgie know it?"

"How the hell would I know?"

"Greer Beck found 'em over behind the haunted house outside Tipeeho." Haunted house? "Greer and some woman drivin' a big black Lincoln Continental car, I heard."

And though George does not look directly at me, I am fairly certain that my car parked conspicuously out front has probably had something to do with his arrival. Vonda does glance toward me and back toward the automobile out front, making the connection. It does not seem to concern her.

"Whur'd Virgie go?" asks George.

"She went over to Claremore to see a lawyer she got."

"She got any idea 'bout what's goin' to happen to Earl?"

"No," snaps Vonda.

"Well, hell, Vonda, I didn't mean to ruffle yer feathers. Christ. You know we all think the world of Virgie." Vonda remains noncommittal.

"And anyhow, them Stoples deserved killin'. Old Earl ought to git him a medal. If he done it. Ain't nobody proved he done it yet." George waits for a moment, and when there is no response he rises casually and edges toward the door.

"Tell Virgie we're all prayin' fer her," he mumbles on his way back out the door.

"He's mean enough," murmurs Vonda as the door bangs behind George. Involuntarily I glance toward the closed door.

"Not him. Not George. Earl. Earl's mean enough to a done it. If he didn't, he's done about as bad. Don't matter."

It is not clear just who Vonda is talking to: me or herself or that unseen but occasionally heard presence back in the kitchen.

"Kids'll grieve ya. You got kids, you got grief," says Vonda. "Maybe it's their way of gettin' even with ya for bringin' 'em into this pissant world. You got any kids?" I realize that she's talking to me.

"No."

"I got four. Cain't live with 'em and cain't live without 'em." She says it grimly. "My youngest girl, she about drives me up a wall about half the time. But they cain't carry a candle to what Earl's put Virgie through. He's her youngest, and I wonder how many times she's wished she'd a stopped short a him?"

I do not understand just why I am being included in this little melodrama. Or perhaps not a melodrama. Perhaps it is a full-blown tragedy, a Greek tragedy, and I am the lone spectator and Vonda is the chorus, delivering a commentary on the action. And is Virgie Hecuba, the grieving mother? Stella Dallas?

"Vonda, I got to get home," comes the voice from the kitchen, a woman's voice, young, I'd say. "Billy's home from school and I got to get her to that dentist."

Ah. Is it Billy or Billi, I wonder?

"Go on. I can take care of it. Virgie'll be back soon. Don't worry about it."

I ask Vonda for a knife so I can cut my partially eaten hamburger in half to make it more manageable. She delivers the knife and then sits amiably down opposite and sighs as if relieved to rest.

"See ya tomorrow," comes the voice from the kitchen, immediately followed by a slamming door.

I work on the hamburger and Vonda stares silently and glumly out the front window. At last she says, almost as if she were making small talk, "So you found the Stoples, huh?"

Before I can say anything, the kitchen door slams again and a woman makes a sudden appearance behind the counter. She carries a pocketbook over her arm and the expression on her face is weary.

"Hi, Virgie."

Ah. Enter Hecuba.

"Lynn had to go home. She just left. Had to take her kid to the dentist."

"Kids are always inconvenient," murmurs Virgie. If she means anything in particular by it I can't tell.

I would like to imagine that Virgie is a commanding presence, a Judith Anderson towering in grief and tragedy. But the truth is, she is not. She is nondescript, not disparagingly so; she simply fits no particular description. She is probably ten years older than I am, while Vonda, I would guess, is ten years younger. Beyond that there is no describing Virgie. She is neither tall nor short, fat nor thin. Her hair is neither gray nor brown and her eyes are, what, hazel perhaps? Hazel, that catchall for eyes that are not gray or brown or green or blue. Virgie wears a dress. It is a squarish kind of dress, topped with a squarish kind of jacket. The pocketbook is K-mart plastic. I could have walked past Virgie a thousand times without ever recognizing that I had passed her before. She is the eternal woman in the checkout, a soft sculpture at a bus stop.

"How'd it go?" asks Vonda solicitously.

Virgie sets her pocketbook on the counter and slips out of her jacket, coming around the counter to hang the jacket up. "That lawyer thinks he ought to just plead no contest and go fer manslaughter or self-defense. I don't know." She sighs heavily and stares out through the front window. "That lawyer, he didn't seem much interested."

"You see Earl?"

"Yeah. A little while. He just keeps sayin' that he hasn't done nothin'. For all the world like he used to do when he was a youngin and got in trouble at school. Never would admit to nothin', no matter what evidence they had."

I am once more spectator to this drama. Or is it merely a soap opera? One spectator hardly constitutes audience enough for high tragedy. Ah no, that's not right. In this age of television the highest tragedy, the greatest spectacles are staged for a small audience, sometimes only one, or even none, a single viewer sitting in bed dozing or eating grapes or drinking beer. For him Hamlet falls mortally wounded, musical extravaganzas rise to crescendo, sport records are broken. The barbarians sack Rome while John Q. Viewer flips idly through the *TV Guide*.

"This lady here's the one that found them Stoples this morning."

And thus am I, the audience, pulled into the drama.

Virgie is not surprised. I suppose she, too, has seen the telltale Lincoln parked in front. Quietly I explain how it happened that I was at the "haunted house."

"Murphy?" murmurs Vonda. "You know any Murphys around here, Virgie? The only ones I know of are dead," Vonda goes on, without giving Virgie a chance to answer the question she asked. "Over at Sweet Briar Cemetery, just east of I-44, there's a little old cemetery. Gary's got people there and so we go over sometimes on Decoration Day. There's four great big white stones that all say *Murphy*. But I don't know any live Murphys, except of course you," she adds.

"As far as I know," I say, "I am the last of that line. It will end with me."

"Hey, that's terrible," says Vonda, and the concern on her and Virgie's faces is very real. "Well," I say, "Murphy is a common name. Perhaps I've got some cousins around that I don't know about."

"There's a big department store in Tulsa called Murphy's. Maybe yer kin to them," says Vonda. "I don't never shop there; it's too rich fer my blood."

I let it pass.

"Well," continues Vonda, "anyway, I got kin comin' out a the woodwork. I'll be glad to lend you some if you need 'em."

I thank her with a laugh and promise to look her up when I feel the need of some relatives.

"I suppose that's sad," says Virgie, "to be clear out of kin. But at least you don't have nobody to worry about but yerself, do you? Sometimes I think that wouldn't be so bad."

"Yeah," murmurs Vonda.

Virgie has seated herself and Vonda rises to bring the older woman a mug of coffee, which she accepts without comment. And then Virgie begins to talk. It is a long, rambling monologue, unemotional, matter-of-fact. I am not required to speak; I am her audience. I do not have a speaking part. The evening settles over us early, for daylight saving time has only recently gone south for the winter, and Virgie unburdens herself, her tale nourished by the empathy of an anonymous audience, the end of a line. I hear her through to the conclusion.

VIRGIE'S STORY

"I come from a big family. I guess eleven of us growed clear up. There's seven left now—scattered—a bunch in California. You cain't really count yerself a real Okie unless you got kin in California, you know. My mom played it smart. She had three girls first, got three girls before she got down to the serious business of havin' babies, so by the time she had a house full of runny-nosed, shitty-butted kids, she had us girls to hep out. We all raised kids—wipin', smackin', huggin', whatever was needed.

"I always knowed when my ma was p.g. She'd commence to movin' furniture. But it never hepped. Tough as a old oak stump and regular as a milk cow, she'd drop that baby—none was ever born dead, either, though some died later.

"I growed up, 'spite of it all. I guess as happy as most. I was one a the older ones. I got in on the affection before it begun to dry out, and I like to think I give some affection, too.

"I used to go to church some when I was young. They say that helps. I don't know. Sometimes it seemed to, but I ain't sure God was ever actually lookin' in on us. I don't go to church much now'days, though. I quit goin' to church when the preacher got younger'n me; I quit goin' to the doctor fer the same reason. I cain't say I have much dealin' with God. I don't guess I ever did. Do I believe in God? Well, I really dunno. But if I didn't believe in God, lord, what would I believe in?"

It is not a question I am supposed to answer, so I wait for Virgie to continue. I can't tell if Vonda is listening to the story. She pads in soundless sensible shoes through the hard light from the overhead fluorescent fixtures, wiping and straightening ketchup bottles and sugar and salt containers, pushing chairs carefully under tables. Virgie stares quietly straight ahead for a moment. Vonda's expression is noncommittal. Has she heard the story before? Is it Virgie's story that she knows, or is this, rather, the metaphor of womanhood, eons old, Virgie's differing only in detail from the memory of the race? Virgie's monotone interrupts that thought as she continues.

"My family fought the Civil War, too, on the side of the South. I guess we always was a wrong-headed bunch. My grandaddy's daddy fought at the Battle of Pea Ridge and Grandpa was all full of stories his daddy told him about it. He loved to tell about the preacher that met a Rebel soldier after the battle and the preacher asked him what outfit he was with. 'Confederate,' said the soldier, 'and what outfit you with?' 'Why I'm with the Army of the Lord,' said the preacher, and the soldier said, 'Well, then, you are sure a fer piece from headquarters.'

"I guess the moral is that war is hell. I lost a boy in Vietnam. I don't know why he was there; I guess he didn't, neither. And I haven't got the smarts to argue the point one way or the other. All I know is I raised that child up from nothin' to a big, strappin', decent man and all I got fer my efforts was a nice letter from his commanding officer and a folded-up flag. I still got both.

"I married a soldier. Right after the war. Ever notice how people refer to the Second World War as *the* war, as if there hadn't ever been any other? I married Billy Ray when I was eighteen because it was the kind of thing you do when yer eighteen. I cain't say I planned any kind of life. I don't suppose I thought more'n a day in advance. Even if I did, if someone'd told me I'd be happier never married, never raisin' kids, that I'd be better off in the long run if I just opened me up a café and made a life fer myself, I wouldn't a believed it, not at eighteen hungry fer a man. Married was what you was when you got growed if you weren't queer or crippled. There wasn't much other choice. We never thought about bein' liberated, only married.

"Billy Ray was just back from the war in 1946, it was, n'en he had on a uniform and his shoes was shined to where you could almost see yerself in 'em. Some a the girls told me he was sweet on me, and one thing led to another. We got married anyway. Went into Tulsa to one a them marriage chapels, got hitched and spent the night in a tourist court. I was a virgin then. I guess Billy Ray wasn't. Anyhow, he climbed on board like he knowed what he was doin'. Gawd, that hurt, and when it was all done I thought to myself, 'Is this what I got to expect fer the rest a my life?' I thought maybe it'd get better, but Billy Ray took a turn about onct every hour that night and by the next mornin' I was so sore I couldn't hardly walk straight. 'You'll git over it,' he said, 'you'll git used to it.' And he was right. I did. I never could say I ever got much kick out of it. It's messy and inconvenient, but the boys seems to like it.

"Billy Ray went on back to the army fer a few months till he got his discharge. I went on home like nothin'd happened. But it had, 'cause I was already p.g. Kids wasn't as wise then I guess as they are now. Almost everybody got p.g. within a month or two of gettin' married. We didn't know it could be any other way. When Billy Ray came home, he lolled around the house till my ma told me we had to git. She had too many mouths to feed as it was, an' I was Billy Ray's responsibility. I guess Billy Ray hadn't never thought of it that way, either, because he seemed pretty shocked that he was expected to take over. We moved in with his folks fer a time, but it was like livin' in a prizefight ring. What time the old man and the old woman wasn't fightin', the old man was tryin' to make out with me, and me already four months along.

"Billy Ray finally got enough of a job that we got us a little furnished room and made do, that is, we just let ever'day take care of itself until we had a baby and then another and finally three.

"Billy Ray just got crankier and meaner with ever' kid and took to punchin' me around. Well, I growed up in a big family an' I could take care of myself, so I didn't take that fer very long. One day I throwed a teakettle a hot water at him. Didn't much git on him, but I warned him that the next time I'd scald his face off. He must a believed it, 'cause he left me then and never come back. He sent a little fer the kids fer a while and then that stopped an' he got a divorce so he could marry someone else."

Virgie pauses, sighs and stares softly into the distance. Vonda has been leaning against the counter for some minutes. At length she turns the lock on the front door and flips the sign in the window over so that it reads CLOSED instead of OPEN. She lifts a coat from the rack by the door, slips car keys out of her pocketbook and with only a cheery wave retreats through the kitchen and bangs out the back door. Virgie briefly acknowledges Vonda's departure, sips at the cooling coffee, stops and, rising stiffly, goes behind the counter, pours two cups of fresh coffee and returns with them. I take the cup of coffee as it has been offered, without comment. Virgie starts talking again as she seats herself.

"Well, there I was, hardly votin' age, three kids to support and no way to do it. But I've found you do what you have to do. I ironed fer folks, canned fer people, made me a garden, baby-sat, and lived hand to mouth till I got a waitress job.

"I was no newcomer to hard work. I'd done it all my life, so I worked hard at a little café off Highway 66, sometimes not gettin' off work till two or three o'clock in the mornin'. My little sisters took turns heppin' out with my kids. Wasn't much of a chore. 'Bout all they had to do was put 'em to bed an' sleep there overnight. I slept when I could. I fed and clothed my kids and saved a little money.

"You'd think a person would learn, wouldn't you? I guess some is just slower'n others. Anyway, to make a long story short, I married Curtis McCullough. He was a truck driver. Least, that's what he told me. What he didn't tell me was that he was out of work most of the time 'cause he couldn't stay away from the bottle. First thing, a course, I was p.g. again, that was with Maxine. And by the time I got Curtis about figured out, Earl was on the way.

"I cain't say I threw Curtis out and I cain't say that he left. He just slowly drifted out of our lives. He's been gone fer years, but there's still clothes of his hangin' in the closet. Last I heard from him, someone said they'd seen him sleepin' drunk on a street in Tulsa. Probably about right. If he ain't dead by now, he's nothin' but a wino. I don't want him back but I never got divorced. Long as I was married, I figgered I was safe from gettin' stuck a third time. Me, I don't really think it's natural livin' without a man, even a halfway decent man'd do. But I just ain't goin' to take that chance again.

"I got a sister-in-law. Well, I guess you'd call her a sister-in-law. She's Billy Ray's brother's wife. I guess we ain't really legal kin no more. We growed up together. I've knowed her all my life. Billy Ray's brother Bud, he ain't no better'n Billy Ray was. But Bet sticks with him, always got a bruise or a black and blue mark or welt to show fer it, too. Neighbors all say what a noble, long-sufferin' woman she is. Well, I'll go fer the long-sufferin' part, anyway. The rest I figger she brings on herself. Bud ain't no better'n he ought to be, but look at his side of it. What must it be like to live with somebody that's forever forgivin' you?"

Virgie pauses to consider that thought and smiles wryly as she speaks.

"Well, I raised five kids with almost no hep at all. All the hep I got from ther fathers was in gettin' 'em in the first place. I've noticed a man's always willin' to give you a start thataway. I lost one of 'em in the war, like I told you, and my middle girl, Karen, got p.g. before she got married. She did git married, but not the right one. But she did git someone'd take her. Then I got Earl and he ain't been nothin' but trouble from the beginnin'. I done the best I could with him. I ain't goin' to lie and say I was a perfect mother, but I tried and I stuck with him. I ain't takin' the blame.

"Sometimes ther ain't nothin you can do. Earl was born mean. That's it. He was meant to be mean and I cain't really say how come. I don't know why. I suppose I could blame him on his daddy, say that he got that meanness from his daddy—Curtis come from a long line a bad . . ."

Virgie sighs profoundly but leaves her speculation unfinished. I do not know why I am sitting here listening. I do not know why I am needed, why it is necessary for me to hear the story. I could put it down to curiosity, but it is more than curiosity. It seems intensely important that she speak and that I listen.

"Earl got mixed up with them Stoples about a year ago." Virgie sighs again. "He come draggin' 'em in here one day. Ken and Terry Stople and LaWanda. LaWanda was supposed to a been one of em's wife but they acted like they couldn't never remember which one's. My guess is they took turns screwin' her, and Earl, he did too. They wasn't nothin' to 'em, took all together they wasn't worth a washin' a soap. LaWanda in particular was a trashy sort, you know the kind, jeans cut off so short that her butt hung out below 'em, and she liked to wear halters or a black baby-doll top with no underwear underneath. She wasn't pretty. Dirty and sloppy, on the fat side. All three of 'em acted strung out most a the time, and I told Earl flat out that what he done was his own business, but I didn't want them hangin' around.

"Well, I suppose they was into dope. They all say they was and that when they tried to cut Earl out of his share he shot 'em and I guess buried 'em out behind that deserted old house out a Tipeeho. Anyway, the sheriff picked him up in ther bloodstained car with a bunch a money and no explanation about where the Stoples was. I don't want to question but that the sheriff knows what he's doin', but to tell you the truth I never knowed Earl to put out that much effort on anything in his life."

Virgie pauses, smiles tiredly and says, "I guess that's my life. Would it make a book, you reckon? Not much, I guess. By and large, I got no serious complaints. I've had my hard times like ever' one else. And there been times when I wisht I didn't have no kids at all and times when I just plain wisht I was dead. But dead is the easy part. Anybody can die. And anyway, a person just cain't seal therselves up in a mason jar away from it all. Ther ain't much to do when you find yerself borned but to git out and mix it up.

"Of course I expect to die someday. I don't expect any exception to be made fer me. But I don't sweat it. I guess I been dead before, not alive, at least. I do think about dyin' sometimes, but you know what I wonder most about it? It's silly, I guess, but I wonder who will have the last memory of me? Do you know what I mean? Who will think the last conscious thought of me? It won't necessarily be kin, I wouldn't think. It'll be far down the road, too. Maybe somebody that's not even borned yet when he's real old will come by here an' think, I used to buy hamburgers there in that building when I was a real little tad; some crazy old lady run the place. An' that'll be it. Nobody will ever recall me again. An' then I'll really be dead, won't I?" She smiles again.

"But fer Earl, my kids turned out pretty good, with a few missteps, of course. An' I'm pleased with this café. I'm proud of it and I enjoy comin' to work here ever'day. It's clean and the food's edible and the prices're fair. I know it's not much. You been to better, I can tell, lots better, but I done it myself and that's what's important. And I do look back sometimes an' think I would a been far better off to a got into a café and never had husbands or kids at all. Far better. I'd a had all the pleasure and none a the grief. But that's not the way it's meant, or that's the way it'd a been. If ever'one thought that, the whole human race would die out pretty fast. I just don't understand why, if the Lord wanted us to keep the race alive, He didn't make it easier. A old woman I used to know—I wonder if I'm the last person to remember her; she's been dead for years and years—I heard her say one time that pain is a gift from God, so you'll know yer alive. That the only emotion people have that animals don't have is heartache. Now, ain't that a happy thought?"

Virgie's story has wound down, and it is night, but not dark. Though what passes as a streetlight on Hubbard's Main Street makes little light, there is a bright moon, the harvest moon of late October shining fiercely out of a royal blue sky.

I ask to use Virgie's phone, for I know I'll be in for it if I miss dinner without reporting to Nanny. I call her and I can hear that she is put out, but also relieved. I do not often take a day off and wander away without explanation. It has been thoughtless of me; only I hadn't expected to be gone so long.

When I leave, Virgie has on her squarish coat, her pocketbook over her arm, preparing to turn out the lights, and as I pull away I note that she is pulling the door closed and locking it, a bright night light shining through the window.

It has been a mixed-up kind of day, like nothing I have ever experienced, and the sensation of being caught onstage during a drama still clings to me. The first act is a ghoulish Halloween story, a ghost story, replete with haunted house and corpses. The second act, what, a soap opera? No, these simple people are not the stuff that soap operas are made of, nor high tragedy either. It is a drama from Arthur Miller or William Inge, a spur-line tragedy. And what of the third act? The drama is certainly unfinished.

The rolling hills are almost as beautiful in the glow from the moon as they are with the sun highlighting the colors of fall. But there is a dreamlike quality to them that sunlight could never afford. And in a like dreamy trance I go over the events of the day, not in any order, but in fits and starts, bits and pieces, like a crazy-quilt dream.

Virgie is the grieving mother, but she is tough, tough as old Hecuba. Her grief has calluses around the edges. I think of the Stople brothers; have they a mother, one who cares? And is she grieving or is she relieved to at last be rid of those twin burdens? And LaWanda is nothing more now than turquoise-decorated remains. Remains. That term has more meaning to me than it used to. LaWanda is indeed only a remnant. But somewhere is there a woman grieving her, a woman who bore her in suffering and raised her to this end? I don't know. Perhaps all of that will come out in whatever legal proceedings there are. I am a long way from high-fashion merchandising, at any rate.

When I arrive at home the house is ablaze with lights, indoor and out. Nanny has turned them all on, the way she does when she is alone in the house. And then instantly I see Leroy's late-model pickup parked in the street. So she is not alone. Sure enough, Leroy is sacked out on a couch in the sitting room, glumly watching television. Nanny greets me at the door and only nods briefly toward Leroy, who rises, greets me and then sinks back on the couch.

I can see that Leroy is planning to spend the night. It is not the first time he has done so. Charlaine has thrown him out or he has stormed out. He will spend one, perhaps two nights here before he and Charlaine settle whatever differences they have.

I am not long in finding out what those differences are.

"He got mad when Charlaine tol' him to go ahead and sell their house to the city. Said they could buy a big old place, said they need the room and they could work and fix it up."

I had forgotten about the city's condemnation proceedings.

"He gone to a meeting yesterday and them city folks tol 'em dat dey definitely was goin' through with buyin' out 'at some future date.'"

"Well," I sigh, "at the rate those things go, Leroy and Charlaine may be retired and living on a fishing boat before the city gets around to doing anything. I wouldn't worry about it yet."

"But he do worry. He hates to be pushed around. He's got a temper, too, an' he say dat dey ain' goin' to push him around. An' den Ah worries."

She turns to answer the phone, which is ringing. We are both startled at the sound, for the phone rarely rings here at this hour. I have made it plain that I do not like to be disturbed at home on business matters, and I have few social calls.

"It Mr. Cloud," says Nanny. I take the phone.

"Hello, David?"

"Ah, Elizabeth. Excuse me for calling at this hour, but it's important. We have lost my father, I'm afraid. He just slipped away from us."

"You mean he's lost!" A hundred-year-old man out wandering around?

There is a long pause at the other end. "What? No, no. He's dead."

Dead? For a brief moment I feel like bickering. I feel like yelling into the phone something like, "Well, why the hell didn't you just say it? Why pussyfoot around? Dead is dead. And lost is lost. They are not the same thing!" But I do not.

"Ah, David, I'm sorry," I say and I murmur the appropriate things about Daniel's having lived a long and rewarding life and offer condolences to the rest of the family and make a note tó have Shirley send flowers to the funeral home and fruit to the family.

I hang up. "Old Mr. Cloud died this evening," I say to Nanny, who has already figured that out.

"Well," she says, "he was a long time agoin'. You know his soul died a long time ago. His body was just slow acatchin' up to it."

"Yes" is all I can think to say. I stand by the sink with a glass of water. The chain is broken. The last link with my past sundered. The old house in Tipeeho, even the ghosts have fled there, replaced by what, the ghosts of the Stoples?

No, I think not. I think perhaps I believe in ghosts, but in a kind of selective way. Some people have enough spirit to leave behind, others like the Stoples and LaWanda are spiritless, possibly even soulless, and leave behind nothing more than bits of cheap turquoise and a few bitter memories, which fade quickly. Daniel and Levi, I think, might muster up a chain or two to rattle. About the others, Obediah and his ladies, I can't say.

Then Virgie's thought comes back to me. Daniel has put my spirits to death. They are now dead, for there is surely no other person alive to remember them. And I wonder, speculate in that futile way, which of those he remembered last? Who of those did he keep alive until his own end?

ELEVEN

THE DAY THEY BURNED NIGGER TOWN

"Good morning, Father. And thank you for that most generous gift."

"Ah, good morning, Levi," I said. Inez slipped his breakfast plate in front of him. "I trust that you will spend that money wisely, perhaps invest a part of it?"

"Well, I had thought to use some of it for a pair of fine riding boots, at least"—he hesitated—"but if you'd rather I invested it . . ."

"No, no, not at all, not at all. If you need a new pair of boots, why by all means use your gift for that." I could not but feel a little smug that I had a son who on his sixteenth birthday still deferred to my opinion in all things, when so many other of my acquaintances had sons who seemed almost always at odds with their fathers. I thought of Otis Wheeler's fourteen-year-old, who by Otis's own account made life around the Wheeler household uncommonly difficult.

Indeed, I had presented Levi with a generous cash gift to celebrate this important birth year, but I did not wish him a happy birthday, nor did he expect it, knowing as he did that the anniversary of his birth was likewise the anniversary of his own mother's death. And though I had never in any way insinuated that he had precipitated that unhappy circumstance, he, sensitive boy that he was, could not fail to realize that he had been a cause, no matter how inadvertently, a guilt reinforced by his mother's family, who blamed me and the infant for their kinswoman's death and so shunned both of us. Levi's birthday, then, was never cause for celebration.

"And have you made plans for your holiday from school?" I asked by way of making conversation, for he was just home from military

266

school in Missouri and, I suspected, was anxious to make use of that newfound freedom. Though a shy and introverted boy, he did have a few acquaintances and liked to hunt and fish and ride with them, plans that he confirmed in some eagerness.

"Fine," I said. I would allow him a few days, perhaps two weeks, of leisure before I put him to work. Sixteen, I thought, was certainly not at all too early to begin the serious business of learning merchandising, as a prelude to learning other kinds of money management. *LEVI MURPHY and SON, DRY GOODS* was already announced by a fine sign across the front of my enterprise. It was time Levi started earning his place on that sign.

Inez waddled through the breakfast room door and announced, "Mr. Copeland is here to see you, Mr. Murphy." It was hard for me to imagine that Inez could get any fatter, but yearly she confounded me in that matter, until she has gotten so immense that I wonder how she bears up under all that weight.

"Ah, ask him in, Inez. And inquire if he has breakfasted. And perhaps Levi would like something else?"

"No, thank you, Father. I am anxious to get started today." And he rose as Booth Copeland entered, tossing his cap toward a chair. Good breeding had still not caught up with Booth, in spite of his wealth. I am not sure it had even left the starting gate yet. Still, for all his crudeness, Booth generated a vitality both ageless and attractive, attractive in that broad sense. He attracted people as he attracted wealth, and though I knew that he had got older in the sixteen years that we had been associated, that age did not show.

"Hey, Levi, out of school already?"

"Yes, sir. How are you, Mr. Copeland? If you'll excuse me, I was just on my way out."

"Well, certainly, yes certainly. Don't," yelled Booth after the departing boy, "hang around any loose women, y'hear? Yer at a dangerous age, y'know?"

"Yes, sir," replied Levi quite seriously.

"That'll be the day, now won't it?" muttered Booth after the boy had disappeared through the dining room door. "I don't suppose that boy'd screw a whore without askin' yer permission, would he?"

"He is an obedient young man."

"Pity."

"I am quite satisfied with the situation," I said. Because of his own independent and rebellious streak, I suppose, Booth has always found those of us with more conventional values suspect. I have always taken Booth as he is; and he has no choice but to offer me the same regard. It has worked to our mutual advantage these past sixteen years, and we are both considerably wealthier for that arrangement.

Still, I saw no reason to remind Booth of the boy's birthday. It would only occasion another of his lectures on the unnaturalness of living a celibate's life and of prolonged grief.

Nor would it do any good to try to explain to him and to others who less boldly hint at the same thing that I do not grieve, that I have been forever denied the solace of grief, that mine is an unhealing open wound that will ooze horror for as much eternity as God affords me. There is no word for this devastation of my soul, rather, for the emptiness where a soul ought to be. Rather than being the one to stem the evil of that heinous line which begat me, I became indeed its most hideous fruit, the culmination of generations of bad seed. It is with the knowledge of truest evil that I live. It is the strength and power of my maternal line only that keeps me upright, that gives me strength and resolve to live with the almighty venom that courses through my veins. It is not death I fear but eternal life.

"I come by to tell you that we have brought in three more wells on the Easterly lease." Booth made no attempt to disguise the smugness of his tone, and with good reason. That lease, shunned by other oil experts as worthless, has yielded a small fortune of its very own. I have indeed heard it said, sometimes in outright envy and antagonism, that everything Booth Copeland touches turns to oil. Booth himself is quick to give credit, claiming that I brought him luck, an irony that I have always let pass.

Actually it was the money I brought him when he failed to find ten men with $5,000. I, in the recklessness of fresh despair, had with little hope and no collateral turned over nearly $35,000 to him, money that has been returned to me a hundredfold at least and shows no sign of abating.

"Well, turn the papers over to Daniel. It all gets too complicated for me."

"That'll be the day," murmured Booth. It is one of his favorite expressions, denoting disbelief, I think. "I already did," Booth continued. "I took the papers by his offices yesterday. It's been a while since I was in there. He's added some more people and expanded space, hasn't he? All on account of your business, too, I bet?"

Booth has never been noted for his tact, a lacking other people often hold against him. Tact, I think, is a civilized virtue, much like using the proper spoon for soup. It is a rule I observe in my own dealings, but I set no particular store by it one way or the other. Its absence does not bother me. Besides, Booth has always balanced that tactlessness with incisive understanding and sharp reasoning. He might be accused of boorishness and tactlessness, but he will never stand accused of ignorance or stupidity.

And indeed Daniel has prospered, mainly on my account, since I recalled him from his firm in St. Louis. I needed his loyalty and acumen and I have not been disappointed.

I called him and he came, almost eagerly. Nor can I say exactly why I wanted Daniel, just that he seemed the only one to fill my need. I did not intend to add insult to injury or to attempt atonement, for there is no atoning my evil. Atonement is the principle business of the lesser gods, so self-centered that they are willing to forgive most any sin for a little propitiation and a few abject apologies in their names.

No, I called and Daniel came and it has been mutually satisfactory. We have grown much alike in our middle years, he, as far as I can tell, as celibate as I, given to long hours of work and little recreation. Nor is there any special bond between Daniel and young Levi. In fact, they rarely meet.

Booth rose, preparing to go, turning down the offer of coffee and breakfast. "Already et," he explained and added, "If you ever want to go out and take a look at them wells, just give me a call. I got a new car that makes the trip a breeze."

"Perhaps I will. I'll think about it. Sometime."

Booth eyed me. "That'll be the day," he said at last and I only smiled. My personal aversion to automobiles has been common knowledge for years, though the antecedents of that antipathy remain my own secret.

I have over the years learned to live with my hideous secret, even to rise above it, though revulsion and terror attack my consciousness on occasion, coming without warning and striking much as a winter fever strikes. For the most part I live an unexciting life. I have no particular desire besides peace, and that is unattainable in this life and probably in the next.

In those infrequent hours when I am struck by self-hatred most terrifying, I call up the memory of that vehicle lodged in the ditch, the dying woman reclining in the backseat. And I remember how I walked away from it, branding the memory into my consciousness as if to cauterize a wound.

I walked away, striding purposely in the wrong direction, carrying that frighteningly small bundle wrapped in the down comforter, that same down comforter which lies on the foot of my bed each night so that, even when the boy is not present, I have a reminder of my own evil.

I was not more than a mile gone, thinking of nothing save my rage and the desire to keep moving, when I spied a figure on horseback some distance away on the knoll of a hill. He hailed, a farmer or cowboy, and waved, too far away to be able to distinguish much about me, save that I was afoot. Horse and rider paused on the hill and then turned as if to ride on. In that moment the horror of what I was doing washed over me. I was bathed in the hot sweat of remorse and I screamed out and waved frantically.

The horseman paused a moment and then galloped toward me. A young cowboy, by the look of him, reached me and with a grin howdied. I took him by business, that my wife had given birth and that I was looking for assistance.

"Yer goin' the wrong way, mister," the cowboy said. "Ain't nothin' back this way. But the Mullinses live about mile and a half back up this road. There's Mrs. Mullins and her mother that lives with her. Between 'em, they probably had a hundred youngins."

The young man was joking. He seemed a kindly sort and was trying to make light in the face of what he supposed was a frightened new father. He pulled me up behind him and I clung to my burden, so heavy to be so light. It was not until we reached the Packard and the cowboy saw Elizabeth's condition that he realized the seriousness of the situation.

"Hey," he said, "I'll ride on and get hep. They'll be here in a minute and then I'll go on to town and roust out the doctor." He did not say what town, not that it mattered. He galloped away, spurring and yelling at his beast. I would have been grateful to him had there been room in my breast for one more emotion.

I was torn by fear, hopeless fear and abject misery. What had I done? Where had such evil impulse come from? I laid the babe on the seat beside his mother and bent over her, crying her name. She was hardly breathing. I could not in truth be sure that she did still breathe.

"Elizabeth!" I shouted her name. "Elizabeth. It is a boy. Elizabeth. A fine son," I cried. She made no move, nor could I tell if she heard me. "He is not dead, Elizabeth. He will live a good long time. Forgive me. Forgive me. Forgive me." There was no response. If I could have believed that she heard and understood, it would have lifted my burden slightly. But there was nothing.

A wagon bearing Mrs. Mullins and her mother arrived in short order, but there was nothing they could do save minister to the babe. By the time the doctor arrived, it was clear that Elizabeth was gone, and I sat frozen in grief on the side of the hill, my head buried in my arms.

The doctor came over to give me the news. "If I had not been so stupid," I sobbed. "If I had not wrecked the car. If I had not—"

"No, my boy, no. Don't blame yourself," said the doctor. "There was nothing you could have done. Had I been in attendance from the first pain, the outcome would have been no different. This woman was singled out by some peculiar fate of genes to die with her first birth. Her only hope was to remain a maiden. But how could anyone know?" And thus the doctor, without realizing, absolved me of all guilt in Elizabeth's actual death. It was not I who had started her on the path to her end, but Daniel.

But that was no crime. It was one of nature's sneak attacks, no one's fault really. My sin, nay, my evil, was an act of commission, of intent. I bore full responsibility, step by step. Of that there could be no gainsaying.

I buried my love in a place of my own choosing. I would never put her, so innocent, near to that villain Obediah, though it was as if he had from the grave reached out for her. I did not inform her people that she had died in childbirth for some days afterward. One of her brothers came, then, in a wagon and asked if he could take the remains, but I told him she had already been buried. He did not ask where, nor did I tell him. Nor did he ask to see his small nephew. In taciturn silence he left, and there has been but little contact since, though at one point when Levi was small I did make honest effort to introduce him to his mother's people, failing finally in that effort. I waited several months before I informed Daniel of her death, but of course named no date. He returned a note of sympathy immediately.

I spent that summer more bereft of spirit than anything, slowly reclaiming life only as small Levi grew, demanding and imperious as infants can be. Black Inez cared for the baby, bringing in a succession of her own kin and acquaintances to wet-nurse him as needed. Bred in secret passion, birthed in deceit and death, nursed on darky milk, that babe became a strange obsession to my stricken soul. There were moments when I loved him with a passion so dark it frightened me, and other times that I would as lief have dashed his brains out against a rock. Whether Inez understood such conflicts I do not know. I doubt that she could have given voice to what she sensed, but I know only that she stood between me and the babe, protecting him with a fierce maternal love of that sort which I had never really known and which I could only finally dumbly respect. To her I owe thanks that eventually my ambivalent feelings toward the infant came into balance and I realized that it was now up to me to raise him and to provide for him.

Levi Murphy II was the bastard namesake I had sought. It was as I had planned. I would end that stained line of Obediah Murphy with a bastard, and yet the triumph I had thought that culmination would yield did not come. Having spat at the memory of the dead lecher brought me no peace, and I have lived these years a kind of numbed existence, going through the motions, doing what needed to be done, reaching decisions and working hard, the boy I raised to near-manhood both my only joy and the paramount manifestation of my torment.

And it is an irony that such existence has brought me the wealth that others desperately covet, wealth that brings me no particular pleasure. Having wealth seems somehow to require, however, the accumulation of more wealth. I could not turn it off if I wanted to. As every species of plant and animal begets its own, so wealth seems likewise to beget more wealth.

"Mr. Levi," Inez said as she came in to clear the breakfast dishes, "it's time to spring-clean, and I goin' to need some hep."

I could have said to her that it was well past time for spring-cleaning, May pushing June; but as Inez's great weight slowed her down, I did not demand much of her. And though we had lived in this completed house only just past a decade, it was already beginning to collect permanent dust and dirt in the corners and crevices, not so much because of Inez's negligence as because it was simply too much house for one person, particularly one as heavy and slow as Inez, to maintain properly. Twice a year she generally called in extra help, but that was not enough. I was loath, however, to hire more help permanently, not because of the cost, for that was negligible, but because I valued my solitude. It was a paradox. I needed this large, commodious house, so that I could lose myself in it; yet it was really too large to be kept by one aging darky. So be it. Let the dust collect.

Dewey Lane might turn over in his grave at that thought, for he had been most particular of this house and it was, indeed, the last that he worked on before he died. I let him take his time with it, and it was years in the construction. I suppose that was our compromise. I did not rush him, and in return he built it as I had specified, except for those details I had planned that my wife decide. Those Dewey did as he wanted, which included ornate and heavily carved molding in every room, dust collectors that I suppose a woman would have recognized as such. Inez has given those moldings but grudging attention, but they were Dewey Lane's pride and joy.

While Dewey went on his leisurely way, ordering special woods and trims from all over the world, actually, and only occasionally having the good grace to apologize for the cost, my small family, that is, Inez and Levi and I, resided in the rooms behind the store, rooms that were in and of themselves quite commodious. We could, I suppose, still be living there, but that the expansion of the store necessitated our removal. I suppose I had intended all along to settle ultimately in this enormous house overlooking the river and the Osage Hills beyond, but I did give voice to the prospect now and then of selling the place once it was completed. And indeed it would have fetched a fine price, for the mansions had by then begun to go up all over town and I found myself with a choice house in a choice location. But in my heart this spot was my own from that time I had shinnied up the tree to ascertain the view from the topmost floor. It is that same view that I now ponder daily, in all seasons, watching rain or wind or smoke or dust rise beyond the hills on one side or spread over the plain on the other. If there is any gentle pleasure in my life, it is the view of a summer sunset from my own rooms. And when I am called upon to account to the Almighty I think I would meet Him eye to eye from that same perch. What will happen at that calamitous moment I cannot, being yet mortal, conceive.

"Whatever help you need, Inez. Only get sufficient that your chores may be accomplished quickly; for the dislocation such projects afflict upon the household I find very trying."

"Yes, sir. I got a man fer de hebby work awreddy and I know two colored ladies dat really deeds de work. I aim to put dem to washin' winders and polishin' woodwork." She said that last with some relish.

My walk to work has always been brisk, for it consists of several blocks. I shun the use of automobiles for all but necessities; indeed, I have never owned another since I left the Packard stranded in the ditch, only telling that cowboy who aided me that it was his for the taking. Horses in these modern times have become inconvenient; consequently I walk most places I need to go, for they are few.

LEVI MURPHY and SON, DRY GOODS is a jewel among Southwest merchandising, modern and well equipped by even Eastern standards. I have never stinted on searching out improvements for the store, for profit is of little account to me, while energetic activity is. But the irony remains; such improvements only seem to draw more trade, and money spent is once again returned triplefold.

I have a secretary, Mr. Perkins, who has been with me almost from the beginning. He was at first clerk, then, when business prospered, he began to help me with the bookkeeping. Now I have two full-time bookkeepers and find that I have business enough left over to keep Daniel and his firm as busy as they want to be.

"Mr. Cloud is waiting in your office," Perkins mentioned almost casually as I walked through the door. He would not, of course, admit just anyone to my office before me, but Daniel is not just anyone. Nor have I seen Daniel in several weeks, keeping in touch on business matters by telephone only. Daniel, not being overly fond of walking, has most likely driven his car the few blocks between our enterprises.

"Ah, Daniel. Good morning, you're out and about early."

"I was just driving by and thought to stop. I have some things you need to look at."

"This is a little out of your way, isn't it?"

"Ah well, there's a little disturbance around the courthouse, and I thought to avoid it."

"Disturbance?"

"Darky disturbance. I heard only that a young buck was booked into jail for making an unseemly remark to a white woman in an elevator, and some of his cohorts are expressing displeasure. It doesn't seem to amount to much. It's spring, you know, and young blood tends to run a little hot this time of year."

"Levi is home from school," I speculated aloud. "I trust he will avoid that area." I was certain, of course, that he would if he realized there was trouble, but of course he might accidentally stumble into it.

"The police seem to have matters well in hand. They're the ones who are directing people away from the disturbance. As I said, it does not amount to much, but of course there are always those who would like to stir such things up further. It's a wise precaution on the part of the police. I think perhaps I'll write a letter to the editor, commending the city officials for their handling of it."

"Does it warrant that much attention?"

"Perhaps not." As he talked he produced a stack of neatly typewritten papers and put them before me.

"Just show me where to sign. I don't have time to read through all of this even if I wanted to," I grumbled.

"Vell! Neffer, effer set yer signature to vat ye an't read! How many times I told you?"

So perfect was Daniel's mimicry that I looked up with a start and he laughed.

"You look stricken, Levi. And did you think that Louisa One had come back to haunt you?"

"I had forgotten," I mumbled.

"I hadn't." Daniel laughed. "I never glance at a stack of papers with an inclination just to sign them without reading them that her admonition does not jolt me. Remember how she used to chastise Obediah? Until my dying day I will remember how guilty and how pitiful he would look when she would find out that he had signed something without her permission." Daniel laughed again. "Vell, you vill be da death of me yet, Obediah," Daniel mimicked again. Such horseplay has always been typical of Daniel. And though he is a good and trusted worker, he still makes light of everything in conversation. You cannot get a serious word out of him. It is a certain shallowness of character, perhaps. Or perhaps it is a defense.

" 'Guilty' and 'pitiful' are hardly words that I would use to describe Obediah," I said dryly.

"Well"—Daniel shrugged—"you always took the Old Bastard much more seriously than I did, you know."

I let that pass. I cannot account for Daniel's never marrying, nor for his apparent celibate state. In one of a more serious turn I might have ascribed it to prolonged grief, but such grief is, I suspect, more the stuff of storybooks than of real life. Certainly Daniel's situation does not in any way parallel my own. He loved and lost, but that is not particularly unusual among young people, who generally shake off such loss and find someone else in short order.

Daniel has remained to all intents and purposes affable, charming, engaging . . . and what? Distant, I suppose. "Distant" is a good word for it. Over the years he has made scant reference to Elizabeth—Betty he calls her. My marriage to her does not seem to have cast a shadow over our relationship, at least not since he returned. But he still remains detached, as if waiting, but charmingly so. His quips are almost a trademark. I am constantly having them repeated to me. And many a good woman would like to see her daughter married to Daniel and, I suppose, to me. For we are neither so old that we are not viewed as eligible.

"Wealth tends to prolong one's marital eligibility, I have noticed," once quipped Daniel in passing reference to that situation.

"I will sign these and get them back to you as soon as I have read them." I waved toward the stack of papers before me.

"Oh well, no, Levi, I was only joking. You don't have to read them. I can be trusted with the family silver, you know."

"I will read them."

"No need to get in a snit about it."

"I am not in a snit."

"Have it your way."

"I probably will."

Just why something like that will get under my skin I don't know. It was Daniel's passing jest concerning Louisa One and Obediah that set me off this time and he was right. He and I hold very different views of the Old Bastard, but he does not share the secret of my birth, so how could he be expected to understand my antagonism?

I have speculated before on the propriety of setting the record straight, of writing down, as I once set out to do, my history and my memories. But I am not sure that I would be capable of confessing my own guilt, and with such an omission, how useful would that history be? Perhaps someday. Some distant hours when time has mitigated my own crimes I will set down the entire story for anyone who might care. But I know not who that might be.

Daniel left, as always, cheerfully, though his visit had left me short of temper and morose. As far as I knew, not another soul on the face of the earth remembered the Old Bastard except Daniel and me, and perhaps what I wanted from Daniel was an ally in the absolute detestation of that memory. That I did not get, for Daniel's attitude toward him was that toward an errant but lovable relative. And his jocularity about the rascal always left me out of sorts. It was Perkins who suffered the effects of that ill humor for the rest of the morning. He, fortunately, was by nature patient and long-suffering, and I was by noon in better humor.

"There is some commotion nearabouts the courthouse, I'm told," Perkins said as I prepared to walk home for my noon meal. "Best to avoid that area altogether," he added.

"Yes, thank you, Perkins. I had already been advised of it, but I'm glad you reminded me."

And indeed my course did take me close enough to the courthouse that I could ascertain that there was quite some activity in that area, somewhat more than I would have expected from Daniel's description. I determined that I must advise Levi to stay clear of the area, for I would see him at lunch; he, being more punctual, I suspect, than most boys his age are wont to be, rarely missed an appointed mealtime. I might suggest that he simply stay around home and perhaps read until the police had got this thing, whatever it might be, under control.

I had forgotten that Inez had planned serious cleaning activities, or perhaps I had not realized that she had intended to get them started that very day, so that when I arrived home I found darkies scurrying energetically about and the dining room so torn up with their enterprise that we were obliged to eat in the kitchen.

"We have h'it all back together by nightfall," Inez promised. She had set two places at the kitchen table and, as expected, Levi was waiting for me there, his growing boy's hunger possibly adding to his natural punctuality. We sat and Inez served us.

"Now I sorry we didn't git the dining room put back together fer lunch," she apologized.

"Ah, that's no problem, Inez. I really do not mind." And that was true, for the window beside which we sat looked out upon the garden, which in the spring of the year was always at its loveliest, flowering bulbs and annuals spreading out beyond the languid laurel, its own graceful boughs weeping over the boulder that Dewey Lane had so objected to; nor had I ever seen a snake in that Eden, despite his ominous warnings.

"Who is that?" I asked abruptly, for there was a child playing beyond the garden, a Negro child.

Inez looked out the window. "She come wid dem women I got workin' on de winders. She ain't been no trouble; dey jist didn't have no place to leave 'er an'," Inez added reluctantly, "things is kinda stirred up over wher dey lives and dey didn't want to leave her alone."

The little girl was earnestly involved in some imaginative activity of her own devising, the way children can be, collecting sticks and leaves and sorting them, and from the look of it carrying on some sort of one-sided conversation. She was a very fetching little girl, fetching in the way that colored children often are, like a puppy or a kitten, perhaps. Even Levi, looking at her, could not conceal a little smile at the innocent activity.

"Levi," I said as we finished our meal, "perhaps you had better plan to spend the rest of the day at home."

"Father?"

"There is some sort of disturbance, turmoil, having to do with"—and here I lowered my voice—"the darkies up in colored town. Those things can occasionally become quite unpleasant. I would be happier if you were to stay home."

"But, Father, we had not planned to go that direction."

"No, Levi."

There was a disappointed droop to his shoulders and perhaps a slight sigh, but no argument. He had learned long ago that I did not brook argument, and he always deferred to my judgment. I supposed he had plans, but they would keep, though a sixteen-year-old boy cannot always be convinced of that truth, patience being probably the last hurdle to adult maturity that a young person must pass over.

He had stepped out on the porch with me, and I noted that the little Negro girl had left off her playful activity and was engaged in some sort of hiding game beneath the laurel and around the boulder. I did not care to have children playing in the garden.

"Levi," I said abruptly, "would you ask that little darky to play elsewhere and not in the garden? Here," I added, pulling a coin from my pocket, for I did not want to seem harsh, "give her this and explain about the flowers."

The little girl had apparently heard me, for she looked up and quickly slid off the rock and, much to my surprise, marched right over to where we stood.

"Ah'm sorry, mister," she said in a surprisingly mature tone for one so young. "Ah didn' know Ah wadn' 'sposed to play dere."

"Quite all right, little girl, quite all right," I replied, much impressed at her dignity. And I offered her the coin.

But she only shook her head and said, "No, thank you, mister. My mama say Ah ain' 'sposed to take no money from strange men."

Levi looked at me and we both struggled to suppress smiles. "Your mother is a very wise mother," I said quite seriously.

"Yes, sir. An', Mister," she added with that same dignity, "Ah is 'colored.' Ah is not a 'darky.'"

At that instant one of the Negro women came around to the side of the house with a stool and pail and cleaning rags in her arms. "Nancy!" she snapped. "Nan!"

The little girl glanced at the woman and began to edge away. "Ah is 'colored,'" she said quickly, "'cause Ah is part Indian. Ah got me two colors. Red and black."

"Nan-cy! You git on about yo' bidness, girl!" cried the woman.

"Yes'm, Aint Clarice. Ah goin'," and she darted, half running and half skipping, around the corner of the house.

The woman looked as if she was trying to think of some way to apologize, but I cut her off with a smile. "She is a very charming and mature child," I said.

"She too fo'ward sometime," sighed the woman.

That was so obviously true that I said nothing more on the subject.

"Father," said Levi, "are you planning to go back to town?"

I was surprised and perhaps a little touched at his obvious concern. "Certainly, Levi. I have a business to tend to."

"Mightn't it keep until things are settled?"

"Oh, Levi, I didn't mean to alarm you. There will be no serious problems, I'm sure. It's just that boys, young men," I amended, "tend to let something like this excite them all out of proportion. I doubt that you and your friends would do so, yet I simply will feel more comfortable knowing that you are not out on the streets. Do you understand?"

"Yes, sir."

My walk back to town was still brisk. That walk four times a day afforded me most of the exercise I got, but I suspect it was sufficient and more than many of my automobile-riding acquaintances managed.

In the space of a few minutes I was passed by several automobiles carrying young men toward the activity near the courthouse. I trusted that the police would turn them back, for I was apprehensive of what a confrontation between two sets of young men—one white and one black—might afford. And passing again near the courthouse park, I was not pleased to note that the crowd had swelled in the hour that I had been gone. I had indeed been wise to remand Levi to his rooms and was pleased that I could be certain that that was where he would stay.

I had taken great pains with the raising of that boy. He was as a child no more docile, I suppose, than any male child. It had taken no small effort to get him to the point that he now was. In those months after his birth, once my ambivalence toward him settled and I realized that he was indeed my responsibility and mine alone, I spent long hours pondering the rearing of a young man destined to wealth and position and influence. I read widely, discovering to my amazement both the magnitude and variety of tracts on the raising of the young, from classical times to the present. Yet in pursuing that course, I found but little from Genesis to Plato to Locke to Dewey that truly met the standards I was determined to set.

Having at last quelled the tumult in my own breast, I had set my life on an unswerving course to its eventual end; but that course, no matter how much industry I indulged, would of necessity be painful because of its precedents. In youthful lust I had stolen a wife and a son; and in unreasoning rage I had turned my back on a dying request. I could blame all of that on the tainted blood that coursed through my veins; but nothing could erase those facts. But the course I now set myself would at least be lacking in those fitful passions that had undone me.

I would set a like course for Levi: a course of industry without lust or pride or rage, the sort of course a young man is not capable of setting for himself. Without the tainted blood of Obediah, that young man, once firmly set upon that course, could take pleasure from the fruits of that path without suffering any of that pain which life daily afforded me.

That decision was long in the making, and though the learned treatises I studied on the subject offered some valuable insights, I at last had to devise my own method and my own rules and to adhere steadfastly to them.

The primary tenet of the philosophy so devised was that the boy stay close by my side, so that I could afford him a model to emulate, a practice that afforded me a reputation as an exceptional parent, and my devotion to the child was often remarked upon, particularly by those ladies whose husbands showed indifference to their own offspring.

Except for the few hours a week I allowed him in the public schools among those of his own age, the greater part of his education I afforded him. Part was simply practical information, which he came by in accompanying me in almost all of my activities, listening intently as I carefully explained a wide range of areas to him; and part of his education was more formal. As time permitted, we explored more fully than the school's curriculum allowed those basic subjects of mathematics and language and science.

I handled my charge with great care, never losing patience or sight of my goal when he was ill tempered or dilatory. Having read and reasoned much about the educational processes, as I said, I had formed my own philosophy; for I knew that one could not beat a child into compliance, nor force information upon him. He must be handled much as newly churned butter, gently worked and squeezed, pressure applied in just the right amounts until a finished product was accomplished. My patience had eventually paid off in an obedient son whose intellect ruled his passions. I was certain that he would in no way ever disgrace the memory of his mother and he would bring to an end the lustful line of Obediah in dispassionate dignity, indeed a fitting end.

Quite frankly, I did not intend that Levi marry and continue the name. From the beginning I had determined that, and though he might struggle against that dictum at some future time, in the long run I knew I would be doing him no disservice.

By midmorning rumors of confrontations between white and black had begun to fly around my store, alarming, unnecessarily I thought, the women clerks in my employ and in truth some of the men.

I sent Perkins out to see if he could ascertain the seriousness of the situation, and as I waited for his return, the telephone upon my desk jangled and startled me, as it almost always did when it rang. It proved to be Booth Copeland, not surprisingly, since he was inordinately fond of using that appliance or any other kind of gadgetry he came upon.

"Levi, y'know there's been some shootin' and burnin' over in nigger town," he said without preface. "It's beginnin' to look like there's goin' to be some bad trouble."

"My word, Booth, this is the twentieth century."

"I don't give a damn what century it is. A riot's a riot. And they don't none of 'em ever get better till they get worse. I'm puttin' armed men over in the yard around the tanks, anyway."

"Well, as you see fit, of course."

"That ain't why I called," said Booth. I did not think that it was, as Booth Copeland was not given to asking my advice or permission in any but the purest financial considerations.

"I seen yer kid Levi over there in the park, the other side of the courthouse, him and a bunch of boys that didn't have no business there. Just come to watch the fun, and that's dangerous. I believe I'd get him off the streets if I was you."

"Levi! Oh no. You're mistaken, Booth." I was certain of that. I knew where Levi was because that was where I had told him to be. "Levi is at home. I gave him strict orders. You've mistaken some other boy for him. Sixteen-year-old boys can all look remarkably alike, you know."

"Well, I don't know. You better check. I'd bet that was him."

"Ah well, yes, thank you, Booth. I do appreciate your concern." I let it go at that. I had no intention of undermining my confidence in Levi's judgment by checking on him.

When Perkins returned a few minutes later, he confirmed that indeed the situation was bad and growing worse. "Perhaps," he suggested, "we ought to close early and let the employees get safely home before dark."

"Yes, Perkins. I was just thinking that myself."

"And, Mr. Murphy," he began diffidently, "I, uh, think that I recognized Master Murphy with a group of boys out at the court-house. I thought perhaps you'd like to know."

There it was again. I felt a little thrill in the pit of my stomach, an apprehension.

"Yes, well, thank you, Perkins. I'll look into it. Advise the customers and employees of the situation and tell them that we are closing early and will remain closed until we are sure the situation is in hand." In one thing Booth had been correct. Riots are ugly and tend to get uglier before they improve.

I picked up the telephone and made a rare telephone call, for I was never enamored of that instrument even though I recognized its value.

I apprised Inez of the situation and said, "You had better get those people working with you started toward their homes. I fear for their safety."

"Dey already gone."

"You might be careful to stay in the house out of sight, Inez. Master Levi will be there with you until I can get home. I doubt that there will be any real problems, of course."

"Master Levi ain't home."

Not home! That knot of apprehension twisted in my stomach once more. "Where is he?" I asked, keeping my voice controlled.

"Ah don' know. Jest said he was goin' to de ribber. He left a couple hours ago. Some a his frens come by."

I carefully replaced the telephone receiver in its cradle and sat at the desk with my hands folded. I did not know if it were fear or anger or a combination of the two that I was experiencing. I was, however, extremely agitated. I could not believe that the boy had so flagrantly disobeyed me; it had been years since he had opposed me on even the slightest issue.

I could feel the anger winning out over the fear. Had I misjudged him entirely? Had he been deceiving me all these years? If he could so casually disregard direct orders, what other mischief might he have perpetrated that I was ignorant of? I stood in sudden anger and paced the floor and then sat abruptly again. Control of self was what I had aimed at for all these years and what I had tried to instill in Elizabeth's son. I must never let my own self-control come undone. Obviously, my work with the boy was not as complete as I thought. That was all. I had more work to do. But he was the child. I was the adult. I would, of course, overcome.

The first thing to do was to ride out this ugly racial situation. I would simply search out Levi and take him home with me. From there we would work more intensely on molding his character. I captured my hat and started through the store, only to be confronted by Perkins and two armed roustabouts.

"Mr. Murphy," said one of the men, "Mr. Copeland sent us over to set with yer store till all this," and he nodded in the direction of the courthouse, "is over."

Ah, Booth. He was thinking for both of us, fortunately.

"And is it all that serious?" I asked.

One man shrugged only and the other said, "Oh, probably not. Ther goin' to burn down nigger town is all. Them niggers got all uppity and ast fer it. Cain't do nothin' but give 'em what they ast fer, kin we?" He winked. "Mr. Copeland jist wants to make sure none of them old boys gits so excited with the fun a burnin' niggers out that they go on a rampage down here, too. You never know what'll happen when a mob gits together."

I did not say anything more. I was so appalled at such a speech from what passed as a civilized man that I could only cast my eyes down, somehow shamed for him, and walk quickly out into the street.

There was no question now of violence. The smell was in the air from the smoke north of the railroad and the noise was in the air, filled with raucous yelling and occasional shots. Carloads of armed white men were riding around town, a holiday air about them. I saw no dark souls and genuinely hoped that there were none in the vicinity, for they certainly would not be safe. I hurried toward the courthouse, not fearing for my own safety or for Levi's were he still in that vicinity, for our skins were the requisite color and the darkies had been driven back.

Momentarily I thought of Inez and speculated upon the advisability of sending an armed guard to sit in my house with her. But I rejected that idea. I was on my way there anyway, and I wondered where I might find a guard willing to protect a colored on this day. She, at any rate, would surely be safe, for my house was far removed from this disturbance.

I found Levi with relative ease among a large group of boys, all excited and shouting, mainly just noise, but some encouragement. I took the boy by the elbow and he looked with some surprise at me. "We are going home, Levi," was all I said, without rancor but with firmness.

"Oh, Father," said Levi excitedly, "they're only going to burn some coons." So out of character was such a statement that I could only assume him to be emboldened by the circle of companions about him.

A startled expletive escaped me and Levi stepped back, his flushed face turning pale. I could not believe that he had said such a thing, and it's possible that he himself suddenly realized the import of what he had said, for he lowered his eyes as if loath to meet mine.

"We are going home, Levi," I said in a quiet and carefully controlled tone. "Come."

He came. Nor did his companions seem to notice his defection, for they were jostling and yelling and generally behaving as if they were at a Fourth of July celebration instead of a lynching.

I did not trust myself to speak, and so I did not. We strode side by side quickly down the sidewalk, ignoring the commotion about us. Levi walked with his head down, wondering, I suppose, what this misadventure would cost him.

Once beyond the downtown area, the streets were quiet and the residential area seemed quite unaffected, except there was not a single person in evidence when on such a quiet spring afternoon one might have expected to see many; and most doors were closed tight and shades drawn. The air seemed ominous as the air before a coming storm.

It was Levi who stopped suddenly, looked around and said, "What was that?" He had heard something that I had not, and I, too, listened, inclining in the direction that he pointed. There was indeed some commotion coming from an overgrown lot between two houses. The cause for that commotion was evidenced when three men emerged from the bushes dragging a Negro with them.

I caught my breath sharply, for the black man was torn and bloody, hanging limply between two of his tormentors. I clinched my teeth and for an instant wondered how Levi would react if I were to say, "Well, it's only a coon that they are burning." I would not in any case have said such a thing, even had the look on Levi's face not been pale and stricken, he having come face to face with naked violence unadorned by festive garments. I heard him breathing hard.

"Father," he whispered. "Father?"

I do not know if I was frightened or outraged; but I could not simply let that black man be dragged away. I stepped forward. "What is the meaning of this?" I demanded.

"We found us a pickaninny," drawled one of the assailants. "And we aim to *pick* him." He laughed and with one hand grasped the black head and pulled it back. I was looking into the terrified eyes of a boy, a boy not much older than Levi, a gangling colored youth, whose split lip and missing teeth gave testimony to the beating he had taken. The look from those wide, dark eyes was desperately pleading.

"Please," he whispered to me, "please."

"Shut up, boy," said one of the other men and fetched him a cuff to the ear. The sound the dark boy made was somewhere between a sob and a gasp and was matched almost identically by a like sound from the boy at my side.

"Father," he gasped, "Father! It's Joab. Father, help him. It's Joab."

"What?"

"It's Joab. Mrs. Wheeler's Joab. He works for Mrs. Wheeler. I know him, Father. Help him, please. Please."

"What do you intend to do with him?" I demanded.

"I told you. We goin' to teach them niggers a lesson this time. They'll know ther place and they'll stay ther, I tell you. We goin' to shoot this 'un and throw it in the middle of nigger town."

"But he's only a boy!"

"He's big enough to mouth off! An' he's big enough to fuck yer daughter if he gits a chance. That's what he wants, too. Just let 'em git out a line an' see what they do!"

Joab was staring at me, too weak to stand, too terrified to speak.

"Father," pleaded Levi. "Make them put him down. Make them leave him alone."

"He cain't make us do nothin'," snapped one of the men. "Anybody tries to stop us is goin' to git his in like measure. You all in your big houses and fancy clothes, you don't know niggers. They'd eat you alive if it wadn't fer us. You ought to thank us fer takin' the trouble. Serve you right if they fucked yer sister to death," he snapped at Levi. "Come on, les git him to the river."

At that moment a car filled with armed white men pulled to the curb. "Hey, lookee here," yelled one of Joab's captors, "we caught us one. Come on, foller us down to the river and join our nigger roast."

"Father!"

"Please," whispered the black boy, and "Please" again, so soft that it was hardly a sound, only a movement of his battered lips.

There was nothing I could do, but I tried again. "If you do not leave this boy, I'll have the law on you," I threatened, but the threat was lightly taken.

"Now you jist do that," said one, and the others laughed and cheered.

"Here," yelled someone from the car. "Tie the rascal on the fender and we'll drive y'all on down to the river. Pile in."

They dragged the helpless boy between them and I realized in horror that that was exactly what they intended to do: display him on the hood of the car like fresh-killed game.

"Father!" I turned to Levi. He was holding a revolver, his eyes wild. I had no idea where he might have got the gun or how long he had had it stuck in his belt.

"Levi, no!" I said, almost under my breath. The group of men involved in tying Joab to the hood of the car paid no attention to us. I wrenched the gun from Levi, for he held it limply, hardly having any idea what he was going to do with it, and threw it into the weeds. He stared vacantly at me.

I turned back to the car, now loaded with men, inside and out, and as the motor started over the laughing jests of the occupants, I heard the loud screaming of the boy on the hood of the car. He screamed and screamed and screamed. As the car moved into the distance and around the corner, I could still hear the screams, like the sound of a siren, diminishing.

Levi had wilted to the sidewalk. I helped him up. "They only mean to scare him," I said. I did not believe it, and I suspected he did not either. "They know I recognized them. They'll not take the chance on killing him," I went on. "They are mindless creatures. There will be more yelling and shouting than anything else. It will all be over tomorrow and we'll forget about it quickly." But the look on Levi's face denied me that surcease from guilt that I sought. I could have said again that there was nothing we could do, that jeopardizing our own safety in a futile gesture was insane. But I said nothing more for the moment, for the helplessness I felt was a strange and unsettling sensation.

I guided Levi home. He was dazed, and I settled him in a chair and went in search of Inez, who had not answered my calls. The adrenaline was still coursing through my veins from that encounter, and in the silent house a sudden sense of apprehension, approaching dread, settled over me. "Inez," I called. "Inez."

Levi had followed me, dumbly, like a puppy. I went into the kitchen. "Inez!" I shouted.

"Father." Levi was pointing out the kitchen window toward the garden. I think I knew what I would see even before I looked. Inez's great bloody bulk lay spread out beneath the laurel beside the boulder. There was no life to her.

It was an easy matter to reconstruct what had happened. The trail of blood that the black woman left came from the trash pile behind the shed. She had obviously ignored my warning and carried trash outside. The shed was close to the street on one side. Probably an automobile passed at that moment and a single shot was fired, perhaps with serious intent, perhaps not. But the effect was the same. This great black lady lay dead, a victim of that racial violence which did not, as I had predicted, pass quickly.

It lasted for three horror-filled days until the colored community was all but leveled and hundreds of both color were injured and upward of three dozen lay dead, with many unaccounted for. I stood at night at my windows and watched the smoke rise from the rubble of what had been a thriving and decent darky community. That view gave rise to speculation upon the nature of evil, and I could only conclude that the Mob is not evil; for evil, like its counterpart, good, requires a capacity. The Mob has no capacity. It is as mindless as rage is mindless, and lust. And as hateful and abhorrent as those things are hateful and abhorrent.

The smoke eventually cleared and we began trying to put the memory of those days behind us. Levi made no mention again of Joab, and when I suggested that it was time to begin to learn seriously the business, he complied almost eagerly.

I heard no more of Joab. I scanned the published lists of victims, but those were admittedly incomplete. At any rate, his name was not there. One day I asked Otis Wheeler if he knew what had become of Joab.

Otis only shrugged and said, "He disappeared that day they started burnin' nigger town."

TWELVE

LOUISA GETS RELIGION

*I*t was better than ten years after the Civil War ended that Louisa Varner Murphy learned the fate of her oldest son, Danny Varner, and that in a most casual manner, for he walked, rather, limped, through the gate of their Mount Vernon farm and stomped into the kitchen as if he had been gone only a morning and was returned for dinner. Clean-shaved and youthful and tall, he had hardly changed since his mother had seen him last, though he was at that time past forty years of age.

Nor was Louisa, though happy and excited, completely surprised to see him; she had been expecting him for nearly a decade. He had merely been slow in arriving. She was satisfied. She had sent four men to war and three had at last come home. The last, Henry Varner, she did not expect to see again. She had suspected from the beginning that he was dead, and although she received no formal announcement of that, her slim hopes faded as months and then years passed with no word.

But Louisa One (which designation had at last been settled by her husband's inability to make clear just which Louisa he had reference to) had not really expected to see Danny Varner anytime soon after his side had lost the war, for he had a stubborn streak to him; she had waited patiently for word from him. Without actually viewing his corpse, she would never have given him over as dead. Nor was he. Crippled he was, dragging one foot slightly, and unduly quiet and even on occasion sullen, but dead he was not, and proved it by seating himself at the midday table and dispatching a disproportionate share of the prepared victuals.

When he had finished eating and had been apprised of the family history, that his youngest brother was dead and his beautiful niece victim afar of a battlefield fever, Danny Varner came close to forgiving his family for winning the war, that victory having cost them much. Yet he kept aside a small plot of anger and cultivated it against the day he might need it, nor did he ever entirely forget that they had been winners, doubly so, for they had prospered considerably, and he had been loser, losing everything, both dignity and wealth, to the victors.

Louisa learned quickly that she must take care in conversations with him, for he retained that tendency to flash rage unexpectedly, which he had always had, and even violently, though it passed quickly, like a single crack of thunder from a passing shower.

"Mine Obediah will settle ye on yer own piece of property," said Louisa One, "as he done for Charlie ven he married." That last she added with a view toward finding his state, whether married or not. But Danny Varner only grunted, and in his own mind questioned the prosperity so obvious all around him. He did not believe that so much could simply be the product of Obediah's industry, though he remembered his stepfather as a good and determined worker.

Had he questioned Louisa One directly, he probably would not have come away the wiser, for in matters financial she kept her own counsel and even Obediah, though he had participated in that wartime arrangement with Adam Springer, had no idea of the extent of the success that enterprise had met with and the range of investments his wife, Louisa, had made. Nor did he know that she kept beneath her mattress a box of gold, which she referred to herself only as her "mattress money." Obediah only knew that he never wanted for cash and so could buy as he needed, nor was he a wastrel with money, only spending a sum annually on his personal dress, his ruffled collars being handsewn and hard come by. He understood but vaguely that Louisa One had land and investments, for he was often called upon to put his signature to papers for her, which service he was always happy, even eager, to perform.

The piece of land upon which Louisa settled Danny Varner was a recently acquired property, which lay between her extensive farm and the town itself.

"It is good land," she affirmed to her firstborn. "Ye kin make a right good livin' from it. Only know dat on the fer side beside the spring near to town lives a vidder and her daughter. She pays a little rent, but not so much, as her husband vas killed in dat var dat also took mine Henry. Ye may collect the rents from her or I vill, fer I vould not have the vidder St. Cloud turned out."

"It does not matter to me," said Danny, who had not bothered to thank his mother.

"Vell, den I vill do it. I collect dem rents once effer six months," she added, though in truth she had not bothered to collect the rents at all. Louisa was not one to collect from widows and orphans on any account, particularly not widows so near to destitution as the widow St. Cloud, who had settled on that spot only months earlier on the recommendation of a mutual acquaintance.

With the arrival of Danny Varner, Louisa was at last satisfied. She was at the time sixty-five years old, though she paid no attention to that fact, and was at last settled on the land on which she presumed she would live out the remainder of her life, for she was convinced that Obediah had at last outgrown his randy ways and had settled into the life of a gentleman farmer on a prosperous farm in a civilized country, the southern part of Illinois being at that time settled and passing properous, with a railroad running through it and coal mines and good farmland abounding. And the Indians who threatened the safety and prosperity of early settlers were themselves removed and mostly civilized but for the far western tribes, who still tended to resentment that their lands were invaded and their food supply destroyed. But none of that mattered to Louisa One, for she had made her home. Others could go fight Indians, not she or hers.

With some great regularity Adam Springer would call upon Louisa Varner Murphy to deliver more interest on the principle that they shared, he being, as Louisa had correctly surmised, a reliable man to do business with, were you in partnership with him, at any rate.

"Vat?" she would say on those occasions. "More money? Vat vill ve do vit more money?"

Adam might shrug and say something to the effect that there was usually something to do with money. "Invest it if you have to."

"It don't make no sense," Louisa might return, "to have so much more money dan you know vat to do vit it, but to invest it so it makes more money dat you don't know vat to do vit it." But Adam Springer noted that she always took the money.

It was on such an afternoon that Louisa One and Adam Springer sat talking in her parlor, for that was where she customarily conducted business, it being where her ornate little secretary was established, when Louisa Two answered a knock on the door and admitted a striking and comely woman who asked for Mrs. Murphy.

"Ah," said Louisa One when the visitor was admitted to her presence, "now it is Mistress St. Cloud come to call. Dis"—she pointed to Adam Springer—"is Mr. Springer, vit who I haf business dealings. And von't you set and ve shall haf tea."

Adam Springer had risen and was staring in open admiration at the woman, a fact that Louisa One noted with some surprise, as Adam was securely married and she would have thought above such things.

"I have only come to pay my rents, Mrs. Murphy, as you have not sent anyone to fetch them. I did not want you to forget them."

"Oh, dat's all right. I am in no hurry," said Louisa. "Do set. Please. Louisa," she directed her daughter, "put on the kettle and fetch the tea." Louisa Two gave her mother a scathing look but rose at last to do as she had been bidden.

"I would not trouble you. Mrs. Murphy."

"Nuh, nuh, nuh," murmured Louisa, who correctly surmised that the woman had not had a good cup of tea in a long time. "Louisa," she yelled toward the kitchen, "put some cookies and some biscuits on dat tray. I know Mr. Springer is hungry. A man is always hungry." It was as well that the mother could not at that moment see the expression on the daughter's face.

"I really do not want to intrude," said the widow St. Cloud. But she seated herself anyway, and Adam Springer remained standing, still ogling the woman fiercely.

Alecia St. Cloud was indeed the kind of woman who elicited that response in certain kinds of men. Her beauty, though more subdued than that of some of those fortunate women born with arresting or at least regular features and figures in decent proportion, ran deep. She was passing tall and slim, nor were her features regular—the nose a bit too large, the mouth a little too full, the cheeks higher than was generally admired in woman—but the eyes, almond-shaped and a startingly deep gray, held the other features together, so that the whole was more striking than its parts.

Still, the widow St. Cloud's beauty, arresting as it was in person, would not have been so pronounced in a picture, for it was of a sort that depended on expression, voice, posture, a turn of the head, a tilt of the chin, more than on regularity and pleasantness of features. It was a total womanliness that turned the head of a man of experience, and the longer that Adam Springer sat in Alecia's presence, the more affected he became, until Louisa One finally spoke.

"Ah, Mr. Springer, an' I seen Mistress Springer at church Sunday last and she looked uncommon good. And has she quite recovered from the fever of the last vinter?"

"Oh, uh, yes, certainly," answered Adam Springer distractedly.

The mention of Mistress Springer's health was actually of little consequence, as that woman, being barren, was given, as the childless often are, to an exaggeration of her own symptoms, so that a slight cold became a fever, a sore toe the gout, a paleness of complexion the jaundice and so forth. Although Adam Springer had long given up serious concern over his wife's complaints, it was customary for his acquaintances to inquire regularly after her health.

Louisa said no more on the subject, only speculating briefly, as she had on other occasions, on the importance of sexual attraction for the efficient operation of the male person. She was of half a notion that without that attraction the entire masculine population would fall into a decline and so perish without so much as a whimper, so dependent on it were they for inspiration, and even for life itself.

But as Louisa One was not of a philosophical bent, she did not bother to try to carry that thought further, but only noted to herself that Adam Springer seemed definitely smitten and wondered if the widow St. Cloud might return that interest.

But Alecia St. Cloud was not a woman whose sexuality dominated her life. She had married Benjamin St. Cloud when she was quite young, he being her first serious suitor, and they had had three children, two dying early, one at birth and one later of the fever. A daughter only survived when Benjamin had gone off to the war, whence he did not return. Benjamin St. Cloud had never provided too well for his family, and in death he left them little but debts and a slight war pension. Alecia had sold most of what she owned to pay the debts and had moved onto the small plot of ground that Louisa One owned, so that she could raise a few vegetables and some chickens and so make ends meet. She was a proud woman and not above thirty-five years of age.

Adam Springer was nearing forty-five at that time and stood only slightly above average, being of a stocky but firm build, with a thatch of graying hair and, Louisa was aware, a growing fortune. It would not, she thought, be a bad match were it not for the fact that Adam was possessed of a wife who, despite regular attacks of this or that, did seem uncommon robust and potentially long-lived.

Adam Springer made no move to go until the widow St. Cloud had drunk her tea daintily, thanked her hostess, produced the few notes she owed on rent and had at last departed.

"Had I my carriage, I should drive you home," said Adam to the departing lady, cursing himself roundly for not having had the foresight to realize that he would meet a lovely princess at Louisa Murphy's and so need to have his carriage at his disposal in order to prolong his contact with her, and he glared accusingly at his saddled horse as if it were that dumb animal's fault that it were not attached to a carriage.

"Thank you, Mr. Springer," replied Alecia; "it is not far and I do not mind the walk."

"I vould not haf her to pay me dese rents," said Louisa after Alecia had departed, "fer she is near-destitute as it is. But she is a proud voman."

"Ah yes," sighed Adam and shortly made his own departure.

"I do hope," murmured Louisa One to Louisa Two, "dat Adam has more sense in his head den he has got in his rod."

"Humph," muttered Louisa Two, who had reached over and was attending to the buttons that Louisa Three had managed to undo, leaving her undergarments and her budding bosom exposed.

"I do not understand vy you do not make her garments vit the buttons on the back," snapped Louisa One to her daughter.

"Because I don't want to," snapped Louisa Two right back at her. "She's mine and I'll dress her as I please."

"Ye only do it dat vay to spite me," said Louisa One, which was true.

It was only one Sunday a month that Louisa One met her son Charlie Varner and his family, and that was at church, after which Charlie and his family joined the Murphys for Sunday dinner, and though Danny Varner did not accompany them to church, he was always on hand for dinner. Louisa and Obediah could actually have gone to church services more often than once a month, for such services were held regularly each week. But Louisa, having spent her life upon circuit-riding preachers, was of the opinion that regular worship more often than once a month was excessive.

And Obediah was content with that arrangement, for in truth he was just as happy not to have Charlie Varner's family in attendance at Sunday dinner more often than they were, for Charlie had, once he got started, proved adept at fathering children on his wife, Margaret Ann, starting with a set of twins and producing regularly each year, until he had a house full. They were quite noisy.

Within a few months of his return Danny Varner had settled into the life of a southern Illinois farmer, his bitterness, if not subsided, at least controlled. And had it not been for a chance encounter that he and Obediah had in town on a Saturday market day, that bitterness might indeed at last have faded away.

"Hey there, it's Colonel Murphy," came a raucous cry from the vicinity of a Main Street saloon.

"*Colonel* Murphy?" That title or its reason for being had never been called to Danny Varner's attention.

"Colonel Murphy! Hey! It's me, Tommy Timmons. We fought them red savages at Pea Ridge," the man cried out, that last more for the information of onlookers than as a reminder to Obediah, for he quickly recognized his fellow warrior, the hard-drinking, hard-fighting Tom Timmons. And all came back to Obediah in a mighty rush, those moments of high glory when he rode pell-mell through the savage battle, exhorting the troops, lifted on a wave of gallantry that kept him still from realizing the carnage he had passed by. Nor with it did he recall the killing of the Indian or of Eli Case, for Obediah's memory, selective as a healing wound, shut out any infectious thoughts.

Though Tom Timmons had been drinking, probably a great quantity, he staggered only slightly, so great was his natural capacity for strong drink, and he hastened over to Obediah with his hands outstretched.

"Colonel Murphy, my Gawd, my Gawd. I figgered you to be in Washington, D.C., at least by this time." Obediah felt his spirit soar at this reminder of his own past glory.

"Colonel Murphy," repeated Danny Varner. "I do not understand."

"Colonel Murphy, now," announced Tommy Timmons to the group that was beginning to form and listen, "was ever as fightin' a soljer as ever was. At Pea Ridge he single-handed almost led us to victory. Had he not got wounded there, he'd a marched us through the South itself and on to Appomattox. No doubt!"

If Danny Varner was ill pleased with that intelligence, the group surrounding them was not, for the war, though ten years or more gone, was yet a fresh topic and any new hero was welcome, the crowd not yet having wearied of tedious old soldiers as it one day would.

Now, to Obediah this was a welcome breeze, for he had not so much mellowed, as Louisa, his wife, believed, as simply become superfluous. His opinions were no longer sought out, though he was respected, as wealthy men are always respected. His voice was stilled, and even the pretty girls did not often call him with their eyes and the flick of their bustles.

He no longer lived on a frontier; this was a populated area, and commerce and industry were the words of the day. And Obediah understood naught of this, nor did Louisa, his wife, bother to explain to him, for she was busy with her accounts—stitching busily on her quilt top—and her interests and her principle and her mattress money and had little need, beyond occasional signatures, of Obediah. He did not raise his voice in sonorous discourse anymore, for he did not know what to say, nor did anyone particularly care. Civilization had caught up with Obediah and had gone beyond him. He did not quite understand that and he was saddened.

His dream of naming a city for himself seemed too distant now, for nearby was already a Murphysboro and likely another was not needed, and his vaguely realized plans for honors and achievements had never got much beyond that state. He could not speak of notes and commissions or grain or hog futures, and even if he could, that lofty language that he had learned at the feet of the Reverend Joshua Trafalgar Mason would not suit these subjects. Obediah Jonah Micah Murphy had gone out of style.

"I do not care to listen to this," snorted Danny Varner and stalked away. Obie, however, hardly noted that departure, so raptly was he listening to his virtues as extolled by Tommy Timmons. And when Tommy finally ran out of anything to say and the group of listeners drifted away, some with parting slaps on Obediah's back, Obediah said, "An', Tom Timmons, will ye come home to dinner with me, fer my wife and daughter are good as cooks as ever ye'll know?" That offer Tom Timmons was not slow in accepting.

Procuring their mounts, the two set out for Obediah's farm, walking and leading their horses at least until they were out of town. "An' tell me, Tom Timmons, what d'ye do these days an' where d'ye live?"

"Oh, I do and live as I please, Colonel," answered the other. "To tell ye the truth, I've found it uncommon hard to settle. I been a fightin' man too long and would be still, but they think I'm too wild fer duty out in the West. Can ye 'magine that?" he snorted. "Too wild to fight the wild savages? They want all spit and polish, and whilst I got plenty a the one, I'm passin' short a the other. They turned me out."

"Ah," murmured Obediah in sympathy, understanding what it was to be in the prime of life and not to be needed.

"I ere a fightin' man, Colonel," repeated Tom Timmons, "an' I hardly know what t'do with no war to fight. It seems to me that there just an't enough wars no more. It's them Republicans, y'know. They only want to make money, an' that an't no fun."

Obediah had to agree. Indeed, people around him seemed to make money all the time and yet had no fun. He knew that Adam Springer made money, and Louisa, and neither of them that he could see had near the fun of fighting a battle like the battle he had fought. Tom Timmons was probably right. What was wrong with the world was that there were not battles enough to fight.

"Hey, now, what's that?" said Tommy Timmons suddenly. He had stopped so short that his mount butted into him, but Tommy did not notice. He was staring at the woman who had come around the house they were passing on the outskirts of town. That woman, with her damp hair hanging about her shoulders, letting it dry from freshly washing it, stared back unperturbed. And Obediah, too, stared hard at her.

He recognized where they were, that this was the piece of their property that was occupied by a widow and her daughter, though he did not know the particulars. He had passed many times this tidy cabin without ever noticing any of the occupants.

"Hallo," said Tom Timmons, doffing his hat; Obediah did not think to remove his. The woman nodded and then smiled at Obediah, for Obediah standing tall and gentle almost always elicited a smile from any woman, they instinctively recognizing him as harmless and kind, and sometimes more.

Now, Alecia St. Cloud, it has already been noted, was a woman of extraordinary beauty, but it was that kind of beauty that a youth in the first fires of his rampant sex might overlook in that headlong rush to fulfill the demands of newly acquired manhood, callow youth having neither the taste nor the experience to recognize and appreciate that patina which enhances true beauty over years of collected experiences and emotions.

But Obediah Murphy was beyond that tumultuous state, and so, too, was Tommy Timmons; and they looked with approval upon the woman with the damp hair hanging around her shoulders, her skin smooth, character and beauty etched in fine and almost imperceptible lines about her eyes and mouth, her form appropriately rounded and her look calm and assured. Tommy Timmons looked at that rounded form and sighed. Obediah Murphy looked further; he looked into her eyes and saw her soul. Obediah for the second time in his life fell headlong in love.

For what he found in those depthless gray eyes caused memory's flood to course through his brain, depositing not images but impressions, and he sensed more than remembered the warm autumn breezes of another time and the rustle of tall grass and the taste of honey upon his lips. And though four decades separated him from that first encounter and though that was earliest manhood against passing prime, the sensation that overcame him was identical to that first one, ageless in its power to stir.

The woman nodded briefly, said nothing, and turned and walked back around the cabin, giving her hair a shake and running her fingers through it to dislodge any remaining tangles, thoughtless of what such a gesture did to the composure of the two men staring after her.

Silently Tommy Timmons and Obediah mounted their horses and slowly walked them toward their destination.

"Ye know, Colonel, sometimes the sight of a woman like that will undo me so's I kin hardly ride astraddle a horse. I don't believe I could stand even a trot, were a whole host of red savages on my tail."

Obediah nodded, for he understood what Tommy Timmons was suffering. And both fell silent, thinking their own thoughts for the rest of the journey.

Obediah presented Tommy to Louisa, his wife, and Louisa, his wife's daughter, and Tommy doffed his hat again and ran a sheepish hand through his thinning hair. Louisa One was cordial; Louisa Two was simpering; and Louisa Three when she finally was found was only vacant.

"She," explained Louisa One, "was struck by the fever back during the war an' she an't been right since."

"A shame. A shame," murmured Tommy Timmons, and he meant it; for the girl before him, but for the vacancy of her expression, would have been passing fair and in short order a full-blossomed maiden.

They all sat to eat, and though no mention was made of the widow St. Cloud, it was that person who possessed the thoughts of both Obediah and Tommy Timmons.

Now, Alecia St. Cloud had, without at all intending to, captured the imaginations of three men, all old enough to know better, only one in any way eligible and that not much by any serious woman's standards. And in short order she would capture a fourth such heart, for not long after her chance encounter with Obediah and Tommy Timmons she came upon Danny Varner and his stepfather mending fences in the field where she picked berries and searched out wild herbs.

Obediah and Danny had worked the morning away, mostly in silence but for Obediah's cheery whistling, for Danny was of a taciturn nature anyway, that taciturnity giving way to sullenness with the defeat of the Confederacy, and indeed became more pronounced with the information that Obediah had been not only a Union officer, but apparently one of heroic proportions. If true, it would have been more than Danny could have tolerated, but he found it hard to believe in all its particulars. He could envision Obediah in an officer's uniform, it was true, perhaps even brandishing a saber. But once his imagination had carried him that far, it would carry him no further. The picture of his stepfather charging through battle, attacking and slaying, leading and exhorting, would not come. Danny Varner had been in battle himself. He had fought at Vicksburg and again at Stone Mountain. He knew battle at its worst, and the stately but often vague gentleman at his side did not fit into that tumultuous picture. Despite testimony to the contrary, Danny could only believe that the history of Obediah Murphy as a Union hero was somehow flawed.

It was Danny who spied Alecia St. Cloud first, as she came from the woods into the clearing, holding her skirts high against the snagging bramble bushes, her bonnet hanging around her neck and a basket clasped in her fingers not occupied with her skirts. Danny caught his breath, for the woman, unconscious of the men, made an arresting picture against the dark green foliage of the wood.

She looked up just as Obediah looked up and, recognizing him, she smiled and then she directed her smile toward Danny Varner, who, though he did not return the smile, felt an unaccustomed weakness overtake him. For though he might contain the expression on his face, he could not contain the flutter that accosted his bosom.

"Ah, good morning, Mr. Murphy," said Alecia St. Cloud as he moved toward them. "An' isn't it a passing warm day?"

Obediah nodded and agreed that it was, a bit saddened that, upon spying the men, the lady had let fall the skirts that she was holding up, camouflaging once more those well-turned ankles.

"It seems sad to me that the berries perversely refuse to ripen when the weather is cool and pleasant, but must wait until the heat of summer before they can be gathered," said Alecia.

Again Obediah agreed that such a situation was not as it should be. Danny Varner remained silent, staring coolly at the woman.

"An' please to wish Mrs. Murphy good day for me," said Alecia, and she nodded toward Danny and passed on her way.

"Who was that?" asked Danny as she had gone.

"That is the widow St. Cloud that lives in the cabin by the spring near to the road," said Obediah, staring after the woman, gentle longing spread across his face.

Danny, who did not notice that, only murmured, "Widow? Ah," his voice carefully concealing the agitation that had overflown his breast and was attacking other parts of his person, particularly those organs most sensitive to that kind of agitation.

Now, Alecia St. Cloud was quite cognizant of Danny Varner's identity and also of his eligibility. For though Alecia did not wish to live out the rest of her life in poverty and celibacy, neither was she anxious to wed just any widower with a houseful of motherless children for her to raise. Danny Varner, though he dragged one foot slightly, was not only reasonably attractive to the eye, but also single and childless, so far as she had been able to ascertain. It was perhaps one reason that Alecia stayed on in the little cabin instead of taking her daughter and going to live with family near to Edwardsville. The possibilities of finding a like prospect in Edwardsville, one so eligible and likewise heir to a large fortune, were bleak. Yet, being a gentle lady, she did not quite know how to capture the man's attention without being forward and impertinent.

It was Louisa One who, with some premeditation, made that meeting possible and also without knowing set in motion a series of events that she would not have set in motion had she the gift of prescience. But she had not.

On the appointed Sunday, Louisas One, Two and Three, along with Obediah, attended church, the elder two Louisas having prepared the usual sumptuous Sunday fare before they left, against the ravenous appetites of Charlie Varner's family.

But Charlie's family was not in attendance at church on that Sunday, and Charlie sent word by his neighbor that they had been called upon to go to Margaret Ann's family on that day and so would not come to dinner. Obediah was pleased at that but said nothing, and

Louisa One only sighed at the thought of the mountain of food that awaited them at home, and so she looked around the congregation to see if there were someone she might invite to dinner. She immediately spied the widow St. Cloud and her daughter, who were sitting not too distant from Adam Springer, who was by himself. Now, Louisa One, who worried about Danny Varner's lonely and celibate ways, had thought more than once of the widow St. Cloud as a suitable match for Danny, he being in her mind too old to court a maiden. Besides, the widow St. Cloud was in need of a husband, it being as unnatural for a woman to live without a man as it was for a man to live without a woman.

Louisa nudged Obediah. "I vill invite the vidder St. Cloud to eat vit us," she said. Obediah felt a sudden flush rush to his face and his spirit soar, and so marked was his reaction that the pastor, who was accustomed to Obediah's dozing through the services, was agreeably surprised at Obediah's sudden intensity, ascribing it to some particularly telling theological point that he had made, though he could not be quite certain which one it was.

At service's end, Louisa and Obediah edged quickly through the crowd, pausing only briefly to shake the pastor's hand, that good man looking expectantly to Obediah in hopes of a good word concerning the substance of his sermon, but he was disappointed, as Obediah only looked over his head, scanning the crowd for the widow St. Cloud.

"Ah, Mrs. St. Cloud," called Louisa, coming upon that woman and her young daughter. "Vould dat you and yer daughter vould share our Sunday meal. You could ride in the carriage vit us, fer dere is room," she added, forestalling any refusal. "Ve haf lots," continued Louisa, "and mine son Danny Varner, he vill join vit us." It was perhaps that intelligence rather than the promise of quantities of food that persuaded the widow St. Cloud to accept that offer.

"Ah, and good morning, Mistress Murphy," said Adam Springer, coming up on them abruptly, having obviously overheard the invitation to Alecia and her acceptance of it.

"I am being bold, I know, but if you have an extra plate, I could join you also, for my wife, Mistress Springer, is quite indisposed this day and I face the prospect of a cold meal, if any at all."

Louisa contained a sigh, for she was not overly eager to have Adam Springer join them, since his attentions to Mrs. St. Cloud could hardly be concealed and Louisa One had entirely different plans regarding the affections of that woman. However, as Adam Springer was a business partner of long standing, there was naught she could do but invite him to share in that meal.

"Ve have plenty," she said quite honestly, "fer mine son Charlie Varner and his family vill not be vit us."

To Louisa's great vexation, it was not Danny Varner who attended the comely widow but rather Obediah and Adam Springer, each vying to catch that woman's attention. Danny Varner sat in aloof silence and hardly glanced in the direction of the woman, though at intervals his mouth tightened and he seemed to struggle to suppress his irritation.

Louisa One did not trouble suppressing hers, for she snapped at Louisa Two, who snapped right back, and at the black girl who served their meal. The widow for the most part kept her eyes demurely on her plate, sneaking only an occasional glance at Danny Varner, while Adam and Obediah vied for her attention.

As Adam Springer did not have Obediah's gift for creative speaking, nor his stock of colorful war stories, he at last had to fall back on his success as a businessman and the foresight he had shown during the late war that had amassed him an enviable fortune.

It would be difficult to say which of those sets of stories most annoyed Danny Varner. But as he was used to Obediah's lofty language and as he must at least admire one fighting man as equal, he found the war profiteering of Adam Springer more distasteful than the heroic posturing of Obediah. He was at least by meal's end barely in control of a seething rage and quitted the table abruptly with murmured explanations of some vague work that needed doing. He stamped out of the house and so was gone.

And through the long afternoon it was Obediah and Adam trading stories and lively anecdotes, topping each other's efforts until Alecia St. Cloud was quite exhausted and both Louisas outraged, for Louisa Two, though a little slow, had at last ascertained that Obediah was as smitten with the widow as was Adam Springer, a fact that she blamed the widow for, though her mother, Louisa One, did not and only promised herself that Obediah would have his ears rent ere he slept that night.

The widow St. Cloud's charms had not, of course, been lost on Danny Varner, that fact authenticated by gossip brought Louisa One by Louisa Two, whose circle of friends could move news and information around with an alacrity that would have done proud a wireless operator.

"And my brother Danny, it's told me, is oft seen at the widow St. Cloud's cabin, or so at least his horse has been."

"If his horse is dere," observed Louisa One, "den like as not he is vit it."

"And it's been mentioned likewise that our friend Adam Springer, since Mistress Springer has gone back to Virginia to take the waters fer her lumbago, has been much in the company of that same widow."

"Humph," was all Louisa One said; but she thought to herself and wondered, as she had upon many occasions, how it was that the shrewdest of men could be brought to intemperate acts in the pursuance of a woman. Louisa One truly could not understand it, for she, who was shrewd in business and uncommonly intuitive about a great many things, would never in her wildest moments, which were in truth few, think of pursuing a man, no matter how attractive. There was a difference, she concluded, not for the first time, between men and women in the matter of sex.

"Adam Springer has, it's been told me"—Louisa Two paused, her lips pursed and her eyebrows arched, for in such manner did her expression always preface news of tremendous import—"it has been told me that our friend Master Springer has said that there is no woman without her price, and that he is prepared to meet Alecia St. Cloud's price, whatever."

"Ah!"

"This was heard by the cousin of Mistress Amy Blake's sister-in-law's husband, who reported it to his wife, Mistress Blake's sister-in-law, who reported it to Mistress Blake, who reported it to—"

"Enough! Gawd Almighty an' an't you nothin' else to do but to assassinate character?"

"Well! Well! And I was not who assassinated Adam Springer's character. He has done that well enough himself."

Louisa One turned her back and went on about her needlework, for she was working on a complicated quilt piece that took much concentration. Louisa Two's point was well taken. She admitted that, at the same time remarking to herself that it was not often that Two showed any such depth of perception. But then it did not take much perception perhaps to realize that Adam Springer was behaving like an ass, for One was likewise privy to that story that Two had told, it being quite common gossip.

It occurred to One that, in the interests of getting Adam Springer's mind back on business and settling Danny into calm domesticity, she had best hasten that union between him and the pretty widow. She did not include, though it must also be said that it was in the back of her mind, that her own Obediah would likewise benefit from having the widow no longer eligible for frivolous pining.

With that in mind, Louisa One accosted Danny Varner the next time she had his attention in private. Louisa One might have approached the subject subtly, but she did not, as no matter how subtle she thought she was being, she never was. She said what she thought, the way she thought it. She knew no other way.

"An', my son Danny, I think that it is time you ved vit the vidder St. Cloud and so to stop all dese rumors and get yerself a family to boot."

Danny Varner, who had been sitting staring into the fire on the hearth in some less moroseness than was his normal wont, sighed a lengthy sign, picked up a branch of kindling wood and broke it in two and tossed each piece one after the other into the sputtering flames. And then he sighed again.

"Vell," said his mother, "an' ven vill ye set the date?"

Danny Varner stared into the flames for a long moment before he shifted his weight and looked sadly at his mother. Such a look One had not seen in her son's eyes for a long time, not perhaps since he had been a boy and had found that an adopted baby squirrel or bunny had not survived his careful ministrations.

"The truth is, Mother, that I already have a wife," he said at long last.

"Vell, shit!" said Louisa Varner Murphy.

She waited for Danny to say more, but when he did not, she asked, "An' where is dis vife dat I have not knowed about?"

"She is in Tennessee. It was not a wise marriage. I regret it, but it nonetheless is."

"An' are dere any children?"

"No. No, there are no children. Only a wife. I have promised that I shall return to her. She thinks only that I have gone West to seek my fortune and that I shall return. But I don't know what to do. She is not beautiful and she is not strong. I married her because I was lonesome, I guess. I cannot think of any other reason."

"Does the vidow St. Cloud know of dis vife?"

"No."

Now, many another man in a like situation would simply forget

the undesired wife in favor of a desired one. But Danny Varner, as it
has been previously mentioned, was turned like his mother. He had a
wife, though he did not want her, but he had her and he could take no
other. Nor was it nobleness of spirit or high principles that motivated
Danny Varner, but simply the knowledge that this was the way
things worked and he would not tamper with the nature of things. If a
man had a wife, he simply had a wife.

"Den you must leave off seeing the vidder St. Cloud." It did not
take any complicated reasoning on Louisa's part to come to that conclusion, for there was no other choice. "Don' see her no more."

"Ah," moaned Danny through clenched teeth, "and leave her to
that reprobate Adam Springer, who would try to buy her favors?"

"I don' see vat's the difference. He's got a vife. You got a vife."

"He is a reprobate!"

"Naw, he's no reprobate "

"He's a fool!"

Louisa One could not argue that point; in truth, she thought she
viewed a pair of them, with Alecia St. Cloud, that nice and trusting
lady, being the loser.

"He does not care for her the way I care for her. I would wed her if
I could."

"You think he vould not?" Louisa was having difficulty making the
same distinctions that Danny Varner was making, he in his own
mind, though committing the same felony, more noble in that commission. They were a pair of fools, decided Louisa.

"Go to Tennessee and fetch back yer vife to yer home and so to
make the best of it. Dat's all. I vill reason vit Adam Springer myself.
Dat's all dere is to it."

"Ah, perhaps. Yes, perhaps you're right."

But Louisa One did not reason with Adam Springer, for that man
took care to stay away from her. Nor did Danny Varner heed his
mother's directions, instead only growing more taciturn and irritable.
And when next she managed a conversation with him, he was at first
distant and then defensive and finally outraged at the position he
found himself in.

"I an't an Adam Springer. I am an officer; I am a man of nobility,
of decency, a gentleman! Adam Springer is naught but a merchant, a
manager! And it is such that won that great war, which pitted nobility
against baseness and soundness of heart against the clink of coin. And
it is the coin that won!"

"I do not see the difference," reasoned Louisa, stubbonly refusing to acknowledge such noble argument. "However ye view it, it is two married men, who should both be ashamed, tormenting a penniless and destitute vidder. The only difference is dat at least she knows Adam Springer to be married. At least he don' lie to her."

"Lie! Lie! It is not a lie. It is a secret. It is a secret that gnaws daily at my very being, eating me alive!"

Louisa failed to make that distinction. "Lie, secret? I don' know the difference."

Like an unexpected dust devil, Danny Varner's argument whirled from self-pity to rage, that sudden change of temper that had been his inclination since childhood.

"The fates are against me! They have trapped me. They have bled the South of honor, of dignity, of spirit, of life, of cash. They have turned their smiles on such as Adam Springer; they have rewarded baseness and cowardice; they have smiled on scoundrels. I will not have it!"

At which accusation Danny Varner slammed his fist so hard upon the tabletop that the bowl of fresh eggs on it bounced and jiggled, much alarming Louisa One, lest a day's enterprise of her hens be lost.

"I will not have it!" he shouted once more and stalked from the house, in his anger forgetting even his hat, which lay upon a chair. Louisa One stared hard at the hat as if perhaps it held the answer for this sudden and to her inexplicable rage. The hat, which was banded with a fresh and gaily striped band, bearing otherwise the sweat marks of long service, had, however, no answer for the riddle. And in a moment Danny Varner strode back into the room and without comment retrieved his hat and strode out again.

"My, my," murmured Louisa One to herself, "he got dat temper from mine udder husband, from Daniel Varner. I think that is vy I married to Obediah Murphy; he has got no temper. Vun temper man is enough fer vun life."

It was Louisa Two, she who dearly loved to carry gossip and who made no distinction between gossip about strangers and gossip about family, it was she who brought to Louisa One further news of the differences between Danny Varner and Adam Springer concerning the comely widow St. Cloud.

"Mama," said Louisa Two sweetly, and Louisa One thought to herself, "Oh shit, vat has she got to tell on dis time?" for One could always tell by Two's pleased expression when she had some particularly lamentable tale to pass on.

"It has been told me, in strict confidence, ye hear, that my brother

Danny Varner and Adam Springer have had hard words and that my brother accused Master Springer of being a carpetbagger and a coward and a scoundrel and that Master Springer only just laughed at my brother and sneered at him for being a ragged Reb and that my brother would have pummeled Master Springer then and there had he not been restrained by those gathered around." Louisa Two sighed happily at the end of her recitation, as if she had truly brought some noteworthy news.

"An' is dat so?" said Louisa One, and that was all.

"Well, I thought that it was important that ye know of this ill feeling between my brother and yer business partner," said Louisa Two, much miffed that her information had been so little regarded.

"Men's business is men's business," said Louisa One and then added, "Dey're all fools, I think, in the long run."

But Louisa One sat long that night over her quilt pieces, which she worked on but sporadically, her mind much engrossed by the problem of her son and Adam Springer. It was she, she was certain, who would at last have to resolve that situation, as the men seemed quite incapable of doing so. At last, after considering the problem and possible solutions for a long time, she arrived at what seemed to her the most logical solution.

As it was the widow St. Cloud who was the center of the turmoil, it was she who must be dispatched. Louisa One, in the interests of family harmony and sound business, determined that she would provide the pretty widow with the means to escape her poverty and resettle herself at long distance from the scene of the turmoil. Having got rid of the chigger, she reasoned, the itch would heal itself. And so Louisa Varner Murphy determined that on Sunday next she would invite Alecia St. Cloud to have tea one weekday when the men would not be about, and so explain to that woman the reasons that she must absent herself and settle upon her a generous endowment for that purpose. Louisa One put away her quilt pieces and took herself to her bed and slept soundly that night, for she had arrived at a just and reasoned solution to a vexatious problem and so deserved the rest she got.

But Louisa One was not destined to have tea with the widow St. Cloud, as the events that settled on them with strange rapidity rendered useless that carefully conceived ploy.

They sat in church, Obediah and beside him Louisa One and then Two and Three, Three fiddling with her buttons and Two periodically restraining her from it. Louisa One cast her glance over the congregation, which had only just gathered and was cranking up for the first hymn, satisfying herself that Alecia St. Cloud was indeed present, though Adam Springer, who was usually close by, was unaccountably absent. It was as well, One determined, his absence making her plan that much easier, for he was wont to hover over the widow under all possible circumstances, so far gone was he in his lechery.

Mistress Read, the organist, pumped at the organ with enthusiasm until she had got it huffing and puffing to her satisfaction, that instrument being but newly purchased and a source of pride for the entire congregation, which congregation enthusiastically slid into the first stanza of the opening hymn, praising God loudly if not altogether melodically for His bountiful mercies.

Louisa One did not sing, for she knew herself to be tone deaf and so prone to being off-key, but Obediah enthusiastically rent the air, carrying the folk about him through the first verse, which was all the words he knew, and through the rest of the verses he maintained only a loud hum, patiently awaiting the arrival once more of the familiar chorus.

It was midway through the second verse that Louisa became aware of a commotion at the back of the church and then through the open window noted scurrying activity as several men dashed past. She nudged Obediah, but he, being busy with the chorus, did not notice, and so she leaned toward the window and attempted to see what was going on, as did several other people not engrossed in the singing. At last a gentleman seated in the row ahead of Louisa rose and tiptoed out of the building and so returned in haste and whispered to his seatmate, who passed the whisper on until it spread quietly through the congregation, like an early spring grass fire, leaving only Mrs. Read the organist and Pastor Ellwood ignorant of the whispered intelligence.

"It's a dead man. Someone is lying dead out by the horses and wagons," the whisper said. "They say it is Adam Springer and that he's been stuck with a knife."

And as the whisper made its way around the room from row to row, the congregation, one by one, emptied bench by bench and hurried out to see for themselves, not one, including the ladies, anxious to miss anything so exciting as a knifing and that in broad daylight during Sunday services. Someone at last tiptoed to Pastor Ellwood with the information and he, too, fled, leaving Mrs. Read, her back to the room, enthusiastically pumping away on the new pump organ, blissfully unaware that the entire congregation had emptied into the yard.

Louisa One, her skirts gathered up, made her way quickly to the forefront of the crowd, which indeed at the sight of her fell curiously silent and made way for her. Louisa's heart, tough as it was, was straining against her bosom and the blood was pounding at her temple. She did not want to see what she was sure she would see: Adam Springer lying in the already faded pool of blood, blood that had coursed through the newly made opening as naturally as it coursed through its regular channels, seeping unconcerned into the dust.

The men surrounding the corpse looked away when they saw Louisa and Obediah.

"Mine Gawd!"

"Ah, Mrs. Murphy," said one of the men, Jacob Olney by name, and although neither Obediah nor Louisa One knew, for they neither of them paid much attention to matters of local government, he was the constable and so had taken charge. "And, Mr. Murphy," he said, addressing his remarks toward Obediah, but looking at Louisa, "do you know where your son Danny Varner might be?" At the perplexed expression he received by way of reply he went on. "Do you know whether or not this is Danny Varner's hat?" he asked, holding up the gaily banded, sweat-stained hat that Louisa recognized. It did not occur to her to lie.

"It is," she said.

"I'm sorry fer ye," said Jacob Olney, "but there were witnesses enought that viewed the altercation between Master Springer and Danny Varner that led to this fatal stabbing. Do ye have any idea where Danny Varner might be found?" he continued with utmost courtesy.

Louisa only sighed profoundly and shook her head, for she truly did not, and had she thought about it she would have said that he would be gone and that neither they nor she would ever see him again, for that was true. But she had not yet thought about it. She shook her head again and glanced up, catching the sight of the stricken countenance of the widow St. Cloud, whose horrified look traveled from the corpse and so up toward the hills and woods beyond as if she would seek out he who had escaped in that direction. Louisa looked away, for she did not know what to say.

"I vould go home, Obediah," she said. "I vould go home to mine house."

Once home, Louisa did so uncharacteristic a thing that both Obediah and Louisa Two were alarmed and anxious. She took herself to bed. Without comment Louisa One undressed herself, crawled among the quilts and turned her face to the wall, for she found herself more tired than she had ever been, and weak and confused.

"I must decide," was all she said to her alarmed husband and daughter. "I don' know an' I must decide. I vill call ven I vant you. Go. Go now, go, go," she commanded and closed her eyes.

Nor did Obediah and Louisa Two know what to do, but only wandered around the house getting in each other's way, Two snapping irritably.

And so Louisa One stayed for several days, eating and drinking but little and speaking less, but she was hardly in the decline that Obediah and Louisa Two feared. She was as a matter of fact quite engrossed, for she was sorting facts, adding and subtracting and calculating her life with much the same precision she used on her quilt top. Louisa's orderly and systematic mind wanted to understand just why this tragedy had been visited upon her. She was making a balance sheet.

She wanted to know why in her old age she was down to one daughter and one son, and her grandchild, the daughter of her husband, without a mind. She did not consider Charlie Varner and his family, for they did not figure in her pain, nor did her wealth and her health. She had need only to dwell upon the ill that had been her lot, not on the fortune, which was not, of course, common only to her, as such is the tendency of those afflicted with a depressed mind. She reasoned that there had to be an explanation that she had been singled out to bear the pain that she had been asked to bear, that it was not all just ill happenstance.

Finally, having sorted through her life, balancing the debits against the credits until at last she arrived at a total, she reckoned that her life did not balance because the Almighty was not happy with her performance, which in regards to Him had been but token.

And so Louisa One got religion.

She sat abruptly up in bed, glared at the ceiling, bracing herself with her hands against the feather ticking, and said, "Vell, all right, have it Yer vay!" And she got out of bed, lowered herself slowly and painfully to the floor, clasped her hands before her, squeezed her eyes shut tight and muttered, "I promise dat I vould do it Yer vay from now on. Amen!"

It was with a great deal of relief that Obediah and Two greeted

Louisa's return to health and energy, for neither of them was at all comfortable with the idea of trying to make do without her.

The furor over Adam Springer's murder died quickly, the consensus being that the fight which had precipitated his demise had been a matter of honor and that Danny Varner, having been seen riding south shortly after the killing, could not be found anyway. The matter was never mentioned in the Murphy household, its only trace a further callousing of Louisa's heart.

But then one evening, as Obediah cut across a field, leading a mule which he had worked that day on a distant part of his land, he happened upon Alecia St. Cloud, who was sitting staring forlornly by the side of that stream which eventually made its way past Louisa's house. She did not immediately spy Obediah and so he stood and watched her. There was an air of sadness about her as she sat hugging her knees to her, staring across the stream. Obediah did not understand but still instinctively felt the loneliness and regret of which the cast of her expression and the slump of her figure spoke.

He drew closer to her, dropping the reins that held the mule he had been leading, that animal immediately seizing the opportunity to seek out grass for nibbling. The widow looked around at the noise the animal made and, seeing Obediah, turned a friendly if forlorn expression on him. Nor did she speak, but only sighed.

Obie spoke her name. "Alecia?" She looked full at him and from the depth of those gray eyes something spoke to Obediah. It came to him as a rustle of autumn leaves and tall grass and warm breezes and a taste of honey, and he sat slowly beside her and in her loneliness she settled her head upon his shoulder and he circled her slender form with his arm and so they sat for a long time until at last she yielded to his gentle pressures and they lay together until dusk settled upon them.

When at last Obediah arrived home, it was dark, but by lantern light Louisa One could make out that wistful, gentle expression that she had not seen on his face in many years and she frowned but said only, "An't you late? Yer supper is stone cold, ye know?"

Several weeks passed before Louisa Two brought the gossip from town again. She fairly bubbled and all but ran, only her great bulk keeping her in check. Nor was she circumspect in revealing what she had heard.

"The widow St. Cloud, ye know, that Danny courted, she has wed that drunken Tommy Timmons and they have packed up and left the county."

Obediah sat in stricken silence. Louisa One gave him only a long glance before she murmured, "Is dat so? Dat don' seem so good a match fer her."

"Ah," said Louisa Two jubilantly, "they *say*," and she paused to survey the effect that her intelligence was like to have, "that she was already heavy with child and so that is why she married him."

"Vell," said her mother, carefully keeping her eyes on the quilt top she was working on, "dat's a good reason."

THIRTEEN

THE GHOSTS HAVE FLED

*T*he routine of a funeral is comforting. I do not speak of the ritual of a funeral, for I see little ritual in most funerals. It is the routine of putting away the dead that most of us count on; and grief, when it is put on at all, is put on like a vestment at the door and removed immediately after the service, to be stored against future needs.

I speak here, of course, of normal funerals, those funerals celebrating death as a part of a natural progression, not the tragedy of someone taken before his time, while he is still needed.

Routine is what Old Daniel's funeral is. At David's house before the service there is a buffet of a strange assortment of dishes that kindly people have brought, paying homage to that notion that grief, while it incapacitates the cook, does not kill any appetites. There is also much discussion of who will sit where and ride in which car and what the proper dress will be. Danny is sent back to his room to change into dark oxfords instead of the loafers he has appeared in, and Arlene has decreed a single strand of pearls for herself and her daughters. There is no mention of the guest of honor, who I suppose is just going along for the ride. Since that could only be considered a sick joke, I keep it to myself.

It is sad. But I won't miss Old Daniel. No one will miss Old Daniel; he outlived his need. Had he died abruptly at some much earlier age, he would have been missed, would have left a vacant place. As it is, he simply drifted into decay, like an old building sagging slowly into ruin, so that its final settling is hardly noticed.

Though the funeral home is filled to capacity, almost no one there actually knew Old Daniel; most had never even seen him. They come instead as a part of the routine, to offer condolences to the living, those living being of course prominent and wealthy. They go to the funeral home and peek dutifully in at the corpse, which in truth does look better after the funeral director's ministrations than Old Daniel had looked in life.

Nanny is not there, though she is one of the few who had known Old Daniel in his prime. She had waited around to be invited to go with me; but I could not. I had been invited as one of the family and she could not go. That is not fair, perhaps, but it is the way the routine works. When it became obvious that she could not go with me, Nanny stamped her foot impatiently and announced that she did not intend to go to the funeral at all, that she never went to funerals because they depressed her. That is not true. Nanny loves funerals. She does not, I'm sure, intend to die and immensely enjoys ticking off the rest of the race.

Nanny is probably the closest person to me, yet when I die she will not be asked to sit with the family. And then I smile. I do not want to wish Nanny any harm, but I do hope I outlive her and it won't be a problem. And then I wonder idly as the minister intones the eulogy to a person he never knew just who will sit as family when I die? Perhaps David or David's family? Perhaps Vonda will lend kin for the occasion. I think I will request to be cremated minutes after my final breath and solve the whole dilemma.

Daniel is interred in the same cemetery where Lee and Levi lie, not far away from them actually, beside Thelma, who though much younger than Daniel has been dead for several years. Through the brief graveside service, where I sit with the family, I stare at Thelma's stone, a single stone with just her name and dates and no room for Daniel. It strikes me as odd, like newlyweds sleeping in twin beds. Later in the afternoon, when mourning has been stored away like the leftovers from the funeral buffet, they already incarcerated in containers in the refrigerator or pressed on passersby, I accost David about the stone. "I would have thought that you would have wanted a twin stone for your parents?" I am never tactful with David, nor he with me. We are not so much tactless as to the point, I suppose.

"He already had a stone."

"Oh?"

"Yes. He was very particular about it. It was chosen and carved all but the dates, ready and waiting. I called yesterday to instruct the stonemason as to the final date."

"Mr. Jenks?" I am certain without asking that that is the stonemason's identity.

"Yes. Jenks, the stonemason."

"I have heard that he is quite skilled. I have heard that from knowledgeable sources." I do not say that the Knowledgeable Source is Mr. Jenks himself. "He's the one who carved Levi's and Lee's stones," I add.

"Yes," says David, somewhat to my surprise. "I know that. Indeed, I think that Father's stone is identical to your grandfather's, to Levi's."

Well, I think, and well again. Are there no end to Mr. Jenks's surprises? Old Daniel's stone is identical to Lee's, whose stone is identical to Levi's, whose stone, but I do not tell this to David, is identical to Obediah's and the three Louisas'. Our dying has made Mr. Jenks a living over the years.

The Case of the Identical Tombstones. And where is Perry Mason when I need him? I nudge that fact around in my subconscious for a long time. It bothers me, like a bubble in the esophagus that I can't get rid of.

"Elizabeth?" It is pretty Marci, divested of the pearls and lounging in jeans and sweat shirt, but still looking pensive and solemn, as if she thinks there ought to be more to a funeral.

"I wish that I had known my grandfather," she says, and I understand what she means, for Daniel was too old by the time she was old enough to understand, had slipped over the line into senility. He had never been anything but a decaying presence to her, a withered bouquet, once removed, missed only because there is nothing to replace it.

"He was a good man." It is an obligatory remark. I make it. I do not know that Old Daniel was indeed a good man, but he was not obviously bad, so I will grant him goodness in the end. I actually knew him little better than Marci did and I tell her so. I do not tell her that I knew him only slightly less well than I knew my own grandfather and indeed my father. We were all strangers.

"Well, you know, I've been thinking." Careful Marci slips unconsciously into the "you knows" of her youth. "I've been thinking. Daniel, my grandfather, just think how many lives he touched? He was over a hundred years old, you know? I can't seem to say what I mean. I mean"—she pauses to purse her lips—"he covered such a span. When he was young, he must have known old people, people possibly born in the eighteenth century, and when he was old, young people, people who will live well into the twenty-first century. By the time the last person whose life he touched is gone, he will have personally spanned better than two centuries. Do you see what I mean?"

I do. "It is an interesting thought." And I am reminded of Virgie's curiosity about who will remember her last. And I wonder, are we more than just a collection of personal experiences? Are we in fact the sum total of all of our own experiences, as well as all the lives we have touched coming and going, and at last, the dimming memories of us?

The thought is too heavy to hold on this fading October afternoon. Grief, if there had really been any, has been replaced by relief, a chore has been accomplished, a duty done, a deadline—I use the word advisedly—met, the Salvation Army already notified. The truck will pick up the personal remnants of Daniel St. Cloud tomorrow.

"I've never had any interest in family history," muses Marci, still picking at the subject. "I guess it's too late now. Certainly there's nothing I could find out from Grandfather, and Dad doesn't seem to know anything. Other people have stories, family anecdotes. Why don't we? I mean on my father's side; there's plenty on Mom's side, God knows." I know, too, and I understand the girl's patient sigh. Her mother's family is prominent, busy, anecdotal, and generally tiresome.

"Maybe that's a blessing. Maybe there were things we ought not to know? Maybe that's why there is such a silence from the past?" Marci does not seem to notice that I have included myself in her reverie. "Our ghosts are perhaps avoiding us."

David settles himself into one of Arlene's chrome and leather chairs and sighs. I think that he cannot be comfortable bent into that unusual shape. I think such furniture was made only for photographers to photograph, all planes and angles, planes and angles that no people, at least no people of my acquaintance, actually have.

"David," I say, "what are the legalities in defending a guilty man?"

"Eh?"

"What are you taught in law school, what are the ethics involved in defending the obviously guilty? Are you supposed to get him acquitted?"

"Elizabeth, I'm not a criminal lawyer."

"But surely you know what I mean? If someone is pretty obviously guilty even though he hasn't confessed, what should be expected of his defense?"

"A lawyer is supposed to secure his client all of his rights before the law."

"Even to getting him freed if he's guilty?"

"Well, as a matter of ethics, no. But as a matter of practice, if you're smart enough or if the prosecution is weak enough, well, it does happen. It's not a perfect system. Why do you ask?"

"I know a woman whose son is in jail, probably guilty. I was thinking of helping her get a good lawyer and wondering about the ethics involved."

"Sight unseen, my advice is to stay out of it. Who is this, anyway? You can't know anyone in that situation very well?"

"Just a passing acquaintance. I like her. I feel sorry for her."

"Not good enough reasons. Stay out of it." David is not abrupt or angry. He is matter-of-fact. "If this person is guilty, any lawyer can get him whatever rights he deserves. As for his mother; well, mothers of criminals have no rights before the law in such cases."

David does not ask any more. He sighs and makes an effort to lean back in a chair that by its design resists such familiarity. David is tired. The strain of putting a parent away, even a little-used, stored-away parent, is telling. I can remember that from my own experience and I realize with a slight shock how recent that has been.

The newspaper accounts of the finding of the Stoples, their identification and the charges finally brought against Earl McCullough were routine, so brief that had I not been looking for them I would not have noticed. "The bodies were found in a shallow grave." "Earl McCullough, 25, of nearby Hubbard, Oklahoma, has been charged." "The sherriff's office refuses comment on a motive for the crime." Even Greer Beck is not mentioned, never mind the mysterious lady in the black Lincoln. Poor Greer. I suspect he would like to have seen his name in the newspaper in connection with the discovery. Perhaps a local paper gave the matter greater coverage and mentioned Greer Beck. I hope so.

I do not know, of course, whether Virgie needs or wants any help from anyone, particularly from me. Nor do I know why I feel the necessity of offering. Is it guilt for having been instrumental in the finding of the *corpus delicti*, or is it a kind of admiration for this tough and stoic woman or, more likely, is it simply that I am loath to let go of this little drama I have unwittingly fallen into?

Nanny is not home when I arrive late in the afternoon. There is an October sunset in the west. Only those who have ever seen an October sunset in Oklahoma can know what I mean. Nanny has gone to visit Charlaine and Leroy, who are speaking again, their tiff lasting more briefly than usual.

With a glass of wine in hand, I make my way to my rooms and the company of my designer sheets. But instead of relaxing on the bed, I find myself staring out the window. Below me is the boulder that is the focal point of what once was a garden, and that ancient laurel tree shades almost everything else from view. I peer out the window for that sturdy trellis that I used for entrance and egress back in my salad days. I find no sign of it. I wonder when it was taken down and why I never noticed. My mood is lonely and pensive as I sip my wine, and it is such a mood that calls my ghosts to visit.

Old Levi is the first, staring distractedly at me as I hauled myself through the open window, finally offering me a hand to aid as I scrambled in apprehension through the opening. I had been found out. I wondered if the smell of sex was as strong about me as the smell of camphor and old age was about him.

"It is lust, Elizabeth, that we must leech from ourselves. It is lust that destroys," he intoned.

Oh, shit, I thought, here it comes.

But it did not. He launched then into those notes he called his book, rambling and disjointed until dawn, while I sat tired and nodding, longing for the hot bath that would wash away the night's passion, not to mention ticks, for we had lain near to the bushes along the river's edge and had there assuaged our passion, call it lust. I can't say, then, that I was interested in what Old Levi was saying, but I was, what, mesmerized? He was somehow seeking justification, for what I could not understand. I only noticed that he sounded like President Eisenhower on the radio asking for support of this or that plan that Congress was being disagreeable about. I was, at that time in my hot youth, no more certain of what Eisenhower's problems were, or interested in them, than I was of Old Levi's. Dawn mercifully came and Old Levi slammed closed his notebook with finality and quitted the room the same way. That was the last I ever heard of it.

"Leech," he had said. "We must leech the lust from us." "Leech" is a peculiar verb. Why not "purge" or "cleanse," which sound less parasitic, less draining, less permanently damaging than "leech"?

I twirl the wineglass, nearly empty, and wait for the next ghost to appear. It is Bradley, golden Bradley. "Humanity is the mold to break away from, the crust to break through; the coal to break into fire, the atom to be split."

Humanity to be leeched, but not lust, at least not by Bradley's reckoning. We lay in his room, sometimes on the bed, sometimes on the floor, his head in my lap, mine in his, or side by side or end to end, he reading aloud the verses of Robinson Jeffers, verses that I could barely comprehend, extolling the virtues of rocks and tides and grass and trees and the permanent; condemning the violence and rage and lust of humanity, the impermanent, a lust, however, that Bradley regularly succumbed to. Just a few lines into one of those patriarchal tragedies and Bradley was ready to ball.

That was the part I liked best. I understood it best, or at least I thought I understood it best. In some men poetry is the ultimate aphrodisiac, although in Bradley's case almost anything, a bottle of Coka-Cola, in the female-shaped glass bottles of pre-can and pre-plastic days, would turn him on. He was an expert in matters sexual, at least more expert than I was used to. None of the hot-handed, awkward gropings I had experienced by the banks of the river or in the backseat of a car or behind a deserted building, an acne-scarred youth trying to hold my attention and fit his overeager member into a condom at the same time. Bradley did not bother with condoms. He trusted me to use whatever I needed. That, I suppose he reasoned, was not his responsibility.

He murmured to me of the purity of the act. As opposed to what? Atomic bombs and infantile paralysis and lend-lease? I didn't know. Only that it was pure where nothing else was.

I don't know that I expected anything permanent of Bradley. I know I did not think of marriage. I guess I was alone in that. All the college girls of my acquaintance planned their weddings in great detail long before they had even picked a suitable mate, planned them with the tenacity with which college girls now plan meaningful careers. I did not. I was not brought up in a married state. I did not understand marriage, though I knew people to be married. Bradley was the closest thing I had ever had to a close relationship to anyone, but I did not think of him, or anyone as a matter of fact, as a long-term proposition.

Bradley probably did not realize that, for when I had told him that I had taken my responsibility too lightly and was probably carrying his child, he grabbed his Jeffers and fled, even before I could explain to him about the nearby abortion clinic, which, though illegal, then, did a thriving business. Nor did he know that I had already once been privy to its services.

That first experience in the abortion clinic I do not recall as being very traumatic. Why? I don't know. Perhaps because I was young or because I had no idea who the other party involved had been—some anxious youth in a damaged condom or none at all, having struggled with it and then said the hell with it in his eagerness. Whatever it was, the clinic, which operated almost as openly as the bootleggers did in those days, was actually a small hospital that simply did an unusual number of D&C's to correct certain "menstrual irregularities." It was certainly not a bent coat hanger operation, and the whole thing was over quickly and painlessly.

The second time around was not so easy. Again, I don't know why. Was it because I was older or because I knew who the other responsible party was and that I felt rejected by him? I don't know. Dr. Harvey, the shrink I eventually fled to, told me that the guilt I was suffering was because my mother had deserted me and that I was punishing myself because I couldn't get along with my stepmother. I'm not sure why I expected him to help me when I so obviously didn't tell him the truth. He might have been able to make a much more accurate diagnosis if he knew that I made up mothers rather than admit I had never had one. I described Lucille to him—Lee's wife, who left when I was tiny—in glowing and tragic terms and my stepmother Louise (why "Louise"?) as distant and unapproachable. Dr. Harvey did his best with that assorted misinformation, and perhaps he helped because I did come out of that funk in time. It may only have been a bad case of postpartum depression, actually.

At any rate, Bradley was the last of my sexual encounters. Except for a rare one-night stand, I have been largely celibate.

The lust leeched from me?

My ghosts again?

Nanny found Levi one summer evening unconscious in his rooms next to the windows. At first there was some thought that he might have been struck by lightning, for there was a fierce thunderstorm in progress when he collapsed. But in the hospital it was determined quickly that he had been felled by a stroke. He lay for several days in something like a conscious state before he drifted into his final coma. I remember that we took turns sitting with him, Lee, David, Nanny and I—even Old Daniel.

The night is growing cold. I have stood by the window from dusk to dark. I close the window and it creaks with the effort, like me sometimes rising from my bed in the night to go to the bathroom. How strange, I think, that I have lived so long and can account for so few of those days. They have each come and gone and left few individual marks, only an accumulation of dust in the crevices of my house and lines upon my face and cellulite upon my hips.

At breakfast I am surprised to find Leroy. He is standing glumly at the sink with a cup of coffee and says nothing beyond greetings as Nanny serves me juice and coffee and the Tulsa *World*. For years that newspaper had a little globe situated between the *Tulsa* and the *World*, but that's been gone for a long time. I miss it every time I pick up the paper.

Nanny is strangely silent, too, and I think to myself that I wish that whatever is bothering Leroy and Charlaine would be resolved. It is always a little unsettling to have that unhappy black man morosely hanging around. I read the forecast aloud. Nanny and I share it each morning. And I read the extended forecast to myself. I am an inveterate reader of extended forecasts the way some people are inveterate readers of horoscopes and advice columns. The extended forecast is depressing, for it warns of an impending cold front and winter weather, to be expected this time of year, expected but not welcome.

It is perhaps that threat of ill weather that speeds my decision to make another trip to Hubbard, to see Virgie again. That this whole thing is no business of mine deters me not at all.

It is Sunday that I drive north through the countryside, alarmed almost at the change that little more than a week has wrought on the landscape. A storm or two has obviously gone through, stripping the trees of all but a few straggling leaves, the fallen leaves already turning brown in the fence rows where they have collected. And the cold front, while not actually upon us, is threatening in the damp and low-hanging clouds.

It is the time of year that the small brown hawks come out and perch on the fence posts by the side of the road, waiting for an accommodating automobile to squish something useful, like a mouse or rabbit, for their own food supply dwindles sharply in winter and they rely a lot on the largesse of passing traffic. Unlike the other busy birds, chirping and flitting and pecking about, the hawk is a stoic kind of creature, folding its wings about it like an old-time movie Indian his blanket and sitting motionless on a fence post until something impels it to unfurl those wide wings, rise slowly, survey and then dive, with a pure economy of motion and effort. They are businesslike creatures. That is all.

I am fairly certain that Virgie's Café will not be open on Sunday. I am just as certain that Virgie will not be in church. Didn't she tell me that she stopped going to church when the preacher "got younger'n" her? I am not so certain how I am going to find her house; however, an obliging gentleman leaning against the fender of a pickup, from his dress churchbound, gives me directions. Virgie does not live in a little house in town, as I had envisioned, but on a small farm outside of town.

Nor is she surprised to see me. I knock on the hooked screen door, which vibrates against my knuckles, and she appears almost immediately to that muffled sound. She has probably watched me all the way from my car. I am invited in and offered a chair and coffee, in that order, Virgie still expressing no surprise at seeing me.

I could tell her that I happened to be passing in the neighborhood and thought of her, but I don't. I tell her the truth.

"I have thought of you often," I say. "I wanted to see how you were getting along. The law," I say, paraphrasing David, "makes no provision for the families of those it jails."

"No," she says, "no, it don't. I'm fine. I'm better off, if you want to know the truth, with him in jail." I notice that she does not give "him" a name. "I'm better off. I know where he is and what he's up to. I don't have to worry no more."

Ah, the other shoe has dropped.

"I'm glad you come by. I hoped I'd see you agin", she says, rising. "I got somethin fer you."

I stare at the eternal rings the spoon in my coffee has created as she pads into another room, for though she is fully dressed in a wrap-around skirt and T-shirt, she is wearing large woolly scuffs on her feet. She returns with a wrapped package.

"I'd fergot about this till I got to thinkin' about you and that old house. I had it fer years; had to rummage around fer half a night tryin' to remember what I done with it. Fer a while there I was afraid I'd throwed it out." She offers me the parcel, wrapped in a fairly current newspaper. It is a solid kind of parcel and I am at a loss to understand.

"It come out of that old house; it's old. One of my kids found it years ago and come draggin' it in. It was wrapped in a old canvas bag and stuck up in behind the mantel." She eases the cellophane tape that secures the package and slowly undoes the newspaper covering. "They thought it was a treasure. Well, I dunno, maybe it was." She slowly unfolds what appears to be a quilt top, from the look and smell of it quite old. "I was always afraid to warsh it fer fear it'd come to pieces. I'd fergot about it, but I guess you got as good a claim to it as anyone."

"No," I demur, "no. I don't know that I have. You keep it." I finger the fragile fabric, some of it cracking where it has been folded.

"I don't want it. I think I'd a throwed it out long time ago if I'd thought about it. I ain't one to keep old stuff. I know it's got value to some, but not to me. Old is just old. I don't know what antique is."

"Peculiar pattern."

"Not a pattern at all, to my way of thinkin'. An' I cain't think what kind of bed it could a been meant fer, long and narrow like that."

Virgie is right. It is really not a pattern at all, though for some reason it seems to have a purpose to it. It is like a poem that runs on long past the need. The strange geometric shapes are embroidered with slashes and circles and there are a few bright patches of pink in the very center and then none. I have a sense of having seen one like it before; it is vaguely familiar. Perhaps it is a particular style of quilt that a history of quilting—I'm sure there is such—would reveal.

"I have no use for it. If you know anyone who might like it . . ." I let the offer trail off at the end. I have no need of anything else in my house that smells old and dusty.

"I b'lieve it probably belonged to yer people. There was an old newspaper wrapped around it inside that canvas bag. I always meant to save it, but somehow it got away from me, got shredded and tore, so I finally throwed it out. It was dated before statehood. I do remember that. You take it or else I'll probably just throw it out."

"Well, I wouldn't want that. I'll take it and have it looked at. I might even donate it to a museum. Maybe the State Historical Society would find a place for it? I'd donate it in your name. 'Donated by Virgie McCullough' the plaque would say."

"Oh my, no," Virgie objects, but she looks pleased.

Our conversation is not exactly strained, but Virgie seems a little more restrained than she did the first time I met her. She is wondering, I suppose, why I am here, what it is that I want. I can't tell her; I don't know.

We talk about her little place, the farm and the house. I rise to peer out the window toward the few outbuildings.

"I bought this myself," she says. "I bought it and paid fer it an' I don't owe a thing on it. I paint it about every year." She laughs. "My second son, Lester, always laughs at me and teases me. He says that if a tornado hit this house, it'd take everything but the paint. 'That's all right,' I tell him. 'I want her painted an' I'm going to have her painted.' I lived too many years in unpainted shacks. I don't have to no more."

"Chickens?" I say. "You raise chickens?" I am looking at some hens pursuing their interests around back near the garden.

"A few. When these are gone, I don't think I'll get no more. It costs more to feed them than what you get out of 'em. There's got to be more rewardin' hobbies than cleanin' up chicken shit."

I laugh and agree. "Uh oh. Is that a chicken hawk?" I am looking skyward at the hovering presence high in the sky.

Virgie joins me at the window, looks up but merely shrugs.

"Any kind a hawk's a chicken hawk if it gets half a chance." She returns to her chair at the kitchen table. "Actually, I don't mind hawks that much, even chicken hawks. They're not bad to get into the chickens if there's plenty of other stuff around. There's lots of grain and corn around here and so there's lots of mice and so there's lots of hawks. I'd hate to think what would happen to the mouse population without the hawks." She stares ahead of her with a smile before admitting, "The hawks do their share, and they ain't ashamed to grub when they have to."

I rejoin Virgie at the table and there is a long moment of silence, but I know that Virgie has something to say.

"Miz Murphy," she begins, for she calls me "Miz" as I call her Virgie, both for the same reason; she would not be comfortable not calling me Miz Murphy nor would she be comfortable not being called Virgie. "Miz Murphy, do you b'lieve that everybody has a soul, is born with a soul? Every human?"

"Well. I don't know." I think I know what she is getting at.

"I mean, is it possible to be born without one, like a empty eggshell?"

"Is there such a thing?"

"I don't know. I never seen one; but I've heard tell."

"I think there are certain conditions in which people have no sense of right or wrong, if that's what you mean. Have no apparent feeling for anyone."

"I mean, if a person was born without a soul, then he couldn't really be blamed for acting like he didn't have one, could he?"

"Earl?"

"Earl, yes, the Stoples, people like that, do they have souls? Or does God fer some reason make a few people without souls? Like flies or ticks or mosquitoes. I know they ain't got souls." She laughs uncomfortably. "What I really want, I think, is fer someone to say 'Virgie, it ain't yer fault, you done the best you could.'"

"Hasn't anyone said that?" It seems a strange omission.

"Well, yes. But they're the ones I'd expect it from. I know they mean it and, don't get me wrong, I'd be willin' to take the blame if it was mine." She sighs. "I still haven't said what I want to say. It's you, yer the one I want to tell it. You set there and you seem so calm, so unaffected, so distant, like I could pour all my miseries into you out of a pitcher or a fruit jar and you could hold 'em all fer me and it wouldn't hurt you. Like you had none of yer own. That's the way I felt the other day when I wound up an' told you all my troubles. I wouldn't a told all that to nobody, I wouldn't a thought. Why you? Because there's such a distance?"

I don't know and I can't say. Virgie stares down at the table and then looks at me.

"I guess I believe in God. I don't know." She pauses. "What do you think, about God, I mean, God and all?"

I think that God created man in his own image and immediately self-destructed.

That's the thought that pops into my mind, but I do not say it. It skirts the edge of flippancy too closely to be comic relief. I only shake my head.

"Would you like to see Earl?" asks Virgie. "Would you like to meet him?"

"Yes," I say, "yes I would." Indeed that's exactly what I want. That is why I came; I know now. It is as a matter of fact intensely important for me to see Earl. I need to know if this is tragedy or comic opera. And Earl is the only principal player whom I have not yet seen. Even the Stoples I have seen. I would see Earl McCullough.

We drive toward Claremore and the Rogers County Jail in the black Lincoln. Virgie does not even protest. I don't know if she is too modest to offer a ride in her tiny import or if she just wants a ride in the Lincoln. From the way she fingers the upholstery and leans back against the cushioned seat, I would tend to suspect the latter.

"Earl's daddy, Curtis, had some Indian blood in him down the line. His grandfather, they said, was part Indian and he was hung along with a bunch of outlaws down near Sallisaw, oh, a long time ago. But you know what they say about Indians and drinkin', and they said that was why Curtis was so bad to drink, because of that Indian blood. That might just be a tale, though, don't you think?"

"I really don't know," I say. I wish I could answer some of Virgie's questions with something other than "I don't know."

Virgie has lapsed into something like diffidence. She does not seem quite the unbreakable bough that she seemed when I first met her. It may have something to do with the Lincoln; or it may be that the spontaneity of that night's confession now in retrospect disturbs her. I am, she has said, valuable to her because of my "distance." I must not get too close. I am along only to put things in perspective, proof to Virgie that there is a wider world, a world that holds her personal tragedy insignificant in the scheme of things.

I am not totally unprepared for a visit to a jail. I toured a prison once, with a group, many years ago. The tour, I recall, included a pair of teenaged boys who kept badgering the assistant warden who guided us to let them see the electric chair. And I was hauled in summarily once many years ago for ignoring some parking tickets, and of course I went to the police station when the children vandalized my house. Besides, I have seen a lot of jail scenes in movies and on TV.

I am actually expecting more than I get. We are ushered into a small, white room with folding chairs and an aging oak desk. It is a room that could be almost anything. If there were pictures on the walls, it might be an examining room in that now defunct abortion mill; if there were diplomas on the wall it might be a college counselor's office; if there were a picture of the current President of the United States, it might be a civil service office. But the walls are blank. There is not so much as a calendar or even an idly scratched *FUCK* anywhere to be seen. It is a room that takes no sides; a blind man's room, as justice is blind, perhaps.

The deputy who brings Earl McCullough into the room seats himself in one of the folding chairs, straddling it backward, his arms across the back, and waits. He may have tuned the conversation out, he may not have. It is hard to tell from his expression, which exactly matches the room's walls.

The room could even be a principal's office as the pouting young man slouches into a chair, his expression defensive, an expression that clearly says, "I ain't done nothin'," as if he had been accused of stuffing paper towels into the urinals in the boys' rest room instead of committing murder.

I had, I think, expected that we would have been in one of those prison visiting rooms, where the prisoner sits on one side of a table and the visitor on the other and they shout at each other through a glass partition. Perhaps the Rogers County Jail does not have such a facility, or perhaps the jailers know Virgie too well to worry about her, and Earl too well to take him seriously.

"Why didn't ya bring somethin' to eat, Ma? I cain't stand the slop they got here," grumbles Earl at last.

The young man before me is moderately tall, moderately thick around the waist, has moderately long hair that is moderately dirty, and has chewed his fingernails down to the quick. He has no particular distinguishing features, and asked to describe him minutes after leaving him, I would probably struggle to recall the exact shade of his hair, the length of his nose, the color of his eyes.

"That lawyer's so dumb. He don't do nothin'," I hear Earl complaining to his mother petulantly, just as a schoolboy might complain that his teacher is dumb and that he will never have need of adjectives and pronouns in his life anyway. There is a numb kind of quality about Earl McCullough, like a shot of novocaine to a lower gum, that gum suddenly out of proportion to the rest of the mouth and at the same time not there at all.

He has stopped talking and is staring at the blank wall before him, which from his expression, an intense expression of nonintellectual absorption, might be displaying a rerun of "Gilligan's Island."

He rouses himself suddenly and briefly. "I ain't goin to no jail," he announces. "I ain't goin to no jail. They cain't make me. I ain't done nothin' and I ain't goin to jail no matter what they say." I suppose he means "prison" instead of "jail," since he so obviously has already gone to jail.

Virgie's comments are commonplace, a few anecdotes and some questions. Does he have enough underwear and do they furnish him toothpaste?

"You could at least bring me a hamburger when you come. This slop here. I cain't eat it," he whines.

I watch Earl's face and listen to his voice in search of what? If not a soul, then a capacity for great evil? I find clues to neither. The absence of good, I suppose, does not necessarily imply the presence of anything, evil or anything else. It is only an absence. Perhaps evil implies a soul just as good does, evil requiring a capacity for feeling, just as good does, mirror images. Earl McCullough's casual killing of his own kind is only that, random and haphazard. Perhaps there is such a thing as a hollow egg?

An acquaintance of mine, a doctor, a few years ago in a fit of civic-mindedness sat in on a Pardon and Parole Board hearing. He came away shaken, not at the sin and violence and corruption those pleading prisoners represented, but at the casual mindlessness of their crimes and the routine reaction to the recounting of them years later. "I'd have turned them all loose," said the doctor. "I'd have turned them all loose. They were all so dumb, so ignorant. They didn't even understand the charges against them. I'd have let them all go," he exclaimed.

I am not sure that turning such mindlessness loose on society is necessarily wise, but I think I understand what he meant. He had gone expecting the vicious and the violent and had found only the vacuous.

I look at Earl and see only the banal. I could not see how he could be convicted of anything. A jury could not have any moral jurisdiction over the likes of Earl. He is not guilty, not guilty by right of having been accidentally born into the wrong age. He belongs in an age where the clubbing down of anyone who gets in your way is not a great matter. Cro-Magnon man could not be measured against the laws of the enlightened. Could he?

But a jury will indeed sit in judgment on Earl McCullough, affording the murdered Stoples a justice their lives probably never merited, just as in death they were afforded the dignity of a limousine, a dignity life never would have afforded them. In the eyes of the law the crime against the Stoples is a crime against the citizens of Rogers County and the citizens of the State of Oklahoma and the citizens of the United States of America and the Brotherhood of Man and must be so avenged. Never mind that the Stoples were themselves in life an offense against all of those things.

"That lawyer says I got to have a haircut and a suit of clothes and a tie," growls Earl.

"Well, we'll just do what he says," replies Virgie. "He knows what to do."

"He don't know shit."

Earl McCullough is not the first person to question the credentials of trained professionals. It happens all the time. The letters to the editors of newspaper are examples, as are the fans sitting halfway around the field who routinely argue close calls by trained umpires.

And almost no President has the God-given sense about economics and foreign affairs of the early morning coffee drinkers in places like Virgie's Café. I don't suppose it hurts anything. Or means anything either.

As we rise to leave, the deputy already nudging Earl toward the door, he whines, "Ma, next time bring me a hamburger, will you?"

"We'll see," murmurs Virgie, for she has the upper hand. There is no way that Earl can force or intimidate her into bringing the hamburger.

The drive back toward Hubbard is silent for a time until Virgie, without preface, asks, "You suppose they'd hang someone fer killin' somebody like the Stoples?"

"No," I say quickly, "no, they wouldn't." I don't point out to her that the method of execution in Oklahoma has recently been changed to lethal injections, that anyway the condemned have not been hanged in this state in many years. But that is not why I hastily reassure her. If Earl McCullough is executed, it will be far down the road. Far, far down. There is no point in thinking about that for a long time.

"Are you hungry?" asks Virgie and without waiting for the answer says, "I am. Let's stop fer a hamburger."

I glance at her to see if this is some perverse suggestion to prove her independence of Earl. But her expression is benign.

"Where?" I ask.

"We'll stop at my place, my café."

"You're not open on Sunday."

"Oh, I often go in on Sunday. Sometimes to clean or do books and sometimes fer a meal. I don't always keep much food at home. It's a chore to buy fer the restaurant and then turn around and buy fer home, too. Besides, it's just easier fer me to cook up a hamburger at the store than at home. I been doin' it so long."

The idea of one of Virgie's hamburgers is appealing, for I have not eaten since breakfast. But the clouds are low and getting lower.

"I can't stay," I say. "It looks like we're in for some weather."

"It won't take long. I'll hurry."

There is something ominous in an after-hours visit to a business establishment, as if you don't belong and are somehow resented for disturbing the silence. I have felt that sensation in my own store, those occasional times that I must go in on Sunday to pick up some work or check something. Those hours when the people are gone and the fluorescent lighting, without movement to break it up, is heavy in its brightness. "Resentment" is the best word I can think of, a resentment of the spirit of the place at having its peace broken.

Although my store is so much bigger than Virgie's place, the tapping of my heels echoing endlessly along display cases and aisles of ready-to-wear, silenced only in the plush carpet of the designer areas, is exactly duplicated in Virgie's empty café, only on a lesser scale. The same sense of resentment comes from the suddenly violated white enamel refrigerator as from a display case of designer scarves. It can seem infinitely lonely in a place of business in those hours when no one is supposed to be there.

Virgie perhaps senses the same thing I do, for she is quiet and distracted and she slowly puts together a pair of hamburgers. But when she finishes them and fishes a pair of cold colas from the intractable refrigerator, I feel the isolated sensation begin to abate. And so, too, perhaps does Virgie.

"You don't want to fergit yer quilt top. You left it at the house, didn't you?"

Ah. Yes. I must remember to take that with me.

"You got to love them 'cause you can't git rid of them."

I know that Virgie has switched from hamburgers and quilt tops back to Earl.

"Love is funny," continues Virgie. "You think of love as being good and pleasing; but it ain't necessarily, is it? Love is about equal parts pain and pleasure, I'd think. Don't you think so?"

It is hardly a profound thought, but I am struck by the country-Western possibility. "Is my glass half-full of love, or half-empty of misery?" I do not, however, share that idea with Virgie, who might not appreciate the apparent flippancy.

I shake my head. It is a question I can't answer. I've had little experience of love as in pain or pleasure, and I suppose that's sad. And then I think how convenient it is, because I would not be in Virgie's shoes right now for all the love in the world. As an onlooker, it seems to me that Virgie's life has had a disproportionate share of the pain. I wonder how she would define pleasure?

Happiness is a hamburger with pickles and onions?

There is a slam of a car door outside the building and Virgie and I look at each other as heavy footsteps approach and the handle of the door is rattled.

"We ain't open," shouts Virgie at the unseen presence. The door rattles again and I feel a little thrill of apprehension at the unknown and unseen rattler.

"Hey, Virg, it's me, George Kellbaum. You in there?"

"Oh shit, George, what do you want?" Virgie rises heavily to open the door to admit George, that same George, it turns out, that I saw on my first visit to Virgie's Café. Bright and eager George, peering past Virgie toward me as if expecting me. He probably is. He has seen the telltale Lincoln and wants to know what's going on.

"We was just leavin', George," says Virgie, not caring, I suppose, that our half-eaten hamburgers make a liar of her.

"That's okay. I just saw you in here an' wondered if y'all knowed about the fire last night?"

"Fire? What fire?" asks Virgie.

George cannot keep the pleasure from his face, pleasure, I suppose, at being the first with an important piece of news.

"Why, that old house, you know, where you found them Stoples, it burned last night, clear to the ground."

"Well, I didn't know that," murmurs Virgie. "I didn't hear nothin'."

"It was all over so quick, and it was late. Nothin' left to it. I was by there this mornin' on the way to church."

I am overcome with the sensation that I am a spectator-performer again in some continuing drama, that I am both a part of it and distant from it, that Virgie's Café is the stage and George is what, the spear carrier, the messenger who brings distant news onstage?

"What happened?" I ask. "Who burned it?"

"Who knows," replies George, delighted, I think, that I have addressed a question to him, fattened his part, so to speak. "That ain't so unusual, to have an old house like that burn in the night. All kinds of people, kids or loafers, out cattin' around. Sometimes they set things a-far apurpose, sometimes accidental. They go in and play cards or drink or whatever"—here George looks slyly at Virgie as if the "whatever" he refers to is a private joke between them.

"It is all gone?"

"Ever' board. Burnt like tinder, they said. Somebody said like the house knowed its own reputation and finally just self-destructed."

"Reputation?"

"I don't know that it was a haunted house really. Kids get to callin' any big, old deserted house 'haunted.' Now, when I was a kid they always called it 'dead man's house,' which was more to the point."

"They did?" says Virgie. "I never heard that before."

"Oh, yeah, they did. 'Dead man's house.' I don't know exactly why, except the story was that the feller built it died before he ever moved into it, and that after that a whole lot of people that lived there died. So they took to callin' it 'dead man's house.' It's been since I was growed that they started callin' it 'haunted.' I don't think myself that it was haunted, unless you count a bunch a pissants screwin' around up there 'haunted.' Beg pardon." George amiably excuses his own language and waits for a reaction.

"I cain't say I mind," says Virgie.

I don't know what I think.

"I cain't say I mind. Ever' time I go by there, it just reminds me and it reminds ever'one else. Now it'll grow up into grass and people won't be so apt to remember."

There is no need to ask, "Remember what?" Even George understands that, I think.

By the time we leave Virgie's it has begun to rain, a slow, cold fall rain. I drive her home and retrieve my quilt top. Our farewell is brief. I am anxious to beat the rain home. If it gets colder the rain will begin to freeze and I don't need that.

Still, I cannot keep myself from driving by the old Sears, Roebuck house, or where the old Sears, Roebuck house used to be. It is, as George advertised, burned down to every board, including the old carriage house. I pause in front of it, making no move to get out of the car. I cannot say how I feel. I look at the package on the seat beside me, the package containing the strange old quilt top and wonder idly if it, too, will be snatched from me as my pictures and papers and now my house have been snatched.

For some reason, each time I reach out to touch a part of my past, it is pulled back. I feel not unlike a donkey after a carrot on a stick. Or, more ominously, the end of a line, all traces of which are being systematically eradicated. I think, ruefully, that I should drive cautiously home, lest I join those disappearing relics.

Virgie is right. The old house will be reclaimed by the weeds until there will come a time that no one will remember where it was. "There was an old house around here," some ancient will remark, "an old house when I was a kid that we called 'haunted,' and one day they

did find a grave with three bodies in it and then the house mysteri-
ously burned down. It was around here somewhere. If you look, you
might find traces of the foundation."

*And will that be the last memory of that old house? And then will it be
dead?*

That is enough of a thought to start me on the road home, a road
that proves mercifully uneventful. Even the rain abates and does not
freeze. By the time I see the skyline, the City of Faith dwarfing by a
trick of perspective the BOK Building, a clear light has begun to show
around the western edges of the sky. Sunset will be accomplished in
spite of those clouds.

"Whur you been?" Nanny asks suspiciously, for I had left while
she was in church with only a note that I would be back in time for
supper.

Nanny is not only the only person alive who would ask me such an
abrupt question, she is also the only person who would get a diffident
answer.

"I've been antiquing," I say, holding out the parcel. "See what I
found?"

Nanny does not ask why I would want an antique. She does not
even comment on the obvious fact that never to her knowledge have I
ever collected anything, much less antiques. Instead she takes the
parcel I extend, unwraps it and stares curiously at it.

"What is it?"

Nanny, of course, knows what it is. Her question is an all-
encompassing one; "What is it?" translates to "Why is it imporant?"

"Funny-lookin' thin', ain't it?" She sits and drapes it over her knee
and inspects it.

"It's quite old, I think," I say.

"Smells like it."

"Have you ever seen a pattern like it?"

"Not no pattern to it? No," she answers the question then, "no, I
ain't never seen nothin' like it. Not finished either, is it? Cain't see
what someone must a had in mind." She flips the top over and examines the back of it, the intricate handstitching that makes the quilt
top interesting.

"I'd say," says Nanny, "that this top was either put together by
more than one person or, maybe, whoever done it done it over a long
period a time and got old doin' it." She examines the quilt more
closely, frowning.

I had not really intended for her to make such an inspection; it seems to have piqued her curiosity, though. She studies it for a long time before announcing at last, " 'Spect this was put together by some lady that got old doin' it. See"—she points to the stitching in the very center of the top, around the pink pieces—"see how neat that is. Now, that is stitchin'," she says in admiration. "That is stitchin'. But down here on the edges, how raggedy the stitches are, like maybe she couldn't see no more or was shaky."

"Why, Nanny, what in the world? You're a regular Sherlock Holmes. You've missed your calling; you should've been a detective."

Nanny gestures deprecatingly, but she looks pleased. "It's just an idea. This stitchin' on the edges 'minds me of a quilt I got that my old granny done when she was old, probably the last she ever done, and the stitches is the same. My granny was pretty shaky then and couldn't see too good. You don't have to be too smart to figger things out, if you just notice things. What you goin' to do with this?" she adds suspiciously. "You better not try to warsh it."

"Oh, we won't. I think I'll have it appraised and offer it to a museum, maybe."

Nanny only shrugs and carefully begins to roll the quilt top.

"What are you doing?" I ask in some curiosity.

"I'm rollin this up. Hit's been folded too long. You want to give it to a museum, you don't want it cracked and faded whur it's been folded." Nanny is as practical as she is wise.

"Now we'll find a plastic bag to wrap it in," she says, satisfied with her work. I think she is impressed with the idea that this relic is bound for a museum. I seem to have committed myself to that, and I find all at once that I am not so eager to part with the smelly thing as I thought I was.

"Leroy ain't here," says Nanny. "He went home early."

I am taken aback by this abrupt announcement as to Leroy's whereabouts. I hadn't missed him, hadn't noted his absence or even remembered that he had been hanging around for the better part of a week.

"Well, did they patch up their differences?" Nanny obviously wants to talk about this, otherwise she would not have so summarily brought it up.

"Oh, I don' know," she sighs and she cups her chin in her palm, resting her elbow on the rolled-up piece of patchwork. "I don' know what'll happen."

"Is there a problem?" What I mean, and I'm sure that Nanny understands what I mean, is: Is there something serious beyond Leroy and Charlaine's normal propensity for fighting?

"Charlaine's pregnant again and Leroy wants her to get a 'bortion and she don't want to. He say dey got too many kids, she say she know it, but she still don' want no 'bortion. What you think about dat?" Nanny looks at me quizzically. "What you think 'bout dat? Dey was a time when only white wimmin got 'bortions 'cause dey was illegal and expensive. Colored wimmin didn't get no choice. White wimmin got 'bortions and colored wimmin got babies."

"Well," I say, reciting the liberated litany, "it's Charlaine's choice, you know. It's her body."

"No, hit's bof of 'em's choice. Dey both got to raise it and dey bof had a hand in makin' it. Leroy he say dey got too many kids, ain't got room enough. Charlaine say dey git a big old house and fix it up; Leroy say no, he like it just the way it is. Dey been fightin' fer a week." Nanny pauses, frowning at the patchwork. "I don' know what's right, do you?"

"I'm afraid not, Nanny." Indeed, increasingly I do not know what is right, what is right about anything.

When I chose to have abortions, there was no moral ambiguity about it. It was wrong, in the eyes of the law and in everyone else's eyes, too. But then it was also wrong to screw when you weren't married, to screw and get pregnant, so that the abortion was often only the extension of that original sin.

What it boils down to here, I suppose, is choice. The human species is the only species that has such a choice, the biblical knowledge between good and evil, to make a moral judgment about a natural function.

But, alas, even good and evil are relative, it being routine to screw, to get pregnant and to have abortions, and if there is a moral objection to that, it has become considerably weaker.

And if indeed the highest purpose is to keep the race alive, then Charlaine and Leroy have done their duty and deserve some peace. But I? Well, that's a thought to sleep on.

"I don't know, Nanny. It's a decision Leroy and Charlaine will have to make." I leave Nanny with the rolled-up quilt top still on her lap and ascend the staircase to my own rooms.

It is not quite dark.

FOURTEEN

WHERE THE SPIRITS DWELL

I marveled at Booth Copeland's nonchalance as I often had. He popped into my office, outlined briefly a proposed project and hardly waited for my agreeing nod before he popped out the door again. That such apparent carelessness of detail and casualness of attitude could have amassed not only a fortune for me, but an almost staggering one for himself seemed remarkable enough. But that he could have with the same carelessness not only weathered the hard times that have driven other men to acts of desperation, but added, almost as an afterthought, substantially to his already immense fortune, was even more remarkable.

Staring at the door he had banged through, I mused that the man who was, I was certain, older than I by at least a decade seemed sprightlier and more youthful by that much. Was it I who was preternaturally old, or was he simply confounding nature as he confounded everyone else, indeed growing younger while everything else grew older?

Still, I had no complaints. My and Booth's business venture profited us both, and that in a time of severe depression elsewhere. And while other giants of commerce were flinging themselves from tall buildings, Booth was happily building taller ones or buying them and, for that matter, almost anything else that caught his fancy. Though he and I shared our original oil wealth, I had continued successfully my own retail business and Booth had barged into first the cattle business and the aviation business and a raft of lesser projects—all successfully, so that he spent as much time out of the city and the state overseeing his enterprises as he did in the state. I saw him infrequently, but his visits were always profitable.

Perhaps Booth Copeland was one of those men whom history
loved, who had a magic—call it luck or destiny—to have been born in
the right age. He was a man of that busy and commercial age, a man
of his time. I wondered how he might have fared in another age, an
age when his strengths were not particularly valued.

I, on the other had, have been a man of no "time," no historical
designation. I am certain I could have survived in any historical con-
text. Could that be my alleged Jewish blood? Would that it were.
Would that I had that anchor, that eternal tie to a definite divine
being, that Patriarchal God of Thunder and Wrath, who cast out
Lucifer in mighty combat that shook the heavens.

But I am not the son of Judah. I am the incestuous issue of incestuous issue, a product of lust without spirit or soul. I have no god to
answer to.

Even without Booth we would have withstood the onslaught of
fortune far better than most, Levi and I, for though we had a certain
amount of paper capital that was lost, we were able to hold on to our
real capital and even make some judicious investments, investments
possibly only because we had ready access to cash, which was sorely
needed in many areas.

Over the years Levi has shown a clear facility with figures and an
industriousness most admirable in a young man. From the time he
began serious business considerations during his seventeenth summer—that bitter summer of the race riot—until now, he has exhibited
little interest in anything save business. And the business has profited
from that attention.

After attending the University of Missouri for four years and
applying himself diligently, he returned home and persevered beyond
my wildest hopes. That slight waywardness which caused us to stumble onto that pitiful spectacle of the colored boy Joab's molestation has
from that moment been exorcised, perhaps by that very violence.

I do not know what memories Levi holds of that event, the death
of Inez and the disappearance of Joab, but for myself that day returns
now and then, a memory that pokes and prods me as if there is
something missing, something I must be reminded of, something I
must make amends for. I would that that memory would quit my
subconscious and let me be, for I have too many such memories and
they tangle and fight with each other until there are times, usually in
the loneliness of my rooms, that sense seems to be deserting me
altogether.

I shoulder no guilt for the deaths of those two coloreds. There were many that day just like them, and I tried to help those two unfortunate darkies. I warned Inez at least and said only what could have been said in Joab's defense. But it was not enough, and they return at odd times to tell me that it was not enough, though I cannot think what they would have me do. Are they only lonely ghosts who want vengeance? I do not know. I only know that they were casualties.

Levi, during the twelve years since that event, has made no mention of it, nor ever remarked upon Joab's torments. I doubt that he has forgotten the event, however, for he is a deep and silent man, as befits, perhaps, the end of the line of Obediah.

Death has seemed to be an inordinate part of my adulthood, beyond even the normal circumstances of the comings and goings of lives. I think I fear death more than most, not actually death itself, but the spirits I must face beyond, for there are none there that I am eager to see again, and scenes of death now and then rivet themselves momentarly to my memory. I see Old Louisa Two dead before the hearth, sitting straight up, that ridiculous piece of wedding lace clutched triumphantly in her fingers to the dismay of Louisa One, snatching to little avail at the lace held thus deathly tight. That is the least of my memories, which include the Old Bastard, peppered with gunshot, his life seeping out of several wounds; and Joab screaming, tied to the hood of the car; and Elizabeth Brady asleep and then dead. These ghosts and more parade themselves before me in my darkened rooms, which is why, I suppose, I often work to exhaustion, thus keeping them at bay.

Bah! These ghosts are a sorry lot, finding excuses for their own behavior, but none for mine.

"Mr. Murphy?" I jumped at the sudden voice breaking the silence in an unexpected jolt. "Mr. Murphy?"

I was surprised to find myself still at my desk. My reverie had taken me so far back in time that it had all but cost me my consciousness.

"Yes, Perkins?"

"We're locking up. Will you be needing anything before we go?"

"Ah, thank you, no, Perkins. I must be off myself. My son Levi will be home tonight. I am eager to see him."

"Yes, sir."

I stared after Perkins. If he had gotten any older over the years he had hidden it well. His hair, always thin, had gotten no thinner and his voice, always weak, had gotten no weaker. He seemed already decked out, when he arrived at manhood, in the trappings of age.

I had let the time get by me, uncharacteristically losing myself in thought at my desk. I was anxious to see Levi again, for he had been gone to St. Louis for nearly six weeks and his communiqués had been but brief and businesslike. I wondered if indeed he treated this annual trip to St. Louis to the trade fair as pure business, as he seemed to. It was hard to imagine that he would not dabble in some of the pleasures that city had to offer. Nor did I mind that thought so much. He was young and strong. That he would suffer the lusts of that age would only be natural.

He was free, as far as I was concerned, to spread his seed where he would, so long as he produced no heirs that I, or he, could claim. That was a very fine distinction, I realized. I wanted only that he end the known line, that upon his death people would say, "That was the end of the Murphys," that Obediah's spirit, hovering, would fade and disappear with that, and my own, too, I sincerely hoped.

This, of course, I had never discussed with anyone, though Daniel, who has proved more perspicacious than I might have imagined, has commented upon what seems to be my talent for inspiring celibacy in others.

Ah, would that I could, would that there were some way to keep the race alive without the attendant lust; for in my own mind I have long been convinced that it is such lust which is at the root of all human failings. That, of course, is not a new thought. While not actually in favor of genocide, I have often wondered what difference it would make if the race of man were to disappear from the earth.

It is just such thoughts as these that kept me working late, accomplishing much, surviving the economic vagaries that nearly destroyed the nation. I did not care to be alone with such thoughts. But as I have grown older, they have begun to seek me out; they will no longer remain at home, secreted behind closed doors.

God! what torment!

Perhaps what has saved me from near-panic has been my daily walks to and from my store, for I still lunched at home and so walked briskly that distance four times daily in all kinds of weather. It was that exercise, that forcing of the outside world upon my consciousness, that conversation with people passing me, that let light into my often cloudy mind. I tipped my hat and spoke to those I passed, even the children, and now and then caught an admiring glance shot my way by some lady or other, for I was quite aware that, even being past the half-century mark, I had worn well, stood tall and straight and was in the eyes of many a striking figure of a man, that image, I'm sure, reinforced by knowledge of my wealth. I have rarely returned any of those feminine glances, as I have held myself aloof from any kind of social consort with that fairer sex, for I would not risk that my body betray me. I would be master over the flesh.

"Good evenin', Mr. Murphy," Mrs. Conrad greeted me at the door to my house. She was the latest in a succession of housekeepers who had followed black Inez, all of them white. For my ghosts now numbered those two black people and I wanted no converse with people of that color. I was too haunted by Joab's final screams.

But, in truth, none of the housekeepers had proved as satisfactory as that departed colored woman, nor did they seem inclined to stay very long. Only one had ever given but the vaguest kind of reasons for going and she had confessed, "This place is gloomy and I'm scared the hell of it."

Mrs. Conrad had been with us for two years; both her eyes and her hearing weak, she perhaps was not attuned to that gloominess. Neither was she attuned to the accumulation of dust and disorder, but she could cook. That was enough.

"Is Mr. Levi here yet, Mrs. Conrad?" I was aware that his train should have arrived early in the afternoon and was a little surprised that he had not already called me on the telephone, although he had, I knew, developed the same sort of antipathy toward that impudent instrument that I had. There is no teaching good manners to a telephone; like a two-year-old it will interrupt and demand attention no matter what you are engaged in.

Mrs. Conrad hesitated and looked a little distracted, "Well, uh, yes, I guess, yes, I guess he is. I, well, he, uh, come in earlier this afternoon." She looked as if she would say more, pursed her lips and then turned back toward the kitchen muttering something indistinguishable.

It was nice to have him back. When he was absent, my routine was disrupted. I did not like to have my routine interrupted.

"Father?" I turned eagerly toward Levi's voice. He stood on the landing, smiling. Incredulous, I stared at the picture before me, caught my breath and exhaled carefully. There are built into the human organism certain safety valves, which work to keep that organism from destructing of its own volition in times of extreme stress. Such seemed at that moment to be my salvation, for at the same time that the blood began to pound uncontrollably at my temples and my knees seemed in danger of collapsing beneath me, the adrenaline began to course through my system and perspiration sprang to the aid of my beleaguered body. As an outward manifestation of my agitation, however, I only caught my breath quickly and let it out in something like a restrained hiss at the sight of Levi, my son, standing smiling and proud on the landing above me with an extremely handsome woman on his arm. I knew what he would say before ever he said it.

"This is my bride, Father, my wife, Lucille."

It is said that a drowning man's life flashes before him in a matter of seconds and I have never doubted that; for I have noted on other occasions how much the mind can absorb and process in an instant's time, as, in the case of an unexpected fall, the victim on his way to the ground from a standing position not only has time to realize what is happening, but to ask himself if it can actually be going on and to determine what his reaction will be when he finally hits the ground. Such was the case as, in the time it took to extend my hand and force a smile, I reviewed my recent years with Levi and cursed myself for a complacent fool, undone by that very complacency. My hand had not yet reached the woman's proffered fingers by the time I had determined that the best course for the moment would be to mask my disappointment, assess the situation and make plans accordingly. And by the time my hand reached hers I was calmly in control of myself and I grasped the hand firmly and felt the pressure returned in kind; a firm handshake in a woman is a rare occurrence.

"I am in shock, Levi," I said.

"I knew you would be happy, Father," burbled the young man quite uncharacteristically, for he was by nature solemn and, if you like, perhaps a little dull.

"He did not say he was happy, Lee," corrected the woman. "He said he was in a state of shock." And she smiled at me. At the "Lee" I looked down at her and she returned my glance in like measure, her expression as firm and controlled as her handshake, and I found myself staring right into her eyes; nor did she avert her glance but met mine head on. I have always been a connoisseur of women's eyes, for in spite of my largely celibate state I have never ceased to be drawn, as any normal man is, to that terrifying sex, though I have found them to be shallow and for the most part suited only for the most ordinary kinds of conversation.

The eyes that I looked into on this occasion were of that same deep blue-gray that Levi's mother had had, though he himself had inherited Daniel's faded brown. It was the blue-gray of moving water, water pulled toward distant rapids or whirlpools. That allusion, perhaps too precious, was, however, the one that struck me immediately. And in those same few seconds that an entire life can pass through memory, I had isolated the adversary and I knew her to be a formidable one.

"Well," I said, releasing her hand at last and taking Levi's, "in celebration we must break out some libation or other. Do you have a preference, Lucille? We do have a fine stock of wine and spirits, if you care for them. I'm afraid we are a little outside the law in that regard." I smiled.

"Bourbon," she said as quietly as if she had asked for tea with sugar. "Seagram Seven, if you have it, Lee," and she smiled up at my obviously smitten son.

"Lee?" I said.

"It is a nickname, Father."

Ah. Levi had never before exhibited a preference for nicknames.

"Two people in the same house with the same name is always confusing, don't you think?" asked Lucille.

"It has never been a problem, until now, since I am 'Father'; in business, most people manage to make the distinction."

"I suppose I am inconvenient," murmured Lucille. "Perhaps I could just refer to you as Levi One and Levi Two and,"—here she smiled at Levi—"when we have a son he could be Levi Three."

I glanced sharply at her, but there seemed to be no dissembling about her. It was, I was sure, only happenstance that she had said that. She was carefully sipping the drink I had fixed for her. I examined her as obliquely as I could manage and was forced to admit to myself that, like a beginning fisherman, Levi had managed to land a prize; and by the time dinner was called, I realized that not only was his a prize to view, she was a person of some intellectual capacity and, I feared, strength and determination of purpose. All of that, coupled with that kind of magnetism, that sexual attractiveness which is less external regularity of form and feature and more some powerful call to that in man which is base and lustful, would prove her, I was certain, to be formidable indeed. The sooner she was out of our lives, the better. Her continued presence boded no good.

The history of this relationship had been lengthier, apparently, than I had at first thought, they having met the year before at the trade fair.

"You seem quite knowledgeable in retail affairs?" I observed to my new daughter.

"My first husband was a wholesaler in a very small way. We have exhibited at the trade fair for several years."

"You're a widow?"

"No." She looked at me serenely, quite obviously intending that I force the issue. Levi had focused all of his attention on the plate of food before him and refused to look up.

Casually I removed the conversation to another area. This attractive interloper would not dictate the terms of our relationship. I intended that her stay be brief, and I was by then certain that she recognized the threat that I posed. I felt something like elation at the coming battle, an elation tinged with apprehension, in much the way, I am sure, an athlete approaching an important contest must feel. It was the kind of sensation that I had not felt in a long time—something to anticipate; the vague sense of dread and futility that had long been my constant companion faded perceptibly.

Levi did not, I was sure, comprehend the undercurrents of our conversation, though from his slightly nervous demeanor he did sense that something he could not fathom was going on between Lucille and me.

After Lucille had retired to Levi's rooms on the second floor, he and I smoked a few moments in the library, I filling him in on general business information relative to his six weeks' absence. But Levi was inattentive, fidgeting, nervous and, I suppose, excited.

"We will take a holiday soon, Father," he said abruptly, interrupting what I was telling him.

"Oh?"

"Yes, a honeymoon, I think."

"Well, I'd appreciate your postponing it for a few weeks, perhaps. I had a visit from Booth today and I suppose I might as well be frank with you. Things are not looking nearly as good as I had thought. If this damnable depression is not soon over, I fear for what will happen to all of us."

"Father?"

Levi might well be surprised. So far as he knew, we were in an excellent financial situation. Though he had been, of course, privy to our circumstances relative to the retail business, I had not yet entrusted him full intelligence on all matters of business, so that there was much of which he was quite ignorant.

"We need to consider some extensive consolidations in the next few months."

"Well, yes, of course, Father."

He made no mention of separate housing; had he done so, I would have argued against it. I had the feeling that Levi, having jumped the traces in the matter of his marriage, would be most docile in all other matters for quite a while. I wanted the couple under my roof and I wanted Levi busy. I did not know precisely what I would do, something along the lines of divide and conquer, I supposed.

Although Levi was obviously beyond himself in passion, I did not think that his bride reciprocated with any fervor. I was fairly certain, as a matter of fact, that her main interest in him lay in the fortune he would inherit. Consequently, I had little guilt concerning my attempts to separate them. I knew, however, that I must move quickly before Levi managed to impregnate this woman, both strengthening their tie and prolonging that line which I would destroy.

That latter thought, I discovered with some surprise, did not distress me quite as much as I might have expected it to, perhaps because, after all, it was only a symbolic ending, as I was myself in fact the end of that line. Still, having for so many years been obsessed with the notion of having the last laugh, so to speak, of ending that branch of whatever tree we came from with a spurious bastard, if you will, I would not let go that idea entirely. I did not want Levi, to become a father either in name or in fact. Nor did I want this winsome witch to lead him up the primrose path, a path he was completely unsuited to travel.

All of this was like an electric shock to my system, and though I suffered the same sleepless nights as before, my agitation was exciting and I paced the floor and plotted, though only in a general way, for events would needs determine my eventual course of action.

"You do not sleep well," observed Lucille at breakfast one morning.

"I'm sorry. I did not realize that I was overheard," I apologized. "No, I do not require a great deal of sleep and I often pace at night and so seek solutions to problems or make plans. I find the late hours the most creative part of my day. However, I shall in the future attempt to be quieter."

"Oh no. Please don't worry about it on my account. I only hear you upon a rare occasion that I happen to wake, and it doesn't bother me. I always sleep well." With this she stretched and yawned more broadly than I thought seemly in a woman, particularly one in the presence of a man other than her husband, for Levi had already gone to work. That gesture she prolonged, pulling the wrapper taut across her bosom, a bosom firm and round and quite out of proportion to her otherwise slender form, ending at last by running her fingers through her hair and giving it a quick shake. It was a typically feminine gesture, one that generally undoes any observing male, particularly if the female involved is well formed and attractive. Nor was I immune to that sudden sensation, being merely mortal.

Still, I recognized the ploy for what it was, and though I might enjoy the sudden thrill of masculine pleasure that attacked my parts, I was far from overcome. Poor Levi. He could certainly be no match for such as this.

Levi I kept busy. I ran a constant stream of crises past him, each more dire-sounding than the next, so that he was physically and emotionally drained whenever he returned from work, certain that our fortune was tottering in the general malaise of the economy and that we were likely to be toppled at each set of figures I put before him. Levi had little time or energy to enjoy the pleasures of marriage, for I am certain that he understood, if but vaguely, that his continued possession of his prize was predicated upon his continuing fortune. Even Levi was not so dull as to believe that Lucille would stick by him through poverty and hard times. I preyed upon that fear and, if I say so myself, I became quite adept at creating crises and ensuing panic.

I hoped that boredom would attack Lucille, or perhaps the gloominess of the environment that had cost me so many housekeepers. But Lucille proved a patient woman and her very presence lifted the gloom from the place. Now and then she eyed me with what seemed to be a twinkle of amusement. She even went so far as to make suggestions for improvements around the house, suggesting lighter draperies, a vacuum system throughout and new appliances for the kitchen.

"We are quite satisfied with things as they are," I told her at one point, and exhibited anger only when she made suggestions for redoing the garden. "It's gloomy," she said. "It's too shady. We must get rid of that big old evergreen tree and that rock. We need some sun and some bright sun-loving annuals."

"*We* like the shade," I said abruptly, by inflection making clear that while her "we" had been inclusive, mine had been exclusive. She was not one of us.

It did not seem to bother her. She only gave me a crooked little smile and rose a little too slowly and deliberately from her chair, brushing her skirt aside as she did so. There were odd moments when her gestures and glances unsettled me considerably.

"Your daughter-in-law is a lovely woman," drawled Booth Copeland at one point. "It is hard to believe that young Levi could do himself so proud."

"Yes" was all I said. He could take that as answer to either question he had posed. I did not ask, nor did he volunteer, where he had met her. Close as we had been in business matters for so many years, we had hardly any more social consort than I had with anyone else. I had as a matter of fact met Mrs. Copeland only on one or two occasions, that lady as elderly as Booth was youthful. I had been told that that lady collected oriental rugs. That was all I knew of her.

"Do you not intend some sort of reception for the newlyweds?" he inquired, with somewhat more interest in my personal affairs than I could be happy with.

"No."

"You are a queer bird, Levi," was all he said.

"Perhaps."

After several weeks, I realized that my subtle stratagems were unlikely to effect any immediate change in Levi and his wife's relationship. Levi, both busy and dense, seemed satisfied with things as they were, and Lucille was nothing if not infinitely patient. I would tighten my grip.

With Lucille I became more distant and colder; with Levi I became more demanding. In addition, I began to drop broad hints about his wife's possible unfaithfulness and to note her obvious willingness to seek her fortune. "There are, I'm afraid, Levi, a great many men far better off than we," I said to him bluntly. "Steel yourself against the possibility that Lucille will leave you for one of those, as she left her first husband."

I had already ascertained, by the simple expedience of hiring an investigator, the circumstances of Lucille's divorce. And it was quite obviously just as I stated it to Levi. He had come along, his prospects much brighter, and Lucille, with no apparent regard for anything save bettering herself financially, had dumped Orson Reynolds, her first husband, in favor of Levi. Levi, though often dense in matters personal, was not that thick. In his heart he knew how things stood. Nor did he even have the strength to resist my suggestion.

"Never mind, Father. I am quite capable of managing my own marriage" was all he said, and that without rancor. It was possible, even, that I detected a hint of defeat already in his weary slouch, for I had nearly convinced him that our fortune was in an irreversible decline.

In that frame of mind I dispatched him to Memphis to see to some properties that had been in the family since Old Louisa's time, properties which were indeed in serious decline and which I wanted dispatched quickly, lest they cost us greatly. Contrary to what I led Levi to believe, in addition to the success I enjoyed with Booth Copeland, I had also strengthened our personal resources by means of letting go of much marginal property and picking up other properties at bargain prices, and the prospects for our growth were great once this economic decline was reversed, as I was sure it would be.

On the day after Levi's departure for Memphis, Daniel called on me at my office on the pretext of presenting some papers for my perusal. But as Daniel had always been largely transparent in his actions to me, I realized that he actually had something else in mind and I waited for him to disclose it.

"Your daughter-in-law called on me today," he began. I stiffened. "She called on me, she said, as a family friend. She was quite distressed." He paused to await my reaction. I did not give him the satisfaction of any.

"She is unhappy that you seem very distant to her and that her husband is overworked and distracted and is alarmed that the cause for all of this is impending financial disaster. And she wanted advice on how she could help. She wanted me to talk to you and tell you that she would be happy to help, to take a job if needs be; she was quite concerned. I, of course, assured her in the most general way that she need have no fear; that the Murphy enterprises had never been healthier."

"Goddammit!"

"Levi, what?"

I had never been given to extraneous epithets. I saved them for only the most serious situations, and Daniel knew that. He realized with that expletive more than I probably could have explained to him in many sentences.

I spoke very slowly, keeping my voice low and my outward demeanor calm. "I do not want that fortune-hunting bitch apprised in any way of our business situation."

Daniel sat for a long moment before he spoke, and then he said quite coolly, "Levi, I don't know what's stuck in your craw, but I think you do that lady a disservice. She is quite lovely and warm and concerned."

"You have no business talking to her about my fortune," I repeated.

Daniel bristled. "I did not speak of your fortune but in the most general way, and I have never known you before to be paranoid and suspicious. That gentle lady does not deserve it!"

"The woman is a parasite," I said coldly. "Good day, Daniel."

Daniel slammed the door on his way out and I stared hard at that elaborate piece of carpentry as if it held some answer. So. Daniel, too, was smitten. I had underestimated my adversary. She had gone to Daniel knowing that he would relay that information to me. And thus was the gauntlet dropped. She would have it out with me. Well, I had no intention of such a direct approach; it was one that could only work to her advantage. I would play dumb.

But that resolve did not quite last the day, for Lucille met me that evening as I returned home. "Mrs. Conrad was called to her sister's bedside in an emergency and left me to serve dinner. I think I can manage." She smiled.

"Ah. I'm sure you can" was all I said, and all through dinner what little was said was only commonplace. Lucille was quite lovely by candlelight; her cheeks rosy from standing over the stove and the top button of her bodice undone, for she habitually wore her waists too tight. She shot me several quizzical glances and returned smiles to my most ordinary comments.

"Shall we have wine?" she had asked and then produced glasses and decanter before I could respond. I thought her flirting quite transparent, but it was obviously what had turned Daniel's head.

I was equally certain that Mrs. Conrad had been called away by no emergency, but had been sent away. I was interested to see what the evening would bring. I felt a rush of excitement, as one preparing for battle. I had the utmost confidence in my ability to parry any of her thrusts. Her weapons were only the weapons of any female and all too obvious.

"Shall I play for you?" She motioned toward the piano as we sat with coffee in the sitting room. Ah, this was truly antebellum. Play for me, indeed!

"Thank you, I think not. I have plans to retire early. It has been a trying week."

"I went to see Mr. St. Cloud today," she said suddenly.

"Yes. I know. He mentioned it."

"Did he indeed?"

She rose, and though her lips displayed a smile, her eyes did not. She stepped quite close and I rose, standing tall over her.

"You do not like me, Levi. You do not trust me."

"*Like* has nothing to do with it. Trust? No, I do not trust you. You married Levi in order to secure a sound financial advantage. It was a business deal. And sound business is never predicated on trust."

"Business? That seems so crass, doesn't it?" She looked up at me and at the same time lightly touched my sleeve. I could feel that touch, however light, through the several thicknesses of cloth as if she had indeed touched my bare flesh, and I looked down at her and caught her eyes full glance and the resultant tremor set off my internal circuitry as if a switch has been thrown. I did with the greatest difficulty control my voice.

"Bear in mind, Lucille," I said, her hand still lying across my arm, "that as far as I am concerned you do not represent the best interests of my son. I cannot say what will happen. Good night." And I gently lifted her hand from my sleeve and then with uncharacteristic drama I lifted it to my lips, before returning it to its owner with a slight bow. If she would be antebellum, then so, too, would I. I turned my back and, mustering all of my self-control, slowly took the stairs and made my way to my rooms, where I stood beside the open windows and stared out at the fading sunset.

I stood for a long time trying to still the agitation of my body Lust was what it was. Lust that I had thought long dead. It was lust and it was manifesting itself in the throbbing of my temples and the dampness on my forehead and the hollowness in the pit of my stomach; it was, I thought, like no sensation I had ever experienced. Was the intensity so great because it had been so long stilled, or had I simply forgotten what a force the lust of the flesh could exert? The woman was a demon. But she was an uncommonly bright demon. She had but one set of basic weaponry, but she was mightily skilled in the use of those weapons. If I had planned to divide and conquer, she had turned my strategy upon me, with what was, I feared, far more resourcefulness than I possessed. Damn Daniel! If she thought we were destitute, she would fly the coop immediately.

I heard a step behind me. I should have been surprised but I was not, and I turned toward the open door at my back where Lucille stood. I stared at her and remained aloof, though the pounding of my heart and the coursing of the blood through my veins made normal speech all but impossible.

"What do you want?" I articulated slowly and carefully.

She stepped toward me, and I noticed that two more buttons atop her bodice were undone and her hair was falling loosely about her shoulders. I did not need a road map to determine what route she was following. "What do you want?" I said again.

She did not speak until she stood directly in front of me. Glancing down, I could see the flesh of her rounded bosom. I did not dare look higher, for I was suddenly in terror of her eyes, those deep blue-gray eyes, the same kind of eyes that had once before pulled me into that whirlpool of mindless lust.

"I want security and position," she said slowly. "I want it and I am willing to pay for it," she added deliberately.

"A whore has her price," I said.

"Indeed?"

Even as I reached for her, my consciousness was beseeching me to leave, to turn my back upon her and retreat until I was in a more defensible position. But as I touched her, all my defenses collapsed and I pulled her fiercely to me and she came with a willing laugh. I buried my face in her soft neck and all but sobbed aloud. I was completely undone, while I was certain she retained complete and cold self-control. I avoided her eyes for only a moment and then I stared into them, caught in that unfathomable vortex and whirling into sensation completely devoid of reason.

We stood a moment in searching embrace before she settled herself upon the bed.

"Undo my buttons," she whispered languidly. "I am very tired." And she stretched as I struggled to do as I had been bidden, releasing at last her breasts, which because her rib cage was so slender seemed almost pendulous in their fullness, the rosy nipples engorged and pulsing. I would have dawdled there all day, but I was at a stage in my passion that I dared not tarry and I divested myself of my own clothing as she slipped out of her skirt. I took her body to mine and lay back only moments later, my passion spent, my defenses shattered.

Twice more that very night I rose to the occasion and only lightly noted Lucille's pleasurable sighs and her murmured "You are more the man than your son, you know?"

We slept the night away side by side, and in the morning I discovered to my relief that Mrs. Conrad had not yet returned from her

emergency leave, nor did she return until the day before Levi returned from his mission. And then she said nothing of any emergency
but only commented upon the rest she had had as a result of her
vacation.

I had been bested, nor did it occur to me to complain of that fact,
for we lay those several days together—morning, noon and night—
and I tasted pleasures that I had been certain were forever denied me
and discovered capacities I never suspected. For Lucille was no ordinary woman. If she was blunt that she was buying her fortune, she
did not haggle the price and could have bought a man's soul for the
goods she offered.

"I have been poor, Levi. I will not be poor again. Ever! But all I
have to barter is all that any woman has: it is what is between my legs.
But I will give as good as I get."

In my rashness I gave no thought to what the future would bring,
what I would do when Levi returned. It was enough then that my
passion be sated, and in truth, it seemed all but impossible that it
would be. The years of self-control and self-denial had perhaps been
cause for that accumulation of desire. I did not know. I only knew that
with that rupture my ghosts had flown; the weight I struggled with
those many years had been lifted and the tension from which my
sleepless body suffered was gone; I slept at last.

But my rest was short-lived, for Levi did return. He returned and
his wife went to him, without a backward glance. If Lucille regarded
me at all, it was with only a cursory glance, a fugitive smile that
seemed neither to promise nor to remember; I felt both used and
defeated, overcome by feminine wantonness and masculine lust.

With Levi's return, my ghosts came back, slowly, one by one. The
first was Obediah, ridiculing, laughing. "The last laugh? Indeed, the
last laugh?" he seemed to say. "And can I be vilified by such as you?
For you are me. Lust and treachery. You have betrayed your brother
and you have deceived your brother's son. A woman is only a woman,
but you have made cuckold of those most dear. And you count me
despicable? Lecher. Fornicator. Adulterer."

Louisa One, that obese old Pennsylvania Dutch woman, cried
from my subconscious, "Levi, Levi, you have already a dark side, a
dark side." And those two dark ghosts. Ah. "You're turned your back
on humanity, Levi Murphy. It's a greater evil than any other, Levi
Murphy."

In the darkness of my rooms I saw them with my mind's eyes and heard them with my inner ear and I agonized and cried out. "I have suffered; I have suffered. Leave me in peace." I stood by the open windows and stared down at the boulder below. And through one entire night I paced past those windows, the blood pounding at my temples marking time for me, the cold sweat on my brow the single manifestation of the terror I felt. There would be no peace for me, even in death, for I owed too many debts; I would be damned if I lived and damned if I died. At last, with the first light of morning when the birds begin to wake and communicate, that hour when the dark shadows regain shape and lose their terrors, I felt the old control begin to reassert itself.

My evil was no greater, then than it has ever been. It had only been reinforced. My mission still stood: to best the Old Bastard in the end. And to that I added yet one more goal. As I had determined a way to best the Old Bastard through eternity, so would I best that wanton bitch, Lucille, for she and he were cut from the same lecherous cloth. My spirit was far from broken and she would know my vengeance. As the light slowly spread from the east, dispatching my shadows to whatever nether land they had come from, I knew that, as events had led me to redress from Obediah, so they would also lead me to redress from Lucille. For she represented that same evil that he did, and both would be exorcised.

"Father?" said Levi, coming unannounced into my office a few mornings later.

"Eh?"

"I've interrupted you. Forgive me."

"No, no. All right, all right. Just wrestling with a problem."

"You ought to take a rest, Father," said Levi, putting some papers before me on the desk. "I truly worry about you. You look so tired and distraught. Lucille and I are very concerned for your health."

"Indeed? Well, you need not be. My more pressing problems are on the way to being solved. I believe I shall rest easier from now on."

"Ah yes," said Levi, smiling. "It is good to know our straits are finally loosening."

I said nothing. I had in no way intimated to Levi that our financial situation was improved. He had, I'm sure, got that information from Lucille, possibly then checking it out himself. That ploy was dead. But there would be others. I would best Lucille as I would best Obediah. I was certain of that.

But Lucille was not yet through with me. I continued, it seemed, to underestimate the woman; for the girl child Lucille gave birth to followed near to ten months that period when Levi had been away in Memphis and could have been fathered by either of us.

By the time I realized that Lucille was with child, it was too late to do anything about it. Lucille and Levi took their belated honeymoon, and when they returned, her condition was obvious to all. Levi claimed that Lucille had urged him to keep it secret, lest she miscarry as she had on some previous occasions and so disappoint us all. I do not know that there would have been anything I could have done. I did know an obliging surgeon who could have undone the damage and I toyed with the notion of offering Lucille a sizable fortune to do that very thing, but it was by then too late. It is possible also that I might even have killed the woman in my first fury had I had the chance. I cannot say. I only know that once more in my life I was undone by a woman birthing a child.

When I accosted Lucille and demanded to know which of us had fathered the child, she shrugged, and the only expression from those eyes, which were then the color of a becalmed sea, was mockery. She shrugged again. "Who knows? Maybe neither."

"Bitch!"

"Bitch? Yes. I've never denied it. But, Levi, I have been willing to pay the price. Anyway, you are not exactly without blame. But I will be a good wife to Lee. On my own terms. I will be a member of society, a fine lady, beloved of my husband, admired by all others. I will not live in this gloomy house, alone and aloof from society, waiting for you to die. We will be a happy little family and we will open up our house and our hearts to the outside world. That's all I want. In return I will be a docile and loving wife and mother. Simple!"

"You are the intruder, Lucille. You have no right to be here. None!"

"Oh, but I have. I am irrevocably tied to this family now," and she patted her extended abdomen. I turned and left her with no further comment.

I have suffered from sleeplessness often enough in my lifetime to realize that it is possible to get by on very little sleep; how little, however, I was only just discovering, for in the following weeks it seemed almost that sleep had deserted me entirely. I prowled my darkened rooms and strode through the deserted neighborhoods for long, dark hours, my soul in turmoil, a seething anger almost always caught in my throat, bitter as gall.

In the suffocating darkness of my rooms, my demons attacked and there were moments when reason seemed to leave me completely. This woman was surely sent from the hell where Obediah dwelled to torment me. Even in death he taunted and teased. Lucille and Obediah. They were one and the same. He she, she he. She was Obediah returned in that tormenting guise. She was the devil, he was the devil. Together they tormented me. All my ghosts, all together, were reincarnate in this one demon woman and the demon child she would produce. Incest out of incest. She would reproduce me; she would reproduce Obediah. Obediah would roam free, lusting and fornicating once more. It was the plot. I had uncovered the plot to loose him once more on the world.

Those were my nightmares, nightmares, however, of a sleepless mind. With the coming of the day, such irrationalities generally faded, those dark spirits working their villainies mainly during the blackest hours of the night. Still, the sleeplessness took its toll and there were moments even in the brightest hours of the day that I feared for my reason, for my very sanity. And it was with a curious kind of relief that I greeted the birth of the girl baby, a relief immediately shaken when Levi announced that they would name the baby Elizabeth.

"For my mother," said Levi. "It was Lucille's choice. I am very pleased with it."

It was almost as if this woman were privy to my innermost thoughts, as if she had read and studied my very psyche. I struggled to believe that it was not deliberate, that she had not been sent to gouge at ill-healed wounds.

"It is a lovely name" was, however, all that I said.

Then, as quickly as it had departed, my reason returned. In a single instant, I was able to view with clarity my circumstances and I understood. I knew the enemy: Lucille, Levi, the baby Elizabeth. They were the enemy; they plotted my death. They wanted me gone, so that they would be free to misuse my fortune and to extend the abominable line of Obediah across the infinity of eternity.

In understanding there is power. The confusion of my mind cleared; I was once again able to sleep. Understanding was my defense. The three of them—with Obediah directing—were no threat to me. I realized that none could do me harm, though they had directive from hell, so long as I had knowledge of their perfidy, and I passed my days in something like contentment.

Daniel came to me, then, in the fall of the year and announced with little preamble his intention to marry.

"Ah, Daniel, my friend. I am surprised, for you've certainly taken your time in this matter, but I offer you my sincerest congratulations."

"Thank you, Levi. I guess it has at last come to me that if I intend to leave something of myself behind, I had best get at it. I would not," he said as if in afterthought, "die without issue."

And so it was that Daniel took with little ceremony Thelma Henderson to be his bride, she being the elder daughter of his long-time housekeeper, some years beyond the normal marrying age, but still quite younger than Daniel himself. She was a placid and pleasant sort, neither large nor small, dark nor fair. Daniel had got himself the kind of wife that a middle-aged man might expect to have, even had he married young. And in short order Thelma produced a son, whom she named David. Thus was that household established and Daniel's claim to continuity assured, and that with what seemed almost negligible effort.

In the meantime, Elizabeth, that child of hell, who would never be able to name a father with any surety, had progressed, as children do, from all-fours to two feet and staggered happily around the house and garden greedily acquisitive of information and sensation, adorable as toddlers are adorable, nothing about her to suggest the sinister.

I searched that small countenance daily for some recognition: something of Daniel or of Betty Butler to confirm her ancestry. But the child confounded me by developing singularly her mother's features. All I saw in her was Lucille.

Try as I might to stand aloof from the baby lest she snare me with deadly charm, I could hardly do so, for she was as warm, loving and happy a child as ever I had seen and lifted the gloom of our mansion with happy yelps of excitement and a cheery smile.

Despite her promise to be a docile wife and a loving mother, Lucille proved to be neither. With the birth of the child, she seemed to withdraw into herself, observing, when she bothered, the rest of us with a sort of bemused smile, and except for occasional bursts of affection, she distanced herself even from the baby, hiring a nurse to do not only those less pleasant chores of motherhood, but also those other maternal activities that most any mother would have retained for herself. Nor did it seem to bother Elizabeth, so absorbed was that surprisingly wise child in the world around her.

I think that I was not particularly surprised the day Lucille presented herself to me at my office. She was got out in traveling clothes and announced that she was leaving.

"Oh," I responded, "and for how long?"

"I am going for good, Levi. I think you know that. I am divorcing Lee. I have found something better. I have never lied to you, Levi. I will better myself in the only way I have. I have found some oil money in Texas that is more attractive than the department store money in Oklahoma, and the man with that fortune is also possessed of some charm and warmth and there is precious little of either in your house."

"What about your baby?"

"I am not taking her."

"Not?"

"Perhaps I'll return for her; but right now she would be an encumbrance. My intended does not want my child, though he wants me. I'll leave her for you and Lee to fight over." After a pause she smiled. "You think I'm callous, don't you. Lacking in maternal love? Perhaps. There are times and situations, I think, when self-preservation, not maternal love, is the greatest instinct. My intentions, believe it or not, were ultimately honorable. But had you twice the fortune that you have, I do not think I could tolerate this existence any longer."

With that, Lucille departed our lives and with her Booth Copeland, for it was his oil money that had lured her away. Though the ensuing scandal was not so great as one might have imagined—Mrs. Copeland, I was told, hardly glancing away from her oriental rugs—I was more scandalized than I might have expected. But I should not have been surprised. Booth and Lucille were in many respects remarkably similar.

Had it not been for that small girl, I am not sure that Levi would have survived. As for myself, I felt not so much despondent as deflated, a peculiar sensation that left me feeling as if something important had not been completed.

Lucille came back into our lives briefly a few years later. She came for Elizabeth and went directly to Levi, bypassing me completely. The news of her confrontation with Levi came to me indirectly by way of Mrs. Conrad and Erica Parsons, who was nurse and governess to Elizabeth. The session had apparently been stormy, Levi rising to the occasion and ordering her out. She demanded her child and he had refused even to let them meet.

"You are not a part of our lives," he had shouted, all of this quite uncharacteristic of the placid Levi; "you withdrew from our lives of your own volition. You shall not have this child and no court of law would uphold your right to her."

The argument lasted for some time, though the good ladies could not apprise me of any more of the dialogue, as the voices, which had been raised, became too quiet for them to hear, though I am certain they gave it a good try.

In the long run I took but little triumph from that confrontation, for whatever Lucille told Levi, and I could guess with some accuracy what it was, his manner changed with that visit and he became quite cold and distant and disappeared into his rooms for several days before he emerged haggard and ashen.

Some weeks later I received formal notice from a set of attorneys that I was not familiar with that Levi Murphy II was no more, that he had had his name officially changed to Lee. The reason behind that strange act I could only guess, for he never told me and his demeanor remained calm, detached and distant.

The pain that all of this brought me was unaccountable. I had thought that I understood, that I controlled the spirits from the past, yet each time I felt that I had bested them they came again in a new guise. In that place where hatred toward the vixen Lucille ought to have been, there was nothing, only a kind of numbness, an overwhelming absence, as overwhelming as great pain might have been.

For the first time in many years, I at last sought refuge beneath the great laurel tree, sitting in the late hours upon that rough and cool boulder, beneath which rested my ghosts. For this was where the remains of my beloved wife lay, where Dewey Lane with his helpers had quietly placed her, that garrulous artisan strangely still as if he at last understood my need. And with her rested the souls of my three Louisas, for I had destroyed their stones so that they could flee, and left that great white monument standing in the old cemetery, imprisoning, I hoped forever, the soul of Obediah, the Bastard.

A strange peace filled my soul. I sat upon that rock and felt the anguish drain from me, and suddenly benign spirits spoke to me.

Levi, the son of Louisa, the mad woman, and Mendel, the peddler, that wanderer of a wandering race, there is only one God and He is Jehovah, He

Who will judge, not your sins and transgression, but only the depth of your evil, your depravity. There is only one God and He is just and terrible.

And that admonition, strangely, comforted me, almost as if the other shoe had dropped. I would wait out eternity for my judgment. I felt a deep kinship for that distant peddler, who had planted his seed and gone on, trailing down through the ages, Mendel the Jew.

Yet at other times in my own rooms high above that meandering river I sank again into despair, for it was not Mendel the Jew who had fathered me, but my own grandfather, and yea, too, my own great-grandfather. Where others had three, I had but one ancestor. The incestuous seed of incestuous seed, I would be odious to all gods, denied peace in death, consigned to the limbo reserved for those abhorrent in the eyes of nature. And Obediah, who begat me, my mentor, my guide through eons of restless wandering.

And so I was torn, pulled, alternately cajoled and threatened by my spirits. Indeed, I could no more name my own father than the baby Elizabeth could name hers.

And I knew myself at last to be going mad, that in that madness lay my only hope of peace. The more I pondered that thought and the more I looked forward to that consummation, the more reasonable it seemed. I had been so long in understanding. I should have realized long ago that in this life only the mad survive and rationality is the greatest transgression.

This was what my ghosts had been trying to tell me, why they had been hounding me. I was at once the son of Mendel the Jew and of Obediah the lecher. I must go mad. Madness was my heritage.

I had but one thing to do, no, two things to do, before I surrendered at last to that mindless peace. I would write my own history and so leave behind what could only be a wretched but fascinating tale, begin again that journal I had, perhaps wisely, destroyed so many years ago before I understood. And I must confess to Daniel. It was the only debt in need of discharging.

And so one evening, with that in mind, I placed a telephone call to Daniel.

"Daniel, my friend, you must come to me at once. For I have something of great importance to confess to you. It will not wait."

With that, I hung up the receiver and the sense of deflation that had been with me since Lucille's departure, the sense that something had been left undone, departed me and I felt infinitely rested.

FIFTEEN

DANIEL'S LETTER

October 8, 1938

Dear Levi,

I suppose it has to do with a lifetime of lawyering that I am only able to summon up ideas and arguments after long delay—postponements, if you like—and then only after I have researched them, rewritten them, revised them and subheaded each in its turn. All of this is by way of explanation for the delay in reacting to your startling revelations of several days ago. Had I been a trial lawyer, I might have been able to have responded to you on the spot, as you seemed to think was warranted. But alas, I am only a corporation lawyer, that dull, slow, stodgy arm of the legal profession that can never accomplish even the simplest task in short order, much less think on its feet.

But then you were hardly realistic. You demanded immediate investigation, confession, trial and verdict. But this is a lifetime we're considering, isn't it, Levi, what is getting to be a rather lengthy lifetime, or lifetimes, if you will? Lifetimes should not be summarily dealt with.

You are probably right; I am a shallow sort (was it to excuse yourself or blame me that I was accused of shallowness?), though to be greeted at the door with such an accusation was disconcerting, at the least. However, until I was so accused, I had not really thought of myself as shallow; but upon serious consideration, I must plead guilty to that indictment.

There have been few incidents in my lifetime that have motivated me to look much beyond the stack of lawbooks at my elbow; and, as you are possibly already aware, despite their ponderance and detail, there is probably nothing more shallow than lawbooks, for they are soulless things. Morality, good and evil, these are the considerations of philosophers, not the province of legal libraries. Lawbooks tell us only what we can and cannot do; they have no interest in why we can or cannot do a given thing. They do not care that God or man forbids an act; only that the courts forbid it, and that prohibition itself is limited by certain restrictions. God might say THOU SHALT NOT KILL, but Blackstone says THOU SHALT NOT KILL, except under certain contingencies and constraints, *vis-à-vis*, being under attack or under the influence of alcohol or temporarily out of your mind or accidentally or any combination of the above, a merciless lack of depth.

Indeed, Levi, I plead guilty, guilty of shallowness under the law, a moral flaw that may merit me in the hereafter a cursory tongue-lashing and perhaps a stay on that rung of purgatory reserved for the shallow; but I shall not be alone. For there are many of us who, like leggy water bugs, have only skimmed the surface.

Perhaps. But I shall return to that idea.

I left your house the other night quite shaken. Indeed, anyone, I think, would have been shaken, if not by your revelations, then by the maniacal presence you presented, padding around wild-eyed, wearing Old Louisa's down comforter, a moldy and disintegrating hair shirt, spouting pronouncements and anathemas like an Old Testament prophet.

My immediate reaction, once I had reached home and anesthetized my consciousness with a large glass of scotch whiskey, was that you were in fact quite insane, that that lifelong obsession with the Old Bastard had at last unloosed you at the hinges. And I must admit it is an appealing diagnosis, for it absolves me of any responsibility for reacting to that obsession and to the evils that you confessed. I would simply like to think, Levi, that you are crazy, dotty as a dodo.

But I fear that is not entirely the case, even though for years you have exhibited a kind of lopsided paranoia. You may yet go off the deep end, but you have not yet done so.

I know what you want of me, Levi. You want to be condemned, castigated, detested. I recognize that need; but alas, I am not able to help you. Perhaps because of the afore-mentioned shallowness, or perhaps simply because the statute of limitations has run out.

I cannot think of young Levi as my son, my flesh and blood, the result of my passion for his mother. It has been too many years and he is a separate adult entity. I have given him nothing, except—as you claim—life. In all matters of parenthood, he is yours, possession being, I suppose, nine points of the law.

My consciousness can absorb the facts of his birth, but it is only an intellectual matter. A lifetime of ignorance cannot be made up in a moment, or possibly ever. I have a son who is my son both in fact and spirit. Levi I leave to you.

I think perhaps that I have always suspected your perfidy in this matter; or if not that, at least that somehow in a panic that lovely young woman, finding herself with child, turned to you for help. I know that I recall dimly certain irrational thoughts and plans when first I realized that I had lost my prize. But that was too long ago. Time has dimmed not only those memories, but the memory of that girl herself. She has been dead for a long time, Levi, and I am comfortable in the worn-slipperedness of my existence. I will not stir from it.

I did love her, Levi. I did feel robbed and bereft both with your marriage and with her passing. Yet had I married her myself, she still would have produced that child and she still would have died and I still would have been bereft. In addition, I would have borne a lifetime of guilt, irrational guilt, to be sure, but guilt nonetheless. You have, in a manner of speaking, shouldered that guilt for me, and perhaps I should thank you for it.

Your sins, Levi, real or imagined, are not so calamitous as you would believe. I do not find the great evils about which you ranted. I do not see Jehovah, the Terrible, sitting in judgment upon you, damning you to endless eternities of torment. I see perhaps a lesser god or two prodding you a bit for your sins of the flesh, demanding a token atonement. Your drama reads like popular tragicomedy—Harold Bell Wright out of Edgar Allan Poe.

If you subscribe to the theory that all is fair in love, well then, there is little that I can accuse you of; for as I came in and took the prize from you, so you retaliated, whatever your motive, which gibberish about the end of the line of Obediah I find to be poor tragedy. Ah, Levi, those who have done far worse that you with no pang of conscience are many and many.

"Denounce me! Denounce me!" you cried.

Alas, Levi, there is little to denounce you for. We are two old men growing older. There is little future and no past. I will not look back.

I must confess, Levi, there is always the possibility that, in deny-ing you, I am withholding that absolution which, though you deny its existence, you so obviously court, a penance for your overriding guilt. If your guilt does not exist, ergo you cannot be absolved of it. You see, Levi, I am ever the lawyer, never running out of contingencies, allow-ing the letter of the law to do my dirty work for me.

However, I think not. I think that I am only too old and too weary to let much of this seep past my conscious understanding. Am I being shallow? Perhaps.

Consider your sins toward me absolved. I bear no grudge.

Only think on this: whatever gods there are will not sit in judg-ment, Levi. We more likely will be ignored. For we have, you and I, destroyed our gods, we have leeched them as we have leeched our own humanity; we have isolated ourselves from the race of man, and its gods owe us no allegiance. I have held the belief for a long time that we create our own gods and they depend on us for survival, just as the race itself depends on us for survival. Eternity is a chain, a continuum that we are already a part of, and you and I have been guilty of consciously trying to sunder that chain, an act abhorrent to the natu-ral order of things.

If that is too dramatic, too metaphoric, too precious, let us attack it differently. Let us start with Obediah, that Old Bastard of memory. Ah, Levi, the Obediah of your memory never did exist. I have never believed in history, Levi, nor trusted to memory, for, if you will allow me an aphorism, I am suspicious that history lies and memory is an ill biographer.

But however much I may mistrust memory, I still am certain that mine is more reliable than yours. The memory I have of our ancestor is fond; the memory you have is loathsome. It is hard for me to understand how two people growing up in the same environment could come away with such divergent views.

I give you that the Old Bastard (and that appellation I apply fondly) was not a moral man; but I will not grant that he was therefore immoral. He was neither. Perhaps "amoral" is the word, but I think not, for that implies a kind of evil, and evil he was not. Obediah was not a giver as history has its givers, nor was he a taker as history has its takers. I think that he was a carrier, a spreader—a carrier of life, of continuity, of humanity.

Like the dog that services the bitch in heat, because that is in the natural order of things, Obediah is not to be condemned. He was not evil, for that requires more depth than he possessed, as does great good, those being to my mind two sides of the same coin. Obediah was more like the wall against which others bounce a ball, he returning it only as it was sent. Or he was the surface of a still and shiny pool of water, reflecting what was presented him.

He was, most important, a necessary link in that chain of human continuity that ensures the race not only its existence, but also its vitality. He was that vitality.

It is, I think, a matter of uncluttered humanity.

It occurs to me, Levi (this is something of an aside), that this particular tribe in the race of man, this twentieth-century enlightened tribe, went a long way toward abandoning that vitality when it removed its excretory activities from outdoors to indoors. I do not intend to be crude; it is only an observation. But as children, didn't we piss blithely on trees and shit behind them? And did we not, the three of us, you and I and the Old Bastard, with much giggling and playfulness, standing at angles to each other, cross our streams, aiming for a particular pattern or spot, all three caught up in the sheer play of it?

Ah, Levi, I recall the smells of the wooded air, the heavy summertime smells, the crisp wintertime smells. They wave over me sometimes, untainted by the smells of burning petroleum products or the exhaust of many automobiles. When we ran among the trees and across the fields, Obediah often led, scampering like a colt though he was already a graybeard. We flew with boys' feet across the fields and woods and hills of childhood, until you and I at last left it behind, our steps slowed, our strides purposeful, while our ancestor continued to dart through an endless youth. I am not sure but that he does not do it yet, that ghost of ours, darting through some uncharted netherworld, being seduced by maiden spirits, who would infect their race with that vitality.

And did I say "our" ancestor? Indeed, Levi, at the risk of distressing you further, I think that it is time that we cast off that fiction that we have lived under these many years, you and I. And at the further risk of falling into a childish you-are-not-I-am-too singsong, I will simply bluntly tell you that while I seriously doubt that you are the son of Obediah, "incestuous issue of incestuous issue," I am fairly certain—and I think so, too, are you—that I am the bastard son of Obediah. This is a certainty that I have lived with since I was old enough to hold such thoughts. Nor is that certainty without foundation, the product of wildly circumstantial evidence, as is the claim that you make.

I have but few memories of my early childhood, of that period before I came and usurped your throne, for usurp it I did. Unintentionally, perhaps. For when I came, was deposited so unceremoniously on your doorstep by that vaguely remembered mother, I knew you to be the prince of the household, exacting homage from all those doting adults, though you were quite a small fry. You understood your power and wielded it effectively. And instinctively, as children do, I understood that this was your territory and made no attempt to dethrone you.

It was amazing enough that Obediah immediately made room for me on that throne, but that Old Louisa did, too, has always been a source of wonder, for I cannot recall that I was by any standards exceptional, being at once gangling and shy and unhappy.

My earliest memories are of mistreatment at the hands of my mother's husband, whom I probably thought to be my father. For that reason, I suppose, I was sent to live with my mother's relatives, nor did my mother surface again until I was a quite big boy and then only long enough to tell me that it was time that I went to my father's people, for they were well off and could care for me as she could not. I only recall then that she held me close and there were tears in her eyes and I knew that she loved me.

We came then to Louisa and Obediah's house, and there I recall vividly standing aside as my mother spoke with Obediah and then with Louisa and Obediah and finally as she followed Louisa One into the house, a house which I thought the most fantastic that was possible. And strangely, though you stood and eyed me as an interloper and I felt the shyness and awkwardness of one, it was Obediah who studied me and patted me and offered me candy—candy that I suppose he kept for you—and then he paced, obviously nervous, outside the door where Louisa and my mother had disappeared, coming back abruptly to pet me some more. I think you must have hated me then, and him, and were I Freudian I might suggest that at that moment was sown the seed of the contempt and hatred that you would forever bear Obediah, like a jealous wife, love and hate.

When the two women reappeared, they solemnly hugged and then my mother came to me and told me that I would stay and that she would come for me one day, if ever she could.

Well, obviously she never made it, nor have I any idea who she might have been. I wanted to ask, but I was afraid by the time I was grown, I was afraid to know, for fear perhaps that I might once more be rejected.

I think that I have always known that I was the son of Obediah, an illegitimate wanderer. That Louisa One would not only take me in, but take me in with warmth and love, I can only ascribe to her near-idolatry of her husband and her anxiety—perhaps that's not the word—her need, to let him have his way, to see him happy. As for Louisa Two, she was as kind to me as her nature allowed, for she was not by nature a kindly sort. At any rate, I was at home and never felt the stranger, except with you.

And eventually we got on, partly because I deferred to you—you have always intimidated me, Levi, and from the beginning I always deferred to you—and partly because you were a boy and, boylike, you needed a friend, and so we, like siblings, played and fought and played again. But there was always a dark side to your humor, Levi. It was often remarked upon, your sudden bursts of temper, followed by sullenness and silence; your insistence on always having your way; your solitary times when no one could reach you.

It was at such times that Obediah remarked on your ancestry. "That damn Mendel, that peddler; it's the race. The son of the wandering race and the son of a mad woman, what can ye 'spect?" Louisa One would only murmur about your "dark side," and Two usually mumbled only that you were spoiled, which in truth you were and she was probably closer to the truth than anyone.

I do not know the story of Mendel the Peddler, but I know there was one—at least a story, if not a peddler. And as for your incestuous grandfather, ah, Levi. The entire race is incestuous. We are all of us the products of eons of inbreeding. Good or bad, I don't know. I only know that humanity interweaves and overlaps and the total variety of genes over billions of human beings is probably remarkably small. We are all cousins twice and thrice and multiple times over and over. It is what has kept us as we are, hindered us or perhaps kept us from deteriorating. I am no geneticist, and my thought is more metaphorical than scientific, I suppose. But a little incest does not alarm me, my old friend.

But as for your being the direct issue of Obediah and his own daughter—oh, shades of ancient myth—I see no tangible thread of evidence to support such a theory. I have examined your testimony with a trained eye and find it lacking in anything even closely resembling fact. Your accusation, I must conclude, is only wishful thinking.

Yes, "wishful thinking." I am certain that you are as convinced as I, that I am likely the bastard's bastard, while you are only his grandson. It is rivalry of the rankest sort that you have determined that you will be the son of Obediah, like it or not.

And, Levi, I do understand that this is not a legal claim, rather, jealousy as old as Cain.

Now, I am not sure what you are thinking. It is not clear to me or, I think, to you whether you are claiming Obediah for a parent or Mendel the peddler, or both. From your ravings of the other evening, I fear that you are not yourself certain of that.

But before you lose your grip entirely, I can only advise that you simply accept your own bastardy for the mystery that it is and make some attempt to come to terms with your humanity. For if I fault you for anything, it is for that lack of involvement in the human process that I have blindly followed after you. We both have missed life. I do not exactly propose the life of Obediah, only his human vitality. We have been as barren soil, Levi, denying our place in the human chain. I look back on a life bereft of meaning, and so, too, do you, and young Levi shows little promise.

You always intimidated me. You seemed so certain of your course. I felt, I think, more inclined toward Obediah, but he was a man of a different time—perhaps a better time, perhaps not. I followed your lead out of blind duty, I suppose, duty and an unhappy disinclination to do anything but stay on the path of least resistance.

Life is for the living, Levi. The ghosts touch us only from memory, not from fact. If you do not live your life, Levi, it is no one's fault but your own, ghosts or not.

I have written and rewritten this letter many times. I have tried to cover everything as rationally as the subject allows. I went so far, even, as to list your purported ghosts and to fit them in. And it is Joab and Inez, those two murdered darkies, who speak the loudest and who urge you to join with the living and plead with you not to turn your back on life. Those large black presences, more than any others, cry, "*Life!*" as vividly, as vitally, as ever did the Old Bastard.

We are all of us bridges from the past to the future. In that only is there meaning.

I remain your friend.

As ever,
Daniel St. Cloud

SIXTEEN

LOUISA LOSES HER RELIGION

*L*ouisa One, having made her pact with the Lord, went at her newfound religion with a fervor that startled everyone, possibly even the Lord Himself. Certainly Pastor Ellwood, that kindly, albeit casual, tender of the flock, was startled at the vehemence with which Mistress Murphy all at once attacked her faith, for that good man, a foot soldier in the Army ot the Lord, although not one enthusiastic about even long marches, much less spirited battle, found that goodwife's sudden stern attention to religious detail unsettling.

She in turn discovered that though for nearly seventy years she had been satisfied with first the irregular attendence upon the circuit rider and then the monthly ritual of Pastor Ellwood's placid services, all at once her agreement with the Almighty behooved her to more fervor than could be afforded even in weekly trips to Pastor Ellwood's congregation. Louisa One needed more religion than she was getting, and in pursuance of that she removed her membership from Pastor Ellwood's congregation, to Pastor Ellwood's considerable relief, as her continual clamor for spiritual urgency had increasingly discomfited that man of the cloth.

Louisa was anxious to make up for a lifetime of spiritual neglect, lest she fall by the wayside without having secured her own hereafter. Nancy Hawkins, her dear old friend, having recently passed to her reward, a victim of the exigencies of age, Louisa One was faced with the realization that she probably would not live forever, though it was her avowed intent to outlive Obediah's randy ways, and there were moments when she thought that, to do that, she might very well have to wait out eternity.

Spiritual urgency spurring her on, Louisa finally removed her church affiliation from Pastor Ellwood's Presbytery to a rather non-denominational group that not only preached sound hellfire-and-damnation doctrine and carefully spelled out right and wrong, but also threw in salvation, healing, signs, wonders and miracles. They met three times weekly and twice on Sunday.

Louisa was welcomed eagerly into that group, for though she shouted "Amen" and "Praise" as loudly as the male membership and contrary to the congregation's belief that women and children should be voiceless during sermons (including crying babies and fidgety toddlers), she tithed liberally enough that the elders of the group could not find it in their hearts to dampen her obvious religious enthusiasm.

Try as she might, however, Louisa could not convince the rest of her family to follow her example. They preferred the comfort of Pastor Ellwood's services, though Obediah had on occasion accompanied Louisa, his wife, to her newfound spiritual home, only to be put off by the considerable shouting and crying and speaking in tongues. Louisa, recognizing her limitations, did not attempt to speak in tongues, for she had not the gift of language, as Obediah had. She was, however, quite put out with him because he would not use those considerable gifts in the speaking in tongues, for she knew that he would outshine all others, possibly even the Apostles themselves. But Obediah demurred.

"It don't make sense," he murmured. "I don't make no sense to stand up and jabber. You tell me what to say an' I'll say it," he quite reasonably added.

Louisa One was disgusted. "I cannot tell ye vat to said. It's got to come from yer own soul."

"Well, I dunno what to say." And they left it at that. Obediah ceased going with her to her services altogether and took what spiritual nourishment he got from Pastor Ellwood's more meager table.

Louisa Two was put out and chagrined at her mother's sudden religious fervor, which she viewed as tasteless and crude. The God she knew, she was certain, would not even allow such to come to the back door for handouts, and she said as much.

"I'll see you in hell, den," her mother announced, not explaining how that might be accomplished, it being expected that she would herself spend eternity elsewhere.

"She'll get over it," said Charlie Varner, who, along with Obediah and his children, suffered considerably by the way of hunger pangs on those Sundays that they all waited out Louisa One's now lengthy pre-dinner supplications to the Lord.

"An', please it, Lord," added Charlie under his breath during such supplications, "that we do not all starve clean to death this day. Amen."

But, contrary to her family's expectations, Louisa One remained firm in her faith, outzealoting what was an unusually zealous congregation, until even the minister to this group deferred to her, for he began to think her marked by the Lord Himself.

All in all, it was a most uncomfortable time for Obediah Jonah Micah Murphy. He did not have anything against religion in its place, but as far as he was concerned, its place was every fourth Sunday for a duration of not more than ninety minutes.

On the first evening that the peddler Mendel appeared at Louisa One's kitchen door, she was on her way to services. She looked quickly over the contents of his cart of wares and bade him return the next day, and she left in the carriage driven by her colored boy. Encouraged by Louisa Two, Mendel the peddler stayed for a time while she examined the contents of his wagon and Louisa Three, grown fetching as a gossamer web and as fragile, came and stood silently staring at the bins of buttons he displayed, and she smiled her faraway smile. Mendel the Jew stared at her in admiration, it finally dawning upon him reluctantly that her delicate beauty and distant expression hid a tragically damaged mind, and Mendel sighed. It was a sad and lonely sound.

The next day Mendel returned with his goods and Louisa One studied them in a businesslike fashion, and though most of what he displayed could be bought from the stores in town, she was intrigued that they should be brought to her; besides, Mendel sharpened knives and scissors and blades of all kinds and, given time, fashioned shoes, for he was a skilled young man.

Obediah came and stood by the wagon as Louisa One shopped and bargained and dickered with the young Jew. Obediah was fascinated with the young man's voice as he negotiated, gently and soothingly, his accent similar to Louisa One's, yet softer and more appealing; but his expression, like Louisa Three's, was distant and vaguely sad. All told, he was, however, persuasive, so much so that in the end he had not only contracted with Louisa One to sharpen every blade in her house and to fashion her a pair of boots that he guaranteed to be a comfort to her aging and bunion-burdened feet, but also had sold a quantity of items to her and to Louisa Two. To Three he offered a small collection of delicate buttons, which in obvious delight she accepted and rattled in her hand and smiled her distant smile. Again the lonely Jew sighed at the thought that one so lovely could be so damaged and thought to himself—not for the first time—that he truly did not understand the ways of the Lord. And again—not for the first time—he excused himself to the Lord for such thoughts.

Mendel encamped down the stream a ways from Louisa's house, declining the offer of the cabin, now empty, but once inhabited by the widow St. Cloud; for Mendel understood that any show of permanence was an invitation to trouble. He was headed West, he said, far West, where there were few merchants and enough business that his peddler's cart would not be resented by established merchants, who tolerated such as Mendel only if they kept moving.

But it took several days for Mendel to fashion the boots, and by the time he had done so to Louisa's great satisfaction, both Obediah and Louisa Two had commissioned boots and likewise Two decided that Three should have a fine pair of winter boots. So Mendel the peddler was several weeks encamped by Louisa's stream and only Colonel Murphy's reputation as a fierce fighting man and Louisa One's reputation, hardly lesser, as being strong of both tongue and arm kept the increasingly restive merchants in place.

And in truth, Louisa One would have kept the gentle Jew on her payroll forever if she could have, for his presence seemed to bring an unexpected measure of calm to her household. Even Two's shrillness was stilled and Three sat quietly by the hour watching the young man's busy and facile hands, putting together and stitching the heavy leather. But it was Obediah who spent much time visiting and talking with the peddler. For Mendel, though young in years, was old in experience and he had already walked across half the European continent and visited great cities before ever he came to America and landed in New York City and had at that time walked halfway across the North American continent.

"And have ye seen a world's fair?" asked Obediah, who never had but who had heard of such.

"I know not of world fairs, but I have been to fairs, many, many fairs, again and again. Little fairs and big, some enormous fairs," said Mendel the Jew. "I go to fairs. I have no trouble, you see, at fairs." And he described the fairs for Obediah as his fingers molded at a shoe. He told of country fairs and of small-town fairs and big-city fairs. He described the dances and the noise and the pretty girls and he sang the songs, for he had a mellow voice and a good ear. And when Mendel the Jew sang, whether softly and slowly or quickly and loudly, Obediah Jonah Micah Murphy joined him, whistling softly or chirping gaily as the measure called for, and the two men together made a pleasant and harmonious sound. Obediah grew fond of the gentle Jew, so much so that when the time came for Mendel to go and when he had packed up his tools and his wares and had shaken every hand and even placed a soft kiss upon Three's pale cheek and had at last departed, the pots and pans and tools of his trade making a tune in rhythm to the leisurely step of the old horse, Obediah felt a hollow of loneliness beneath his rib cage.

"Perhaps I will see you at a fair sometime, I hope," Obediah called out after the peddler. "Perhaps, for I go to many fairs."

But the peddler only waved and passed around a curve in the road and so was lost to sight.

A few days after the departure of Mendel the peddler, Louisa One joined the rest of her congregation in revival services that featured the Reverend J. T. Carney, Minister of the Gospel, Layer on of Hands and Purveyor of the Healing Powers of the Almighty. The crowd that gathered for his services was eager to witness this man's gift, for he represented to them the signs, wonders and miracles that they espoused.

And indeed the Reverend Carney did take his ministrations seriously, witnessing himself certain of those signs and wonders and miracles that he boasted. He knew for a fact that he had cured a severe case of carbuncles and that a dangerously ill old woman, clinging to life, had risen under his hand, shouted praises to the Lord and skipped, albeit awkwardly, up the aisle, though her own husband was heard to mutter that she was not so sick as she thought she was and he could not see that the minister ought to get credit for healing someone who was not sick to start with. The minister could not be so certain of all his ministrations, though not a few of those so treated did profess to feel better, although two or three that he knew of had died. Still, his record was not so bad, as he had just begun the serious pursuance of his gift.

"It is not I, brothers and sisters," he told the congregation, "it is not I who am the healer; it is Almighty God Who heals you, and I am but one of His loving tools. Come forth, come forth and feel the pain and sorrow melt away as the spirit of God flows through me and over you. Amen, brothers, amen, sisters."

"Amen!" they all returned to him and filed slowly up the aisle and in front of the pulpit where the Reverend Carney stood, hands outstretched, eyes closed and face turned toward heaven. "Bless you, brother; bless you, sister," he intoned until the last soul had passed under his lifted palm.

Louisa One stood by the side of the pulpit and waited until the Reverend Carney opened his eyes and glanced toward her.

"Sister?" he intoned, for he was not unaccustomed to being accosted by sufferers desiring more personal attention.

"I vould like, Reverend Carney, fer ye to touch the head of my granddaughter and so to drive da madness from it."

"I will do that, sister, I will do that. Bring her to me, and through me the Lord will bless her."

"I vill not bring her here. I vould dat ye come to mine house. I vould not bring her to a public place fer such as dis."

This was not a new request either for the Reverend J. T. Carney. "I do not usually go to the house of the afflicted, sister, for the Lord His wonders works in strange and mysterous ways and my gift is more certain with the full spirit of the congregation working as one with me in the healing process."

"I vould tithe ye good," said Louisa One. "I am a good tither, and though I know dat ye vould not take pay fer dis blessing, still da Lord's vork needs funds."

This was a little different appeal than the Reverend Carney was accustomed to, and he gave it all serious consideration.

"It's true, sister, what you say, and though mine is a gift and as such is not for sale, yet do I depend on the succor of my holy brethren for simple sustenance. I could visit your house, pray with you, take sustenance and rest. But I promise nothing. It may yet be necessary to bring your granddaughter before the full congregation so that the Spirit of the Lord will work."

"So be it," said Louisa.

So it was that the Reverend J. T. Carney (which initials stood for Joshua Trafalgar, a combination of names that the Reverend Carney found cumbersome, not to mention too easily familiarized—he took himself too seriously to answer to Josh) came to spend the duration of his time as revivalist at Louisa Murphy's house and was only slightly taken aback at the number of women in the house bearing that same name. Nor did the minister encamp as Mendel the Jew had, nor occupy the unoccupied cabin once occupied by the widow St. Cloud, but stayed in a bedchamber on the second floor, between Louisa Two on the right and Louisa Three on the left.

"I don't know," said the Reverend Carney upon viewing Louisa Three, "that it be the Lord's will that she be treated, for it is said that such are angels unto him."

"Vell," said Louisa One, "it's also said dat da Lord giveth and da Lord taketh avay. Vell, He gived dis girl da brain fever an' now he could took it avay." She said this in a tone of voice so matter-of-fact that it brooked no argument to the contrary. Louisa One's faith was great and sure.

"If it be the Lord's will," mumbled the Reverend Carney and he closed his eyes and lifted his countenance heavenward. He placed one hand upon Three's hair, which he felt to be fine and silky and passing soft. His other hand he placed upon her cheek, which he felt to be tender and warm and curved. He opened his eyes and glanced down at that infinitely sweet face staring up at him with deep blue eyes, eyes incapable of any expression save trust, her fingers working at the buttons on her bodice, loosening them at last to reveal the twin rises of womanhood, and he felt a slight but unmistakable tremor go through his parts. He closed his eyes quickly and began to beseech the Lord in His own Son's name to reconsider the damage done to so tender and fair a maiden.

Over the next several days the Reverend Carney worked with the girl, praying, touching, stroking, a suppliant to the merciful God. He even imagined that he began to notice some improvement.

"Ah, did you see that, did you see that expression, as if she might have understood for a minute? Did you see it?" he would say to the girl's mother and grandmother.

Louisa One might nod her head solemnly, trying to convince herself that she had indeed seen whatever it was that the minister had seen. Two was less inclined to such conjecture and kept her arms more or less continuously and suspiciously folded across her bosom.

"There is a devil here," cried the young minister at one point, "there is a devil here causing all this pain and suffering." At which Louisa One nodded, while Two and Three merely stared at the man. Nor did any of them realize that the devil he spoke of was quite real to the minister, but was inhabiting his own soul rather than the soul of the girl, for that man's physical longing relative to the maiden had advanced agonizingly until he could hardly sleep at night.

"There are times," he told his congregation, "that I have my own devil to wrestle with."

"Amen, brother, amen," they responded.

But valiantly as he might tussle with the devil, that evil at last held sway, and on the last night of his stay, the Reverend J. T. Carney slipped into the unlocked room beside his own and viewed the sleeping girl, in sleep more beautiful than ever, for evidence of her illness was not then apparent.

The minister made one last attempt to quell the beast within him, and failing that, he slipped at last into the bed beside the girl, who woke then to his gentle, low words and searching touch and smiled through the dim light toward him. Her eyes asked no question, though she did cry out, he stifling that cry with his hand and his soothing words, for she understood pain as any dumb animal understands pain. At last he slipped from her and lay for a long time beside her, petting and soothing her until she finally fell back asleep, and he made his way to his own bed, where he spent the rest of the night praying and beseeching forgiveness.

When morning came and Three appeared, to the Reverend Carney's vast relief there seemed no evidence of the lust of the night before, save a little unsteady and awkward gait that only he noted. Nor was the maiden frightened of him in any way, for dream and reality were one and the same to her. The Reverend Carney took those signs as proof that the Lord had forgiven him his weakness of the flesh. Still, he was in haste to get away.

Then abruptly he asked if Three had ever been baptized and, informed that she had not, he insisted that that office ought to be performed immediately by him ere he left. And so, stripped to her petticoats, the mindless girl was led into the stream near to where Mendel the peddler had camped, and with a few brief words the Reverend Carney doused her, declaring her baptized in the name of the Father, the Son and the Holy Ghost and trusting to himself that any evidence of lust clinging to her body had been thus washed away with her original sin ere someone in helping her dress might notice.

Both Mendel the peddler and the Reverend J. T. Carney were largely forgotten by the time that Two began to notice the suspicious thickening around Three's waist. She watched that waistline expand for a time before she went to One with that intelligence. The two of them kept watch over the girl until all signs were positive and they knew for certain that she was with child. Neither asked the other the obvious question until finally they went together to Obediah and faced him with the news.

Now, Obediah, while not altogether bright, was neither altogether stupid and he understood their silent accusation and he rose up to his full, towering height and in sonorous tones decried them their lack of faith.

"It is dastardly," he intoned, "nor would I ever think of such a thing."

Louisa One knew Obediah to be truthful, and so, too, did Louisa Two. In relief they greeted his incensed protestations of innocence. And the three of them began to ponder just who the father could be. The suspects were few, for Three was rarely out of sight of someone in the house.

"It was," said Louisa One finally, "either Mendel the peddler or Carney the healer."

When Three at last gave birth to a strong and healthy male bastard, Louisa One determined that the babe should be named Leviticus in honor of her uncle the Philadelphia lawyer, Leviticus Rippert, but Obediah suggested that he should be named Levi, which would likewise honor that distant relative, and also, "It is a Jew name," he said. "And I would rather that he be the son of that good Jew than the son of that preacher that fussed so long and ate so much. We will name him Levi." He said it as if the name itself would confer definite parenthood. "And if I ever see that peddler at a world's fair or a county fair, I will knock his block off."

But Louisa One, watching the babe grow strong and fair, saw in him the features of the minister and not the features of the Jew, until at last she bit her lip and looked heavenward with a bitter sigh.

"An' this is vat I get, is it? Dis fer all mine tithes and all mine vorship and hard vork? Dis is vat I get? Vell, I don' like it, how You do business. I been better off, I think, vit old Paster Ellvood. Right now I don' care. I'll take care of mine own hereinafter, thank you." And with that Louisa One lost her religion and ceased attending religious services altogether, to the consternation of the congregation, which had come to depend on her largesse and was considering ordering a pump organ like the one the Presbyterians had. Nor did Louisa One have anything more to do with religious ritual until many years later, when she came under the spell of Manasquatch—Old Four Lumps—whose reliance on chicken innards and other natural signs appealed to the practical Louisa One (she thinking it meet that there be some useful function for chicken "enters"). Manasquatch was not interested in the hereafter with its potential rewards and punishments; he only used his gifts to foretell, mainly the weather and that only one season at a time. Thus was Louisa's slight need for the superstitious satisfied.

The baby Levi grew and prospered and brought both joy and fear to the hearts of his elders, for he was as bright and clever as his mother had been as a child, and they remembered.

"They say," said Louisa Two, "that the Lord takes the best."

"Da Lord, posh fer da Lord," said Louisa One, who was still out of sorts with that deity.

Though Levi might have the brightness and quickness of his mother as a child, he did not possess her winning disposition, for he proved to be a small, imperious and demanding dictator, understanding quickly that the three adults could be brought to their knees by so little as a cough or a fretful sigh, a discovery made early and employed often. Still, he was a source of pride to Louisa Two, who loved to dress and fuss over his handsome figure, and to Obediah, who longed to teach the boy all that he knew and hoped that one day he, too, could be a soldier and feel the strength of the horse between his legs and thrill to the sounds of battle and charge mightily through smoke and fire. And in his secret heart he dreamed perhaps that Levi might one day have a city named for him and that the city would have a fine fair and that people would come from far and distant places to the Murphystown Fair and that Levi would modestly proclaim, "I owe it all to my wise and noble grandfather."

Obediah took the youngster out into the woods and fields with him and tried to teach him the things that he himself knew of those places, but the boy did not like getting his feet wet in the dewy grass, nor did he like the slap of branches and the snag of briers against his legs, nor the feel of an unexpected cobweb across his face. He preferred playing near to the house where the ground was bare and smooth and carefully swept, both One and Two employing the skills of their Pennsylvania Dutch forebears.

Obediah whistled to the youngster, the sounds of the birds and the wind through the chimney cracks, of soldiers marching to battle, and Levi listened enviously to those sounds, trying futilely to emulate them, but he had no sense of rhythm or tune and in truth could not begin to master the intricacies of maneuvering air along tongue, through teeth and between lips. In his frustration he stamped his foot and demanded that his grandfather not whistle anymore, for it made him nervous and he did not like it. Sadly Obediah ceased his music unless he was by himself, thinking that if Levi did not like it, perhaps he had lost his gift, and no one else cared to listen to the sounds he made.

Though a robust child, little Levi did not care for rough-and-tumble games, preferring instead to play for long hours gathering and sorting stones in neat piles and making intricate designs.

"It's the Jew in him," said Obediah. "That's the Jew peddler in him."

But Louisa One, who had never made any attempt to disabuse Obediah of his notion that Levi was the son of Mendel the peddler, was more inclined to think that the boy had inherited her own tidy and systematic tendencies.

Louisa Three loved and petted the boy, watching over him fretfully, trying somehow to understand what needed to be done with the small person, as if some instinct, undamaged deep within her mind, told her that he needed caring for and that he was hers. And Levi, though he treated the rest of the family imperiously, often contemptuously, was strangely gentle with this silent adult and in that matter mature beyond his years.

It was in Levi's sixth year, when he ruled all that he saw by acclamation, that Daniel St. Cloud arrived to challenge that supremacy.

Daniel at about eight years of age had hardly the presence of a challenger; indeed, he was already developing that lengthy ganglingness that would stay with him for the rest of his life, and though he was passing shy, for he had absorbed many blows in his few years, he had developed a carefully friendly demeanor of that sort which is a protection of its own kind. He had learned that a pleasant disposition and a quick quip could turn away wrath that an aggressive nature would only aggravate. So that while Levi was imperious and demanding, Daniel was friendly and engaging, and while Levi was prone to sulking fits and ill temper, Daniel was eternally cheerful and helpful. Levi hated him on sight, and Daniel from experience recognized the symptoms and went to work to distract little Levi, likewise finding Levi as intimidating as the adults found him.

The widow St. Cloud, with the boy in hand, arrived on foot walking that dusty road that she had walked before, her head erect, her bearing forthright.

She spoke with Obediah first. "My son belongs here, for I cannot care for him; it is only right that he be with his father's people." She did not whine or haggle, nor was she aggressive or angry. She was only matter-of-fact. "I cannot care for him, for my own husband will have nothing to do with him. So I have brought him home and I ask that you take him in and raise him until that time when perhaps I can come for him."

Obediah was at first astounded and then enraptured. He stared at the lady. The passing of eight years had shown her no favors, for she was thin and faded, though traces of beauty mingled with her natural dignity and Obediah felt once more the familiar thrill.

He took her hand and looked at her. His first thought was, she has brought me my son. His second thought was, Louisa must let me keep him. It did not occur to Obediah that asking a wife to raise her husband's bastard was not generally done. He only knew that the son he had longed for was before him; that he had fathered a male child on the woman of his dreams. It did not occur to him that Louisa could do aught but love that child, too.

Louisa One, when she heard the widow's plea, only sighed, while Louisa Two stared in absolute disbelief and, opening her mouth wide, started to speak loudly to that point, but her mother shushed her.

"I vould confer vit da vidder St. Cloud," she said.

"Mrs. Timmons," the woman corrected.

"Yes, so it is. I vould confer vit you by yerself in mine parlor. Come."

The minutes that the women were gone were like hours to Obediah, for it began at last to dawn on him that it was quite possible that Louisa One might well refuse to take the boy, disallowing his parenthood, perhaps, or from simple stubbornness. And panic, which was a strange and frightening sensation, began to wash over Obediah, panic that once more a son would be snatched from him, and he began to try to form arguments, persuasive reasoning with which to cajole Louisa, his wife; but alas, Obediah, though he could have moved the bark on the trees given lines from some other source, could not frame any coherent or logical arguments of his own. Nor was his situation helped by Two, who was standing muttering loudly about the propriety of raising someone else's bastard, apparently ignoring the fact that

Louisa One had in effect raised the bastard child of Louisa Two and Obediah. Little Levi stood beside his grandmother Two and stared in outraged silence at the frightened child, whom Obediah was petting and offering candy and smiling stupidly at, when he was not pacing distraught around the clean-swept and barren yard. Daniel stood in one spot, not daring to move, holding his cap in his hand and trying to put on an agreeable expression, though his heart was pounding madly in his chest. The boy hardly knew what was going on and wondered where the father that his mother had spoken of was; certainly it was not the old man who chuckled incoherently at him and then strode wildly about the yard. Daniel wished that he were somewhere else.

In shorter time than Obediah would have thought, Alecia Timmons and Louisa One came out the door, stood on the porch and embraced tearfully. Alecia came down the steps and reached out for her son and held him close as Louisa called out to Obediah, "Obie, get fer Mistress Timmons a carriage and da boy to drive her back to town; fer she must catch da train." Turning to Alecia, Louisa One admonished gently, "Remember. Remember vat I told you. I cannot tell ye vot to do but you tink upon it; it bears tinking upon. Levi"—she turned toward that thunderstruck boy—"ye take Daniel St. Cloud and ye show him da house and da barn and such as might interest him. He vould stay vit us fer a vile until his mama could come fer him."

So unaccustomed was Levi to receiving orders that it did not occur to him not to obey. He nodded toward Daniel and the two of them started around the house. Daniel stopped to wave at his mother before he turned the corner.

"You tink on vot I said," Louisa called after the departing carriage. She stood along time looking after it and then turned slowly away, sighing. "She von't do it, though. I haf never understood vy a vimmin has to stood vit a vortless man just because she's married to him."

"Because," said Two, though One had not been addressing her, "she's got no other way to live, most likely."

"Nah. I give her money and I vould give her more if she vould leave da scoundrel."

"Money? Mama!"

"Oh, hush. You don't know nothin' dat I know. Hush!"

Before little Levi had time to react to the interloper, Daniel had begun making admiring overtures, laughing at Levi's little jokes, deferring to him, obsequious enough that for a time Levi lost his resent-

ment of this stranger in the opinion that he had merely added yet
another vassal to his court. Little Levi, being but five years old, had
only limited experience to rely on and that experience told him only
that he could do no wrong, was without blemish or peer, and that
everyone was aware of that fact. But little Levi was also uncommonly
astute for one so young, and in a short time he began to realize that
some of those attentions and favors that he had taken for granted were
being funneled off toward the young stranger.

It was an outrageous situation, one that demanded instant remedy,
and Levi set about working such remedy. He began to sulk; as it had
worked in the past, he saw no reason that it would not work its usual
magic; but it did not.

"He's got a dark side to him," said Louisa One.

"It's the Jew blood in him," said Obediah.

"He's spoiled," said Louisa Two.

"Let him be," said One.

Only Daniel worried some about Levi's fits of temper and went to
him and offered him a handful of smooth stones that he had gathered
from the creek. Levi took them and threw them disdainfully on the
ground.

"Come, Danny," called Obediah, "leave the Jew boy alone."

"Don' call him 'Danny,' " snapped One.

"Come, Daniel. Come and I will show you where the Banty hides
her eggs," called Obediah.

Daniel turned and dashed after the tall old man. Levi sat a moment
suffering. He also wanted to see the Banty eggs, but his wounded
pride would hardly allow him to run after Obediah. However, curiosity being after all a more demanding force in small boys than pride,
Levi jumped at last from the fence post upon which he was perched
and ran after Daniel and Obediah. The Banty eggs were in a hole in
the straw back behind the manger, from where the Banty chided them
shrilly for their intrusion.

"Now, don't touch 'em, boys," said Obediah, "er she'll peck yer
hand off."

The boys stared wide-eyed at the tiny bird, both taking literally
Obediah's admonition. Daniel backed slowly away; but Levi stood his
ground and stared at the Banty hen guarding the nest where her tiny
eggs lay. When Obediah and Daniel had quitted the barn, Levi picked
up a stick and gingerly poked at the setting hen. It took several pokes
before the hen retreated reluctantly from her nest, and Levi reached

quickly into the nest, gathered up as many eggs as his small hand would hold and with a deep breath and a malevolent glare hurled them against the wall, retreating himself quickly ahead of the shrill cackles of the hen. "Jew boy," was he?

"Come, Levi," called Obediah. "Now leave her be, understand. She gets upset."

"All right," murmured Levi. He felt better.

It became obvious finally that the fits of sulking would not have their intended effect. So Levi took another tack. He started wetting the bed. The first time he did it, Two clucked and frowned but took his ticking out and hung it over the fence and washed his bedclothes. The second time he did it, Two spoke sharply to him and warned him about going outside "fer relief ere ye go to bed"; then she took his bedding out to air. The third time he wet his bed, One said, "If he likes a vet bed, so be it." And he was forced to spend several nights in the smelly bed. Levi was a fastidious young man, and when the bedding was fresh once more he decided against defiling it again.

Things were not going in Levi's ordered world the way they should, and he felt betrayed and alone. He did not know whom he hated more, Daniel or Obediah. He could not hate One or Two, as those two huge presences were the deities upon whom his existence— and regular meals—depended. But he hated Daniel. He hated him for listening enraptured to Obediah's whistling, his young body wiggling and twitching in eagerness to join the music; he hated Daniel for chasing after Obediah through the damp grass and the high weeds and wading the creek and skipping stones. And he hated Obediah for whistling when he had been bidden not to, for showing Daniel how to skip stones across the smooth pond and how to piss on a tree without splattering and how to whistle a tune, which, though Daniel could not do it well, he could do a little, which was more than Levi could do.

In a fit of temper, Levi called Obediah an old bastard and he pushed Daniel into a mud puddle. And then the unthinkable happened; Levi got switched, switched just like the black boy was switched for sometimes being too dilatory with his chores. Levi was switched by Louisa One.

"Yer a bad boy," she said, as he sat on the ground nursing his stinging shins and crying. "Yer a bad boy. I von't have it. Ye'll be nice to yer grandfadder. An' ye'll be nice to Daniel, fer he is our guest. Ye mind dat er ye'll feel dis sapling again."

Grudgingly Levi eased his campaign and finally settled into something like an uneasy routine with Daniel and Obediah, joining them reluctantly in their outings, lest by staying behind he lose more control. And in truth, he and Daniel grew to be something like friends, for Daniel deferred to the younger boy, winning him slowly with casual jests at his own expense, a uniformly cheerful disposition and an agreeableness that bordered on the obsequious; for Daniel truly was intimidated by Levi and did not want to incur his displeasure, all of which suited Levi just fine. Though in his heart he harbored disdain for the boy and anger for the man, the years of their childhood passed with little of note until the day that Obediah announced his intention of taking the two boys and attending the World's Fair in Chicago.

"Vat!" said Louisa One. "Vat! Yer seventy-five years old. Yer too old to go to vorld's fairs."

"I an't but seventy-four," said Obediah in some pique, for he was beginning to be self-conscious of his age. "I just turned seventy-four."

"Anyvay, dat's too old to be runnin' around all over to vorld's fairs," said Louisa One.

"No it an't," said Obediah, and in truth, though his years were many, they hardly showed; for he was still straight and tall and his hair was only peppered with signs of age and, except for some stiffness upon rising, he got around as young as ever and hardly slowed the boys down when the three of them romped through woods and fields.

"I want to go to the world's fair; it's all they're talking of in town. They say there are great displays of fireworks and lights and music, they say. And there are people," he said, "ever so many people, more than a body can imagine, and a gigantic Ferris wheel."

"Vell!"

"We shall go by train," he said. "I will take both boys. They should see a fair ere they're growed. An' ther an't so many fairs no more," he said sadly.

And so it was that Obediah set out for the Chicago World's Fair with the two boys, both well past young childhood. Levi was thirteen and Daniel sixteen, and neither had ever been on a train, nor had Obediah, who had never been far from home except for a trip to Chattanooga and those months spent doing service in the Army of the Potomac. But Obediah remembered the fairs he had been to and he particularly remembered the Lewisburg Fair of his boyhood, and he could not imagine that any fair could be finer than that, though he knew that the Chicago fair was. Only he didn't believe it.

He regaled the two boys with the wonders of the Lewisburg Fair during the train ride, which took them to St. Louis first and then cut back east toward Chicago through heavily planted fields and small towns, which at last gave way to larger cities and the colors and smells of many people and much smoke.

They stepped off the train into a bustle of noise and people and confusion, the World's Fair nowhere evident. Obediah was for a moment as suddenly intimidated by the big city as the boys were, and to cover his confusion he laughed and spoke too loudly, and several people turned to stare at the towering old man and the two tall boys. "We'll find the fair," he said, "an' no tellin' what we'll see there. But we'll see all that's to be seen and see ever'body that's to be seen. Why," he cried in sudden inspiration, clapping Levi on the shoulder, "mayhap we'll run into yer father the Jew. Now, wouldn't you like to see him? He always said he loved to go to fairs. Wouldn't that be something?"

Suspicions, like weeds, once sprouted need little cultivation. A heaviness, near heartbreaking, settled over Levi. He hardly heard as Obediah fussed around and at last found his way out of the gigantic train station and so to a hack. He could not share the eagerness of Daniel over riding in so handsome a vehicle toward the hotel where they would be lodged, nor hear the happy chattering of the other two. So this was it, that other shoe that he had been waiting for since the day that Daniel arrived? He had, he was certain, been brought here under pretext of attending the fair, when in fact the old bastard intended to desert him, to turn him over to that father that he had never truly believed existed. It was a plan, a plot, and he wondered if the two Louisas were in on it. Probably, he thought, for they, for whatever reason, had always preferred Daniel. They had only been keeping him, Levi, until he was old enough to join that peddler.

Levi was devastated and that devastation turned slowly to horror as he tried to imagine over the steady clop-clop of the horse pulling the hack what that Jew would be like. He could only picture that entity as dark, faceless, stooped and perhaps with pointed teeth, a sinister, frightening personage who had deviously, perhaps supernaturally, impregnated Louisa Three and produced him, Levi, unnatural product of unnatural lust.

"Levi, lookit. Yer not lookin'," shouted Obediah. "Ye'll like never see such fine buildings again in a long time. What're ye frownin' fer? Lookit. Lookit."

"Yessir," mumbled the unhappy boy. But he did perk up some

when he finally realized that they were indeed passing through a fine city with tall buildings.

"The fair," called the cabby, anxious to impress these country people with his knowledge, "is over that way, and at night you could see the lights forever."

"I can't wait; I can't wait," cried Daniel and both the cabby and Obediah laughed, enjoying the boy's excitement.

"Now, Levi, and an't you anxious, too?" asked Obediah.

"Oh yes," murmured Levi, but with such lack of enthusiasm that Obediah looked sharply at him, wondering if the boy had eaten something that did not agree with him.

Through the afternoon, as they first settled themselves in the hotel and then made their way to the fairgrounds, Levi harbored a sense of dread, which only grew stronger the nearer they came to the fairgrounds, slowing his step as if he were marching through mud that caked his shoes and trapped his feet.

"Hurry, hurry," shouted Daniel, in a haste to get there. "Hurry, we'll miss something!" The boy did not know precisely what they might miss, but whatever it was, he did not want to miss it. The first thing they saw, which stopped the three abruptly in their tracks, was a great jet of flame powered by a natural gas jet that they happened onto, hardly suspecting, caught up short at the towering magical flame.

"Ah," sighed Obediah. Levi and Daniel said nothing but only stared open-mouthed at the spectacle. They had no frame of reference in their limited experience to match it against and could only wonder if the stars up in heaven, viewed at close range, could be so spectacular, or, thought Levi, the flames of hell itself.

Daniel tired of the spectacle first. He absorbed as much as he could and then decided that he needed an ice and said so. But Levi stood more stupefied than anything that such a wondrous sight could indeed exist on their planet, much less in their very own country and state. Levi sighed a large sigh and the dread he had experienced lifted from him for a few moments and he was caught up in the excitement of the World's Fair. He forgot the Jew and for a time the suspected perfidy of Obediah in the wonder of the sights, sights that Daniel was surfeited of more quickly than he, for Daniel had a growing boy's appetite that would not allow for uninterrupted sightseeing.

Still, after the initial delight, Levi found the sense of dread again descending and he began to stare into the faces of men he passed, those who looked of an age to have fathered him, though to tell the truth he was not quite sure what that age might be, the Jew, he had the feeling, being prematurely aged. And so he found himself staring at nearly every adult male he passed, some of whom stared back with curiosity and a few with smiles full of meaning and enticement. And each time that Obediah, who was fond of talking to those peopling the various booths and displays and regaling them with stories of the old and venerable Lewisburg Fair, stopped to chat, Levi looked around him suspiciously, stiffening, ready for flight should the anticipated Jew suddenly materialize and grab for him, for that was the picture that had finally evolved.

It was in such state of nervousness that Levi found himself one afternoon, along with Daniel and Obediah, standing at the foot of the giant Ferris wheel, the sign of which proclaimed it to be the largest ever built, a giant lighted circle, revolving slowly around to the accompaniment of a leisurely-sounding pump organ. The three stood in wonder before the contraption, Obediah pondering the safety of it, and the two boys pondering the size of it. For the mighty circle held thirty-six enclosed cars, each capable of holding upwards of sixty people.

"You want to ride?" asked Obediah with a twinkle, for he doubted that they did; he knew that he did not. He had no desire to leave the ground for so lofty a view no matter what.

Daniel smiled timidly and shook his head, for he, too, was afraid of heights.

"Well, come, then," said Obediah.

"No. No," said Levi. "I want to ride. I am not afraid. I will ride."

"Ah, now, Levi. Be sure, fer it's very high and a long way down."

"No. I will ride. I am not afraid."

Levi was pointed brusquely into one of the cars with another dozen or so folk, but he might well have been alone, so awed was he, and indeed the exclamations and excited conversation of those who accompanied him were stilled in the reality of the chamber they boarded. Levi took a seat by the window, and with a rumble and a whir the giant vehicle carrying its passengers aloft began to ascend, pausing now and then with a spastic shudder to let someone else aboard. And thus was Levi lifted slowly from the ground, first shoulder-high and then overhead and finally so far up that he could not even make out Daniel and the Old Bastard; and from that vantage point fear deserted him—fear of the height, fear of the Jew, fear of the future—for he could see far, beyond the tall buildings and past the lights and over the plains. It was a clear day, the clearest that they had had at the World's Fair, and Levi thought that he could see the curve of the earth if he had but powerful enough glasses, that he could see beyond time, and he felt at last secure, secure and omnipotent. Below him Obediah waved, but Levi did not see, nor did he see Daniel, his eyes shaded, looking with worried stare toward where he suspected Levi to be. Had I but wings, thought Levi, so that I could soar from here to where I would be . . . Though in truth he did not know where that would be, only somewhere, somewhere where the Jew would never be, nor Obediah, nor Daniel, where he, Levi, could be king.

And then from the pinnacle the Ferris wheel began to descend, slowing, jerking periodically to a stop, pausing and then jerking into movement again, until he was finally stopped and the bar lifted for him. He sat in disappointment, the greatest disappointment he had ever known, until at last the operator of the machine urged him with a curse to get moving. Levi's feet were on the ground again, but his heart was still in the sky, and the meanness of the ground level no longer mattered. The Jew had receded so far into his consciousness that he only surfaced thereafter during fitful dreams, and then it was hard for the boy to tell if it was the Jew he dreamed of or Obediah, the Old Bastard.

When the trio after several days began their trip homeward, only Daniel chatted fondly of what they had seen. Both Levi and Obediah sat in taciturn silence, barely hearing, hardly responding to Daniel's happy chatter. He had enjoyed the visit to the fair, but for Obediah and Levi the trip had been much more than a lark; it had been a significant experience for each, but in very different ways.

Had Levi been able to put into words what he had felt hovering like a dragonfly in the Ferris wheel high above the fairgrounds, looking west toward the future, he could have said that he had been unbound, that he was free. Free of the Jew, free of Obediah, free of everyone, for that matter. He could and would stand apart and alone without fear, for he felt and understood his own omnipotence beyond the ground and beyond even the race of man.

But Obediah had felt the thrill of the fair in quite the opposite manner, nor could the Old Bastard explain it or even understand it. He only knew that the blood coursed gaily through his veins as it had when he was a young man; that there were smiles yet to return, tunes still to be whistled, laughs to be shared, hands to be shaken, backs to be slapped, cheeks to be kissed; that the human race went on and on, forever and ever, and that he was a part of it and life was an endless fair.

But neither man, young or old, could quite formulate his feelings into coherent thought; but could only sit in heavy silence and absorb feelings and sensations that they had not brought with them to the World's Fair. And neither was as satisfied when he returned as he had been when he left.

Louisa One noted the change in both, particularly in Obediah, for he was more silent and thoughtful than was his wont; but she put it down to his age and the strain of the trip and thought no more of it. Of Levi she only shrugged to herself that he was by nature moody anyway and she wasted no worry.

But Obediah continued to pine, and it was not until the day that a letter arrived for him, that letter read aloud to Louisa and Obediah by Daniel, that his spirit suddenly soared and the sparkle came back to his eyes and the spring to his step.

"Honored Commander," the letter began, "those of your command in the 36th Illinois still surviving most graciously request your presence at a reunion of those troops in Springfield, Missouri, on the 28th day of September next, said reunion to commence at 12 noon of that day in the city square."

The letter's signature was not familiar to Obediah, but it did not matter. Youth came back into his eyes and he fairly jigged out of the room and onto the porch.

"Vy," said Louisa One, lifting her heavy self from a chair and following him, "yer not thinkin' to go to nothin' so frivolous as dat? Vy, yer a old man."

If Obediah heard her he did not so acknowledge, but only gleefully cornered Levi and Daniel and began the familiar tale of the Battle of Pea Ridge, which he judged to have been the turning point of the war.

"Yer not goin' to no such reunion," insisted Louisa.

"But yes," said Obediah, "yes of course I am going," he said happily and Louisa sagged slowly to the step and sat with her elbows in her lap and frowned. She was too old for such adventures; she had thought all her adventures used up.

"Den I vould go vit ye," she said at last.

"No," he said, "no, you will not go with me. I shall go alone."

Nor was there any more excited person than Obediah as the time for his departure approached. Louisa One said no more, though Two complained considerably at the silliness of the expedition. Two had grown even more garrulous and temperamental in age and she did not like to have Obediah out of her sight for very long at a time.

And so it was that on the twenty-fourth day of September in 1893 Obediah Jonah Micah Murphy set out for adventure, which would last another ten years and which would ultimately land him in revered age in the Indian Territory of Oklahoma.

The survivors of Pea Ridge greeted Obediah as befitted a legend, with awe, excitement and loud cheers.

"Why," they marveled among themselves, "he don't look a day older'n he did thirty year ago. D'ye mind that? An' how tall and straight he is, just like then. He could move mountains, y'member, with his voice. Recall that?"

Indeed, Obediah was as his men remembered him, for memory being but an ill vehicle, the men remembered their colonel older, wiser, more deliberate than he had actually been; and as he had at last grown to resemble those memories, he was suspected of never having aged at all.

They called upon Obediah for a speech and he rose to the occasion, slowly warming to his topic, which was but general and along those lines that his men best remembered, sonorous of tone, heavy with metaphor of battle and bravery and love of country. He left many of his hearers in tears and others shaking their heads in agreement and perhaps a thoughtful few wondering that had come of the world since those glorious moments when in their salad days they had defended the Union. Some might have said to themselves that they could have asked for better of the succeeding years.

And when the speech was finished, each man could repeat it as he heard it, which in truth was as many versions as there had been hearers. But Obediah was content. He thought that he had never known such complete contentment to be met and hailed and appreciated once more, and he winked at a lively young miss at the edge of the crowd and she winked back.

Louisa One was not really much surprised when Obediah did not return at the appointed time, nor even when she did not hear from him for several weeks. By the time word came from him, written in his own irregular scrawl and suspect spelling, but signed elaborately in that signature hardly shaken by the years, Louisa had already made up her mind that she would probably have to go after him.

Daniel read the letter aloud, struggling with Obediah's spelling and licentious punctuation.

"He has," the young man finally announced in amazement, "gotten himself elected to office in Missouri. He is a magistrate in Stone County, Missouri."

"An is he dat?" said Louisa One.

"But, Grandmother," said Levi, "how can that be? He is not eligible to be elected in that state. He is not a resident."

"Obediah could do vatever he vants," sighed Louisa. "Don' ye know dat?"

"He makes no mention of what we are to do," said Daniel, reading aloud. " 'Me dute er heve.' 'My duties are heavy,' " translated Daniel. " 'My duties are heavy' is all he says. He doesn't even ask for money."

"He von't think of dat until he's got none. Ve vill have to go get him," Louisa One sighed.

Louisa had gone after Obediah before. It was not a new experience, but it had been a long time. Still, she remembered what to do and to the amazement of the two boys packed up as if to remove forever, the last thing on the two wagons she hired to move them being her small ornate secretary. She ordered the big house boarded up and instructed the foreman left with the land, "Ve probably be gone fer a long time. You take care until I contact you." Obediah had never been an easy man to return once he had wandered.

In all of their western removes, he had sometimes been forced by an irate husband or father to move on and sometimes he had, as seemed to be the case, merely wandered away, gotten interested in something and forgotten to return.

"Ve vill be visitin' in Stone County in Missouri," Louisa told her neighbors and Charlie Varner. "Perhaps over da vinter."

Nor did either boy protest the move, since both thought that their fortunes lay with Obediah, not realizing that they could have lived well and comfortably without him. Had they known, however, that Obediah was not the source of their wealth, they probably still would not have objected. For they were boys and a move West was an adventure, an adventure that the boys anticipated and Louisa One dreaded.

They found Obediah without difficulty, for the tall old man with the vibrating voice left a plain trail and was in truth quite delighted to see his family. He was very nearly out of funds; and found lodging for them in the rooming house where he stayed until they found a house that they could settle in. Nor did Obediah ask why they had come or how long they were staying.

There was a spring to his step and a sparkle to his eye and for a moment, as Louisa One looked at him, she felt as she had felt those many years before staring at the handsome young man with the dark curls, trousers tight across his bulging manhood, ruffles at his throat. The trousers, she thought, were still tight, though they did not bulge near so often, and the ruffles he still sported at his neck, a fact about which Levi complained and Daniel joked.

Obediah had been elected presiding judge of the county court, running at the urging of several of his companions from the Pea Ridge conflict. Obediah had not thought to inquire of residence require- ments, nor had anyone else, the population being but lax in such matters in the face of what was obviously a candidate of courage, well spoken and resourceful, those qualities deemed by most sufficient qualification for any office, never mind residence requirements.

Nor were Obediah's duties actually of magisterial proportions, the office of presiding judge being more administrative than judicial in nature in that small county, which sat upon the Arkansas border and through which the 36th of Illinois had marched on its way to Pea Ridge. In most other parts of the country old soldiers were becoming increasingly tiresome, but not in that border land where the war had been fought both on military battleground and through the country- side by bushwhacking guerrillas. The War Between the States was, nearly thirty years after the fact, still a viable concern. Obediah was welcomed into the community as a hero ought to be welcomed.

"I have never been so happy," cried Obediah. "I only wonder that it taken me so long to get into politics."

"I guess ve vould have to buy land here," said Louisa One to Louisa Two. "I don' tink dat ve could get him back home now."

Two merely nodded, but she was not happy. She had left behind her circle of friends, was developing gout in her big toe, did not care for the backwoodsy people she encountered and did not want to share Obediah with his electorate, anyway. Neither woman, however, con- sidered leaving him there and going back without him.

"This is where we'll stay," announced Obediah as if they had, like Moses and the Children of Israel, been wandering the desert in search of the Promised Land for forty years.

And they might well have lived out their lives there had it not been for Obediah's encounter with the widow Whetzel, for he was admired and generally respected by all for the timbre of his voice and the sagacity of his decisions, which were not all that complicated for the most part, and when they were, Louisa One obligingly sorted the problem through for her husband.

Obediah, however, early one September morning called upon the widow Whetzel at her behest, for she had encountered some problem concerning the county's right-of-way on her land that she wanted to discuss with the presiding judge, not being willing to settle for any less. The widow, who was some above fifty years, was immediately charmed by the courtly and handsome man and bade him stay for noon victuals and after noon offered to share a nap with him, for she had been a long time without a husband and for her age was a woman of some beauty with passing strong appetites.

The widow Whetzel was so pleased with Obediah's performance that she invited him to stop by whenever he was in the neighborhood. Now, it had been quite some time since Obediah had dallied with a willing lady, Louisa One being too old and obese to interest him anymore; and still being under injunction from her regarding Louisa Two, he did not dare drift in that direction, either. Anyway, his own appetites lessened by age, he did not find Two so alluring. Consequently, Obediah was both pleased and startled to find his juices still flowing copiously and made occasion to check on the widow Whetzel's right-of-way claims often, sometimes two or three days in a row, which was all right with the widow Whetzel.

And though Louisa One recognized the pensive and distant gleam in Obediah's eyes, she said nothing, only sighing and girding her loins, as it were, for she was of that age that living or dying were one and the same to her, except that in her stubbornness she had vowed to outlive Obediah's randy ways.

"I might never get to die," she mused to herself, going about her business creaking with arthritis and huffing and puffing at the effort.

This was a situation that might have continued for a long time had not a revival come to town, which revival the widow Whetzel attended with great zeal, for she dearly loved revivals. And through those services she sat and listened to others rising to profess sinfulness and redemption in the most glowing terms and she was quite envious of the attention they got until she could contain herself no longer and so rose to announce herself a sinner. In truth, she had probably never intended any but the most general kind of self-indictment, but standing before that crowd, each eye watching her, occasional tongues encouraging her with "Amen, sister," or "God love you, sister," she got carried away and itemized her sinfulness in some detail, at last announcing, "I am a sinner, for I have fornicated wif (for the widow had a slight lisp) an adulterer." And she named his name, tears of joy and repentance coursing down her cheeks.

Now, the widow had seven grown sons, four of whom were in attendance at that same revival, and while they might forgive their mother her feminine frailty, ascribing it to loneliness, they could in no way forgive that adulterer Obediah Murphy, who had taken advantage of their mother in her weakened and lonely state. They would be avenged.

Fortunately, the Whetzel boys determined to go for their other three brothers before they hanged Obediah Murphy, and also fortunately, one of the faithful old soldiers made haste to Obediah with word of the impending festivities.

"Oh shit," said Louisa One. She hastily packed Obediah's second-best pair of trousers and two ruffled shirts and handed him some money and admonished him, "Get to home. Back to Illinois where ye belong and ve'll join ye dere. Don't stop till yer clear shed a dis place, hear?"

Obediah heard and obeyed, except that Louisa One noted with a frown and a sigh that when he turned his horse onto the road, he turned south instead of north.

"Vell," she grunted, "vat now is it?"

Obediah was not disobeying Louisa; he was merely following his instincts. He might not consciously realize that he was on the trail of the widow St. Cloud, Tommy Timmons's wife, but he had heard casual mention from former comrades-in-arms that the "old rascal Tommy Timmons" was known to be alive still and residing with his family in Arkansas—Crawford County, Arkansas, it had been thought. Thus, without plan, Obediah rode south toward Arkansas, and if he had thought about it might have felt the cool breeze upon his forehead and tasted honey upon his lips, for it was his restored manhood that drove him on. As a migratory fowl, he flew south to seek a mate, instinctively certain of the finality of that trip.

Riding south, Obediah discovered many things, among them that mention of the recent conflict between the states ought to be circumspect, for the farther south he traveled, the fewer were those who honored and admired Union veterans. He learned this fact most specifically in a chance encounter with two mountain men on the outskirts of a small village deep within the Boston Mountains, and though there were Union sympathizers in those mountains these particular two were not among them.

His announcement, in conjunction with his request for information concerning Tommy Timmons, that they two had been fighting and victorious comrades in the Battle of Pea Ridge was met with a string of epithets and threats, one of the strangers going so far as to grab a stick and make for Obie and his horse.

It was only Obediah's loud and commanding "Down, sir!" that startled the man into inaction long enough for Obie and his horse to retreat with dignity. Thereafter Obie practiced restraint concerning his military experience, only admitting to the title "Colonel Murphy" without designation, most people being agreeable and assuming that he had been a colonel in the "right" army.

Obediah did not find Tommy Timmons; he did not even find any trace of that formidable fighter and his faded wife. What he found was a legislative district in need of representation in the state legislature. By the time Louisas One, Two and Three and the boys found him, he was an elected official in the state of Arkansas, having assured those few interested enough to inquire that he had been around the state for a very long time, having served in the Battle of Pea Ridge. No one thought to ask him which side he fought on. His announcement coupled with his dignified demeanor and his assurances that he was not a Republican (it did not matter so much what he was so much as what he wasn't), seemed sufficient reason to elect him to the state's governing body.

Obediah's family was nearly a year in finding him, settled and respected in Van Buren. The trip had been a strain on those aging ladies, the one suffering mightily from the rheumatism and the other from the gout. Both Daniel and Levi, when they finally arrived in Crawford County, were quite relieved, their responsibilities for the three aging ladies having been great.

And though Obediah greeted the whole family eagerly, it was Daniel he sought out and admonished. "It's time ye thought of gettin' an edjercation, boy. An edjercation is what it takes, a college edjercation, fer I've found my own learning hardly adequate fer my new duties. A lawyer, a solicitor, he must be, fer them as are has the greatest prospects in politics." Indeed, Obediah had passed but part of a term in Little Rock, and those few weeks he had spent mostly in listening, which gave him a reputation for thoughtfulness, and in repeating to each one who discussed a matter with him all of those arguments that each man espoused, giving him a reputation for wisdom as well as sound judgment. But in only one matter was Obediah possessed of great wisdom. He had that rare insight to understand that he didn't know what was going on. Therefore he nodded much, frowned often and said little, which added to his already growing reputation for sagacity.

"And what shall I be, Grandfather?" asked Levi. "Shall I go to college to become a lawyer, too?"

"Eh? Ah no, Levi. Yer a peddler, ye see. It's in yer blood, ye know?" He might have added, but some insight kept him from it, that as Levi had peddler blood in his veins, so Daniel had politician's blood in his. "Ye'll be a merchant. That's what. A fine merchant, in a fair city." Only Obediah understood that that fair city would be Murphystown, that it would be founded by Daniel in honor of his own father, founded somewhere in the West, he supposed. It would grow to be a great city and Levi could indeed found a fine mercantile enterprise there. Only, Obediah did not know where that might be.

Levi was crushed. Crushed and then angered. He was, after all, brighter and more perceptive than Daniel. They both knew that. Besides, he claimed seniority, though Daniel had managed to weaken that argument some by pointing out that neither one of them was actually blood kin to the Old Bastard. But Levi was, he assured himself, at least closer related by stepparenthood than Daniel, who was naught but a foundling. Even so, it was Daniel that Obediah singled out for future prominence, possibly even the presidency (for Obediah, he knew, could be as expansively imaginative as any boy), while he, Levi, would be *allowed* to be a merchant. A peddler. Jew boy! God damn him to hell!

Louisa One, though suffering the infirmities of age, particularly those infirmities related to the rheumatism, had not wasted her time in the year it took her to find Obediah. In addition to those properties she had bought in Missouri, she had paused long enough along the trail to pick up some timberland in Arkansas, as well as a farm and a mill. The farm was no great buy but the mill was and they went together. But as her account books were overflowing and her quilt top grown to unmanageable lengths, she one day sighed and said to Obediah, "I am passing tired these days, veary it is. I tink dat perhaps ve need a lawyer to help us order our business. See ye can find such in dis gotfersaken place."

So it was that Obediah rode one day into Fort Smith, which was a bustling little city on the edge of the frontier, and inquired of some of his constituents, for he was recognized and hailed often, as to a legal firm which he might do business with. Each man he inquired of had his own recommendation, for there were many passing themselves off as lawyers in those days. Obediah was confused in the matter and very nearly left town without accomplishing his mission when he chanced upon an office which proclaimed to house "Solicitors at Law—Mr. Helms and Mr. Driver." Not lawyers, not attorneys, but solicitors. Were they indeed solicitors, they were surely a cut above all other practitioners of law, lawyers, attorneys and such. And so Obediah took Louisa's business to Mr. Helms and Mr. Driver, those two worthies' business thus improving by about 50 percent. Consequently they treated Obediah with all the respect and courtesy that 50 percent of their business warranted.

Louisa One, though wearied, had not lost all her business acumen and entrusted to Obediah and his solicitors only those matters so routine that there was little danger of malpractice on their parts, while Obediah was accorded a measure of respect that she hoped would at least keep him from straying. And so it did for some few months.

"A man like yerself," said Mr. Driver one day to Obediah, "a man with investments to make, you ought to be lookin' toward the West, ye know? Toward the Indian Territory, where there's land to be settled and properties to be had for a pittance. It's a new land and ye ought to invest." Mr. Helms nodded his agreement.

Obediah thought on that suggestion all the way home, and when he arrived he said to Louisa One, "My solicitors think that I ought to invest in western land."

"Vat do dey know?"

"They're solicitors. And they know what to advise."

"Does advise come out of dere pockets? You ask dem dat. Mine Uncle Leviticus Rippert, the Philadelphia lawyer, he told me a long time ago dat poor men give rich advise. Remember dat."

But the seeds were sown. There was open land in the West, land where cities would rise, cities that would need names and stores and fairs, most assuredly fine fairs, perhaps even world's fairs. But Louisa One was adamant. They would remove no farther. They had gone too far already. She was too old to move again. But the gleam in Obediah's eyes troubled her.

"Yer too old to go no furder," she said. "You von't go!"

But Obediah did go, as she had known he would. He rode off one morning, and when she heard from him again, he was in Tipeeho, a thriving community in the Indian Territory.

"Come at once," Daniel translated, "for we'll settle here." Oblivious to the complaints of Two and the boys, Louisa One once more commanded that the wagons be loaded and sent word to her solicitors as to the care of her properties. She did not bother to inform Obediah's constituents what had become of their legally elected representative. She had never taken that matter seriously, anyway.

"I did not tink," said Louisa One, eyeing her ornate little secretary being loaded onto a wagon yet another time, "dat ve vould go no furder Vest. I haf a feeling dat dis is it."

SEVENTEEN

LEVI'S JOURNAL

*T*his is the best of times.
The worst of times are over, and I, Levi Murphy, feel compelled to take up my pen and address myself to this new century. Though I recognize that there are those who would scorn such act as the presumption of raw youth, I would risk such scorn; yea, I would risk it and return it in like measure.

Confident? Yes, I am confident. Presumptuous? I think not. We have passed into a new century and in a matter of months I shall attain that majority that leaves childhood but memory, memory both bitter and dear. And I have likewise passed into a fresh and new land, a territory nearing statehood, a primitive place awaiting, docilely almost, the imprint of civilized man (though, truthfully, "docile" might hardly be the description of choice on Saturday nights when those dregs of society pushed this far and destined, I'm sure, to be pushed yet farther, make apparent their noxious but probably diminishing presence).

The blank pages before me represent a life to be lived, a promise to be fulfilled in this land and in this century. To record it as it happens is not an act of presumption but an act of foresight and wisdom. I have faith that I would be an important part of that future and those events, and I would leave a record of them through the eyes of one who can not only record them, but who can add detail that lesser men would hardly have access to. If that be presumption, then presumption I plead.

I will call this record a journal for want of a better name. I would eschew the word "diary" with its suggestions of the recorded tedium of day-in and day-out existence. Life is made up of a continuum of trivial comings and goings and doings and undoings. History is not.

History comes in waves, in tides like the great seas, washing men and events before it, depositing them briefly, receding, only to rise and drive further events toward those already deposited.

I would write history, but history of both a personal and a general nature. I would stand dead center of the universe, radiating consciousness over it, transcribing all as it whirls about me.

I will write of the important and let each day take care of itself, for who cares that we rise each day, take nourishment, occupy ourselves in activities and then retire to rest? Jesus, Caesar, Alexander, William the Conqueror, yea, even Napoleon did all of those things and made history between times. And I would do likewise, recording such events as I deem them important for the future understanding of this age. And I care not one whit that the above might seem presumptuous, and even grandiose.

I shall add to my history, then, in paragraphs as they occur to me, inserting dates insofar as they are useful and not as the scholarly decoration of lesser histories.

I consider myself particularly qualified for the task I have set: to both make and record the break with that period of history, and my personal history, which is stagnant, unproductive and, yes, terminal. For I am a bastard. Yea, more than bastard. I have no father to claim me, to demand allegiance of me, and the woman who bore me does not answer to the name of mother. I call myself orphan!

Nor do I care that there are those who might accuse me of lacking feeling. I care not for the opinions of others. The demands that society places on individuals are not nearly so rigid as the demands that I place upon myself, and I count society's good opinion of no import as it pertains to me.

I would record, however, for it is a fact and not an apology, that I am far from unfeeling. I do bear affection for those to whom I am tied by both blood and childhood bonding, though they are few. But those bonds are as strong only as life is strong and none of them, with the exception of that foster brother (which relationship is more titular than anything), Daniel St. Cloud, will accompany me far into this new century.

Those adults who have shaped me insofar as shaping has been possible (for from childhood I have largely borne my own counsel), though they be passing dear to me, have affected me little enough that they can hardly count in this history.

The generations are, however, interesting if only because of their longevity. For among them they very nearly cover the entire century just past, just past and well past, for it tailed off the crudeness and lack of both polish and imagination that has characterized the race of man with precious few exceptions through recorded history. Fittingly, my mother, her mind completely blanked by early childhood illness, represents that break between old and better, the better being that which is coming. For I count the past as coarse and rough as the dark bread that fed it.

I bear those adults of my family no malice, no regret, nor will I forgive them even their callousness, for forgiveness would give such callousness a recognition that it does not deserve. It was not their fault that they were a part of the end of this dying age. And that mindless woman who bore me is the end. I, I rise phoenix-like and herald a new civilization.

Lest it be noted against me (not, of course, that I would care for such censure) that I failed to turn my back on the wealth and property that the line will leave me, I must counter that indeed I will not. That wealth (if there is any such, for I know not where it originates, nor actually how much there is) is mine by right of birth, just as the color of my hair and the shape of my nose are. It is both a right and a trust, and though the possession of it might aid my eventual successes, the lack of it would not deter them. That wealth is the foundation of a better world.

My childhood is a matter of record, I suppose, should anyone be so interested. The three women who raised me all bearing the Christian name Louisa—two more accurately, as my dear little mother was hardly more than an affectionate presence—were my grandmother and her mother. They washed me and taught me table manners and nursed me on those rare occasions that I was ill. I think they had but little influence upon my character.

And certainly my great-grandmother's husband (he was, I hasten to note, only a step-grandparent to me) had no bearing save possibly negative, as I made determined effort to be as little like him as possible, on the eventual dispositions of my talents and sensibilities. However, I am forced to add that I think he did have great influence on the eventual formation of Daniel's character, which I think is too bad. But Daniel, who when he came to us was young and probably frightened and of a malleable disposition anyway, fell under that old man's peculiar charms and has developed certain character traits as a result that are not likely to do him well.

Obediah's charms are great. I will grant him that. That and little else. I have little feeling for him one way or another, save occasional embarrassment. I have never been able to understand those charms that others find so fetching, nor have I been able to understand the power that such a weak personality has over those three women who make up our household. For they orbit around him, even my mother, who follows him about mindlessly and happily as a puppy while both my grandmother and great-grandmother are hardly less attentive. He is boorish, selfish and often embarrassing. Yet they have followed him apparently contentedly across very nearly half a continent.

And Daniel. He and Daniel have been like children together, playmates, while I, I have always been the adult. I do not, of course, begrudge Daniel that; I only wonder at it. But now that he is adult, for Daniel is older in years if not in wisdom than I am, I would think that he would put such silly idolatry away.

Even as a child I was more the adult. I stood back and watched the foolishness of a foolish old man and understood it for what it was, a senile old mind at the least, possibly a mind that never had grown up. But Daniel did not. He listened to Obediah's war stories, to his whistling, to his tales of the Lewisburg Fair, and gave them attention, attention that such nonsense could never deserve.

There were indeed times in my childhood that I think I had the only adult mind.

We chased Obediah across two states to get where we now are, and I suppose that I should be grateful for that. Or perhaps it was meant to be that way. For it is obvious that I had needs get to this location in some manner.

When we settled in southern Missouri, I knew that I could never stay. Nor was it only the rocky, barren land that defied man to make a living from it that put me off. I know only that I could never live in a land where the steep hills covered with thick, tall growth dominated. It is such geography, like a grizzled old man, like God, that is master. There are places where the land forces the man; and there are places where man can force the land. This land of gently rolling hills and spare growth is of the latter. I could never have survived under the dominion of the land. The land would work for me, not I for it.

These thoughts are random as they come to me, random and only background for what is to be. They must serve as introduction to my journal and to my life. The past is almost safely behind me. The future is mine, and I will add to these pages as that future spreads out before me.

Such date as is needed: In the Year of Mankind One thousand nine hundred and one.

EIGHTEEN

A FINALE IN THREE ACTS

1.

The solicitors, Helms and Driver, most probably did not intend to send 50 percent of their business into the Indian Territory. Indeed, it is probable that those stagnating worthies, in offering their opinions on the wisdom of western removal were only giving voice to those dreams they themselves would never achieve, indeed would never even pursue beyond voicing disappointment that they never had and therefore never could. But Obediah was without those involuntary restraints that stall most men at a certain plateau of curiosity and achievement. Were it wise to go West, he would then go West. Being at the time past eighty years of age was a matter of no consequence, for the infirmities of age had not yet intruded on his consciousness as they had begun to intrude upon the two elder Louisas. For Obediah, life was just beginning.

The community of Tipeeho in the far eastern edge of the Indian Territory was a thriving one, with two banks and two newspapers and a citizenry hopeful of securing a place on the proposed railroad line. It was not alone in those many aspects, as there were several other communities of like ambition, only a few of which would ever actually succeed in them, and they mostly modestly. But at that time, the beginning of a new century, there was a great deal of optimism and a good deal of competition.

Obediah chose to settle in Tipeeho and to send for his family, not on a whim, but on reasoned logic: that that community, to thrive, needed a name change, Tipeeho being adequate for a sleepy village, but hardly for a great city. Such name change ought to reflect the influence of the city's most important citizen, and Obediah Murphy, from experience, realized that his own combination of oratorical ability and wealth would be enough to so invest him.

With unusual foresight, Obediah looked around for the most prestigious house in the town, a house that would suit the city's most prestigious citizen. He found it in the nearly completed mail-order house that the citizens referred to as Coe's Folly, Thomas Coe having ordered the house from Chicago, gotten it nearly completed and then died. Ordering a house from Sears, Roebuck in Chicago was silly enough, but to compound it by dying before you could live in it could only be considered complete folly.

"Vell, it's a nice house," murmured Louisa One when she first saw it, "but ven vill it be finished?"

"Oh, soon, soon," said Obediah, for there were still workmen putting on finishing touches and the mantel in the sitting room needed to be refitted, for it did not quite fit.

"I do not know why we continue to follow the Old Bastard into these godforsaken places," grumbled Levi.

"Because he has the money," replied Daniel, quite to the point.

"Well, when I'm out of college, I shall make my own way and I shall repay what he has spent on me and I shall be free of him."

"As you like," said Daniel, shrugging, nor did either one of them actually believe it. Had they strained their imaginations to capacity, they could not have imagined life without Obediah, it never occurring to either that he would ever do so mortal a thing as die.

The settling into the house was quickly accomplished, with the workmen scurrying to finish.

"Daniel," called Louisa, sitting in her armless rocker before the mantel-less fireplace in the sitting room.

"Yes, ma'am," for Daniel had never referred to any of the Louisas by any other name in their presence, nor had he ever been instructed to do otherwise.

"Daniel, I vant yer help. I has dis quilt top. I vorked on it fer, oh, fifty, sixty, seventy years—I don't know. But I'm now tired of it. You wrap it, please, secure it vell and ven dem vorkmens puts up dat new mantel, you put dis package in back of it so it stays here as long as does dis house. I like dat idea."

"Well, certainly, ma'am," said Daniel, whom Louisa knew to be more understanding of such things than Levi. "Levi," she had often said, "has dat dark side; he has not good human understanding." Daniel, in turn, knowing Louisa One not to be a woman given over to whim, did not think to question that act or perhaps to put it down to an aging mentality. He knew better.

Obediah was not long in making his presence felt in that community, if for no reason other than his imposing and still-straight form, dressed in the archaic ruffles and breeches of another age, and his courtly manner and resonant voice. A certain garrulousness was the only sign, indeed, of age, and he told all who would listen of his feats as a soldier and statesman, and he signed with an admirable flourish a petition to have the capital of the new state, when that should happen, placed in Tipeeho, remarking after he was done that a change of name might make that possibility less remote. And upon any opportunity thereafter, he continued that campaign of a name change, presenting his point so carefully and so eloquently that hardly anyone realized that the sum of his argument was Louisa One's own voiced opinion that Tipeeho was "a silly name fer any real place."

Thus they settled into the life of the community as if they had always been there, for that is easily done when almost everyone is new to a place. Daniel and Levi went off to college, but not before they posed for a family portrait, an experience that Louisa One vowed never to repeat, "fer dat fool like to a blowed us up." Louisa Two, however, would have enjoyed sitting for more photographs; for she was impressed by her own likeness, though she was ungainly and passing crippled. In truth, though, she looked better than she had really thought she looked, the flash of the photographer's powder erasing much of time's labored industry upon her countenance.

The very damp winter that followed brought Old Manasquatch the Indian healer into their lives, for Louisa One's rheumatism became excessively burdensome and Obediah, having heard of the wonders worked by the old Indian, brought him to Louisa. Indeed, the old man's ministrations, which included reading the signs from chicken innards after drinking very hot tea spiced with four lumps of sugar, did seem to provide some relief from suffering, if only because his forecast for drier, warmer weather proved accurate. Thereafter, Manasquatch was a frequent visitor in Louisa's sitting room, where, when he was feeling in the mood, he would relate horrendous tales of anguish and suffering, for he seemed to enjoy those the most, relating the maltreatment of the Indian at the hand of the white man. Both Louisa and Obediah were genuinely sympathetic.

"My own sister," intoned Manasquatch, "only in her first bloom, her earliest bud, was raped by a white man, raped and gotten with son. And that white man, he did not ever know his son, nor care for him, and when the great war came, the white men murdered the son of the white man, cut his head off and paraded his body through the camp. They did."

"Ah," said Obediah, truly unhappy. "That's terrible. Terrible."

Louisa nodded in like sympathy and the old man went on, "I'm all that's left now. Just me. And we've had no justice yet. And I shall be the end of it."

Obediah wondered if he could rectify that when he became governor of the new state. It was a new thought to him. But there was no reason that he could not be governor. There certainly could not be, as he had great experience already. And then he could see justice done these poor, misbegotten heathen. He liked the idea so well that he thought of it for several days before posing that possibility to Louisa, whose response was, "Ye do dat and I vould beat yer backside vit mine broom!" It was said with such vehemence that Obediah recalled one other such beating and decided against mentioning the matter again for a while.

There is no Murphystown or Murphysville or Murphysboro in eastern Oklahoma. That there ever might have been is only a matter of speculation, for Obediah Murphy, before he could move to make that a reality, fell victim to the gunshots of an irate husband.

That irate husband was Tommy Timmons, the husband of Alecia Timmons and onetime fighting mate of Colonel Obediah Murphy. Tommy Timmons, who had given his life over to strong drink long since, had made some feeble attempt to wrest a living from the promised land of the Indian Territory; but though the land was promising, it demanded long hours and patient toil before it would deliver upon those promises, and once Alecia Timmons became so crippled by advanced rheumatism that she was largely confined to her bed, Tommy gave up what little fight he had and moved with Alecia and Alecia's daughter and her illegitimate son into the nearest town, which was Tipeeho, relying on his Civil War pension of twelve dollars each month to feed his family and restore his manhood, which restoration resided in whatever cheap bottle of spirits he could obtain. For he was not fussy and, in truth, tried very hard to contribute the largest portion of his income to his family's upkeep. But his dignity was sorely tried and came and went, that dignity being on the upswing when he, only moderately influenced by drink, stumbled upon Obediah Murphy on the street in front of the newer bank.

"An' it's Colonel Murphy," he cried in recognition, and the two old men fell into each other's arms.

"And Alecia, yer wife," Obediah inquired at length, "an' how does she do?"

"She is not well," said Tommy. "Not well a'tall, fer she kin hardly move from her bed most days."

"Ah, and I would see her, I would visit you," said Obediah. "Alecia, she was as beautiful a woman as ere I have known."

Now, that little beast suspicion, once born, grows apace. Tommy Timmons stared for a long, hard moment at Obediah and remembered the child that his wife had borne in shame, for though he had been privy and sympathetic to her condition when he had married her, the actual event so unsettled him that he could hardly stand it and he took it out on the brat, Alecia being forced to take the child to her family lest Tommy in a drunken rage harm him.

"I do not think that possible, fer she don't receive," said Tommy suddenly distant and formal. "Good-bye, Colonel," he added and whirled stiffly away.

Obediah did not give his precipitate action much thought, for he was already deep in consideration of another quandary: how to discuss with Louisa the rediscovery of Daniel's mother and the reaction on her part that that revelation might incite. It was a hard thought, and at last Obediah treated it as he did all hard thoughts; he put it out of his mind, reviving it some time later and at last deciding to call upon Alecia St. Cloud. He could do that much at least.

And so on an afternoon, polished and brushed, he made his way to the tiny shack behind the livery where Tommy Timmons housed his family. He was met at the door by a boy.

"What's yer name, lad?"

"I'm Billy, sir, Billy Timmons."

"Ah, an' are ye the son of Alecia Timmons?"

"No, sir, her grandson."

"Ah, an' could I speak with yer grandma?"

"Well, sir, she's not well. I dunno."

"Would ye tell her that it's Colonel Murphy, Colonel Obediah Murphy, that wishes to speak to her?"

"Well, yes, sir," said the boy, then retiring quickly into the dusk of the house and returning immediately with an affirmative.

The house had but two rooms, both dark and equally smelly, the room where Alecia slept in the back. Obediah entered. He did not see the faded crone with the painfully twisted fingers resting on the quilt. He saw only the eyes of deepest gray and his own photographic flash erased the years and he sensed the autumn wind and tasted the taste of honey and felt his knees go weak.

"Colonel Murphy," she said, and her voice, though low, was warm and deep as ever, "I did never expect to see you again." He reached for her hand, and though she winced at the pressure she allowed him to take it.

"My son," she whispered urgently, "my Danny. Tell me of him."

"Oh, he's a fine man, a tall, fine man, studying fer the law in St. Louis. Ye'll be proud of him."

The woman sighed a gentle and painless sigh. "I would see him, Colonel. I do not want him to know who I am. But before I die, I would see him."

"Yes, certainly," boomed Obediah, startling the frail old woman. "But someday, someday soon, I intend to tell him the circumstances of his birth. I want him to know that I am his father and you are his mother. He's a right to know."

Alecia started, took a deep breath and stared at Obediah.

"Colonel? Colonel Murphy, I don't understand what you mean. No, wait, yes, I guess there is room for misapprehension. I guess there was. But . . ." and she paused a moment in confusion. "Colonel, Obediah, did not Louisa your wife, Mistress Murphy, did she not tell you? I never thought. I did not want you to have that mistaken impression. I am sorry."

Obediah felt his heartbeat, which had been agitated, begin to slow and he felt light of head, for the expression on the old woman's face told him that she would tell him something he did not want to hear.

"Danny is not your son. He is the son of Danny Varner, Louisa's grandson. I thought you knew. I, I only came to you that day because your gentleness warmed me and gave me strength. I should not have, but it seemed so natural and I was already with child. I do not understand that Mistress Murphy did not tell you that my son was also the son of her firstborn. I do not understand."

Dumbfounded, Obediah rose, still holding the hat he had removed upon entering the house. He could not think what to say, nor possibly could he have said it, for the disappointment had found its way from his heart to his throat and he feared that he might explode of it.

"Gawdammit, Murphy, what're ye doin' with my wife?"

He whirled. Tommy Timmons, an ancient revolver clutched in his hands, leaned drunkenly against the doorjamb. "What the hell ye doin' with my wife an' her in her nightclothes? I got ever' right to shoot, ye sonovabitch!"

Obediah was not frightened by Tommy Timmons's threat. He was not afraid of Tommy; he was only nearly sick from disappointment and he was never a man to relish a disagreement, and as Tommy Timmons occupied the only natural exit from the room and as Obediah had no stomach for either the loud words or for pushing past him, he chose the only alternative exit and turned toward the tiny window, uncovered save for a piece of cloth, and without a word hoisted himself into it.

Obediah heard the explosion before he felt the pain and he told himself that what was happening could not actually be happening. He would have Louisa see to it.

It is possible that Obediah Murphy might have recovered from the wound—for it was not immediately mortal—had not his rescuers been so well-meaning and anxiously hoisted him among them and carried him, dripping life, the several blocks to his house, only one having the presence to rush to find the town's single doctor. They laid him on the floor at Louisa's feet and stood and removed their hats, for he was by that time largely gone.

Obediah, beyond pain, looked up into the crowd of faces above him, hardly distinguishing any. It is said that a man's life flashes before him at the moment of his death and it is perhaps true. At any rate, Obediah bemusedly stared at the faces above him and wondered if black Benjamin were among them and the concerned whisperings came to him as the rustle of leaves and he saw smiles and bright colors and heard much music and it was like Christmas Day, or more likely a day at the fair, and he felt like whistling, for it never occurred to him that death was upon him.

Smiling gently toward the faces, he at last distinguished Louisa One and whispered through pursed lips, "Ah, I should have gone out the front door."

And if Obediah could have voiced any disappointment with life, it would have been that he left no tribe, no generations. Only Levi.

2.

I have always been agile, even in age. I suppose in part I owe that agility to my daily climbings of these stairs to those rooms to which I refused to be confined and from which I cannot entirely stay away. That black woman, Nanny, whom Levi so precipitately imposed on me against my will—for I fear those dark people with their dark secrets, they who know hell first-hand— would have bedded me forever on the first floor if she could have. But I thwarted her, for the existence I have, such as it is, depends on the view from this height. Nor does Levi care one way or the other.

How many such storms have I watched making that same approach from the west? Storms with lightning or with wind or both? Eons, I think, I have stood above the earth, eye-level with the clouds. And if I die, for I cannot be sure that I ever will, I will die on this very spot, stalled on this Ferris wheel, secure from the pull of the earth and those who would force me down.

I do no longer fear that end, being one with Obediah and one with the peddler Mendel, father, son and ghost, we are of the sky and the elements therein.

And we have power over the firmament, high above those bending trees, bowing low before wind and rain that never touch us. The imperious crack of thunder, the bright light of rent air and the power surges within us, now and forever.

But the wind would force more air upon us than we can breathe. I do not know; I do not understand. The dark lady; I would call the dark lady, for I cannot shut off the air. There is too much. I cannot breathe; I cannot breathe. God. Father.

"Ah, Lee, I've been waiting for you."

"Daniel, there was no need for you to come; I did not expect you. It is, I'm sure you know, only a matter of time. The doctors hold out no hope."

"He is in a coma, then, and not asleep?"

"I suppose. It's hard to tell. Sometimes his eyes will dart open and I would swear that he wants to say something. Not unusual, the doctors tell me, with stroke victims."

"Well, the nurse said you had only stepped out for dinner; I have sat here watching, thinking perhaps he was asleep."

Asleep, asleep? Why would I be asleep? I have spoken with God; I have seen Obediah and Obediah does not sleep. I would not sleep unless the Old Bastard sleeps. I shall go round and round him, for the wheel circles over his head and he cannot reach me and I am safe from him and from Mendel the Jew. I hover like a dragonfly above them and Joab and Inez plead with me to come down before I fall.

"You did not need to come, Daniel. I know it's a strain."

"No, it's no strain, Lee. At my age nothing is a strain; everything is simply very slow. Elizabeth called and I came as soon as I could. But these days everything takes time."

Elizabeth? I meant to tell, Elizabeth. It's a boy, Elizabeth. You have a fine son. He is ours, dear wife, our son. I meant to tell you. By the way, Elizabeth, it was not good of you to die. I would have told you. I meant to tell you. Ah, Elizabeth, I wrote it all down, all the perfidy, so you would have it, so you would know. Everyone must know. Be sure to tell it just as I told it to you, so they will understand. But I don't know, Elizabeth, I'm not so certain of many things. The Old Bastard knew, but he died. I hated him when he died. Mendel the Jew knows, and the bitch Lucille. Ask them, Elizabeth, make sure that you know your own father; it is such agony if you don't know. "It is a wise man," they say. Indeed it is. I've always wondered.

"It was inevitable, Daniel; he has gotten weaker and weaker the past few months, and wilder and wilder, raving like a madman, calling on the prophets, ranting about Mendel the Jew and Obediah. I do not mean to sound hard, but it will be a mercy to be rid of it."

"Ah, Lee, we should not be too hard on an age-damaged mind, I suppose. Although I have always thought that Levi had been a little unbalanced all his life. I have wondered if the illness of his mother's system did not perhaps infect him while he was yet in the womb, for he was always strange? And then I think that that is silly, too. He was a man of his time, if a little Freudian in his torments. His life, I suppose, reduced, adds up to little more than sibling rivalry and a father fixation."

My life has been a magnificent agony.

"I loved him, Lee. Loved him as an arrogant brother perhaps, but I loved him."

"I'm not sure I can say that. He cheated me of much and I resent him for it."

"Now, Lee, all sons resent their fathers. It is a quite natural thing."

"No, you do not know how he cheated me, cheated me of my childhood and my birthright and tried to make me a copy of himself. I cannot forgive, even in death, his transgressions."

"Lee, it is better to forget. I have forgotten much. It is less painful all the way around."

"He accused me of being a Nazi once, do you remember? He accused me of changing my name from Levi to Lee out of anti-Semitism, remember?"

"Have you made any final arrangements, Lee?"

"He asked at one point to be buried by my mother, and then by Obediah, but it made no sense. Do you happen to know, Daniel, where my mother is buried?"

"No, don't you?"

"Levi and I did not talk much, ever, for he was a distant man. I do not really think he would have told me had I asked."

"I don't know. I do know where the rest of the family—Obediah and the three Louisas—are buried. The last time I was there—that was a long, long time ago—I did look to see if your mother was buried there, but she does not seem to be. Obediah lies there beneath a huge, commanding white stone with the three Louisas spread out at his feet, though they were hard to find, as their much smaller stones had been removed."

"I wonder that Levi let that happen."

"I don't really. I did mention it to him, but he in effect told me that it was none of my business."

"Strange."

"Perhaps. But you see, Levi had a kind of love-hate relationship with Obediah. I can understand the perversity that would let that stone dominate."

"Well. Perhaps I will do something about that. Once he is gone, all our ancestors are fair game, are they not?"

She lies beneath the boulder, secure and safe, safe from the elements, from Daniel, from the Old Bastard. No one knows where she is and no one can discover her, shaded eternally by her laurel, my Daphne, my Penelope, my Ophelia, my love. They are both secured—he beneath that heavy white stone. I would not that he would escape. Let those other gentle souls, all my Louisas, let them roam at will.

"Lee, my aging bones tell me it's time to go. I hate to leave you, but it goes without saying that I am not as young as I once was. David will come later. Perhaps he can keep Elizabeth company?"

"Good night, Daniel. Good night. . . . And now, Levi, it is just you and I again. We have been alone so much. Alone together. I cannot say, Levi, that I am sorry to see you go or that I shall miss you. I don't think that either is true. I am not sorry to see you go; I am not going to miss you or grieve for you; nor will I be glad to see you go. There is no feeling about you one way or the other. All I feel is emptiness. That is your legacy to me, emptiness. God curse you, Levi, for I cannot. I have not even that much feeling.

"God curse you, you old bastard!"

3.

I have never actually been in a courtroom before and I am startled at how much it really is like those movie and TV courtrooms I have seen. The only thing that's missing, I suppose, is the certain knowledge that something dramatic will happen. But something dramatic *will* happen; a man will be sentenced to die, I'm fairly sure, and that is dramatic. But the routine gets in the way of the drama, the drama that I have followed from near the beginning. Reality keeps intruding upon it: small talk, occasional laughter, the glare through a torn shade, the jury foreman's annoying habit of clearing his throat and tugging at his tie periodically. My drama could use the ministrations of a first-rate dramatist to put things in perspective. At the very least there ought to be some celestial drum roll for life's big moments, so we'd recognize them when they happen.

The courtroom is not actually crowded, nor has it been through the whole trial, just comfortably filled. Many of the faces are familiar and there is a kind of camaraderie that comes of having shared the several days of trial, a familiarity attested to by smiles and nod, if not by names. Greer Beck is among the interested onlookers, and two or three of the men who had viewed the disinterring of the ill-fated Stoples. George Kellbaum, the spear carrier, is here, as he was the first day of the trial, though he missed the rest. Having missed the guilty verdict, he is on hand for the sentencing. Vonda is not here, nor has she been at all during the trial. Someone to mind the store, I suppose.

And Virgie. Virgie is occupying the same seat that she has occupied throughout, neither close nor far, neither spectator nor player, disinterested by expression, straight and unemotional. There has been no tear, no sigh, no sagging shoulder. If she has flinched at all, it has been inside, for no one has seen her, she who went down in the agony of birth and brought forth a murderer and raised him and, I suppose, loved him. And I think to myself that, amazingly, tomorrow's murderers have already been born, are lying in their cribs, crying or kicking their feet. And tomorrow's victims have already been born and they are identical to the villains and no one can tell them apart. Not even their mothers.

And I am here, spectator in this drama to the end. But the program does not tell me which act this is, third or fourth, or does it ever end? Will I even know when it ends? And am I the eternal spectator, awaiting word from the chorus or at least an instant replay, involved, safe from any pain save catharsis?

I have spoken only briefly with Virgie, nodding, and she thanked me for coming, as if my presence meant anything in this particular scheme of things.

Earl McCullough pouted his way through the trial and was summarily found guilty, mumbling only in his own defense, "I ain't done nothin'."

There is sympathy aplenty in this room for Virgie, but little for Earl but curiosity, many wondering, probably, how they could have known this murderer from childhood and never realized it, though there is an occasional muttered "Always knowed he'd come to a bad end." It is, as a matter of fact, a kind of choral refrain that runs through the audience. "Poor Virgie. I always knowed Earl'd come to a bad end."

Earl McCullough is guilty; Virgie, his mother, is not.

The audience fidgets and then pauses and waits as the prisoner is brought in, followed by two deputies, only one of them armed. Earl is not even shackled; it is a casual way to mete out justice. But Earl is hardly dangerous, scuffing down the single aisle, no expression save petulance on his face. I glance toward Virgie; I am not the only one. What do we want? Weeping and screaming and remorse or curses? The expression on the woman's face is stoic. She must realize that her son will have to die. And how will she deal with that? I am annoyed at my own morbid curiosity. But didn't I come to see the action?

The judge is announced and we rise, Earl more slowly than anyone else, prodded by one of the deputies, thinking perhaps that he, being star of the show, should be exempt from some of these for-malities. His greasy hair hangs limp about his shoulders and the suit and tie he wears look as if they were meant for another performer. He turns his face toward the window and from the profile the expression remains an angry pout. He does not look at his mother. His eyes do not seek her intervention. His whole posture says, "I ain't done nothin'."

The judge is cursory. He reads the indictment and then the guilty verdict and addresses a few almost casual remarks toward Earl about the injustice done to the Stoples. Perhaps he is only thinking that they deserved killing, which is a commonly expressed opinion, or perhaps he has an early luncheon appointment.

Whatever, he dispatches his grisly duty quickly, solemnly declar-ing, "You, Earl McCullough, having been found guilty of the first-degree murder of Terry Stople, are hereby sentenced to death by lethal injection on the twenty-eighth day of November of this year. May God have mercy on your soul."

There is no sound but the echoing of the judge's gavel. I am not sure what we are supposed to do at this point. Cry, cheer, break into a chorus of "God Save the Queen"? The whole thing suddenly has the reality of *Alice in Wonderland*, and we are all poised for what? I glance at Virgie. Her expression has not changed and she holds her pocketbook with both hands in front of her.

I look back at Earl. His expression has changed. He has gone from the petulant to the incredulous. It has finally reached him. Earl McCullough must die. Soon. He cannot believe it. He is angry and amazed, staring wide-eyed at the judge as if he had expected perhaps only to have to sit in a corner for a specified time or write on the blackboard one hundred times, "I won't kill anybody again."

"But I ain't done nothin'."

"Remove the prisoner."

"I ain't done nothin'. Ma?"

Virgie winces at last. I see it. Everyone sees it or at least senses it. The pain runs through her solid body like a flash of lightning and just as quickly.

"Remove the prisoner!"

Earl McCullough is standing straight now, the slump replaced by righteous anger. "You cain't do that. You cain't do that."

"Remove the prisoner," repeats the judge somewhat testily and the deputies start to attention, one of them reaching for Earl's elbow to guide him around and back down the aisle. At the deputy's touch, Earl whirls and with a quickness belied by his normal slouch, he grabs the deputy around the neck and with his other hand relieves him of his gun, pushes the deputy aside and backs into a corner, both hands holding the gun.

"Well, shit," mutters the other deputy, his first reaction annoyance, glaring at his careless partner.

"It ain't got but one bullet," admits the deputy dumbly, as if that absolves him of his carelessness. "Gimme back my gun," he adds.

"I ain't goin' to no jail. I ain't going to die. I ain't goin' to get executed. You cain't do that, hear? You cain't. If I'm goin', I'm takin' somebody with me. I'll kill some sumbitch before I go. You hear that?" he fairly shouts at the judge. "I got one bullet and I aim to use it! Come and git it!"

There are no volunteers.

"You can't stay like that," says the judge at last. "Remove the prisoner." It is almost comic relief, but not quite. The judge is trying to restore routine. He is not prepared for the unexpected. Routine is all he knows.

"Don't nobody try it. Don't nobody try it. I'm goin' to kill somebody fer sure. Somebody," he hisses at last.

The spectators have all become actors. No one in the courtroom is still uninvolved, curious about the outcome. The spectators have become participants by virtue of having a loaded gun pointed at them. No one can claim disinterest, each person absolutely certain of his own mortality at that moment. The jury foreman has gone white, hanging on to his tie, posed in an instant of time, knowing himself a prime candidate for that single bullet, and the judge, too. Both deputies look embarrassed and uncomfortable and there is not a person in the room who does not think that that single bullet could find its way to him. There is no sound. It is as if we are all holding our breath as one.

And then there is a sigh and a shuffling and Virgie rises slowly switching her pocketbook from her hands to her arm. Seated in the middle of a row, she carefully scoots in front of people, apologetic as a late moviegoer. If there is any other movement in the room, I cannot detect it. It is an imperfect tableau, the main character moving steadily through the other perfectly still forms. Earl watches her, holding his gun straight out in front of him, his expression slowly going from anger to fear.

"I'm goin' to kill somebody!" he yells. People jump; the sound is so unexpected. "I'm goin' to kill someone!"

Virgie continues her journey to the end of the row. Time and breathing stand still and then there is a kind of collective sigh, for we are all spectators again.

"I want you to give me that gun and set down," says Virgie sternly as she walks slowly toward where Earl cowers in the corner.

"I'm goin' to kill someone, Ma. Ma, I'm goin' to kill someone," he whimpers.

"I want you to give me that gun and set down and behave yourself."

"Ma, not you, Ma, not you, not you, not you, Ma."

"Earl . . ."

The sound of the explosion jars the room and echoes and then there is perfect stillness. No one moves. For a moment there is no sound at all except the ticking of an old schoolroom clock on the wall behind the jury. And then there is the collective sigh again and a sob, perhaps pain, perhaps relief.

Virgie stands motionless, her plastic pocketbook hanging from her elbow, and she stares, bemused, at the crumpled form of Earl McCullough, the top of his head no more than memory and the drippings of a self-inflicted mural coursing slowly down the wall behind him.

"Clear the courtroom," says the judge, but gently.

EPILOGUE

"**W**e're glad you could come."

I'm startled at the voice at my elbow. I have just signed the guest book and am looking for an inconspicuous place to sit. The church is crowded, from the look of it mainly by old friends. I see few near to Earl McCullough's age and wonder absently if he had no friends or if they have deserted him in his final hour.

"We're glad to see you," says Vonda again. Her beehive is perfectly intact and her expression friendly. "Virgie was hopin' that you'd come. You be sure to come to the graveyard and then back to Virgie's house after. There's plenty to eat there. She'd like to see you."

I have come again, thinking to close out this little drama, for impressive and horrifying as it was for those of us in attendance, the suicide of the convicted Earl McCullough was worth only a few lines in the newspapers. It is of no great import in the scheme of things. Still, having gone as far as I had, I could not bring myself to miss the last act.

"I wouldn't want to intrude."

"No, no. You wouldn't intrude. Just come on. Virgie wants you."

There is a shuffling that tells all that it's time to be still and the bereaved slowly file to their appointed pews. The casket is closed. No undertaker, no matter how skilled, could have done much to repair what once was Earl McCullough's head.

The service is brief, the words of comfort are general, but the message is clear: "You're better off without him and it's now between him and his Maker." The coffin is loaded on board the hearse—I wonder if it's the same one that carried the Stoples on their final rides. The cortege to the cemetery is longer than I might have expected, but the service there is brief, and for a few moments people break up into small groups and chat amiably, as if they had just been let out of church. There is, if anything, a sense of relief in the air.

"Ms. Murphy," It's Vonda again. "Didn't you ask about some Murphys once? Remember? And I told you about some stones? Well, that's them over there. We come over here ever' Decoration Day and I always stop to look at them stones. They look so out of place among the others, don't you think?"

She has not intended offense, and I take none. I am only curious and I wander over to inspect the four huge white stones, certain of the names I will find, and I am right. I have stumbled onto my ancestors, for here are Obediah and all three Louisas, resting beneath stones identical to Levi's and Lee's, though Obediah's is obviously much the oldest. Maybe I'd better retain Jenks to cut me one before he dies and the pattern is lost.

Well, I have been led by the defunct Stoples and the ill-fated Earl McCullough from my ancestral dwelling to the bones of my ancestors. I wonder if my grandmother Elizabeth is here, too. There is no other such stone and the cemetery is moderately large; it would take some time to hunt through the stones and I do not feel up to crawling around decoding faded tombstones.

"Are these the ones?" asks Vonda.

"Yes, I think they are."

"Well, I'm glad." And she obviously is.

She is not the only one. Phoebe Ruskin will be happy that I am interested again. I don't think she's given up the idea of a history yet. "There was an O. Murphy elected to the Arkansas legislature in the late nineties," she called recently to tell me. "Do you suppose that's the one we're after?"

"I suppose it is, Phoebe," I said to her, we having finally got on a first-name basis. I am always bemused by Phoebe. "Why do you do genealogies?" I asked her once.

She thought for a moment. "I get paid for it." She smiled but I knew she would say more. "It may sound foolish or wishful thinking, but I think the past superior to the present, the further past the more superior. I am fascinated by the individuals of the past, those about whom it is impossible to know anything, actually. The present, our time, is like white bread, the nutrients refined out of it. There is a texture, a character, to the past that is somehow lacking in our time."

"Have you done your own genealogy?"

"Oh my, yes. But it's an almost endless task, you know. One answer always leads to so many more questions. Just recently I uncovered a relative, Leviticus Rippert, a lawyer from Philadelphia and a Revolutionary War hero. But Rippert is a new name to my genealogy and it opens up a whole new line. It's never done. Do you see what I mean?"

"Yes," I said to her, "Yes, I suppose I do."

I stare long at each stone, passing from one to the other until I realize that the cemetery is quickly emptying and the men charged with the last work are eyeing me impatiently. They will not begin until the last mourner is gone. My Lincoln is conspicuous in its aloneness.

I do not feel like an intruder at Virgie's house. The neat little house is open to the pleasant breezes and people in varying stages of dress-up, some ties and coats still in place, some not, are spilling out of the house, many carrying large paper plates filled with food and balancing large beverage cups. The air is jovial; it might almost be a family birthday gathering or reunion. Inside, the rooms are similarly crowded and people are filing by the stretched-out kitchen table, filling their plates from an assortment of casseroles and plastic containers. There is even a big bucket of Kentucky Fried Chicken, its merry red and white stripes more appropriate to a country fair than to such a solemn occasion.

Calm, subdued, Virgie is still a gracious hostess, as if she had planned this successful affair for many months, the only sign of grief the dark circles beneath red-rimmed eyes. These are her friends, her children and grandchildren, her sisters and brothers, some cousins and nieces and nephews, they are circling the wagons, feasting against the common enemy, death. I am treated as one of them and a paper plate pressed upon me. I am suddenly very hungry.

"Miz Murphy," says Virgie later, "I'm glad you could come." She looks as if she would say more but she does not. I think of the quilt top and hope that she does not ask about it. I have found it strangely compelling and am unable to think of donating it anywhere. I showed it to David's Marci at one point and she was equally taken with it. I suppose I'll pass it down to her. It somehow has the air of something that ought to be passed down.

The talk is of general interest, the sort that permeates such gatherings. There is no mention of the event that brought them together, however; and it occurs to me that the play is not over, will never be over. Like a soap opera, it will go on and on, this or that character being written out of the script. Virgie and her cast are forever.

That thought hangs with me as I drive back toward Tulsa, through the greening countryside. I feel briefly desolate. My own line is gone, near to extinction, and when I finally fade out of the scene, I will hardly be missed, the last memory of the Murphys of Oklahoma represented by a few towering white tombstones. "I wonder who those was?" some distant child may ask.

There is a vastness to these rolling hills, a vastness which absorbs the occasional houses and outbuildings. And spring is upon it. I vow never to be surprised by spring again, spring or any other season. Earl McCullough is dead. That is real. I saw him die. One moment he was living, the next he was not, his death more real than Levi's and Lee's and all their forebears', and Old Daniel's and even more real than the decomposing Stoples'. He was, and now he is not. So one day it will be with me and Virgie and everyone else. There is a beginning and an ending. We can catch only a glimpse of what went before and a promise of what will come after. But all we can actually know is that which comes between our own beginnings and endings.

On impulse, I roll down the window of the black Lincoln. I'm not sure but the car may have jerked, as if startled. I have spent too many days, weeks, too many months and years enclosed in things. I like the sudden feel of fresh air against my face, messing my carefully coiffed hair. It is resistance, the air resisting the car, pushing it back, the car fighting forward.

Perhaps I will sell my house, donate it to a worthy institution. Would it make a good museum? I will buy myself a flashy con-dominium and hire an interior designer to come in and fit it out with shiny chrome and glass, surfaces that reflect, that dust could never cling to. Arlene would be beside herself. Perhaps I'll let her do it.

That house, that house, that aging monument. It's always been a museum. It's time it was lived in. It's time it was filled with childish laughter and the busy noises of a gathering family. I could turn it into apartments, maybe. Ah, no. I could not turn it over to the transients of the world.

Maybe I could give it to Nanny. Give it to Nanny and Leroy and Charlaine. With another baby on the way, they need the room. I think of Nanny, excited at the coming birth, all of them happy at the idea, the earlier discontent buried in the reality of Charlaine's swollen belly.

Leroy working happily to keep the old house secure, no longer having to worry about being displaced by "they"; Charlaine whistling through the upstairs and downstairs; Nanny sleeping eternally in her room before the blaring TV set. Old Levi's rooms, so expansive a place for children to play and dream and watch the sun set. But Leroy would have to do something about those windows so he wouldn't lose a kid or two out of them.

The wind has blown my hair loose from its frosted moorings and numbed my cheek and my foot is harder on the accelerator than the law allows. I feel like whistling. I wish I could. I switch on the radio, the words barely audible above the rushing wind, but the beat is strong.

The line of Obediah Murphy made fade out, but the race goes on. The race goes on.

THE BEGATS

And Obediah Jonah Micah Murphy lived to the age of eighty-three, four months and twenty-three days and the issue of Obediah were these:

Obediah begat Rebecca Jane who was the mother of Nancy who was the mother of Alexander who begat Jonathan who begat Ralph who begat *Jenks*.

And Obediah begat Noah who begat Bertha who was the mother of Reeta who was the mother of Leatha who was the mother of Joe B. who begat Raymond who begat *Charlaine*.

And Obediah begat Quewanah and Quewanah begat Sholhonah who begat Cleeta who was the mother of Sampson who begat *Nanny*.

And Quewanah likewise begat Curtis McCullough who begat Ike who begat Billy who begat Curtis who begat *Earl*.

And Obediah begat Patty who was the mother of Joel who begat Ellen who was the mother of Mary Ann who was the mother of Joseph who begat *Shirley*.

And Obediah begat Nathan Beck who begat William who begat Robert who begat Harry who begat *Greer*.

And Obediah begat *Louisa* and *Louisa* was the mother of *Levi*.

And *Levi* was without issue.

And the generations of Obediah are many and continuing into the present.

And Louisa Rippert Varner Murphy lived to the age of ninety-four years, six months and eleven days, and the issue of Louisa were these:

Louisa was the mother of *Charlie* who begat Louise who was the mother of Clem who begat Ruby who was the mother of Maggie who was the mother of *George*.

And Louisa was the mother of *Danny* who begat *Daniel* who begat *David* who begat *Marci*. And Daniel likewise begat *Lee* who begat *Elizabeth*.

And Louisa was the mother of *Henry* who was without issue.

And Louisa was the mother of *Louisa* who was the mother of *Louisa* who was the mother of *Levi*.

And *Levi* was without issue.

And the generations of Louisa are many and continuing into the present.

420